SHE
OF THE
SHADOWS

KERRY WILLIAMS

HOT TREE PUBLISHING

She
of the
Shadows

KERRY WILLIAMS

This book is dedicated to my parents.
How much you both do for me can never be repaid.
Mom, you are the living embodiment of how much strength there is in gentleness.
Dad, you're not fooling anyone with that hard shell. We all know you're soft as anything on the inside!
Thank you both for teaching me what real strength looks like.

CHAPTER 1

LOVELY

Over creaking, haunted floorboards, I pad towards the bedroom where Tino slumbers. The darkened hallway flickers in and out of existence in the light of the single wall-mounted lamp, its illumination traumatised by the spirits passing through the peeling papered walls. Though no heartbeat pounds in the cavern of my chest, nerves dance along my skin. The power of the Furies simmers in my veins, raw sensation waiting to be flexed and wielded, urging me to flay in this land of the living. The strength in the tips of my fingers sizzles and almost burns.

A distant desire calls, something with teeth lurking beneath my surface. *Maim. Maim. Maim.*

However, in this moment, a different kind of hunger entices me towards the bedroom. A ravenousness a thousand years in the making.

Easing the door open, careful not to wake Tino, I linger at the bed's edge, my eyes trailing over the soft curves of his face as he peacefully sleeps. His thick dark lashes, the warmth of his tanned skin, his longish black hair scattered across the pillow, his full lips parted ever so slightly. The carnal urge devouring my insides ebbs from my bones at the sight of my beautiful friend, vulnerable with no clue of the monster who looms over him. Though no tears well at the corners of my eyes, the compulsion is overwhelming, for I so desperately want to cry. His image of safety and warmth is one which I violently clung onto for lifetimes.

Will I ever bring myself to admit to him that during the mere minutes he lost me, I spent a lifetime grieving for him? Ten lifetimes. I already didn't admit to Marie the truth of my awful calling and how my rejection of it resulted in me being held in a prison for so long. How could I? From my friends' point of view, I left this life for ten minutes, not a thousand years. The passage of time in the Underworld is incomprehensible. It passed—kind of—and things changed, though we all remained the same. The guardians, Hero and Leander. Me. *Him.*

Tino stirs, sensing my presence. Peeking one sleepy eye open, he reaches out and threads his warm fingers through mine, pulling me to him. I let myself be swayed. He shuffles over, and I settle into the spot he'd previously occupied, the patch warmed as if a cat had lain there. All his heat makes my head a little fuzzy.

In one swift motion, he brings the palm of my hand to his mouth and places a searing kiss against my skin. Suddenly, his eyes widen, and he drops my hand as he recoils.

'Shit!' he says. 'Lee, I'm sorry. I wasn't thinking of the pain.'

'It's okay.' I half grin. 'Actually, the pain is gone. A weird side effect of dying, I suppose.'

His silence echoes through the room and turns me a degree hotter, his amber-hazel eyes piercing me. I flush at my lie.

My flaming red hair hangs in tangled waves over my shoulders, pooling on the bed between us. I'm still wearing his oversized jumper. Sweat trickles down my spine. My leggings cling to my skin. The clothes of the living world itch to be removed.

In a heartbeat, he closes the distance, and his lips find mine.

His hands become hot and frantic, searching for my skin. I've never been undressed so fast in my life, an urgency I've never experienced. To be so desired, and I am so starved. I haven't been touched in lifetimes. As soon as his claiming fingers begin smoothing along my waist, I'm a quivering wreck moaning into his mouth.

My hands, acting as if having a mind of their own, roam his body, removing his clothing in return with remarkable speed. I need his skin burning next to mine. Having that contact is the same vital bliss as eating again, only multiplied by a hundred. A hundred thousand. His chest is as blistering as flaming coals against my tender flesh. He strokes the soft skin of my inner thigh before moving his fingers to my core, and my head truly spins as if I'm cresting the big dip of a roller-coaster.

It evokes a distant memory different from the searing heat. Charon's embrace was cold, the end, oblivion. For a few seconds when the cool shock of his fingers brushed the same place so very long ago, I had longed to live in that moment. Once—and never again. He never held me again. Never kissed me except for the moment of my turning. All that desire for him balled up, unsatisfied deep in my belly.

This is no time to lose myself in memories of Charon, who is death incarnate. Who only wanted to control me. Yet images of his neon blue eyes flood my vision, how his shadows would twirl around my ankle, the sight of his fanged teeth denting his lower lip. I bite hard into Tino's shoulder, his balmy gasp against my neck sending goose bumps firing along my legs as he slides between them. His heat is everywhere.

Inescapable.

My chest constricts.

Tino's physical weight is heavy against my chest

and abdomen while Charon's mental weight is oppressive in my brain. Tino's skin is parching me. His musky scent, rich with desire, is both overwhelming and consuming. Akin to flames licking a burning building, and I'm being herded further and further into the bowels of the blazing halls. I fight to catch a single breath, but there's no escape from it, and I may just catch fire myself.

My stomach churns. 'I'm going to be sick,' I choke out, throwing Tino off me.

I sprint to his en suite bathroom and unload my guts into the toilet. Sinking to my knees, I continue to heave as every morsel of ice cream and beer and pie splatters the bowl, everything tasting burnt on the way out. The sulphur scent is so nauseating, it makes me vomit even more.

The sudden draping of a dressing gown around my bare shoulders startles me so much that I give another heave. 'You okay? Does this usually happen?' His voice is so full of concern, I'd almost forgotten this is how it is to be around him. How he moves protectively around me.

'Don't. Stay—away,' I order him between retches, not wanting him to catch the damned stench as I recall the feast I indulged in upon being alive again... or whatever I am. Cherry pies, cookie dough ice cream, six beers, probably three packs of cookies—I overindulged. I haven't eaten in so long. Foolish of me.

His fingers are as searing as a brand when they

press against my forehead. 'Jesus, Lee, you're running a fever. We should get you to the hospital.'

'No. Stop it.' I swat his hand away. 'You're making it worse.' I retch again, yet more watery ice cream leaving my body. When I chance looking at him, his expression is bordering on hurt. 'Sorry. What I mean is, your hand is so hot.' I raise the back of my own hand to my forehead and find he's right—my skin is on fire.

'Lee.' He utters my name, nothing more—not giving voice to all the many worries likely swirling around his brain.

Shuddering, I rest on my heels, hopeful that the last of my stomach has finally been emptied. 'It's the adrenaline.'

'That was hours ago.'

Wiping my mouth with my shaking fingers, I try to steady my breathing as dry heat evaporates across my skin. Any moment now, flames will engulf me. Tino is leaning in the doorframe, so he doesn't notice when a few strands of my hair hanging loose by my bare breast sizzle, catch fire, then smoulder when I put them out between my fingers with an audible fizz.

'I need to cool off.' I rise to my feet and shrug off the dressing gown, which only made me sweat even more. There's a small shower cubicle, and I fling back the flimsy curtain. The stark white tiles are a shining sanctuary in this haunted house. I grab the handle of the tap and yank it all the way to the coldest setting possible.

When I turn around, Tino is open-mouthed as I advance on him, naked. 'A little privacy please,' I tell him, shoving him out of the doorway before closing the door. Which is kind of ridiculous and rude because this is his room, but I might actually ignite if I don't cool down now.

The cold water sizzles like fresh rain on hot tarmac as it makes contact with my skin. I plunge myself under the showerhead, facing the spray full-on. Somehow, it's not cold enough.

'Calm yourself, Fury. You don't want to set the whole house on fire.'

The rough voice echoes around the walls, startling the life out of me—so much so that I tumble out of the shower cubicle, almost tearing down the curtain in the process, and clatter to the floor in a heap.

'Lee?' Tino calls through the door. 'What's going on?'

'I'm fine. I slipped,' I reply, breathless.

I stand up and approach the still-running shower as if it might suddenly transform into the ruler of the Underworld at any moment—which is to say, with extreme caution. Poking my foot under the running water, I whisper, 'Charon? Can you claim me through the shower?'

When a chuckle reverberates in my mind, I realise

his voice is completely inside my head. *Lord, I really am hearing voices now.*

'No. I cannot "claim you," Fury.'

Expelling a sigh of relief, I step back under the stream and relish its cool waters once more. 'How did you get in my head?' I say out loud, pushing my hands through my hair, enjoying the feeling of it soaked and clinging to me.

'*You're Fury. I have to call my Furies home to me somehow.*'

'I didn't submit, though,' I say, ignoring the extreme tug in the place where my heart once sat. It has now been replaced with the invisible string binding me to The Ferryman, and it flutters at the mention of home.

'*But you* are *Fury.*' His voice is all mocking and shadow. My skin prickles in a wholly unwanted way, the unsatiated hunger rising once more, and I curse it.

'Do you see me?' I ask, suddenly a little more conscious of the water on my naked skin, the placement of my hands on my stomach.

'*No. I have a vague awareness of where you're located in the waking world.*' Though he's speaking directly into my mind, the loaded pause is crushing.

'But...,' I prompt.

When he responds, his words bite. '*You got what you wanted. You escaped. Now you will reap the consequences.*'

Clenching my fist so I don't slam it into a wall, I grind out, *'Marie pulled me out—I didn't escape.'* I don't know if I'm more annoyed with Charon for his sudden turn in attitude or myself for caring what he believes about my so-called escape. I guess a thousand years as a prisoner cultivated a sympathy for my jailer along with it.

'Oh, your collusion with Kane was a mere stroll through the Underworld, then?'

'You're infuriating!'

'Enjoy your freedom, Fury,' he mocks.

'Charon!' I seethe, only to be met with silence. 'Charon?' More silence.

'Bastard,' I mutter to myself, turning off the shower and stepping out before wrapping myself in the discarded dressing gown. Thankfully, I'm now free of the sensation that I'm about to combust.

I may have agreed to go along with Kane's escape attempt, but perhaps if Charon hadn't been so bloody stubborn and had released me from my cell after the first thousand souls, it wouldn't have happened. I curse the piece of never-ending chalk that Charon had crafted for me to tally the passing souls—my only way of observing the passage of time. I curse the luxurious bed. I curse the ridiculous mockery of the roll-top bath. I curse each fine thing he ever made for me in his attempts to bring me to heel like some bitch of the Underworld.

I'm free. Free of my bars. Although not quite free of

him—and what right does he have to invade my brain?

When I yank the door open, I find Tino perched on the edge of the bed, and though his eyes greedily roam my long legs, his eyebrows knit together.

'Who were you talking to?'

'Myself, of course,' I say, scanning the room for a towel for my hair. I'd been so engrossed in my one-sided conversation with Charon, it didn't occur to me that it might be overheard.

Tino eases himself upright and takes a few paces towards me. The heat radiates from him as if he's a bonfire in summer, and without meaning to, I take a step away.

'Lee.' A weird sort of desperation seeps into his tone. 'Talk to me. What's going on? You're not in pain when I put my hands on you, yet you don't want me to.'

'It's all a bit much.' I try to mentally pivot. 'I died. Again.' I cross the room and perch on the end of the bed. 'Tino, I just want to go home.'

'Home?' The bed sags beside me under his weight as he shuffles closer, and it takes all my willpower to remain still and not shrink away.

'Back to England. I'm done.'

'What is it you remember?' he whispers, clearly not buying what I'm selling. 'What happened to you on the other side?'

'I—' I begin, but I falter—because how do I explain

that I was seduced by Death? That Death told me his name, and it tasted as sweet as sugar on my lips. I agreed to sell my soul to become walking vengeance on Earth, and though the foolishness of my decision came swift, it still came all too late, and he took me as his prisoner. How time stretched differently in the Underworld, and in those lifetimes, he became my only companion. And I craved his icy caress more than anything else. In his presence, I'd never felt more myself. He and I faced our loneliness side by side. Now in the living world again, so full of vibrant colour and drowning heat, I'm staggered by the garish assault on my senses, as well as the affection Tino is so willing to give when I have been so deprived.

'I have no memories of it,' I lie instead.

Closing my eyes, I lean forwards and rest my forehead against his. *It's a period of adjustment,* I tell myself. *I will find a way to be the woman Tino loves.* 'But this world is overwhelming right now. We tried our best to find my purpose, and it didn't work. You asked me before how many more times I would dance with death, and I told you once more. I kept my promise.' He threads his fingers through mine. 'I came back to you, Tino, like I said I would. Here I am. No more death. Let's go home.'

Tino takes a sharp, shuddering inhale, squeezing my hands. 'Home. Me and you?'

I nod, my head still pressed against his, fighting against the heat where his skin meets mine. I pull away, removing my hands from his and placing my palm against his chest.

'I want you, Tino.' I lean in, placing a chaste kiss on his lips. 'I want this, but baby steps for now, please.'

His smile is glorious and warm and safe, and it's all I ever wanted in life.

CHAPTER 2

TINO

When Lee announces our plan of returning to England, Marie is the only one who isn't surprised. In fact, she's pointedly avoiding my eyes altogether, while Lorna almost spits her coffee into her mug. The atmosphere in the kitchen is abruptly at odds with the mouth-watering smell of bacon.

'You're leaving? But there's so much we need to figure out.' Alarm cuts through Lisette's words, clear as day.

Lee gives her a sideways glance, the syrup from the peach slice she has jabbed on her fork sliding down her chin in sticky glory as she hesitates before answering. 'There's nothing to figure out. The mission failed. I returned without my memories. Again.'

Marie descends into a coughing fit so severe, she must excuse herself.

Lisette's knuckles turn white on her cutlery. She shuffles across the table, leaning in to implore Lee. 'You should stay. Please reconsider, Lee.'

At the sound of her name on Lisette's lips, she flinches a fraction. 'I'm tired, Lis. I want to go home.' She devours another peach slice whole, no chewing required.

Lisette's mouth hangs open, her eyes flitting between Lee and Lorna, disbelieving. For someone recently returned from the dead, Lee doesn't appear traumatised. Her pale skin all but glows, and the red of her hair is even more vibrant, its wildness loose to her waist. She wears a simple pale blue vest top, all her scars shining in the artificial light with no sense of shame. Her tongue twists around another peach slice before it slides down her throat with a slurp.

When I glance at Lorna opposite me, her expression reeks of uncertainty, and she gives her eyes to her own mound of food, though she doesn't make any move to eat. Instead, she pushes pieces of bacon about her plate, the metal prongs squealing against the porcelain, setting my teeth on edge. We're all thinking the same thing: There's so much Lee isn't saying. But only Lisette is willing to confront it. The maple glaze of my breakfast turns to ash in my mouth.

'Who am I talking to?' Lisette demands, earning Lee's attention. 'The Lee who died not even twenty-four hours ago was desperate for answers, willing to die to learn her purpose. And now, what? Your calling doesn't matter to you anymore?'

Lee cocks an eyebrow, placing her palm on the table with a deadly slowness. 'What is it you're suggesting? Should I die again? Do we keep drowning me until something sticks?'

'That's not what I'm saying, and you know it.'

Lee glances at me, and I'm shamefaced that I haven't jumped in to defend her, but honestly, I'm curious too.

Her words come out fierce, through gritted teeth. 'I made a promise that this death would be my last.'

Lisette whips her head my direction as if for confirmation.

'She did,' I say quietly.

Lee stands, sending the chair screeching across the kitchen. Her eyes harden on Lisette once more. 'It didn't work. I made a promise. I intend to keep it. What more is there?' She grabs the remaining tinned peaches along with her mug of tea and storms outside onto the rear porch, leaving us to fester in a moment of silence.

With Lee gone, Lisette swings her body fully towards me.

Anticipating her reproach, I raise my palms in premeditated self-defence. 'What she's saying is true. She promised me she didn't want to die—not really. She didn't want to stay with Death. She chose me. She *is* choosing me.'

'Is she acting like the Lee you knew?' She motions in the direction of the kitchen door.

My heart gives a double beat, because how could she be anything different? But watching her sit, scars and all, in the open kitchen gives me pause, her lack of pain gives me pause, her talking to herself gives me pause. Instead, I say, 'What are you getting at?'

'She was dead for ten minutes, Tino. She'd passed on. What Marie pulled out is not the woman you loved.'

'Babe,' Lorna chides, placing a steadying hand on her wrist, 'there's no reason to jump to conclusions.'

Lisette gawks. 'Seriously?'

Lorna hesitates. 'She's a bit off, I admit, but she did die again. Let's cut her some slack. Besides, what's the alternative? Possession? Someone else using Lee's body?'

'No.... I'm not sure. Something isn't right. What Marie did crossed a line.'

Anger builds in my chest as I cut them off. 'All that matters to me is the fact that I got her back. She remembers me and the promise she made, and her word is good enough for me,' I say, almost convincing myself out of the wrongness of Lee's return. So many times in the past, I haven't protected her, but never again.

'Tino...,' Lisette begins to protest.

'What would you have me do?'

'Maybe convince her to stay?' Lorna suggests. 'At least then she's under Marie's watchful eye.'

'Marie?' I respond, incredulous. 'The same Marie who, only a second ago, Lisette reproached for "crossing a line" to save the woman I love? How would convincing her to stay make things any better? And forgive me if I'm unable to find it in myself to be mad at her for doing so. Lee has done nothing but put herself in harm's way for years, and she's finally had enough, and you're *not* okay with that?'

'Tino, this is exactly what I'm saying. If Lee truly lost her memories, she'd be devastated. She'd be harassing Marie for answers. But she's just giving up? That's not her. Either she's lying or something's wrong.'

Now *I've* had enough. I rise to my feet, needing to leave before fury consumes me. 'Am I not a good enough consolation prize? She promised she'd stop when she returned. I'm not saying she's happy about it, about not discovering why she's haunted, and yes, you're right, she's probably upset she'll never learn her purpose. But you want a reason why she's "just giving up"? Well, you're looking at him. I want her to stop, for us to be together, for her to be *safe*. And for once in her life, she's going to listen. Okay? Let her be safe, Lis. Hasn't she earned it?'

Lisette's mouth flops open as if she wants to say more, but the words don't come.

Lorna takes her girlfriend's hand and answers for her. 'Of course she has, Tee. You both have.'

I take that as my cue to leave.

As I approach the door to the porch, I spy Lee through the narrow windowpane. She's in one of the low wooden deck chairs, gazing out at the creeping fingers of the weeping willows trailing their tips in the calm waters of the bayou, where the sun paints them orange. Her hands are wrapped around her mug, her arms exposed to the biting winter air. I turn on my heel to the coat pegs and find a woollen blanket hung there, making to join her when the low tone of her voice freezes me to the spot with my hand resting on the door handle. The blanket suddenly feels too coarse against my skin.

'...you cooled me down. Again.' She pauses, and I peek out the window to check if Marie or Lisette's parents have joined her, but I find no one, though I'm sure I catch Lee's mouth curl into the beginnings of a smile. 'Thanks all the same.' Her words are so soft, I almost don't catch them.

Despite my little speech to Lisette, dread pools in my stomach. The fleeting paranoia that Lee indeed found Death on the other side and she's lying about having zero recollection of him spears me. But she's here with me now. Isn't that what matters more?

I push open the door, and at its creak, Lee jumps a little before a bright grin settles on her face. I wiggle the blanket in front of me as I approach, as if I need to demonstrate that I'm not spying on her, happy for the spicy pepper scent of Avery Island clearing my thoughts and my sinuses. 'Thought you might need this.'

'Actually, I'm enjoying the brisk air. It's refreshing, and I was feeling a tad hot-headed.' She motions towards the kitchen. 'Thank you for defending me.'

Sighing, I take a seat in the deck chair opposite her. 'You heard that?'

'Yes.' She shuffles forwards, and despite the winter air, when she cups my cheek in her palm, her caress is warm. 'And you're wrong, by the way. You're not the consolation prize—you're the dream.'

The sentiment mellows me somewhat, giving me the courage to ask, 'Who were you talking to?' I thread my fingers through hers, still not believing it's possible to touch her again.

Her gaze wavers only a fraction. 'Myself.'

'You're lying,' I say softly. 'You expect me to believe you thanked yourself for something? Tell me, was it Death? I won't be mad. I'd rather have the details. I hate being in the dark.'

Her lips tighten, and I brace for the worst. 'It wasn't Death. There *is* no Death.' She squeezes my fingers. 'Can't we put this past us?'

Her eyes are so hopeful, a beautiful endless blue. More vibrant now than I've ever seen them. I told her before that I was over saying no to her, and now isn't a good time to start, so I nod.

Only her happy expression sours quickly as she gives a sudden heave and is on her feet. She takes a few steps and retches before she throws her guts up again. The canned peaches are the same glistening slugs on the way out that they were on the way in.

'This—is—so—shit,' she spits out between pukes. I rub between her shoulders until the sickness subsides. Once done hurling, she slumps against the rail until she's a crumpled heap on the floor. 'This is so unfair,' she mutters to herself, slicking her hair away from her face.

I crouch beside her, the worn painted wood of the porch rough against my spine even through my T-shirt. 'Perhaps you've reset your factory settings, and you'll have to eat normal-person portions from now on.' She snorts, opening her eyes to meet mine. 'Perhaps this is it for you. No more dead. No more pain. You move on and live your life.'

She beams far brighter than the cool morning sun. 'Let's hope,' she says.

And I smile at her in return, though in my heart of hearts, I'm certain we both understand my false hope is just that. False.

CHAPTER 3

LOVELY

To fly is such a strange sensation. As is the disconcerting itch of wings hidden somehow within my shoulder blades like scarab beetles scratching to break free.

Tino snoozes in the chair beside me while I give my attention to the orange light crystalising on the peaks of clouds outside my window, a delicious dessert in the sky. I'm glad to be returning to England, away from the watchful eye of Lisette. Marie had developed quite the flu before we left, and she didn't support Lisette in her protests that I should remain, which only added to Lisette's suspicions that I'm hiding something.

While I returned from the Underworld hopeful no one ever need learn of my dealings there, things have proven quite difficult. I'm only able to manage the tiniest amount of food before I vomit. Sleep is still a stranger. I'm relieved that I spent so much time lying in bed pretending to sleep during my incarceration in the Underworld; otherwise, I might have gone mad in those silent early hours.

A few times, even Lorna has shot me questioning glances during our final moments together when she's caught me smiling to myself, having inaudible conversations with Charon. When a dizzying hot spell threatens to overcome me, it's only his cooling words that distract me. While I'm not in his servitude, as ever, he has an effect on my body, and when I'm being honest with myself, I miss talking to him. I miss the neon glow of his eyes on me, the draw of his skin wrapped in shadow which, after a thousand years in his company, I never had the courage to reach out to first.

My eyes on the sun-speckled horizon, I pluck that invisible cord still fastening me to him.

'Charon? Are you there?' I whisper in my mind.

Silence. This happens sometimes. I reach out, and he refuses to talk unless I'm about to combust.

'Yes, Fury,' he finally answers.

'Have you ever seen a sunset?'

I bite my lip to conceal the smile that blooms across my face when I hear his annoyed huff in my mind.

'No. I've never left the boundaries of the city. This is my world. I leave the living to theirs.'

'Shame, it's beautiful.'

'*Well, if that's all, I have matters to attend….*'

'*I miss you.*' I close my eyes, my breath tangling in the sun's rays. I didn't mean for it to slip out, but that's the problem when he's in my head—I don't always have control of what pops to mind. It's the truth. I'm so happy to be free once more, but I miss Charon desperately. Kane was right—I'm in the grips of Stockholm syndrome.

His pause is so long, I'm almost relieved that he must have severed the connection before he registered my admission.

'*Then come home.*' His voice is saturated in such longing, I must be imagining things. His desperation curls around my edges and squeezes.

Unable to resist him, imagining his foggy opium scent, I think, '*How would you have me now? Still on all fours?*'

'*Having you in chains might be more prudent.*'

His voice is all smoke—thick and drenched in a dark humour. I curl my toes in my boots. My imagination in free fall, my nails grip into the armrests.

'*Come home to me,*' he begs.

'*I won't go back to that cell, Charon.*'

'*Things will end badly for you on the surface.*'

He doesn't refute the fact that I would return to being a prisoner. I swallow, clearing my mind, pushing all my long-held desire down, and turn to observe Tino's peaceful face. This must stop, talking to and missing Charon while trying to carve out a life with Tino. It's not fair on anyone.

'*You can't give me what I need.*'

'*Come home,*' he demands with a little more authority.

'*I am home,*' I tell him, though it hurts to say. '*Good-bye, Ferryman.*'

'*Fury!*' he yells, but I work on erecting my mental barriers to block him out. I put my headphones in, select the most brutal heavy metal song I own to drown out his rumbling anger, and resign myself to never speaking to him again.

***

THE ROUGH RIVETS OF THE KEY TO MY FLAT SLIDE INTO THE keyhole, the resistance jittering my fingers. Taking a deep breath, I step inside, Tino at my heels. The taxi journey here was a quiet one, and Tino's eyes are now boring holes into the back of my head. I sense them on me as he hesitates on the threshold, my suitcase in his hand.

I should turn and talk to him, but my eyes are busy roaming the home I've been parted from for far longer than mere months. I almost want to laugh at how my flat is even sparser than my cell in the Underworld. I've never given much stock to possessions. I coast my fingers across the soft cushions of the faded, second-hand navy sofa.

'You seem so different,' Tino finally says from the doorway.

Stilling, I drink him in instead. Tall, beautifully tanned, he's everything that is good, all heat and warmth and safety. A sanctuary. *My* sanctuary. Someone to bury myself in.

As though my appraising has unsettled him, he makes a vague motion with his hand. 'I should go.'

'You should stay,' I counter.

His eyes meet mine. He makes no move. The air turns thick and oppressive.

'Please.'

He closes the distance with strong, steady footsteps, halting inches from me, then pushes his fingers through my hair. His contact all the signal I need, I throw myself at him, demanding his lips, his hands— everything. I wish I could crawl into him.

He gives his all, his palms sliding under my top until they are fire on my skin. He tastes like the long-forgotten summer nights of my youth, wild and restless, and when he moans into my mouth, I jump into his embrace. I wrap my legs around his waist, tightening my grip. Catching my ass, he deepens our kiss, swinging me in one swift motion while walking over to the sofa before dropping me onto it with a thud, then landing between my legs. He yanks my top over my head before placing fast, searing kisses down my chest.

I'm pure, shuddering sensation, each kiss setting

me alight. I press my nails so hard into the flesh of his shoulders, I tear through the material of his T-shirt, then rip it off his body.

Tino stills, pulling away with widened eyes as he beholds the scraps of material draped in my fingers. 'Shit,' he chuckles.

I grab the back of his neck, bringing his mouth to mine, and rob him of his oxygen while he pushes his fingertips to all the sensitive places I long for them to be.

'*Cool yourself, Fury.*' Charon's voice is rough in my mind.

'*Get out of my head!*' I scream internally, digging my nails into Tino's arms and eliciting a gasp from him, though it's swallowed down my throat.

'*Do you want to rip his skin off?*' His voice is rich with a sick kind of humour, as if nothing would amuse him more.

I try to ignore him, shoving Tino off and rolling him so he's sitting, then shucking off my jeans to straddle his lap before kissing him some more, trying to ignore the indents my nails have left in his skin.

Tino breaks away from my mouth, needing to breathe, and instead his lips ghost along my neck all the way to my chest. Then he unhooks my bra and brings his lips over the peak of my breast. This time it's me who gasps.

Self-control slips away from me, and I pluck that

golden cord, sending my message along its trembling vibrations. *'Do you know what I'm doing?'*

'I'm aware of your desire, yes.' His voice drops an octave. *'It's easy to imagine what you're doing.'*

I pin Tino between my legs, kiss his earlobe, and bite his neck before licking his skin all the way from the base of his neck to the top of his jaw as his palms knead along my thighs, his soft pants hot in my ear.

'Does it bother you?'

'You should stop.' Charon's voice is thick with something I so wish to call longing; his writhing shadows all but ensnare me all the way from the Underworld.

'Would you like me to rip his skin off?' I tease.

'Yes. He has his hands on what is mine.'

His response is so immediate and forceful, I groan out loud, pushing further against Tino, the hardness of him giving away exactly what having me in his arms is doing to him.

'Lee,' Tino moans, moving to kiss me again. Though his lips lock with mine, his soft call brings me back into my body with a jolt, causing me to scramble to my feet.

We both pant, silently staring at each other.

'Fuck,' I gasp, covering my mouth with my shaking fingers and closing my eyes to compose myself, a wave of wretchedness washing through me at what I was allowing to happen. Having Tino's hands on my body with Charon's voice in my head. Worse, I was enjoying it.

'Are you okay?' Tino asks, his lips swollen from the violence of my kisses.

'I can't do this,' I tell him.

His face is immediately devastated, and I realise my mistake.

I sit by his side, taking his hand. 'No. I don't mean us. I mean this, right now. I need to take things slower. My head is still all over the place.'

He sags with relief, smoothing a palm down my naked spine. 'Sorry. I let things get a little out of control.'

'Tino, you have nothing to be sorry for. Believe me, I want to.' I chuckle, going rosy when I contemplate my behaviour. 'It's just....' I pause, and he waits. 'For some reason, I haven't quite regained full control of my body since I was resurrected. I'm getting there, but between the hot flashes and the nausea, it's taking some adjusting.'

His lips purse as if he might say more on the subject, but instead he nods.

'Will you stay with me tonight?' I ask.

His eyebrows shoot up. 'Sure, if that's what you want.'

'Yes.' I kiss him again, chaste and simple, and his shoulders relax into it. 'Give me two minutes while I change.'

I grab some comfy clothes and head to the bathroom. I turn on the light and throw some cool water on my face, then take a moment to study my reflection. My pale skin now appears flawless except for the shock of scars glittering on my forearms, the red of my hair falls in luscious ringlets to my waist, and my eyes are almost as blue as Charon's.

I skim my palms over my bare curves.

'Charon?' I call in my mind.

'You didn't do it, then?'

'What?'

'Rip his skin off?'

I snort. *'Of course I didn't.'*

He doesn't respond, and I want to curse myself for how much it bothers me. Why do I long so desperately for the thing that doesn't want me? Not in the way I need him to. I wasn't lying to Tino—he is the dream. I placed him on a pedestal for eternities, someone good, safe, everything I ever wanted. Why am I acting so depraved as to crave a being who wishes me on my knees, at his feet, in chains?

'Charon?'

'Fury.'

'How do I shut you out?'

His laugh is brusque in my ears. *'There is no shutting me out. You belong to the Underworld.'*

'Let me go. I'm not coming back. Please let me go,' I plead.

Silence.

'Charon?'

'Charon?'

'Charon? Don't ignore me!' I demand.

'See, Fury?' he teases. *'If I cut you off, you would miss me.'*

'I would. I do,' I admit. *'But it's not going to happen. I will not return. I want to live, and a life at your feet is not living. Please, you need to be the one to cut me off. If you ever cared at all about me, if even the slightest part of you cared for me as anything other than your servant, please, let me go.'*

His response is a long time coming. In the minutes that pass, the thread in my chest tied to him trembles with the need to be near him. Golden, glistening, shining hope tying me through worlds, through time and space to the ruler of the Underworld.

His sigh is so soft, it makes my toes curl. *'Come home, Fury. You will not return to any cell. Just come home to me.'*

I brace my hands against the sink, hanging my head, gasping for air as the need for him grips me so awfully. I long to weep, to thrash against this world. The injustice of how much I miss my prison, the guardians, and, most of all, Charon. It's not fair.

After several minutes, I compose myself before returning to the man I've loved for an eternity and push the longing for the one I left behind deep inside myself, telling myself it's nothing more than our bond.

Tino places a kiss on my forehead with a promise to return to me later before he's out the door on his way to visit his ma. For the remainder of last night, Charon had, thankfully, stayed out of my head. Tino and I snuggled on my sofa, watching reruns of *Friends*. I'd let the familiar scent of freshly laundered clothes that Tino carries with him envelop me like a blanket, making me almost feel normal.

While the heat between us didn't ignite again, Tino slept next to me in my bed, then woke up giving groggy smiles, and we shared a cup of tea this morning while talking about our plans for the day while I thought, *This might be my life with him*. Only, I lied about my plans, told him I was going to visit the care home where I worked, which I had gone AWOL from following my father's death, and beg them to give me my job back. Well, it was only a half lie. I do plan on doing so, but my true plans take precedent.

I pull out my iPad and dial Marie on FaceTime. I've already texted to ask her for the call, so she's expecting me. When she answers, though, I'm shocked by the sight of the woman on the screen. A shock of grey hair is threaded through Marie's braids, and her face is gaunt, cheekbones deathly angular. When she tries to say hi, she viciously coughs instead.

'Marie, are you all right?'

She pats her chest. 'This damn cough.'

'Your hair.'

She smooths a hand over her whitening braids.

'It's come on gradually. I'm looking into this. Don't worry about it.'

I knit my brow and curse Kane for whatever he did that is obviously now taking its toll on my friend.

Marie continues, 'Seriously, Lee. It's okay. What's on your mind?'

I chew my lip. 'I need to tell you something, but you must promise you won't mention it to Lisette or Lorna. I need your help.'

She stills, worrying her own bottom lip in return. 'I don't enjoy lying to them. Lisette is already suspicious that I'm privy to more than I'm letting on. Plus, they'll want to help.'

'Please, Marie—swear it.'

She hesitates, but her arcane curiosity wins, and she nods.

I take a deep, steadying breath before plunging on with my confession. 'I told you before, there's a ruler of the Underworld, but what I didn't tell you was that he and I....' I pause, palming my chest. 'You need to understand, time passes so differently there. I wasn't in the Underworld for only ten minutes—it was more like a thousand years. I've lived lifetimes with him.'

Pausing, I take in her shock as her eyes widen. 'You were *involved* with the ruler of the Underworld?'

'No. Yes. No. Not in the way you assume.' I huff, ignoring how horrible it is to talk about this. How little definition my relationship with The Ferryman has. 'The problem is, even though you pulled me out, I'm still connected to him. He's in my head, under my skin. I need to find a way to sever our connection.'

'So, you *were* talking to someone else back in Avery Island?'

'Yes.'

'You were talking to Death?'

The soft surface of the lip I've been gnawing breaks and copper stings my tongue. 'That's not what I call him. It's not what he is—not really.'

Marie frowns. 'Why didn't you mention this to me sooner? What does he want? What does he say to you? Lorna said she's spotted you smiling to yourself.'

I pound my right eye with the heel of my palm. 'Things are so incredibly complicated. I was his prisoner—I must have Stockholm syndrome. I need a way to sever the connection between us. To keep him out of my thoughts so even if I do wish to reach out to him, his voice will be blocked.'

'What does he want?'

'For me to return. To the Underworld. To him.'

Now it's Marie's turn to sink her head into her hands. 'There's so much you're not telling me. How am I supposed to sever a connection to a being who is Death but not Death? Did you fall in love with him?'

'No!' I say immediately, red colouring my cheeks. 'It was....' I lose my words again. 'Stockholm syndrome, definitely.'

Her eyes turn sympathetic.

'I'm not in love with him,' I repeat, standing my

ground. 'Trust me. Besides, he's a creature incapable of love. I love Tino. He's all I've ever wanted. I'm distracted is all. This is why I need to break the connection.'

Marie eyes me for a moment but doesn't press me any further on my feelings for Charon. 'Okay. You need to give me something, though, Lee. What am I searching for?'

I swallow my fear. 'Have you ever heard of The Ferryman?'

She frowns. 'As in Greek mythology?'

'Something like that.'

'It's not my area of expertise, but doesn't he ferry souls across the Styx?'

I shrug a shoulder. 'All stories start somewhere, right? There's a river there, as I told you before. They never called it the Styx, though. It flows with Charon's blood.'

Spilling his name is sacrilege. His old name revived, out in the world instead of something wholly mine. I slap my palm across my mouth.

'Charon?' Marie coaxes. 'That's Death's name? The Ferryman?'

'Yes,' I whisper. The urge to cry stings my eyes. Charon isn't a name unknown to history, but giving credence to the stories, claiming him as my reality, was something I wished to remain mine alone. But I need Marie's expertise.

'And what are you to him—merely his prisoner?

Why do you have this connection?'

'Do the Furies mean anything to you?'

Marie quirks an eyebrow. 'My knowledge is vague. This is what you are now? You're a Fury?'

'More like half of one.'

'How do you mean?' Marie has moved so close to her screen now, her eyes hungry for information. But I can't bring myself to admit to her the demand for my submission, how Charon would have me on my knees before him. How I wanted something from him he would never give. To admit it would only fuel her belief that I fell for him.

'Marie,' I plead. 'Help me.'

With a laborious sigh, she says, 'Okay. I'll covertly research the Furies, along with their connection to the Underworld. Do more research on Charon—'

I cut her off. 'Please don't speak his name again,' I plead.

She eyes me curiously. 'The Ferryman, then,' she corrects. 'For now, wear crystal quartz. It should help as a defence by keeping your mind clear.'

'Thank you.' I bow my head as Marie descends into another coughing fit. 'Now it's your turn to talk. You're not well. Is it because of Kane, whatever deal you made to pull me out?' I probe.

She shakes her head, coughing into her elbow. I wait for it to pass.

'To be honest, I haven't been at the board to find

out. I did once only to be overcome. I haven't felt Carline's presence since.'

'Marie—' I begin, alarmed, but she cuts me off.

'Don't worry about me. It's some sort of spirit sickness. The girls and I are on it. We'll sort it out. I'll be fine.'

'I should ask The Ferryman what will help you.'

Marie's eyes snap to mine, the corner of her mouth quirking. 'The same entity you're wishing to cut off?'

A huff leaves me as I roll my eyes. 'For the purpose of helping you. You saved me. I owe you. I don't *want* to speak to him.'

'I'm sure even Death would have feelings about being used,' she says wryly.

'That would require him to have feelings at all,' I quip.

Marie's gaze pierces me with all her unanswered questions, though after a moment, she merely asks me not to seek his advice, as he'd likely manipulate me in some way. Though I'm a tad offended, I agree to her request. After all, the last time I asked for her help, I requested she kill me, and look how that turned out.

Two hours later, after becoming thoroughly lost in Birmingham city centre, I've managed to locate a crystal quartz necklace in the markets. I'm fuming at myself over how the place I called home for all my life is now a stranger to me, meaning I barely manage to navigate its bustling streets.

The market is thick with the heady scent of incense and worn clothes. Determined to be human again, I let the lady wearing a tie-dyed T-shirt persuade me into also buying a vintage tan leather jacket, the laughter lines etched deep into the skin around the corners of her eyes mirroring the worn creases in the fabric that tell its story of a life before me, which I appreciate. The coat gives the illusion of armour around me. The crystal quartz is caged in a thin silver wire, and at its cool touch to my chest, I let out a huge sigh of relief.

The shimmering thread that connects me to Charon still lies in wait in the centre of my chest, but rather than test the efficacy of the clear stone, I decide not to tempt fate and resist the urge to pluck at the cord that binds us.

It's surprisingly bright for this time of year. As I exit the market, I tilt my face to appreciate the kiss of the sun's rays on my cheeks. When I pause to bask, it takes less than a second for my enjoyment to die in a pulse of searing agony. Starting in my legs, flame and fear are wildfires spreading through my body before igniting an inferno in my chest and brain. Clutching at my head, I scream, dropping to my knees, startling those around me, who flinch away.

Awful images flood my vision of walking through a car park, being jumped from behind, a chemical taste stinging my tongue. The sinking sensation that I need to fight the arms closing in around me in juxtaposition to my jelly-like limbs. The world turns black.

When I open my eyes again, I'm in an unfamiliar room with shiny plastic wrap covering the walls, and there are tight leather bonds cutting deep into my arms, strapping me to a gurney. The incessant shaking in my bones isn't through fear alone, though. When I glance down at my exposed body, I discover that my right leg has been amputated below the knee. Bile rises in my throat. A few feet beyond the gurney, a figure of a man sits at a table, eating something that is too blurred by my tears for me to identify, but as the loud slapping of his chops rings in my ears, the absolute certainty that what he's eating is my missing leg chokes me.

Blinking the images away, I come to, realising that I'm screaming. Kane's terrified yelps mix with my own. A small crowd has gathered, circling my place on the ground, their heads haloed by the sunlight.

'She's awake,' one says as I shakily rise to my feet.

Not knowing what on earth just happened, I mutter an apology while stumbling away, clutching my head and trying to make sense of the vision. All too vivid, the picture of the amputated limb that felt so much like my own floods behind my eyelids, rolling my stomach. I pause to be explosively sick. Nearby people jump out of my path, their disgusted yells matching my own unrelenting horror. I wipe the sweat from my brow while heat explodes through my body, leaving me gasping for air.

Stumbling along the busy streets, I ricochet off passers-by. My vision spots and blurs, blackness creeping in at the edges. I clutch the clear quartz necklace swinging violently from my neck as I stagger ten paces, strict in not allowing myself to yank it off so I can call out to Charon and demand he explain what's happening to me.

The open space is unnerving, and like the wretched creature I am, I stagger into a quieter, piss-stinking street, where I close my eyes for a moment's reprieve. Which is a mistake. With my eyes closed, Kane's death is a scene painted in crimson, a searing agony so strong, it should flay the flesh straight off my bones. A scream rips from my chest. Though my yells are truly a curse at my own stupidity for ever believing my pact with the wraith wolf could be avoided for long. My liberation from my cell came at a cost: my freedom for Kane's vengeance on his killer. Behind my eyelids, the vision of the wolf's jaws ready to swallow me whole snaps at my skull, and I jerk away. It seems the price is ready to be paid.

When I open my eyes, I'm on the floor outside my flat with no idea how I got here.

CHAPTER 4

TINO

The sight of Lee's door ajar, blackness creeping around the chipped white wood, sets my heart racing. I barrel into her flat, frantically calling her name, but find no one and no signs of struggle. Only my own laboured breathing echoes in the darkness of her living room.

Through the permeating stillness comes the spattering of running water. Without thinking twice, I throw open the bathroom door to find Lee standing in the shower. Naked. The faint smell of sulphur clings to the edges of the room.

All my breath leaves me in a woosh as she turns to face me, shock parting her lips into a perfect O. The sight of her bare has my body singing with need. She's beautiful. All long legs and flame-red hair plastered to her pale skin. Even the angry shine of the scars adorning her arms that she once covered with shame are now worn more as battle scars.

I feel like I stare at her for an eternity, but in reality, it's only moments before I'm moving. I need her—no, I need to be inside her. Crossing the room, I climb into the bath to bring her lips to mine—

Shit, the water is freezing! I instantly retreat.

'Lee. The water is like ice.'

She doesn't respond. Instead, she clambers out of the tub, meeting me in a clash of bodies. Her lips on mine, she's all teeth and nails, her hands on my chest pushing me to the cool tiled wall while her tongue explores my mouth. Leaning her body against mine, she responds to each caress as my greedy palms explore her.

Despite the freezing water, touching her skin is like handling an ember, and while it kills me to put an end to her clawing at me as if she might die if she doesn't have me, I let her go. When I try to pull away, she releases a juddering exhale, pressing her forehead to mine.

Her body trembles, which I might mistake for a good thing if it weren't for the devastation on her face. She's not crying, though she might be moments away, her hands balled into fists in my T-shirt. Her anguish is so intense, I'm lost for words.

'Tee,' she keens. Though when she throws her arms around my neck and pulls me to her chest, it's not out of lust. This is sheer desperation.

I press my splayed palms to her waist, holding her close. Her skin is like the surface of the sun, almost excruciating to hold. We do a kind of swaying dance on the spot.

'I want you to know, I loved you for so long, for eternities. Through eons, ages, you were always the dream.' Her words are a whispered psalm, though they trouble me. They're not wrapped in devotion but sound more like she's trying to convince herself of their truth.

'I love you too,' I say into her sodden hair after a while, steam rising from its lengths, misting my vision. 'You're burning up.'

As if a spell is broken, she pulls away, blinking, surveying me as if for the first time. Then she kisses me, a simple soft brush of her lips, the taste of hot ash there. It's a flavour as bitter as defeat. When she pulls away, her devastation remains.

She gulps, her eyes snagging on my lips before she wipes a palm across her forehead and steps away from me to wrap herself in a towel.

The silence between us unnerves me, so I'm compelled to speak again. 'Your front door was open.'

She doesn't answer, instead fidgeting with something around her neck. A pendant I've never seen her wear before is a prisoner clutched in her closed fist.

I take a step closer to her, easing the white gem dangling from the thin strap of leather out of her hand, only for her to snatch it back from me. 'Where did this come from?'

'It's for protection.'

'Protection?'

She finally meets my eye. 'Yes, protection. I'm broken, Tee.'

The dread in my stomach pools further.

'That's the reason for the freezing showers, the constant puking, my loss of control around you. Why I lose control when I kiss you.'

'I don't understand.'

She heaves a big sigh. Scratches at her neck with one hand while the knuckles of her other turn white on her necklace. 'I lied,' she says, voice small. 'I remember the other side.'

Sickness and anger flood my veins, my body fighting a war over which emotion will win, the horror of what she went through, what she's been withholding all this time, battling the dread of who she's been withholding about. We stand staring at each other, the silence a lead weight around us.

'And?' I demand.

'And—' She takes time with the word. '—my freedom to return to this world came at a cost. To Marie. To my soul. I'm charged with a deadly mission of vengeance.' She starts to stutter as she clutches her stomach. 'I-I'm scared of what will happen if I don't fulfil my task.'

I knit my brow, confused. 'A mission of vengeance?'

Lee nods frantically, the words now tumbling out of her as she paces. 'I blacked out and woke up on my doorstep. I have no idea how I got here.' She wildly thumbs her necklace. 'I went to buy the crystal, and not long after I put it on, I had a vison. An awful vision. It must have been Kane, from when he was human, showing me how he died in agony. His soul was flayed during his murder, and now he demands vengeance. I need to do something. I'm running out of time. The only path clear to me is to find his murderer. Tee, I think I need to kill him. If I have another vision, it might destroy me. Agony doesn't cover it. It felt as if my own limbs were being sawn off.'

'Lee.' I gently take her shoulders, smouldering coals in my palms, feeling both guilty for my own jealousy and awful for what she's gotten herself into to return to me. Whoever Kane is, he doesn't sound good. Another problem to add to my list. Though my priority right now is calming Lee down. 'We'll figure this out. You won't have to kill anyone.'

Her blue eyes are pools of endless ocean as she chews her lip. 'You don't understand. Our bargain....'

'We'll figure it out. There's always a way to undo what's been done. After all, this Kane you made the bargain with, he's in the Underworld and you're not. Plus, you have your necklace now.'

Her fist tightens around the amulet. 'The crystal doesn't protect me from Kane.'

'Then who?' She casts her eyes down. My stomach drops once more. *Please, please don't let it be Death.*

Her lip trembles. 'I'm so sorry, Tino.'

'Sorry for what?' My mouth is dry, but I need it to be said out loud.

Her eyes close softly as she says, 'He's in my head.'

'Death?'

She doesn't answer, but her expression is all I need. The truth is painted over her every feature. She remembers the other side, and Death was there to meet her. Whatever trouble she's in now, he has a hold on her somehow.

I dig the heels of my hands into my eyes, trying to organise the tangle of my thoughts. I'm so mad at her, but at the same time, I'm certain that whatever stupid bargains she's agreed to, she did it to return to me.

I take a few steadying breaths, about to speak, but before the words leave my lips, my phone buzzes in my back pocket. I withdraw it to reveal an incoming call from Lorna.

I narrow my eyes, showing Lee the screen before answering the call on loudspeaker. 'Hello?'

'Tino. Oh, thank God you answered. Are you with Lee?'

'Yeah, she's here.'

'We've been trying to ring her for an hour.'

'Sorry, I lost my phone,' Lee chimes in, a note of panic in her tone.

'Lee, we need your help. It's Marie.' Lorna's voice wobbles, on the edge of tears. 'She's really sick. She was taken into hospital three hours ago.'

Lee grabs the phone, holding it close to her. 'Lorna, what's happened?'

'She's in a coma.'

'No!' Lee drops the phone in a clatter, falling to her knees and fisting her fast-drying hair. She claws at the skin of her face. 'No, no, no,' she repeats as I bend to collect the phone, her forehead now pressed to the wet bathroom floor.

'Lorna, are you still there?' I ask.

'Yes. What happened?'

'Lee's pretty upset.'

Lorna's voice turns urgent. 'Marie is suffering from some sort of soul sickness. Her hair turned completely grey. She was ageing in front of us. The deal she made to get Lee out—we only understand that she made one, but we have no further information to go by....'

I glance at Lee, still clutching her head while crouched in supplication.

'Lee may find it hard to trust us, and if she wants to keep secrets, that's fine, but things are different now. Marie's life is in danger—'

'I know,' I interject, interrupting her flow. There's no need to convince me. 'Lee admitted as much herself. She also made some kind of bargain. She felt compelled to confess. She's had some kind of vision.'

Lorna's sharp inhale ghosts in my ear as I kneel by Lee to implore, 'Marie needs you. This bargain you made—Marie made one too. Have you any idea of the terms?'

Lee gulps air as if she's drowning again, pushing the sodden hair from her face. 'Only that she made a deal. She didn't tell me the details. Though, given it's a deal with Kane she brokered, it'll mean nothing good.'

'Are you getting this?' I ask into the handset.

Lorna's voice is tinny through the crackling line. 'Is Kane a spirit stuck on the other side?'

Lee's eyes are wide and wild, staring straight through me. 'Kane is a wraith,' she whispers.

'What's a wraith?' Lorna's small voice asks.

Lee's skin shudders along her shoulder blades, an alien, inhuman motion, and on instinct, I shuffle away from her. Fear and terror saturate the room.

'A spirit torn apart in a violent death. A soul charred and stained.' Lee's voice quivers, her gaze imploring, a cry for help I have no understanding of how to answer. 'He is a creature bent on revenge. A gigantic wolf who stalks the Underworld.'

I shiver.

Rising onto her knees, she grasps the front of my shirt. 'It's his mission I'm charged with. His savage death is in my blood, seared into my memory. Perhaps Marie will be well when my mission is complete.'

'You're seriously suggesting you murder someone at the behest of a ghoul?' I ask.

Her eyebrows shoot up, eyes wide in terror. 'It is my purpose. It's a living beast, itching under my skin.' She rocks on her heels, her chest heaving as if released from a burden, fist still clenched around her necklace.

'What of Death?' I probe, and she flinches.

'Marie was helping me, trying to find a way to sever the connection we share.'

Lorna is saying something, confused about Lee's confession. But the blood rushing in my ears makes it hard to concentrate. 'Jesus, Lee. Marie helped you escape and was helping you cut your bond. This is obviously all his doing.'

'No,' she whispers. 'No, he wouldn't. He's not cruel.'

'You're defending Death.'

She stumbles to her feet, fast and fierce in front of me. 'He is not Death! He has a name. He is The Ferryman, ruler of the Kingdom of the Underworld. He watches over the river to the next life. He preserves life; he doesn't destroy it. He cares for the spirits there, even the wraiths. He would not hurt Marie.'

Her chest heaves as my jaw slackens. Her eyes close, regret hunching her shoulders as she addresses the phone. 'Lorna, I'm bound to The Ferryman. I need to sever the connection. Perhaps if I fulfil Kane's wishes before we do that, it will uphold Marie's end of the bargain.'

Lorna's panicked voice rings through the phone. 'Are you talking about killing someone?'

'This isn't some promise easily broken. Both Marie's life and mine could rest on this.'

'Lee—' Lorna starts before I interject, finally done with being reasonable and understanding.

'What is he to you, Lee? The Ferryman. This bond. He's in your mind. You defended him. What happened?'

Lee straightens, impossibly tall and imposing. 'He changed me.' She stalks over, now meeting my eye. 'When I was dead, I had but one motivation. Of returning to *you*. The Ferryman gave me that option, to change my very being, to become a Fury. A vessel of vengeance on Earth. The gravity of my mistake came all too late. I should have accepted my fate and remained dead.' She admits her final sentence with a sigh. 'But I didn't, and then I refused to become his bloody right hand in this world. When Kane gave me the opportunity for escape in exchange for the life of his killer, I took it. I betrayed The Ferryman.'

My brain struggles to process the information. I should be asking better questions, like what a Fury is exactly, but all I register is the flicker of pain at the name of The Ferryman.

'Were you with him?' I'm pathetic and jealous for asking when lives hang in the balance.

'No,' she says, softening, and I release a sigh of

relief. 'But....' She rests a gentle palm on my chest. 'I can't be with you either.'

'Lee, we'll figure this out.' I push down the hurt her words cause me. 'You won't have to kill anyone. We'll find a way to sever your connection to the Underworld. It doesn't matter to me that you're a Fury, whatever that means. We'll figure this out together.'

Her smile is a shaky one. Threading her fingers through mine, Lorna forgotten on the end of the phone, Lee draws closer. 'I never forgot about you when I was prisoner there,' she tells me. I frown at the notion of her being held captive, but I don't have time to ask about it as she barrels on. 'I wasn't with him. But... time passed so differently there; I grew... attached. I'm different now. You're my oldest friend. I love you. Believe me, I hate myself for wanting him and not you. My Fury bond to him clouds all my emotions. I'm so, *so* sorry.'

I take a dry swallow. A thousand micro reactions fly through me, fighting to make themselves known. Betrayal. Heartbreak. Disbelief.

This can't be it. This can't be where we end.

Her face crumples as if she's crying, though no tears stream down her face. Her hand remains curled around the cord hanging from her neck. 'It's a constant battle with myself not to remove this to speak to him.'

I try to pull my fingers from hers, but she holds them fast.

'I wish it wasn't this way. Because all I ever wanted was *you* and all your goodness, how you want to take care of me—I so want to be taken care of. That sounds so awful, but it's true. The girl who went to the Underworld held on to that memory for so long. I'm so tired of fighting my way through life, or even death. I'm tired of never knowing who I am. You can't know how much I want to lose myself in you. But I returned broken, and right now I'm the thing you need protecting from. That's why Marie was helping me. It was to escape this wretched connection, not to release us from our bargains.'

Her teeth chatter, and while her admission crushes me, the desperation in her stare cannot be contended with.

'We break your connection to him. This is what you want?'

Though my words are hollow, she nods ferociously.

This time when I step away, she releases me. I told her when she came home, I wouldn't let her go. Am I about to break that promise? Do I want to rage against her over the fact that my deepest fears have come true? She threw herself at Death's mercy and is now recoiling from it. Do I tell her that it's her mess to clean up? In typical Lee fashion, she's dallied too close to the edges of chaos; then, after being burned, she's retreated to the safety of our friendship. Perhaps I've been wrong all these years, and Lee is not a fragile doe in need of protection; instead, she's a wolf masquerading as a lamb, too timid to fully realise it herself.

'Lorna,' I say after a lifetime lost in my swirling ruminations, 'is it possible to sever a connection between a Fury and The Ferryman?'

'I have no idea,' she says after a pause. 'Without Marie, it's a hard task. I'll ask Lis to call in some favours. Please, don't go killing anyone, Lee.'

Lee huffs out a humourless chuckle.

'It's a line that, once crossed, is hard to come back from,' Lorna adds.

Lee's mouth downturns into a grimace.

The line goes dead, and Lee steps to me, not daring to take my hand again. 'Thank you, Tee.'

I swallow thickly. 'We sever this connection, Lee. We do this because I love you, always will, and I don't want to see you bound to anyone against your will. But you just broke up with me. I'm not sure how I feel about *us* right now. I need some time too.'

She nods, lip trembling. 'I understand. I'm so sorry.'

Then, releasing a shriek of ear-splitting agony, she clutches her stomach, bending double at her middle, the stench of singed hair saturating the space between us.

CHAPTER 5

LOVELY

Under the freezing cascade of the shower is where I practically must live, water droplets like tiny bullets evaporating on my skin in shallow hisses. If I step out of the downpour, I might be set alight. I haven't eaten in three days, though even with an empty stomach, I've been throwing up round the clock, plagued by visions of being slowly eaten alive, the stench of sulphur now a living being in my bathroom.

Kane's murderer was one sick, sadistic son of a bitch. Starting at the knee, arm—cutting off limbs with the skills of an amateur but the equipment of a surgeon. Even giving Kane antibiotics—an IV of fluid to keep the meat fresh. My stomach turns, and sick splatters the bath where I'm sitting, all traces of dignity evaporated with my stomach lining. It's all just bile and blood now.

'But the crystal is working?'

I nod at the voice coming from my iPad, which is propped on a chair placed far enough away from the shower spray spitting pinkish residue down the plug-hole, the taste of blood coppery on my tongue.

'If a mere crystal is capable of blocking your connection to The Ferryman, the being who once commanded the Furies, severing your tie to Kane should be feasible.'

I groan, resting my head on the hard, smooth porcelain. 'It's different, though, isn't it? I rejected the Furies' call, whereas I committed to an agreement with Kane. The Furies are Ch—' I correct myself. '— The Ferryman's extension on Earth. My failing to submit means he can't control my actions. I am, however, bound to my word to Kane. And a Fury's word seems to hold more weight than Lovely's.'

Silence. When I glance at the screen, Lorna is chewing her lip, and even Lis, who was furious I hadn't told them the truth straight away, glances nervously at her girlfriend.

'What?' I probe. 'How bad is it? What do I have to do to escape my bargain?'

'Honestly,' Lisette starts, 'this is ancient stuff, and American Voodoo is young magic, so this is a bit beyond us. According to myth, The Ferryman is a lesser god. Hades was the big bad of the Underworld. We weren't certain there was any truth to their mythology until you spoke of it. As far as we knew, the gods have long since died out. There's no precedent for this.'

I shiver under the icy water, the skin of my arms contracting as if a separate creature to me. 'What are you suggesting? That there's no hope for me?'

'Noooo.'

The way Lisette stretches the word gives me pause; this isn't something good.

'We're still exploring some... channels.'

'Channels?'

'They're not exactly friendly,' Lorna chimes in.

'Don't put yourselves at risk for me,' I implore, only for Lorna to roll her eyes.

'Please, who wants an ordinary life?' She smiles, but the worry tainting her eyes is discernible even an ocean away. 'But... well, maybe you should talk to The Ferryman? Tell him what's happening.' She registers my hesitation, speeding on with her line of thought. 'He might be furious about how Kane got one over on him, and if there's anything at all he's willing to do that would help Marie, it's worth a chance. You said yourself he isn't cruel.'

I shake my head. 'It's not a good idea. Besides, Tino hasn't spoken to me in three days.'

'He's hurt,' Lisette answers. 'To him, you were gone for minutes. He'd held you in his bed hours before you came back to life. But for you, so much time had passed. You lived a life with someone else.'

'Don't you think I know that?' I snap, fisting the

crystal so tight, it groans under the pressure. 'If I take the crystal off now, the way I'm feeling—blood on fire, Tino gone, and Kane's death pooling in my stomach.... If... if I speak to Charon now, if I hear his voice in the state I'm in, when he tells me to come home, I'll do it. I'll return to the Underworld, fall at his feet, and he'll never let me go again.'

The couple stare.

Every treacherous cell in my body screams in agony, demanding vengeance. I lurch forwards, clutching the bath lip with talon-like fingers. 'Perhaps,' I continue, 'you could both research Kane's murder. Is his killer even alive? A Plan B, so to speak.'

They exchange a glance. 'It won't come to that. There's no guarantee it would even cure Marie, and we'd still be stuck with your bond to the Underworld.'

'At least my brain wouldn't be scrambled,' I grind out. 'Helping you guys would be physically possible once I no longer have to douse myself constantly.'

'Hang in there, Lee,' Lorna encourages. 'The witches might come through yet.'

I raise my eyebrows, biting my tongue on the argument that this line of enquiry is a terrible idea given Lorna's past dealings with them. I'm even more sceptical now that I'm aware of the nature of the channel they're exploring. Without Marie, we're truly lost. I need to get out from under this water and make a plan. But I'd be lost without their help, so I nod.

'I'll call Tino,' Lisette reassures me. 'Make sure he

comes to check in. You shouldn't be on your own right now.'

'That's not fair on him.'

The corner of Lisette's lips tilts. 'No,' she agrees, 'but you're in pain, too, and you don't deserve that either.'

I've never wanted to kiss her more.

———

My back aches against the cool curve of the tub as I stretch my leg, letting it lounge against the wall, my pruned foot leaving a ghost on the dull magnolia paint. The constant shower spray leaves me sodden, the fabric of my black vest and underwear clinging to me. Though I'm stripped down as much as possible, I keep these on in case I need to take a call from Lorna. *Heavens, my water bill is going to be insane.* Dull but thunderous pounding makes its way over the din of the shower, and I scramble to my feet.

Tino.

Caring little for the trail of water I leave through my flat, I run to the front door, my frozen fingers clamouring with the latch before throwing the door wide.

'Mom?' My jaw drops, my eyes struggling to believe who is standing in front of them.

She barges her way in before stopping short at the sight of me soaked and barely dressed. I don't miss how her eyes rake over my naked arms for signs of puncture marks, then beadily assess the room around me for paraphernalia. Her breaths coming rapid fire, hands braced against her hips, she's come ready to riot.

'As if it wasn't bad enough that I had to learn you'd gone to America with Tino from his mother, now I learn from Tino himself that you've been home for almost a week. I've worried so much about you.'

'You spoke to Tino?'

'That is not the point, Lovely. But yes, Rose has been a lifeline of late, and when I called, he was there.'

I massage my eyes, my head beginning to pound as vile images start coming through like grainy film reel. Kane had lost all his limbs before his killer let him die. Fear has been steeped so deep into his blood, all other emotions are now a stranger to the wraith. I choke on my bile.

'Mom, this isn't really the best time.'

Suspicion grows in her gaze. 'Tino said you were sick with the flu.'

I nod, clutching my stomach.

'Lee, if you have a fever, it's actually very bad for you to try to cool down with cold water.'

'I'll bear that in mind.' I attempt to usher her out before I buckle in agony.

'You're my daughter. I love you.'

I scrunch my eyes closed because, though she means well, the words are daggers to my heart. I'm her daughter no longer.

'Mom, I'm sorry, but you have to go. You don't want to catch this.'

She stands, defiant, though watery eyes betray her. 'I'm sorry, okay? For before, when you were struggling with... everything. I'm sorry I failed you. Please let me make it up to you. I've lost your dad. I don't want to lose you too.'

'Mom,' I plead.

'You don't understand what it's like. There's no guidebook for when your daughter has a mental breakdown. I admit, I didn't know how to cope with it —with you.'

I reach out to her. I want to tell her that it's okay, I forgive her, I don't blame her, and put an end to her suffering. If I could end the suffering of just one person instead of being the cause of it. But my vision blurs while inside my body, a rib cracks under the pressure, and I keel over while images flood my brain: the final cut, the prize of Kane's killer. The one Kane won't live to witness him consume.

This is the end.

Kane's butcher had green eyes, bright and hollow. Though he wore the skin of a man, someone so deranged hardly deserves to be called human. Kane's heart was the ultimate delicacy to him. I clutch my chest as the scalpel pierces skin. I fall to one knee as my mom rushes to my side.

'Lee! What is it? What can I do?'

But the pain is too much. No one should suffer as

Kane suffered. He deserves his vengeance. Deserves it ten times over. The heat in my core rises, water evaporating into steam on my skin. My mom takes a step away from me as a feral snarl leaves my lips.

Tino appears in the doorway. His eyes widen at the sight of my mom, then dart to me steaming like a dumpling and slumped on the floor, clasping my broken rib. 'Lee.'

He moves to help me to my feet, but as soon as his hands clasp mine, I double over in pain again. This time the skin tears along my shoulder as if lashed by a whip, and I cry out, my voice a jagged blade. Bent at my middle, my hair a cascade in front of me, a bead of blood runs along the curve of my shoulder, and I watch it drip to the floor, its minute crimson splash against the white linoleum a vibrating gong in my ears.

I glance at them in time to witness the fear bloom across my mother's features as she demands, 'What's happening?'

Tino's eyes dart frantically between us, all explanation escaping him. 'You should leave,' he says instead.

'Leave? I want you to tell me what's happening to my daughter.'

Fear prickles along every ridge of my spine. Lurching forwards, I dig my nails into Tino's chest, and his fearful gaze meets mine. 'I have to get out of here, Tee.'

With a second lash of an invisible whip, the skin of my shoulder blade splits further, the force of it sending me against him, my body pressing into his. My mom cries out in horror, bringing her trembling fingers to her mouth.

'I've got you,' he murmurs, though now he's trans-fixed by the crimson puddle pooling at my feet. The air is thick and tinged with the metallic aroma of my blood.

Threading my fingers into his hair, I consider his honey-soaked eyes and marvel at my own stupidity in believing escape was possible for me. 'Look at me,' I whisper, only continuing when he meets my gaze. 'Something bad is about to happen.'

When he parts his lips to talk, I capture his mouth with mine. For one glorious second, I live in that sensation, his tongue hot against my own. Then I say goodbye to the girl I once was.

On the third lash, I cry out, Tino swallowing my pain. Bracing myself against him, more than my ribs break—in a crunch of bone and tearing of flesh, the ache in my back is finally satiated. In the space of my tiny Birmingham flat, where the dead once haunted me, the giant wingspan of a Fury dominates the space. My wings flex from the discomfort of being hidden inside my body, black sinew and bone, awful batlike extensions of the Underworld, unseen in this realm for almost three thousand years.

My mom reels, awestruck. Tino takes a sharp inhale as he marvels at my wings.

Already my discomfort is eased, like a snake shedding its skin. The collective power of the Furies surges forth, filling me with the absolute certainty of retribution. One more itch to scratch, and I'll be free. Kane will be avenged by my hand. My rage will be the sharp edge of a blade for his killer. Pain will be his only companion by the time I am through with him.

Taking Tino's chin between my thumb and forefinger, I drag his attention from my wings, forcing him to match my gaze. 'I have to do this.'

'No,' he whispers, hands at my waist. 'Don't go.'

'He deserves to die,' I grind out, sliding my palm over his jaw, letting it descend to rest on Tino's throat. His gulp is a heartbeat in my hand. A life in my grasp.

'Lee....'

'I am Fury now.' I set my jaw, my lips a whisper away from his. Now I revel in my heat, the inevitably of my destruction, the flex of my muscles against Tino. 'Kane died slowly. A death so awful, he recalls nothing but terror in this life. No other emotion. No love. No warmth. Terror alone. Does any creature deserve such an existence?'

'We're past vengeance. We must move past it. We're not living in those times anymore.'

I clench my teeth, seething. 'Tell that to the man who consumed Kane's body, eating him while Kane watched.'

Revulsion flickers through Tino's expression. He says nothing more. I release my grip on his neck.

Nothing more than my mission on my mind, I stalk from my flat, leaving Tino shaking by the wall and my mother on her knees in reverence. An ancient power flows through my veins, flexing and flaring. What I must do and where I must go are now a path as clear as day, paved in blood-soaked steps. Vengeance, for all its bitterness, is a drug more insatiable than one I've ever tasted before.

CHAPTER 6

TINO

'Jenny! Jenny!' I grip Lee's mom's shoulders, shaking her, trying to rouse her to the moment immediately after her daughter sprouted wings and stalked from the flat.

Shit! Lee has wings. Huge batlike wings ripped right out of the skin of her shoulders. Suddenly I'm filled with regret that I didn't research Furies more diligently. Too mad at Lee for the childish hurt that she cares for another man... being... whatever he is.

Someone who understands her.

I swallow the unsavoury thought of Lee in Death's embrace, jealousy acidic on my tongue.

'Jenny.' I shake her more gently this time, her mouth hanging agape as her eyes fill with tears.

'An angel. She's an angel.' Her words come as a whisper.

For a moment, I'm too shocked to acknowledge

them. *That's her takeaway from what just happened?* Lee was hardly a vision shrouded in a halo and feathery wings. With water evaporating off her skin in jets of steam, jaw set with fury, wings of sinew and bone, all pale flesh, only wearing a black vest and underwear, she was less heaven-sent, more creature straight from the depths of hell. *I'm wasting time. I need to stop this before she does something she'll regret. My Lee would never hurt another person, only herself. Though one thing remains true—she still needs saving from herself.*

Jenny collects herself with a clearing of her throat, standing to meet my eye. 'That wasn't my daughter, was it? It was something who looked like her. Lee isn't.... Lee's dead, isn't she, Tino?'

The answer to her question is so much more complicated than I have the time to explain right now. 'It was Lee. I'm so sorry, Mrs Timms, but there's no time to explain. I have to catch up with her.'

'Where is she going? What's she going to do?'

'Something terrible,' I whisper to myself as I walk out the door. She calls something else, but I don't stop, don't look back.

The Birmingham roads are wet and grey, busy with the hum of commuters coming home from work, already dark with headlights casting nightmarish shadows of passers-by, exhaust fumes rich in the air. Yet no one is running alarmed through the streets from having moments ago seen a young woman barely dressed with wings sprouting from her shoulders. I turn my face to the heavens, the rain pelting me. No sign of Lee. Panic writhes inside my limbs as I take my phone out and call Lisette. She called me yesterday to encourage me to speak to Lee, and in typical Tino fashion, I was too late.

'Tino,' she answers by way of hello.

'Lis, we have trouble.'

She doesn't answer, only waits with a held breath.

'Lee's gone. She sprouted wings.' I half laugh because the sight of her truly transformed should be impossible. My heart and my brain war with each other. Jenny was right. Our Lee is dead... but how can she be anything other than the woman I love? A strangle of frustration leaves my throat. 'She's gone for Kane's killer.'

Lisette doesn't say anything for a long minute, and from the rustling at the end of the line, I get the sense she's on the move. When her voice returns, she speaks in hushed tones. 'Lorna would kill me for saying this— she's witnessed first-hand how killing another changes a person, no matter how justified or unjustified....'

'But?' I push.

'But what if this is a good thing? According to Lee, Marie bargained with Kane for Lee's life, and Lee bargained with Kane for his vengeance. What if this saves Marie?'

'An eye for an eye and a life for a life? Is that what

we've come to? We must be better than that. We're not living in the Dark Ages.'

'These are times of gods and monsters, Tino.'

Her words send a thrill of dread through me. One part terror, the other part a twisted sort of excitement at being privy to the world steeped in shadow lurking beneath the modern-day exterior.

'There is no room for morality here,' she continues. 'And yes. I would trade Marie's life for a murderer's. I would trade it for Lee's freedom from being the pet of the Underworld. Damn what that makes me. The people I love matter more!'

The ferocity behind her sentiment has me split between nausea and admiration. It's a barbaric way of thinking, yet wouldn't I do the same for Lee? The question troubles me.

I change the subject with an exhale, sidestepping a man with an umbrella power walking past me. 'We need to do some work and fast. The world is too calm for one that's witnessed a woman take flight, which means she's on foot. Where is she going, Lis?'

'The name Kane alone isn't a lot to go on.'

'Lee mentioned he was eaten. Cannibalism isn't exactly an everyday occurrence.'

'Hmm,' she agrees, pensive.

I chew my lip, my feet pounding pavement even though I have no idea what I'm doing. I stop, massaging my eyes until I see stars. 'Research is going to take too long. I need to help her. She'll regret this forever. I can't let her become a killer—that's not who she is.'

'Tee.' Her voice is gentle, pleading. 'Perhaps she doesn't want to be saved.'

The words sting. 'You don't know her like I do. She would never hurt anyone. This will destroy her.'

Her next sigh is one of defeat. 'What do you need me to do?'

It's a huge ask. 'Use the board. Find Kane. Find where she's going.'

'Shit,' she mutters.

My heart is a caged bird in my chest. One heartbeat. Two.

'Okay. I'll call you back when it's done.'

Clicking off the line, a silence surrounds me, so total I could drown in it. I don't like that I've asked Lisette to put herself in harm's way. But *this* time I have to save her.

Perhaps Lisette is right. Perhaps there's no cost too high to save the woman I love.

CHAPTER 7

LOVELY

As I walk, passers-by avert their eyes as if they're instinctually repelled by the unnatural shape of my wings wrapped around me like a cloak. I half smirk at memories of The Ferryman draped in shadow engulfing me as I stalk. How I longed to be consumed in his icy embrace. To let go. Forget about who I am and what I am—simply be. Revel in the sensation of abandon.

Wait, no. That can't be right. I pushed so firmly against the rule of Charon. I didn't desire his control. In fact, I longed for my own. I just wanted *him*. Craved the luminescent, inhuman blue of his gaze on me. Bone antler crown looming over me. Sharp cheekbones. Olive complexion. Icy fingers trailing my skin. I mutter a curse at my Fury bond, or the Stockholm syndrome, probably both, holding me firmly in their grip.

'This longing isn't love,' I shout out into the bleary night, my steps now taking me through a clearing in a wood. My instincts to get to Kane's killer are so ingrained in me now, guiding my feet as if possessed by the wraith himself, that I'd barely noticed my journey's length, nor the transition from city to country.

Tilting my face, I'm glad of the rain even though it evanesces into the ether from the heat on my skin. Through the gloom of the sky, the moon is a scythe tonight, a fitting omen of my mission. Dirt clings to the soles of my feet, which move on instinct, following an invisible path. With every step I'm surer of what I must do. Images of teeth and bone and scalpels flash in my mind, though no longer accompanied by my agony anymore. Kane's deep growls of satisfaction will soon rumble through the streets of the City of the Dead. The notion of it sets goose bumps firing over my skin.

Unbothered by fatigue or hunger, I walk into the night. Under the cloak of darkness, I spread my wings, arching my back as a cat would shake off a nap. The earth reeks of dampness following the rain, yet the air crackles with the possibility of what is about to happen as my feet hit soft grass and I set my eye on the low-lying structure before me.

A menace in itself, all beige on beige, brick and barbed wire. A place with one sole purpose: to protect the world from those it houses. It's not without a hint of irony that I stalk up to the building, seeking my way in, bringing a harbinger of doom to one of its inmates.

I pause slightly at the sign near the main entrance informing me I've arrived at HMP Long Lartin. Home to some of Britain's worst. My Fury instincts simmer in my blood, Alecto's fiery rage telling me to burn, burn, burn.

But I'm here for one man alone. And I suppose the easiest way in is through the front door.

Though the rain has stopped, the heat inside me has become almost unbearable. So unbearable, the grass around my feet turns to tinder and sizzles. I stumble a fraction, clutching my chest while catching the quartz necklace between my shaking fingers. The scent of smouldering sends Alecto's memories flooding into my brain—cities aflame, the guilt of the one becoming the guilt of the many. Her duty to purge flexes in the tips of my fingers, stifles my lungs. My breath becomes impossible to catch.

No, my bargain is with Kane.

Yet her unrelenting wrath shines through.

Scenes of Kane's bloody murder appear to me so vividly, I'm sick once more on the ground before me. It's not only his death now—there are more images. Victims before Kane when his killer was honing his skills. Anger and pain and so much suffering. The ends of my hair spark, leaving trails like dynamite.

I'm vaguely aware of a guard leaving his booth by the barrier. I think I'm going to pass out, my vision littered with black spots. I need to breathe, but the rage is too much.

'You can't be here.'

The guard's words sound like they're underwater. I'm clutching at consciousness. A last pang of anger pushes through me. This is so unfair—to be so close to the sick, vile degenerate housed in these walls... and fall short.

The dynamite detonates and my hair catches alight, a bright beacon in the night. My wings flare behind me. The guard stumbles and falls to the ground with a yelp. Alecto's call was a battle cry straight from the depths of hell. All cowered before her, but my own consciousness is smoke through my fingers. Her psyche pushes through the ether of time, mingling with my own, its rage too much for my gentle spirit to bear. Her wrath is terrifying, boiling my very blood.

A faint golden thread plucks in my chest, a tiny pinprick in a sea of unrelenting rage.

'*Careful, Fury,*' Charon purrs in my mind, '*or you'll set the whole world on fire.*'

I'm only vaguely aware of glancing down as my world turns black. My clear quartz necklace—I'm still wearing it. Yet The Ferryman spoke to me.

And then I pass out.

CHAPTER 8

TINO

Lisette had taken way too long. By the time she'd called me back with the location of Kane's killer, too much time had passed to make a difference. In my heart, I know this as I hurtle towards the prison, breaking the speed limit, every speed camera flashing as I go.

There goes my career in security.

Not that I care.

Lisette was practically a shade of green after battling to pry a message from the other side. A meaningful one. Lisette is not a skilled medium, and according to her, the spirits coming through from the other side are in chaos. Although part of me deeply suspects a large part of her delay is because a good half of her wants Lee to succeed if it means a chance of curing Marie.

I attempt to grapple with the bedlam of my

tumbling thoughts over what lengths these women would go to for the people they love. Lisette would condemn a man—who is apparently already serving a sentence for his crimes—to death to save her friend. The more rational side of my brain screams that it isn't right—we don't play at being God. But then I think of Lee, of what she gave up. She sacrificed her humanity, all so she could return to me.

Are the depths of her devotion so unfathomable? Am I crazy to want to stop her?

All thoughts of the right and wrongs of morality instantly flee my mind as I come to a screeching halt before the barrier, where there are no guards to be found.

I open the car door and step out, open-mouthed, the last trappings of winter chased away by warm air clogging the breeze, thick with smoke.

Long Lartin Prison is on fire.

CHAPTER 9

LOVELY

Alarms blare, and I feel them as ungodly tremors thundering through my veins. I blink my eyes open, and the world comes into blurry focus. The tips of my fingers are sticky and coated in red. I rub the tacky substance between my thumb and first finger, then marvel at the perforated metal staircase I've found myself on, which ascends further to a metal galley leading to corridors arranged in a square around an open middle. As my gaze travels lower, taking in my unknown surroundings, I try to figure out how I got here. The same substance from my fingers also stains the walls and drips off the lower railings.

I squint against the incessant alarm, noticing for the first time the bodies, necks bent at unnatural angles at the foot of the stairs. I realise what I'm looking at is blood—lots of it.

Glancing down at my still-bare legs, I see I'm covered in the stuff.

'Did I do this?' I whisper, though there's no one around to answer me.

I climb the stairs, thinking back to the last thing I recall—a guard approaching me and Alecto's memories that were so powerful, they made me black out. Brief remnants of rage needle me like daggers, and I stagger to the edge of the walkway to throw up over the railing before crumpling into a heap.

My skin prickles as if with fever, my breath juddering out of me. I need to pull myself together.

'Careful now, Fury. The one you seek is in the bowels of this dungeon,' a voice of writhing smoke purrs in my ear.

'Charon.' His name escapes me in a whisper. 'You were always there.'

'Of course,' he says a little more softly. *'A mere trinket will not keep me from you.'*

I bring my palm to my forehead. Of course it was never going to be that easy.

'You were so intent on shutting me out, I gave you time. Now you're in need of my guidance, if you will take it?'

Gulping, I stare at the trail of bodies left in my wake. Necks bent, batons gripped in their hands, knuckles still white around them, mouths wide in horror. I close my eyes, not wanting to look any longer. 'Alecto—her memories were too strong. I lost myself. I couldn't stop it, Charon. I've killed the guards.'

My stomach is a dead, dread weight.

Charon lets out a soft chuckle. *'I did wonder what would happen with an unchecked Fury in the waking world. It seems Alecto's legacy of wrath will live on.'*

'You knew this would happen?'

'I suspected.'

My skin turns to gooseflesh, and the ends of my hair, which have returned to normal, now sizzle, leaving smoky trails in their wake. That awful burnt-hair smell fills my nostrils, stoking Alecto like a living beast inside my chest.

'Charon,' I breathe, clutching my head, the mother of all headaches threatening to overtake me. 'Charon, help me,' I plead.

'Guidance is all I'm able to offer you right now. I have no real power to stay your hand.' While his tone is sooth-ing, the bite behind it is clear. *'Kane's killer is within the prison. Move quickly and find him. Kill him. And get out.'*

'I don't think I can.'

'You will or you will *lose yourself again, and more damage will be done than is necessary.'*

Perfect.

I haul myself to my feet, allowing instinct to guide me further into the belly of the prison. The corridor is long, with reinforced metal doors lining it, the pulsing of a light near the end casting an orange glow along its deserted length. Over the noise of the blaring alarms, I might have missed it—the sound of pounding coming from behind the door. All the doors. Men shouting. I still, my breaths coming rapid fire. There are at least twenty cells, all with men locked inside them.

My bare feet slapping against metal, I approach the cell closest to me with slow, cautious footsteps.

'*Fury,*' Charon hisses. '*Retreat. Find Kane's killer.*'

But I don't answer. Some kind of morbid curiosity pulls me forwards, somehow satiating the need under my skin. *Is this you, Tisiphone?* Slowly I wrap my fingers around the latch of a small window in the door and slide it across with a clink.

Inside, surprise betrays the man's face for a moment before it turns dark and hungry from his vantage point through the little window. He drinks me in, ogling my long legs where I'm standing in my vest and underwear with bloody hands, taking in my red curls that intermittently catch fire and smoulder into nothing.

'*Fury,*' Charon warns.

But he's drowned out by the pulsing in my ears as the man gives me a leering smile. I know him. Not in the way where I've met him before, but I know that devouring leer, have ducked my head and tried not to be noticed, his unwanted palms lingering on my thighs. Know him the way millions of women across the globe know him.

'Look at you,' he says, letting out a low whistle. 'Like Carrie on prom night.' Flickers of confusion pass his eyes, breaking through the lust. 'What's going on out there?'

My mind is a whirlpool of bitterness, revenge tasting like ash on my tongue for every unwanted grope I've been forced to endure, every bruise, every time I turned my cheek and pretended not to care.

'What's the matter, sweetheart? You need me to sort you out?'

He winks as I move forwards again to the handle of his door. It's locked, but strength flows through me now, and I wedge it open.

'Oh yeah,' he practically croons.

The inside of the cell is thick with his musky, predatory stench. The guy honestly licks his lips as I step closer to him, but before I have chance to do anything, he moves quick, arm lashing out as his palm strikes me clean across the face in a loud slap.

My head whips back, my hair covering my face and masking my attacker's glee from me, though his giggle confirms his pleasure in hitting me. Faintly, Charon's voice is in my head, and my vision fizzes at the edges, but I cling to the fringes of my consciousness. I want to be here for this. I want to savour every moment.

Turning to face my attacker, power surging, I vow this will be the last time he lays a hand on anyone. With his slap I bore witness to it all—all his crimes. The women. The lives he's ruined. This cell isn't punishment enough.

His elation swiftly changes to confusion before

contorting in horror as he clutches his temples. My touch means madness to those who are unworthy. Within a few moments, he's cowering before me, simpering like the animal he is.

I grin.

'Please, please, please,' he begs.

I grab his chin, forcing him to meet my wrath. 'You deserve so much worse than what I'm about to do to you.'

Fear trickles into his expression, and it's as sweet as honey. Sliding my hand down his neck, I let my fingers press into skin, sharp and strong, tearing into his flesh until his screams drown out the alarms. I let it all out, everything I've ever held back, every hurt I've had to endure—I let it out as I tear the limbs from his body. Until there's *nothing* left. Just flayed pieces of meat.

I return to the corridor. Too far gone to heed the hail of The Ferryman, I call upon all my powers as Fury. From my place in the corridor, I slide open every lock and allow every door on the level to swing open. Bemused prisoners stumble from their cells, stopping dead at the sight of me. Not an inch of the bare skin of my hands is visible beneath the blood of the obliterated prisoner. I'm thick with the stuff.

'Run,' I tell them.

The one closest to me makes to attack, but I'm too quick and strong. Grabbing his face, I wrench his jaw wide and yank his tongue clean from his skull before letting it fall to the floor with a wet slap. A moment of silence glides by. Even the alarms seem shocked. Then most of the inmates take my advice and flee.

Those who linger quickly find themselves bereft of a spine. Bones turn to dust in my grasp. Insanity seeps from my pores. As I stalk forwards, palms splayed, my sparking hair finally catches, igniting to flame, and the wings that had retreated into my flesh stretch to their full glory, scraping the walls and ceiling and sending a few of the men to their feet in prayer.

'*Oh, Daughter of Darkness,*' Charon croons in my ear. '*You truly are a plague to the unworthy.*' His voice is a black caress, one I lean into, arching my wings as I snare an inmate before snapping his neck.

'They deserve to burn,' I grind out, surprised by my own volition, unnatural speed and strength allowing me to pull limb from body. 'This is for every victim. Everyone who never had the strength to fight back. This is for them.'

The golden thread binding me to The Ferryman plucks in my chest. I clutch the spot where my heart once thundered. 'That won't work,' I tell him, rage ringing through me, bitter and metallic tasting—or that could be the blood spraying my face from the severed arteries of the man I just beheaded. 'You have no control over me.' I grin.

'*Your wrath is a feast to behold, my ferocious one— truly,* truly *terrible. The river is alive with souls.*' The reverence in his voice sends goose bumps over my skin, and I have a fleeting notion of a vision with Charon on his knees at my feet, not the other way around. *'But a take care. There's a wildfire in your heart, and you will set the whole world aflame if you do not control it.'*

My answering cry is the same battle call of Furies millennia ago, one that has not seen the light of day since we fought alongside the Spartans. Though not only Alecto, Tisiphone, and Megaera are with me but a hundred, maybe a thousand others from before we were known as Fury. Their rage is hot. At my call, the cells around me catch fire, and awful flames like phoenix wings engulf the prison.

I plunge deeper and deeper into the institution until I come to a door, shivering and recoiling at its edges from me. This is it. In my true form, that of terrible, bloody Fury, even the earth can tremble, afraid of my retribution. The door, like the unworthy, is right to fear me. I tear the quaking metal from its hinges.

The man inside sits calm and collected on his bed, as if he's expecting a visit from the Grim Reaper. He pays no heed to the smoke and fire behind me, nor to the wings I have to fold in around myself to fit into his cell.

His soulless eyes stare into mine. Green. Void of humanity. 'I've made peace with my demons,' he tells me.

Through the bond of my word as Fury, Kane's

satisfaction grumbles in my stomach. The Ferryman's anticipation dances on my skin.

'Honey,' I say, offering a maniacal grin, grabbing his lower jaw, 'I'm no demon.'

The smallest flicker of confusion passes over his eyes before I hook my other hand into his mouth, my fingers sliding on his jagged teeth before jerking his jaw upwards and tearing his face in two, a burst of blood and flesh splattering the wall. His remains slump and slide off the bed.

A breath as heavy as a lead weight leaves me.

'*It is done,*' Charon says in my mind. '*Now come home, Fury.*'

CHAPTER 10

TINO

The wailing of alarms is swallowed by hungry flames. The absence of prison guards swarming the inferno informs me of the fate of the prison's inhabitants. Every window is blown out, fire licking, charring the brick with sooty blankets. Nausea rolls in my stomach. Surely it won't take long until the fire services arrive. I need to not be here when they do; I have no explanation about why I should be here in the middle of the night. I doubt anyone would buy my story that I'm trying to save my friend, the rogue Fury, who might have just killed everyone inside.

She might have killed everyone inside.

Though there's something about the terrible sight —along with the knowledge that Lee lit the match— keeping me rooted in place. My delicate girl, driven to so much destruction. I'm unsure how she'll forgive herself for this. On instinct, I dig my phone from my pocket and call Lisette.

'Did you find her?' she answers without preamble.

'Not in time,' I say, the heat of the fire warming my face. 'He must be dead. The whole place is burning to the ground. Any change in Marie?'

'I'm at the hospital now. No change.' Her worry cuts through the phone line.

'Maybe there's a delay in the effects and a full recovery is still possible,' I suggest, though even I hear the lack of conviction in my voice. As I lower myself into the car, a movement on the grass in front of the inferno distracts me. 'Lis, I'll call you back.'

Hanging up without waiting for a response, I slowly track and approach the dark outline of a figure sitting on the grass. Dread pools in my stomach as I skirt around her edges, her wings twitching and trembling, her long legs stretched out in front of her. She's whispering something, one fist clenched around her necklace, her other hand braced in the grass, and she's rocking to and fro. As I round to face her, a singed smell emanating from her every pore stings my nostrils. Her skin is stained, filthy with caked blood. She pays me no heed, her focus firmly on the blaze. At least it conceals my lips parting in shock as I take in one side of her face, which is completely covered in blood, eyelashes matted and half of her mouth crusted with the stuff.

'Rise, Daughter of Darkness,' she whispers repeatedly.

'Lee?' I sink to my knees in front of her.

For the first time, she meets my gaze, and the anguish I find there is a kick to the chest, winding me. She snatches my elbows, holding them fast with claw-like fingers. An unnatural keening tears from her throat, jarring my very soul. It's so desperate, more animal than human. 'At first it wasn't me who did it. Their rage was so much, it took over, and when I came to, I was already surrounded by bodies. Innocent bodies. The Furies may have taken over, but it was my hands that snapped those necks.'

Every hair on my arms stands on end, and I struggle to control my breathing. Suddenly I'm fuelled with a violence towards this creature who enslaved Lee in such a manner.

'But then,' she laments, her voice hoarse, 'then I was just so angry, and it was me. I killed all of them, not Kane's killer alone. They're dead because of me.' She throws her head back and wails into the burning night like a wolf howling at the moon.

The gravity of the situation comes crashing on me in turn, and I grab her by the elbows and hoist her up. 'We need to get out of here, Lee. Move. You need to move.'

She stumbles to her feet, but I'm unable to reach around her shoulders, what with the size of her wings, so instead, I lead her by her blood-soaked hand. The heat of the fire licks accusingly at my exposed neck.

Lee is talking to herself once more. '...*add fire to the fury you will rain upon the living lands...*'

I move the passenger seat as far back as it will go before bundling Lee inside. With her wings wrapped around her, she just about fits. I race to the other side and get the hell out of there as fast as I can. The car is silent except for my thundering heartbeat and Lee's inaudible mutterings, the fringes of panic frazzling my edges every time I glance at her, blood plastered to the side of her face closest to me. The point where flesh meets wing is mesmerising, a seamless part of her.

What a massive fucking mess.

As I pass by Wixford, I remember Lee has family there, but what explanation could I offer them in exchange for letting her get cleaned up? Oh, and the giant batlike wings might be something they would notice. Shit. Where am I going to go? Her flat? My ma's? I drag my hand down my face, slowing the car from the 100 mph I've been doing and dropping to a more legal speed. The last thing I need is to be pulled over.

Lee groans, leaning forwards and digging the heels of her palms into her eyes. 'He warned me this would happen.' She glances in my direction, disarming me. 'This is all my fault.'

Despite the insane atrocity I witnessed only moments ago, ugly jealousy rises to the surface. 'You mean you shouldn't have agreed to your deal with the devil?' I bite out.

'Charon isn't the devil.' She sighs, tilting her head. 'More like death incarnate.'

I give a sardonic smile. 'Oh, in that case, much better.'

She laughs a little, and it dissolves something of my panic.

'I was talking about my stupid decision to be a Fury in the first place. Stupid, stupid Lee.' She shakes her head. 'Do you know the worst part?'

'Do I want to?'

She chuckles again. 'It's not what you think. In fact, it's even more shameful.'

I hold my breath, though her expression is only sad.

'When I agreed, I thought I might do some good in this world after all.'

Her admission kills me. It's so her.

'Lee.' Her name is a plea.

She shifts in her seat, adjusting her wings until her temple is leant against the headrest. She laughs before a wistful sigh escapes her. 'Silly, right?'

For some reason, the soft way she admits it brings tears to my eyes.

We drive for a minute in silence before she asks, 'Where are we going?'

Now it's my turn to chuckle. 'I have no idea. Your flat maybe? Any ideas?'

A smile tugs at her lips. 'Please, not my flat. Keep driving. Let's go to the beach and watch the sun rise.'

Unease pulses through me, and I glance at her. The knuckles of her fingers are touching her lips as she yawns. 'Are you okay? You're so calm now.'

A languid serenity creeps into the spaces of the car around us as Lee's blinks become long and heavy. 'Honestly, I'm okay. It feels like a massive relief, a weight off my shoulders. My bargain with Kane is fulfilled. His killer is dead.'

I glance at her again. Her eyes are now closed. With a final breath, the wings shiver and begin to shrink, creasing like rustling tissue paper as they recede into her body. The skin where they had been seals as if they were never there.

Lee's chest rises and falls with the peace of sleep. I rub my eyes a few times, disbelieving. It's over.

I call Lisette, keeping my voice quiet so as not to wake Lee.

'Hi, Tino.'

'Hi,' I whisper. 'Any improvement in Marie?'

'Not yet.'

Disappointment sinks through me.

'Why are you whispering?'

'I found Lee. She's in the car with me right now. She's sleeping.'

'Oh shit. She hasn't slept in days, so this is a good thing, right?'

'The wings have gone, shrunk into her skin as if

they're nothing. Now her bargain is done, I'm sure the worst of it is over. We should keep searching for a way to cure Marie... and a way to cure Lee.'

'You mean to sever her connection to the Underworld?'

'Yes. For starters. If there's a cure for Marie, surely there's a cure for Lee too. Change her from Fury to human again.'

'Tino.' Lisette emits the sympathy of a mother about to gently pacify her child. 'Try not to hold out much hope for this. Severing her connection is one thing, but there's no cure for her.'

'You're 100 percent certain?' I protest.

'Nothing in this world claims those odds, Tino. I'm sorry, but Lee, human Lee—she died.'

My sharp inhale comes with a shot to my heart. I furiously rub my eyes again. My brain wages war with the notion. Lee is here, with me, breathing and bloody in the car at my side.

After a moment's silence, Lisette releases a sigh. 'You both should come back to New Orleans.'

'Does that mean you'll look? For a cure?'

'There's one person who might have answers. I'm waiting on them. They're not exactly my friend.'

'Thank you, Lisette' are all the strangled words I manage.

Halfway to the seaside, Lee stirs slightly, the night outside as black as the wings now vanished underneath her skin. I pull into a service station and pause, keeping vigil over her sleeping body, blood still crusted over her skin, her arms forming a cocoon around herself. She appears more peaceful than I've seen her in a long time, the skin of her face smooth without the deep worry lines she's worn for days.

Heaving a sigh, I leave her in the car in the darkest part of the car park. Inside the deserted service station, I pick out some clothes for when she wakes. The selection in the gift shop is crazy. The best options are a pair of neon tie-dyed leggings and an oversize T-shirt with a picture of a cat on it. I buy some baby wipes along with a couple of bottles of water before grabbing a double shot of espresso and heading to the car.

As I slide into the driver's side, I see Lee is awake and staring at me. Heavy blinks tell me she woke mere moments ago.

'Hi,' she croaks.

'Hi.' I grin in return before taking a huge swig of my hot drink. It burns my throat, though I relish its heat. Its bitterness is grounding in the most surreal night of my life. At least the stench of dried blood has been replaced by my coffee's rich aroma.

'I slept.' She yawns, pulling down the mirror of the visor and staring at the state of her face.

'Here.' I throw her the bag. 'Not much in the way of choice.'

I glance at her bare legs and force a hard swallow. The glorious night we spent together was weeks ago for me, but for Lee, lifetimes have passed. Though she assures me nothing physical happened between her and Death, it hardly puts me at ease. I try not to dwell on the times we've been close since being alive again, how each time, the slight unease gnawed at me that she was attempting to throw herself into it too much, as if trying to bypass who was touching her, only desperate for sensation.

She removes the T-shirt from the bag and eyes the cutesy cat picture, a smile ghosting her lips. Turning to me, she holds it up to her chest, the sweet design a ridiculous contrast to her bloodstained features.

A chuckle leaves me. 'It suits you,' I tell her.

A crack in her facade drags at the corners of her mouth. 'Only you would say I look sweet after a massacre.'

The stare I hold goes on a beat too long, a heat stirring in my belly, hungry for her. Longing. But she clears her throat and gives her attention to the bag, laughing off our tense moment as she pulls out the baby wipes and water.

'I thought you might want to get cleaned up.'

'You thought right,' she chuckles. Immediately she whips out some baby wipes and furiously cleans her face, her swipes so hard, they must be taking off layers of skin. I observe her in silence, the ocean of words unsaid stretching between us until the tension is too much for me to stomach.

'Have you spoken to him? About what happened back at the prison.'

She stills before resuming her cleaning a little more slowly. 'Tee.'

'Just tell me. I can take it.'

'Yes,' she mutters.

I wait.

She sighs before relenting. 'In the prison. I haven't spoken to him since.'

'Since you've been with me, you mean?'

Her eyes flick my direction. She nods.

Fuck.

I release a breath and wrench the ignition of the car into life, allowing her to get cleaned up in peace, wincing only slightly as she drags wipes across her arms, revealing her scars once more, a reminder of her constant suffering. My constant failure to protect her. Part of me wants to be mad at her—for never embracing what's good for her, for even giving her conversation to such a creature who would use her, wants to own her like every other man she's known. I drum my fingers against the hard plastic of the steering wheel, slick from my sweaty palms, the sanctuary of the service station left behind as I merge onto open road. The glare of headlights is sparse in the dead of night. Each time they pass by, claws of shadows stretch over the inside of the car.

'What did he say?' I ask, morbid curiosity besting me.

'He tried to stop me.'

That surprises me.

'But he couldn't," she continues. "The power of the Furies overtook me, and I was lost to it.' She adjusts her head again, making herself comfier, and bites her lip. 'He was right—an unchecked Fury is the last thing the living world needs.'

'But it's over now, right? Your bargain is done. You won't lose yourself to it again.'

'Right,' she quietly agrees before taking a tiny sip of water.

I hate that, hate everything she's not saying, hate all her secrets—the ones she must have shared with him in the lifetimes they spent together—hate how he means enough to her that she can't bear to be with me.

We drive on in silence. The white chevrons of the motorway are brilliant markers guiding us forwards in the still night, the glow of our headlights cutting through the darkness.

CHAPTER 11

LOVELY

They say it's darkest before the dawn, and as I stare out at the deserted beach, watching the gushing tide retreating into the abyss, I'm inclined to agree. The light of the stars is swallowed by hungry night. The blackness is foreboding, not comforting as I believed it would be.

Nerves radiate from Tino. He's always been one to fill a silence, but instead, he keeps fiddling with the car heater rather than voice whatever concerns he has. A fine sheen of sweat has settled over my skin. Though Tino found clothes for me to wear, I'm still lacking shoes and socks. Not that it matters. As I open the car door, I'm thankful for the cool bite of the night air.

'Wait,' Tino calls after me, shrugging on his coat. 'We should wait until it gets light.'

'Why?' I ask, though my voice sounds a million

miles away as I wander off the asphalt and sink my toes into the freezing sand. It clings to my feet as sharp as shards of diamonds. After the heat of the car, its shock of cold is a relief.

I swallow, and it could be a death rattle vibrating my throat.

For the first time in a long time, nerves thunder through me.

My feet hit the sand harder, faster, dull pounding on damp ground, the black of the coast so total, the world right in front of me is veiled by the greedy night. The anticipation my blindness creates sends a thrill down my legs. It's like being in a horror movie, never quite sure what lingers in the dark edges. That feeling of a hand groping towards you in the void, something ready to eat you alive.

The sea is further than I'd anticipated.

Tino is becoming breathless behind me, his footsteps heavy and laborious in his work boots. 'Lee, I can't see where I'm going,' he pants.

I laugh. 'Me either.'

That's the point.

In a tearing of flesh and fabric, I almost stumble as the skin of my shoulders rips open. I manage to keep moving through the pain as my wings open to their fullest. In two beats, I take flight. My feet leave the cold sand behind. Night air kisses my face, the salt of the sea collecting in the corners of my lips, and when I lick them, the briny taste fills me with longing.

I pause to take my final fill of Tino, who has now come to a slack-jawed halt on the deserted beach. I take a moment to let the heat in his amber eyes fill me before I leave the world of warmth behind me.

'I loved you for a thousand years,' I tell him. 'But I can't stay. I'm sorry.'

Without giving him a chance to respond—or myself to fully absorb the betrayal on his face—I depart. It doesn't sit easy. He's all I ever wanted, the memory of him placed on a pedestal to return to during my captivity, but after my slaughter of the prison inmates and guards, one thing is clear as crystal in my mind: I do not belong here. Innocent people died because of me.

To fly is a freedom beyond comprehension. When I was a girl, I used to daydream about being a bird, how wonderful it would be to leave the world behind. To fly above it all, peaceful. Serene.

When the soft lapping of waves caresses my ears, the first rays of sun peeking over the horizon, I tuck my wings behind me and plummet. Nerves wrap themselves around my core while the golden thread that binds me to Charon glimmers in my chest.

Breaking the water's surface does little to slow my momentum, though soon the dark is a distant thing. While my descent continues, reams of bubbles the same colour spectrum of the aurora play with my hair, riding my skin. The resistance of the water lessens, allowing me to bring my feet forwards so that I'm cupped by the water as I marvel at the world calmly falling away. I'm Alice through the looking glass, drifting through time and space. The kaleidoscope continues around me, dappling my skin in such an exquisite symphony that a grin is impossible to keep from my lips. For a brief moment, my murderous rampage was worth it to experience the passing between worlds once more. To witness what my calling allows me to observe, how the border between life and death is paved with indescribable luminosity.

Once more, a sense I have no name for tells me I'm about to hit the bottom. I brace, though when I land, it's as soft as crashing into a bed of feathers. The black silt ground of the Underworld plumes around me, stealing my vision like the night of the Welsh coast. Only when it clears this time, I'm surrounded by endless grey.

Rising to my feet, I dust myself off. I'm still wearing the fluorescent leggings and cute T-shirt, though the back of it is shredded, making it even more loose-fitting and flapping at my sides. I run my fingers over the leathery skin of my wings, fingering tiny knicks from my last altercation with the wraiths. They feel strangely more substantial. I wiggle my toes into the silt, my weight forming footprints in the gritty substance. I frown at my toes. My last, albeit extended, sojourn here always had a hint of unreality to it.

No doubt due to the belief that I was dead.

I bite my lip. I'm very much *not* dead now. Didn't

kill myself to get here. Now my soul and body both are firmly in this dead place.

A tiny cloud of silt kicks up into the water around my feet as I spin in the greyscale void. This time the nothingness holds no dread. The golden thread that attaches me to Charon strums as if a flurrying violin, singing me home.

I take flight through the watery abyss without worry about my destination, only a desire to meet the guardians again. Will Hero and Leander have missed me? Is Kane at peace, or is he still a menace? Will Charon be pleased by my return, or will he be furious?

The last time we shared the same space, he shook the foundations of the city with rage moments before I was summoned to the land of the living. The thrum of the bond rattles my bones. And then tall spires of a haunted Atlantis loom into view.

UNLIKE BEFORE, I DON'T LINGER AT THE FRINGES OF THE city. Though flight over the high turrets would be easy, I still make my way to the bone gates. Charon has willed me to him. However, I'm still nervous that, for some reason, I'll be denied entrance to the city. The Ferryman might believe it punishment for my disobedience that I remain in the living world to wreak havoc.

As if expecting me, the bone gates creak as they

stutter open with a low groan. A fleeting spear of disappointment that no one is here to greet me is quickly overshadowed by the scene before me. The City of the Dead can hardly be called a city anymore. Rubble lies scattered everywhere, piled almost as high as the boundary. A faint shimmering of dust infuses the water that fills the city. Buildings lie in ruins, though the most intact structures are those closest to the river.

Boats carrying souls of the dead continue down the black river onwards to their next lives. The slick glisten of the water sends a sudden rush over my skin, reminding me that it flows with the blood of The Ferryman.

I take a tentative step into the city limits, half expecting alarm bells, Charon's enormous shadow to flood the watery sky, for the guardians of the river to float effortlessly over, chastising me for being late. Instead, the silence fills me with dread. I continue for a few paces, too aware of my lurid outfit in this landscape of devastation. I frown at myself for even caring what Charon will make of this ridiculous get-up. I've been gone for weeks; how much time has passed in the Underworld? A hundred thousand years? An eternity? How many souls has Charon ferried to the source? Perhaps he's found another Fury, the stars having aligned for a new Drowned One. Every time we talked, he never mentioned *this*.

A shift of shadow to my right brings me out of my

ruminations. Out of the darkness, bone, and rot leers the giant wraith wolf, Kane.

'I never thought you'd grace these eldritch roads again,' he says with a lazy yawn, stalking around me. 'Then again,' he chuffs, 'maybe I'm not too surprised. This place has gone to the dogs since you left.' He ruffs a chuckle, raising his nose in the direction of the rubble-filled city.

'I'd hoped...,' I fumble.

Kane arches a rotting eyebrow. His form is just as awful as when I left him. He reeks like a rotting carcass, yet I sense no menace. That is, he hasn't yet tried to maul me with those awful teeth.

'I'd hoped you'd be at peace.'

'You fulfilled your end of the bargain. Make no mistake, Fury—my vengeance is done.' The corner of his snarl rises. 'A wraith rarely moves on, though, and I have little incentive to do so when things have become so... interesting around here.'

The hairs on my arms rise. 'What do you mean by that?'

He continues to circle. 'A Fury has never escaped before. Wild, unchecked in the waking world, wrath personified unleashed upon the living. And yet so many wraiths remain within the city limits, with more appearing over time, their will strong and unfulfilled. The Ferryman is without his hands, his weapon snatched from him.'

I gulp, starting to lose sensation in my legs. 'Is he terribly mad?'

'Oh, there is madness enough to go around, Fury. This city is rife with it.'

'Kane...,' I falter again, now doubting my desire to return—perhaps I will do no less damage here. Certainty now fills me that I will be thrown into a cell for the rest of time when Charon gets his hands on me, and a new Fury will be called as soon as possible.

'It was a poor choice of words earlier. I merely *wished* for our paths to never cross again.' Kane barrels on, hastening his pace, the hackles of his spine rising. 'The truth is, I've been waiting for you, guarding these gates in case you returned.'

'You waited? For me? Why?'

'When you accepted our bargain, our touch was our bond. You not only saw into my torn soul, but I glimpsed yours.' His words come hushed and fast at my shoulder, his rotting breath almost making me gag. 'Your greatest strength is also your greatest weakness. You're here on a fool's errand. There's nothing here for you but pain.'

My jaw drops. Part of me wants to fight with the wolf. Argue how I would cause far more pain in the waking world, but rubble gently cascades nearby, a rogue rock bouncing to Kane's paw, a judder shaking the ground beneath us. A new spindly shadow elongates on a crumbling wall of a nearby wrecked street.

'Run, Fury,' Kane commands, though I only stare at

him in shock. He cocks his head, black sludge dripping from his jowls. 'That is, unless you want to be charged with yet another unholy mission?'

I don't need telling twice. On foot, I flee the prowling threat along a nearby abandoned street. The Underworld has become a wasteland. As I barrel past smashed-in homes and dusty piles of grey rock, I marvel at the destruction of the wraiths, my wonder as bitter as it is awestruck. I run until my muscles burn —until I'm so deep into the city, I have no idea where I am. I'm utterly alone.

Leaning my shoulders against a broken wall, I attempt to regain a semblance of composure, stretching my wings while clutching my chest. The thrum of the golden cord lassoing my empty heart is so violent, it's almost unbearable, stealing my breath as I drop to a knee. I wanted nothing more than to escape—escape my fear, escape my cell, escape the land of the living, escape myself. And now... now... now I'm terrified of facing Charon, yet escape seems like the last thing I want. I squeeze my eyes shut tight, asking myself, *What is it you do want, Lovely?*

The sensation that I'm not alone forces me to my feet. When I peel my eyes open, a giant tarantula of a wraith is at the end of the narrow street I've taken refuge in. Pincers chipped and twitching, shadow oozing into its path as its legs on the right side creep along nearby buildings to accommodate its size. Its eight eyes are hollow, hungry, trained solely on me.

The awful stench of decay permeates the space between us.

The proximity of the wraith causes my hair to sizzle, then catch fire, lighting the enclosed space and casting even more ghastly shadows of its approaching shape. A walking nightmare.

The path is too narrow for me to take flight. My wings flap uselessly against the too-close walls, brushing the rough brickwork. The beast's excitement is palpable, pincers click, click, clicking. I freeze, cursing myself for every stupid decision that has led me here. The City of the Dead was supposed to be a refuge, but instead, I'll be leaving once more with a mission, bent on more blood on my hands. That's if he doesn't rip me apart in his attempts to secure a bargain.

The ground rumbles beneath our feet, toppling a building and sending the spider sideways, its screech at so high a pitch, I'm forced to cover my ears. The building that was holding it upright crumbles, and the monster rolls away from me, allowing more dim light into the space. I whip my head towards the end of the alley where a tall wolf looms, dead eyes gleaming. Next to him is a figure cloaked in shadow, the antler crown of the Underworld atop his cloaked head, only the luminous blue of his eyes visible in the shadowy depths of his hood.

'Charon,' I whisper.

Whatever words I'd planned on saying next are

lost to the shriek of the tarantula. I shrink into the corner as it rears out of the rubble.

'She's mine,' it cries, its voice as jarring as breaking bricks.

'No, Dorian,' Charon commands, raising a hand, pushing the wraith away from me with an invisible force and stepping into the path between me and the spider. 'Now is not your time.'

The spider wails once more as Charon edges closer to me, Kane snapping his jaws at Dorian, who's in turmoil as he's forced to retreat, eight legs dug into the silt and rubble sending plumes of debris everywhere until he's lost in a cloud of dust as he withdraws. A lead weight settles on my chest. It's so easy to forget because of their grotesque forms that the wraiths are human spirits. The spider. Dorian. He was once human, a man with hopes and dreams. A man who was most likely murdered in the most awful sort of way.

My whole body constricts. I keel over, bending at my middle. I've doomed the entire afterlife. I'm too dangerous to reside in the living world, too pathetic to reside in the dead one, depriving the wraiths of the Underworld of their vengeance.

Kane prods my arm with a rotting nose. 'Don't faint on us now, Fury.'

Charon's imposing figure stands before me, unmoved by my anguish. I force myself to straighten and stare into the unworldly blue of his eyes. Try to imagine the emotion there. Lost to the depths of his hood. So unlike The Ferryman I was once familiar with, uncloaked and lying opposite me in my giant bed. *Whatever became of that bed?*

'You can't remain in the open,' he says, voice cold as he turns his back on me.

CHAPTER 12

LOVELY

Stumbling, I struggle to maintain pace with Charon, snapped back into my body by the ice in his demeanour. Kane trots a little way behind us, dripping sludge and shadow.

Now annoyance flares in me. 'Is that all?' I demand.

'What more is there?' Charon asks without turning or slowing his pace.

'How about, "Are you all right, Lovely? So glad you've returned, as I've been *begging* you to do."' *I'm happy to see you* are the words I wish he'd say, though I don't voice that particular foolish notion.

'I've hardly been begging,' he scoffs, his voice a tone darker.

I snort, and Charon's hand clenches into a fist at the sound.

'What now?' I ask as he glides through the city

while I practically run to keep up. 'Am I to return to the cell?'

Charon's hooded brow tips towards Kane. 'The cell was destroyed.'

'And you haven't rebuilt it?'

'I've been somewhat preoccupied.' He motions to the piles of rubble with a mercury-ridden hand.

'Then you haven't called a new Fury? You're not going to replace me?'

At this, he stops, rounding on me, and though his expression is masked by the hood, his shadows writhe around him as if ready to rebuke me for all the trouble I've caused. They flare, snapping dragons of midnight, but he restrains the shadows cloaking him from reaching out to me, no errant whisper wrapped around my ankle or finding its way into the flame of my hair.

Charon's own fury simmers beneath his surface. He takes a step closer, and I hold my breath.

'Even if I wanted to, it wouldn't be possible. Gods are not born every day.'

'Oh' is all I say to that. So much for being special. He'd replace me if it was an option. A Fury needs to be called into the shadow of a god. I vaguely remember the guardians telling me that. Whatever the hell being born in the shadow of a god means.

He doesn't move. Neither do I.

My hair crackles. His shadows shudder at his edges.

Needing to fill the loaded silence, I grapple at the first words that spring to mind. 'You don't seem pleased to have me here.'

The grind of his jaw crunches within the depth of his hood, and even Kane, still a few yards behind us, huffs.

'Do you understand how much trouble you've caused?' Charon bites out, clearly magnetised by the audacity of what I've just said. He looms closer, his opium scent fogging my thoughts. 'You are a danger to the waking world, yet you're a menace to mine. The wraiths are in revolt. Your creation calls to them, yet your denial is an insult.' He takes a final step, his antler crown casting tree branch shadows across my face. 'They are ruining my city, Fury. No peace for the lost souls lingers here. There is no refuge to be had. Only chaos.'

'I'm sorry. I didn't know,' I whisper. 'What will you do with me?'

'I should have you in chains,' he growls. 'On your knees. Dragged behind me for the wraiths to witness your contrition.'

My lips part, but no words fall out. A tumult of emotions crashes inside me. Guilt at what I've done here and in the living world. The blood on my hands from the prison and the ruination of the sanctuary of the City of the Dead both. Anger at Charon for wanting me only for the purpose of appeasing the wraiths. But most of all, annoyance at myself for my foolishness for ever considering that my relationship with The Ferryman was anything but that of master and slave. And how, like an idiot, I'd considered my own feelings to be something more. That I am bound to him as Fury is a fact I should never forget.

But it's so easy to forget it, and stupidity begets stupidity.

I reach out to push his hood from his face, longing for the sharp edges of his features to be exposed. Believing things might be better between us if only his true self were bare before me.

He recoils from my touch. 'Don't,' he snarls. 'What you want, I cannot give you.'

Gulping down my embarrassment, I snatch my hand away, instead bringing my wrists together and presenting them to him as if I'm a sacrificial lamb, recalling the Furies before me offering themselves in supplication. On their knees. Always on their knees.

Bowing my head, I raise my wrists and steady my breathing. 'The chains?' It may not be the submission he wants, but it's all I'll allow myself to give. To return to being his prisoner and accepting how it's the lesser of two evils. Better that than wreak havoc on Earth.

'You would make it that easy, wouldn't you?' He sneers. 'Poor Fury, always the victim.'

Mortified, I drop my wrists, the heat pooling in my cheeks. 'How dare you.' I reel back from him, landing my palms on his chest and pushing him away from me, though I only succeed in propelling myself backwards. 'This is your fault too. You tricked me into this. You didn't tell me all the facts. That I would be bound to you. How bloody my hands would be.'

'It's the way it has always been.'

'Well, your way is arcane and ridiculous,' I spit. 'The other Furies were too young and too stupid to recognise when they'd been taken advantage of. You forget I know a thing or two about being used.'

His laugh is a cracked thing. 'Of course the blame is all mine. The massacre at the prison, the wraiths' unrest, the souls forced on because they're denied sanctuary. My fault alone.'

Frustration rises in my chest. 'That's not what I'm saying. You're twisting my words.'

I close the distance between us once more, my vision a wall of black and neon blue. Kane stalks off somewhere. Charon grasps my wrists, bringing them together. I almost forgot how freezing his skin is against my own, how I can shrink to a single point of contact. I half expect him to clasp chains made of shadow around them right then and there.

'What are you doing here, Fury? Why come back?' he asks, gentler now, though I don't trust it.

A shudder dances along my spine at the sensation of his palms still wrapped around my wrists. 'You asked me to. You told me to come home to you.' My voice wobbles with shame that I ever considered it would be a welcome return.

'Oh, so you submit?'

'No.' I pull my wrists, but he holds them fast.

'Why are you here? What do you want?' He's closer still, antlers twisting into my hair.

'Charon... I don't know.' I pull and pull, but he lifts my hands higher, holding them tighter. A vice. I'm forced to meet his cool gaze.

'You won't submit. You won't kill. What will you do? What use are you?'

'Please let me go.' I yank against his grip and find no quarter.

'Where will you go? You're under my protection. The wraiths will eat you alive. You'll kill the humans. What are you going to do, Fury? Your human isn't here to wrap you in cotton wool and lie to you about how all will be well.'

I cry out at the pain in my wrists and the hopelessness of my situation. I only ever wanted to be safe, and yet I'm so sick of having to be saved. 'What do you want from me?' I shout, and with all my strength, I whip my hands away and shove Charon from me, sending him into a nearby wall, my wings stretching out. The golden thread of our bond warms my veins to a shimmer cascading over my skin.

Charon rights himself. 'I want you to fight!' he roars. 'Stop feeling so sorry for yourself. This mess is of your making.' He gestures to the destroyed city. 'What are you going to do about it?'

Panting, I stare across the landscape of desolation. *What could I possibly do about this?*

But I don't have time to react before Kane comes cantering over, halting just short of Charon. 'We've got company,' he announces.

We move swiftly, but not swiftly enough. The tarantula, Dorian, has returned. He scuttles over the caved-in roof of a nearby building, pincers twitching. At the end of the street closest to Kane comes a wraith I've never laid eyes on before. It's taken the form of an elephant the size of a mammoth, bunting of rot threaded across its goliath tusks. Its wail shakes my bones. A crack in the opposite direction alerts us to a third. Shaped like a tiger, its fur is matted and claws sharp.

Charon positions himself between me and the tiger, raising an outstretched palm. 'Back,' he commands.

Though the tiger obeys, my head snaps towards the elephant, who has gained ground.

'Charon,' I whisper.

He switches, raising a palm to the elephant now. It stomps its foot, silt rising in the water around us. At this, the spider inches closer, its leg going through the broken roof. Bricks tumble down, narrowly missing Kane.

'Occupying them all is impossible alone,' Kane tells Charon. 'When you're distracted, one of them will strike.'

'Obviously!' Charon grinds out. 'Are you going to help?'

The wolf guffaws. 'I suppose that might be amusing.'

Charon growls. Actually growls, and unbidden, the image of his fanged mouth springs into my mind and warms my core at the memory of his tongue against mine. The flames of my hair crackle, causing him to glance in my direction. 'You must get to the river,' he commands me. 'The guardians will be there. Find them. They'll ensure your safety.'

Kane snarls at the nearing Dorian.

'Let me help you,' I plead.

'Unless you want another bloody mission to the surface, your only use is to hide right now,' Charon snaps.

Though he's said nothing that isn't true, it still wounds me.

Before I have chance to reply, Kane's snarl turns into a shuddering howl. He pounces on Dorian, causing them to sail through the wall of the crumbling house, taking out the entire top story. Charon mutters a curse; then with supernatural speed, he's on the elephant, his huge palms wrapped around its tusks. He slams the beast to the ground, dislodging so much silt that I can barely see three feet in front of me. I fumble in the melee.

Believing the tiger will pounce at any moment, I propel myself blindly into the air, clearing the tops of the buildings. The silt dissipates just enough for me to witness the tiger vaulting off a nearby roof, claws extended but thankfully only swiping air as I tuck my feet to my body in time so all it grazes are the hem of my ridiculous leggings.

Now airborne, I head towards the river. Charon and Kane are more than capable of taking care of themselves. Chancing a peek over my shoulder, my stomach drops at the sight of Dorian scurrying along the rooftops in chase. Even worse, when I return my gaze to the river, the dim glow of its safety is hindered with the dread outline of a cadaverous eagle. An entire wing is so bone withered, I have no idea how it has the power of flight.

I'm so screwed. With the eagle in front and Dorian behind, I have no choice but to change direction from the river. Instead, I retreat to the depths of the city, both creatures in pursuit. I'm too vulnerable in flight, out in the open, so I must take refuge in the streets, where I have more chance of losing them.

The crack of tumbling bricks causes me to glance behind me. Dorian is gaining ground, eight hairy, decaying legs stabbing at building tops, lashing out and swiping at my feet. My inexperienced wings burning, I brace for a painful landing, picking a street to disappear into while hoping my halt will be so quick that it will take a moment for the spider to right himself, and by that time, my course will be in line with the river.

Holding my breath, I close my wings, dropping to the gully of the street as if I'm a missile, overshooting it a small amount so as I hit the bottom, I careen into a wall and take the skin off my shoulder. I cry out, though as I turn towards the heavens, my yelp of pain turns to one of relief. The crashing of brick and tile in the near distance confirms my hope. Dorian's momentum was too great, and he's been thrown off balance at my sudden change in direction.

I spare myself a single moment of respite before I'm on my feet again and sprinting in the direction of the river. I hurtle along street after street, pure instinct guiding me to the sanctuary of the guardians, adrenaline thundering in my veins. How I've missed them. I almost want to cry.

By the time I register the shadow, it's already too late. The speed of my run coupled with the force of the impact sends me against a window. The glass splinters, shatters, and I tumble to the ground in a shower of shards. I choke on silt, wanting more than anything not to face my attacker. Only the hot putrid snort on the base of my neck forces my gaze to meet the hollow eyes of the beastly caribou, decay settled into its antlers, rot gnawing its hooves.

It brings its head down, ready to strike. I yell in protest as I throw my hands up defensively, catching its antlers in a way similar to how Charon had the tusks of the elephant. Only I'm not strong enough to throw it off as it tries to spear me, and my bare feet slide in the silt until my wings hit stone.

It strains against me, and my muscles shake with

all my strength until my arms weaken. The beast continues to push, the tips of its antlers beginning to press into my shoulders until the pop of my skin breaking rings in my ears.

'Charon.' I mean to shout, but it comes out as a whimper.

The caribou releases its hold, withdrawing its antlers from my shoulders. The relief is so sudden, I drop my arms as dead weights before it lowers its head as if to spar and throws them into my soft stomach with a squelch.

All terror leaves my body, and for a moment, all I focus on is a soft glugging noise. *Where is it coming from?* Raising my palm to draw it eye level, I see that it's slick with shiny crimson glinting in the gloom. With a cough, my own blood pumps out of my mouth in soft gasps, gelatinous and coppery tasting. It splurges in torrents over the snout of the caribou, who has me pinned to a derelict wall. I slump forwards against its forehead, a rag doll in human skin, my body contorted at a weird angle.

Amidst my confusion at what's happening to my body—*surely this should be agony?*—flashes of another life flit before my eyes: sepia snatches of dirty dishes on the kitchen table, walls damp with mould. My back aches from the belt. Shouting is coming from the bedroom, and I hide under the table. My name is Jamal. Today was my birthday. My sixth birthday. Now the steel grip of a hand is around my foot, and I'm screaming.

'No,' I try to cry, but blood bubbles on my lips, popping like gum. Already Tisiphone whispers in my ear, *'How sweet Jamal's abuser's death would taste on my lips. They are a family of monsters, violence passed from father to son. We should decapitate the head of the snake. End their line.'* The golden threads of a family tree begin to shimmer in my mind.

I squeeze my eyes closed in protest. The final vision of Jamal's father arrives, the silver knife illuminated by twinkling lights, the air thick with the tang of rage. Before the knife finds its mark, the vision shudders, and I slip to the ground in a heap. No longer impaled, I lie drowning in a pool of my own blood. I crack my eyes open a fraction to witness Kane driving Jamal from my body, jaws snapping against his neck, spilling shadow instead of blood. Though the Underworld has been painted red from my opened veins, sympathy for Jamal and his awful fate washes through me.

My eyes want to be closed. A heaviness lists about within me. Sensation tingles out of my legs. The corners of my mouth lift as my soul starts to detach.

I'm such an idiot for returning to this place. Did I believe I'd simply retreat to my cell with Charon's shadows wrapped around me for eternity? Playing chess. Counting souls. In my haze, I wonder what became of the bath. Did Charon ever pull the pearl across his own skin? Did he toss my chalk into the Stix? I drift in a reverie. If I die here, will I become a ghost of the Underworld? Perhaps I'll haunt Charon. That'll serve him right for binding me to him. I want to laugh, but it would take too much effort, and I'm so sleepy.

The crunch of teeth around my arm startles me awake. My first thought is that Jamal must be back to finish the job, but when I peel my eyes open, my arm is in Kane's maw. *Just like old times.* I'm filled with the sick urge to giggle again, though the desire swiftly leaves me when Kane runs at breakneck speed through the city, dragging me behind him. The friction burn against my skin and wing is enough to make me want to be sick even though my insides must be on the outside right now.

When I glance behind us, Jamal is no longer in sight, only the trail of blood I leave in my wake.

CHAPTER 13

LOVELY

Peeking my eyes open, a flicker of a smile passes my lips at the odd sensation of lightness—it would be so simple to float away. I'm by the river, basking in the golden hue of souls passing on, their glow the main light source for this entire dreary place. The City of the Dead is comprised only of shades of grey except for their sheen, the passing of one life to the next. And I feel so at peace, it would be too natural to drift right along with them. It would be as easy as closing my eyes and going to sleep.

A musical lilt sings somewhere at my edges. 'Poor child.'

Wait.

A suckered limb slides across my cheek, popping as it goes. Hero. I attempt to open my eyes again, but my lids are so heavy, I quit trying.

'Where is he?' croons another gentle voice. Leander.

I wish I had use of my body to embrace my friends.

'Settling the wraiths,' Kane snarls. 'We're lucky they're not storming the river.'

'They would never—' Hero starts before being interrupted.

'This is your doing, beast,' Leander snaps, though it's hard for the soft-spoken octopus guardian to actually sound angry.

The ground shudders, and I sense more than witness a cloak of darkness drop over me. For the first time since arriving back here, my body glitters with cold rather than the strange sense of nothingness.

'You left her out in the open?' Charon's rage rattles whatever structures are close by, shaking their already unstable foundations.

'We thought it best, what with her condition,' Hero replies.

'The wraith almost split her in two dragging her here,' Leander interjects while, I imagine, directing a scowl in Kane's direction.

'Time was of the essence,' Kane growls.

They grow quiet again. My broken body must be confused, because I'm floating. Levitating with the grace of a feather playing on a gentle breeze on a cool day. I'm filled with the anticipation of landing on the Earth's surface again. The feeling is so alien, I force my eyes to peep open to find myself scooped up in

Charon's arms. One of my wings is completely torn from being dragged by Kane. It hangs uselessly over Charon's arm while I drip blood all over his cloak. Though the red is quickly disguised, as my body is swathed in his shadows, I'm almost sad that my kitten T-shirt now bears no trace of said kitten. And yep— there's definitely some of my intestines spilling out of me.

If I look at that mess of guts long enough, I'll puke. So I loll my head, instead focusing on Charon, his face buried in the depth of his hood. My head bouncing around is bringing on nausea too. I think I preferred the nothingness to the sickness being in The Ferryman's arms has caused by bringing me back into my body a little. With the remaining strength I have, I draw my head up to rest on his shoulder, its steadiness a relief. The cool of his palms frosts crystalline fingerprints on my skin.

I let out a little sigh, prompting Charon to turn his neon blue eyes on me. This close to the glow of the river, the depth of his hood is intermittently illuminated with flashes of skull and skin, echoing like strobe light.

'Charon,' I whisper, though when I do, my throat is as rough as sandpaper, making me regret the exertion.

'Shhh,' he hushes, cutting me off. 'Save your strength.'

His words are soft and, for some reason, reassuring. *Save my strength.* This isn't the end. He's not going to send me floating down the river in a boat of my own. In fact, the world is calm around him. Everything is right. But my head is becoming light again. Maybe I should rest my eyes for a few moments.

'Stay with me, Fury,' he whispers.

When I blink my eyes open again, I must have dreamed the words, because Charon isn't here. Instead, Hero's cerulean luminescence is almost blinding.

'Hang in there, sweet girl,' they greet me.

'Where are we?' My voice is gravel, my lips so cracked, they split and bleed at the effort. I try to wiggle my toes to no avail. I have no idea if my lower half is still connected. The metallic stench of blood pollutes the water between us.

'In the home of The Ferryman.'

I wish to peer around and see how Charon's home is now adorned, but the world beyond Hero is blurry. 'Home' escapes my lips so softly, I'm not sure I voiced it out loud. I'm not sure why I said that. My eyes flutter closed once more.

'Do you have it?' Charon's voice.

I decide that if I'm dreaming of him, then it's my dream, so I'll make it a good one.

'Here,' Leander's disembodied voice replies.

Go away, Leander—this is my dream.

My neck screams as my head is forced upright. I protest against it with a gurgle of pain.

'Drink,' Charon urges someone.

He must mean me, because the cold edge of a vessel is being pressed to my lips. But this is my dream, and I don't want to drink. *I want....* Liquid slicker than the surrounding water wets my closed mouth, almost oil-like as it moistens my cracked lips. But when I lick them, it tastes rancid.

'No.' I splutter, forcing my eyes open.

Charon is standing above me again, his crown looming over me. I wish I could reach up and push back his hood to reveal his face so I would be better able to detect some kind of reaction from him, but my arms won't cooperate, and words fail me.

'Drink,' he says again. 'It's the only thing that will help.'

This time I do as he requests. I swallow the foul liquid, allowing him to pour more and more into my mouth until it dawns on me what the ghastly stuff is. River water.

VAULTED CEILINGS ARE THE FIRST THING THAT BLUR INTO focus when I open my eyes. No longer drowning in the need to sleep, I raise my fingers to rub the weariness from my eyes. It takes me a couple of moments to realise what I'm doing, and releasing my eyeballs, I marvel at the dexterity of my digits. Smoothing my hands along my stomach, I find no intestines hanging loose, just sensitive bare skin. Glancing down, I see I'm no longer wearing my cat-print T-shirt. Instead, a bandage of black silk is tied across my chest. I'm still in my garish leggings, though they're covered in dark splotches. My whole body aches an incredible amount.

I push myself up onto my elbows to take in my surroundings.

'You're awake.' Charon inches closer to the table I've been laid on. He's still crowned and hooded.

'I ache,' I complain with a grimace.

'You did go a few rounds with a wraith. I'm afraid you were by far the worse off.'

At the gentle taunt in his voice, my stomach does a little flip.

I peer at my bare abdomen that bears no hint of a scar. 'You saved me.'

'It was a joint effort,' he counters.

I sit up, then stretch out my wings, which are also now repaired, and massage the base of my neck.

He stills at my side, then lays a kylix with black liquid swirling in it near my fingers. 'A sip or two more should do. Then you'll never know you were attacked.'

I take a tiny sip of the awful stuff. Running the fingers of my free hand over the smooth silk of the bandage, I quirk an eyebrow at Charon.

'Don't worry, the guardians tended your wounds. I didn't touch you.'

My face falls. That's so not what I meant.

A moment stretches out between us. Breaking the spell, we move at the same time. Charon makes to step away while I catch his fingers in my own. I gasp at their coolness as his shadows instantly wind up my arm, the sweetest poison ivy.

'I missed you,' I confess.

He says nothing.

The thread of our bond simmers in my chest, making my ears rush with white noise. 'Did you miss me?'

He drops my hand and turns from me. 'I'll call the guardians. The wraiths demand my attention.'

He is gone.

A different type of ache fills my chest. My escape truly destroyed everything between us.

I catch myself. There is no *us*. Only the Fury bond. Now I have no cell to return to, yet it's not safe for me to roam the city. Is this my life now, forever, not fitting anywhere? Charon's home is now even sparser than the first time I saw it, before I turned Fury. In fact, the table is the sole piece of furniture in it. No chairs, no chess set. Nothing.

I swing my legs off the table as Hero and Leander glide in.

'Lovely,' they chime in unison, swimming over to wrap my arms with their tentacles and helping ease me to my feet. They run their limbs through my hair, across my freshly healed skin that no longer stinks of blood. They must have cleaned me up. Only the faintly earthy scent of the silk remains.

They carry on speaking alternately.

'We missed you so.'

'What a relief to have you looking well once more.'

'You truly were cut in half.'

'The Ferryman should have serious words with that wraith.'

'He almost tore your arm off.'

Without Charon here confusing my emotions, fogging my brain, I'll better contemplate the situation as a whole, I'm sure. But first, I hug them. My friends. Because they truly are. Despite everything, I'm glad to be reunited with them. With their happy chatter and beautiful luminescence, they'd been my constant cause for cheer for so long.

They're quiet as they return my embrace with all sixteen of their limbs.

'I made such a mistake, my friends.' I sniff. 'Charon hates me.'

Hero smooths a tentacle over my cheek.

'How could he hate you? He saved you,' Leander tuts.

Their partner continues, 'It would have been easier for him if he didn't.' Hero chuckles.

My mouth drops open.

Hero shakes their head. 'You were all torn up. It would have been nothing for him to pop you into a boat and send you on to the next life.'

'Hero,' Leander laments, 'let's not terrify the girl.' They wrap a tentacle around my shoulder. 'The

Ferryman is fair. He would never throw you in a boat and force you to move on.'

'Just as he doesn't to the wraiths,' Hero chimes in, catching on to my growing horror.

'If he'd sent me on, he wouldn't have *any* Furies,' I counter. 'He said we're only called when a god is born, which means not often.'

'Exactly.' Leander pats my hand.

'Although...,' Hero falters, swishing through the water in front of me. 'You being alive is a herald to the wraiths. If you were gone, they would be more likely to settle or perhaps even move on.'

I sink my head into my shaking palms. 'This *is* all my fault. The city is destroyed because I escaped.'

'The wraiths were more easily managed when you were imprisoned, as they merely believed it a matter of time before their will would be done. When you broke free, they were furious. But it was The Ferryman who failed them,' Leander explains.

'Though Kane has had somewhat of a guilty conscience. If it's possible for a wraith to comprehend such an emotion,' Hero adds, and Leander sighs.

'*I* failed them, Leander,' I correct.

Hero shifts uncomfortably, knocking the kylix over so the river water—*blood*—spills onto my leggings. Leander sucks in a sharp inhale.

'What?' I probe, disregarding the essence of the river.

'Leander,' Hero cautions.

'Child, it's The Ferryman who is at fault. It's only natural for you to flee from him. His actions before your escape are to blame. He allowed himself to become too familiar, didn't do enough to ensure your submission. We believed the time of gods long passed. The Ferryman has long been without Fury. However, a new god is unleashed upon the surface. Gods are bloodthirsty, soul-eating things—they require the energy for the creation they wield as well as their destruction. That's why the city was already in disrepair. Life is not passing through our gates. The Ferryman needed you to restore the balance of souls. He needed you too much. A foolish misjudgement. And then you escaped.'

I'm completely shocked to hear Leander questioning him in such a way and for Hero to not be checking them. Instead, Hero's sadness twinkles in the list of their limbs.

'What's happened to the other souls? The ones trying to make contact with the living world?' I ask.

'They've mostly moved on,' Hero answers, desolate.

I swallow hard, panic tinging my fringes. 'There was one called Carline, a spirit guide to my friend. Has she moved on?'

'There have been too many to keep track. But if I were you, I'd assume so. The spirits have no peace here anymore.'

When I speak, my tone is shrill. 'What would you

have me do? Should I submit? Would the wraiths be at peace? Would the spirits have sanctuary?'

'The Ferryman has always been the mediator between Fury and vengeful wraith. He negotiates the terms and sets the Fury on their path. Once the bargain is fulfilled, the wraith remains but is no longer bent on vengeance, harmless to the residents of the city. Perhaps if you do submit, he'd find a way to mediate the terms....' Leander pauses.

My hands will not cease their trembling. There's something they're not saying, and it fills me with dread.

'What Leander is trying to say,' Hero interjects, 'is that much has changed in your absence. You are a single Fury, and the wraiths are many. The city is in ruins, saturated with their anger. Even if you were to submit, we're unsure how The Ferryman could broker a deal. They fear him, but they do not trust him. The wraiths who linger have never known a time of the Fury. Perhaps... the time of the City of the Dead is over. Everything comes to an end eventually. Charon will hold on for as long as it is possible for him to do so. If there's nothing to be done, he will see you on.'

My hands are no longer the only thing shaking— my whole body now vibrates. Is it possible for a Fury to have a panic attack? My mistakes have ruined lives and worlds. I've always dallied too close to the edge since my drowning, but consenting to be Fury was the worst error of all. Now the wraiths are in revolt, destroying the city. I'm a danger to the living world. Lost souls are forced from their sanctuary into the next life, and on top of it all, Charon is losing his grip on the only home he's ever known. Will he journey on to the next life? Or will he effervesce into the ether?

'Lovely.' Hero steadies me in their limbs.

'What should I do?' I manage to get out, my throat closing. I will the tears to come. I long to expend this wretchedness, but nothing will come out. There's no outlet. No way of calming my churning ruminations— nothing to help me. A high keen escapes my lips. 'Help me. What do I do?'

I drop to my knees, still grasping on to Hero. 'It hurts.' I clutch my chest, another animal cry leaving my lungs, one that should beg the hearer to end its suffering. 'Help me, Hero. Please send me on. I can't do this anymore. I have no idea how to fix this. How can *I* save Charon?'

Hero betrays their panic at my breakdown, bioluminescence sparking, moving like an ultramarine phantom across their skin. 'If we had the answers, sweet girl, we would surely give them to you, but we have no advice to offer. You are so unlike any Fury before you.'

That makes me feel in no way better. I continue to weep tearlessly.

'I am not the Master of Boats, Lovely. It's not in my power to set you on the path to your next life. You must find your own way,' Hero says.

Hanging my head in shame, I try to catch my breath. When did things get so dire? Yet making a break for the surface would somehow be worse. Confronting Tino's heartbreaking expression, fearing every person I come into contact with. I'm so tired of being afraid, yet fear is my constant companion.

The door blowing wide, cracking on its hinges, shocks Hero out of my grip, and I fall to the floor in a heap. Charon's darkness floods the room, anger vibrating to such a pitch that I shrink from him too.

He sinks to a crouch before me. 'On your feet, Fury.'

'Let me go on, Charon, please. Let me die. It's the only way to calm the wraiths,' I cry.

'Stop this.' He shakes me, rattling my bones. '*You* returned *here*.'

'I killed all those people.'

'They deserved it,' he snarls.

'The guards were innocent.'

'Every war has collateral damage. Those guards were seen on to their next life. The circle goes on.' I drop my mouth open to argue, but Charon continues with renewed vigour. 'It's only you who continues to disrupt the way of things. You may have defied me, your calling, turned your back on the wraiths, but I am still the master of the river, and you will *not* journey on. I will not allow it.' He pauses before adding, 'You can die when you've fixed what you started.'

I blink, taking in his words. 'What I started?'

'You broke my world. And you are not going anywhere until you repair it.'

'Are you serious?' I gasp, faint traces of anger clouding my vision. 'How am I supposed to fix the City of the Dead? Send me down the river. Do what you can to appease the wraiths. I'm not The Ferryman. I have no power.'

'No power?' he scoffs. 'Your decisions have left my city—the city I built brick by brick with my bare hands—in ruins.' He plants a shadowed finger on my chest.

'With your bare hands? Really?' I ask, distracted by the notion.

He rises, taking me with him to a standing position. With his face cloaked, only his antlers push into the flame of my hair. His freezing hands on my arms bring me more and more out of my panic and into the moment. 'Every house, cathedral, lute, lamppost. Every king and queen on every chess set, every needle. All were moulded by my hands. Gifts for the spirits who live here. Gone. Do you believe that if I simply gave you the gift of your next life, the wraiths would be forgiving? They'd help me rebuild?'

I shudder. Tearing my eyes away to stare over his shoulder, I attempt to steel myself against hopelessness, but the pressure of his hands jolts me back to the passion in his otherworldly eyes.

'Fight,' he demands. 'You need to find your fight. Fight what you're feeling now. Fight me if you must.

Turn the despair that threatens to choke you into rage.'

'I... I don't think I can. Charon, that's not me. The prison was a mistake. I don't want to hurt anyone.'

'More will be hurt if you don't,' he counters coolly.

Charon takes a step away from me, releasing my arms. I'm both sad and relieved at the same time that he no longer has his hands on me.

Raising them, he wraps his fingers around his crown before discarding it to the floor with a dull thud. Then his fingers move to the clasp of his cloak, loosening it at the neck and letting it fall to the floor, where it appears to be a black hole through space and time. For the first time since I've returned, he reveals his face to me, his features unnaturally angled, too beautiful to possibly be human, skin olive and smooth as marble, full mouth over fanged teeth and eyes of blue neon, hair black as shadow.

He advances a step. 'Fight me.'

I retreat from his next stride. 'No.'

He takes a hard swallow and runs his tongue across his fangs, which sends a shudder of anticipation along my skin. He diverts his gaze to the guardians hovering nearby.

'Leave us,' he commands them.

CHAPTER 14

LOVELY

The guardians linger for a moment, discomfort radiating from them in the twitching of their limbs, but unlike me, they're under The Ferryman's thrall, so it's not long before the door to Charon's home is closed behind them.

I may not have a heartbeat, but the golden cord attaching me to Charon thrums wildly. I swallow and swallow again as he advances on me. Although his cloak is discarded, the shadows still whip around him, his anger stagnant in the air.

'Fight,' he commands.

'No.' I can barely get the word out. As I retreat, my wings scrape against the window, obscuring the view of the river.

'Your only wish is to defy me?' His delicious mouth quirks a little. 'Is that it?'

But I can't think as his hands slide to the window, bracketing me. He towers above me, clouding every single one of my thoughts. In my world's time, I'd been gone for three weeks, and it hits me that there wasn't a minute when I hadn't thought of him. Longed for him. And now, I have become his doom.

Annoyance at my silence rolls off Charon's being, though his voice is rough and soft at the same time. 'No more weakness, Fury.' He moves his hand to my hair, wrapping a tendril of flame around his forefinger. 'You are made of fire.'

I push my palms against the cool glass. I'm not sure I have full control of my body. My chest heaves inches from his. My eyes on his, the moment stretches on for what could be years given its intensity.

'Call me by my name,' I say after a while. Soft. Only half daring to dream that he might. If we're both doomed, we might as well burn together.

Charon cocks his head, a fang dropping over his lip, and then his finger is no longer wrapped in my hair. Instead, it trails along my jaw, sending a thrill over the skin of my arms until a sharp nail tilts my chin towards him. His gaze drops to my lips. Looking at Charon is akin to being set on fire and plunged into a lake of ice simultaneously.

His mouth twists, savage and utterly tempting. 'How was he? Your human? Did he taste the way you remember? Did he make you feel all those things I so cruelly denied you?'

Embarrassment and anger both pulse against the shameless desire I felt moments ago. This time he's ready when I try to push him from my orbit and doesn't budge, though he also doesn't stop me escaping from his trap around my body.

'Fuck you,' I spit. 'And fuck this bond I have with you polluting my thoughts. Fuck it all.'

'Sore point?' He turns with a sneer as I face him again, a shiny dagger in his hand. 'You want the bond gone so that, what? You can return to him, give him your body that you would willingly give to so many, and call it love? Is that it, Fury? Is that what you're desperate for? For someone to hide behind for the rest of your life while this world crumbles?'

'As opposed to you?' I seethe. 'A being who wants me as a servant. Why the hell would I choose that? Besides, the guardians said that it may be too late. The wraiths might not accept your deals.'

He steps closer, blue eyes churning with a thousand stars, and for a moment, my breath is stolen. His hands find mine, though his eyes never leave my face. Into my palm, he slips the dagger.

'You were the one who broke *our* bargain,' he says. 'What are you going to do about it?'

The knife slides against my skin, as frigid as an icicle, and when I look down, I discover that it is just that—an icicle so sharp, it could slice through bone. Its handle is swirled, mimicking a flame.

'What are you doing?' I ask him, while on some

instinct, I hold the ice dagger to his throat. 'Do you want me to kill you?'

'I'd like to see you try.' He arches a brow. 'I'd like to see you do *something*.'

'How did you make this?'

'I make everything here. There isn't much I can't imagine into existence.'

That distracts me for a moment. I can't recall getting so close again, the briny tang of his breath making me lick my lips. I'm so close that the dagger is indenting his skin as I lean into his chest. The sight is mesmerising. His opium scent seems to be burning the fight out of me, and I'm melting, soft and compliant against him. After a moment, I realise his hands are on my hips, then sliding up my waist, and I'm almost certain he doesn't know he's doing it.

I press the dagger further into his skin, and he takes a shallow gasp.

'What do *you* want?' I ask him.

'You. On your knees.'

'My submission alone?'

'Yes. It's the only thing left.' His hands slide further up my back, thumbs pressing into my ribs, and my head is becoming foggy at his proximity. 'Now, tell me what you want.'

'You,' I say simply.

It's clear he expects some kind of further explanation as to how I want him. And what the fuck do I say to that? My brain is scrambled from the impending destruction of the city, and my body is its own traitor. And Charon, the ruler of the Underworld, is just standing there, holding me to his chest, knife at his throat, asking what I want, asking how I'm going to fix his world. It's too big. It's too much.

Reaching out into the ether of my brain, I give voice to my next thought. 'Chains. I want chains.'

His brows knit together. 'Your requests were always rather singular.' But he says nothing more, removing his grip from my body and taking a step away from me. When he motions with his hands, the water shimmers around him like a mirage until the beginning of something appears, slowly working its way into existence.

I stand a few feet away, icicle dagger still raised, though I'm not sure why—only that I feel better with it in my palm. As the chains materialise, they become monstrous things, made of what looks like bone.

Moving closer, I run my fingers over their coarse surface, an uneasy judder passing over my skin.

He holds up a section, looking a little perplexed himself. 'If you plan to restrain the wraiths, we'll need much more, and though it'll hold them, it's only prolonging the problem. More wraiths will appear, drawn to you. It will only be a matter of time before one breaks free. Then there will be the issue of where to house them....'

I snatch the chain out of his hands and sling it over

my shoulder before flying the short distance to the beam of his vaulted ceiling and hooking it over.

'The chains are not for the wraiths,' I inform him. 'They're for you.' I've obviously lost my mind, but I'm rolling with it, and now I'm guiding Charon beneath the hanging chain, and he's moving, allowing me to shepherd him into place. I figure I just need some time to catch a breath and think of my next move without him breathing down my neck.

Charon's gaze is fixed on my face as I put one wrist and then the other above his head and chain him to the ceiling. He's tall enough that he can still stand on his toes, though I have to flutter my wings slightly to bring my face level with his.

I move closer, my lips a hair's breadth from his, and breathe in that delicious scent, allowing myself to be soothed by its heady effects. My eyes drift to his mouth, though I can feel his penetrating gaze remaining firm on me, surprised and waiting to see what I do next.

'Now you're mine.' My breath mingles with his. I wonder if I'm the heat to his cold. If he feels me that way.

'Your prisoner?'

I'm not sure when the room became cloaked in darkness. I can't even see the glow of souls from the river.

'Yes.' Somehow the dagger is back in my hand and

pressed against the exposed skin of his throat. 'How do you like it?'

He tilts his head slightly, easing himself further onto the blade. 'You realise these chains cannot hold me. I am the master of this place.'

A ghost of a smile passes over my lips. 'Isn't that the point, Charon? That you can, yet you won't.'

A growl sounds from somewhere deep in his chest. 'Okay.'

I feel a flicker of surprise, the knife relaxing in my grip. 'Okay?'

'It's something new.' His lip quirks a fraction. 'The guardians will not be amused.'

'You will command them not to enter this room,' I tell him, the words quickening in my stomach before they leave my mouth.

For the first time, Charon pulls back to survey me fully, pulling on his chains with a clink. 'What are you doing, Fury?'

'I have no idea,' I admit. Then he betrays only the slightest wince as I finally press the knife hard enough into the spot where his neck meets shoulder that black blood wells from the wound. The tang of the rancid river water is a living memory on my tongue, and in this moment, I need all the strength I can get. I lower my head and lick the blood oozing from his neck. Charon shudders, but he tips his head back to allow me better access.

This is no river water. This is bliss.

THOUGH SUSPENDED ON THE TIPS OF HIS TOES, ARMS raised, Charon betrays no hint of discomfort. After several minutes of Hero and Leander banging on the door, Charon had done as I'd requested and told them not to enter, to guard the river and only call if the wraiths are planning on disturbing the passing souls.

I'm seated in front of him, my wrists resting on my knees and my wings reclining behind me, more relaxed than I've felt in God knows how long. I don't think I've ever breathed so deep. I need to be thinking of a plan, but the bliss of his blood has dulled my panic, and I've pushed it far from my mind. Having him this way is far too interesting.

'You know,' I remark, arching a brow at him, 'the blood of the river tastes rancid.'

'That's a weird way of giving me a compliment.'

'In fact, it is. The river is filled with your blood, and it tastes rank, whereas you—well, you do not.'

'I see the guardians still have no idea when to stay their tongue.'

'Don't be mad at them,' I say, although his tone was far from abrasive, more observational.

'I cannot account for its taste; it is a river, after all.'

'If your blood is what flows in the river, why do you turn the Furies with that? Why heal me that way? Why not straight from the source?'

He stares at me for a long moment. 'Allow me some dignity.'

Something about his expression makes me take a hard swallow. 'What do you mean by that?'

'You were made of my blood, as were your sisters before you. The city is crafted by my hands, and my essence carries the souls on. When you are the master of all, when the whole of the Underworld draws upon your being, well, let me just say, you may not want that level of intimacy.'

I frown, rising to my feet, inching closer. 'But you *were* intimate with them—those who came before me.'

His laugh is so dry and so slight, I might have missed it. 'Your predecessors lived lifetimes in the human world. They had many human lovers, those who worshipped them. But a human life is temporary, and I could provide my Furies something none other could—longevity.'

I step closer, our chests grazing. 'They loved you.'

'No,' he breathes, our lips so close now, though his eyes remain on me. 'I am not a being of love. I mean the end, nothing more.'

'But when the souls move on, they're recycled, so nothing truly *ends*, right?'

'True. But I remain outside that cycle.'

'Sounds lonely.' I slide my hands onto his chest, and for the first time, his gaze leaves mine, and he draws his eyes shut.

'Stop,' he urges. 'You will not submit to my will.

You will not bow. I concede to you my willing freedom. I make a gift of my blood and a knife for you to take it with. But I cannot give you this. It is the sacrifice I cannot make.'

'Why not? Why can I have your blood but not your heart?'

His lips part, a pained sound escaping them. 'Your bond to me. It's clouding your judgement. Free of it, you would return to your human. Without it, you would choose him. Every. Single. Time. Dignity, Fury —allow me a little of it as I stand here in the chains I willingly crafted for you, needing your help.'

Shame swallows me, and I retreat, giving Charon some room. How can I deny what he says? Before I died for the final time, Tino was my main incentive to return to the living world.

Clearing my throat, I stalk around the table, tracing my fingers across the ice dagger. I decide to change the subject, mollified somewhat that Charon is acting out of self-preservation and is not wholly indifferent to me. 'So, you control everything here? Why can't you just lock the wraiths away or forbid them to wreck the place?'

'The wraiths are still human souls. My job is to provide sanctuary, even for them. I created Furies *for* them, to help bring them peace in their death. To send a soul on who is not willing.' He shudders. 'To force an unwilling soul on is a fate worse than death, incredible suffering.'

'It sounds like you really care about them even though they're destroying your life's work.'

'All who reside here are in my charge. Even you.'

'Did you just admit that you care for me?'

'It's my job to do so.'

'And who gave you this job?'

'There is nothing else. I have always been. My role is as instinctual as the moon's orbit of the Earth.'

I frown, and he tilts his head up, his neck already healed from where I cut him. 'How long am I to be your prisoner?'

I stalk back to the table, take up the knife, and turn it on him, bringing it to his throat, then trailing it along his clavicle. The garment he's wearing splits as if spun from the finest silk, revealing the hard planes of his upper chest. The sharp whistle of his sudden inhale through clenched teeth cuts through me, and I pretend not to feel the shudder along my arms, the thrill that moves up my legs.

'I'm deciding my next move,' I say. In truth, I have no clue what to do. 'Does this bother you?'

'No.'

'Does this?' I push the knife into his skin, drawing blood.

'No,' he whispers, dipping his head back again as I bring my lips to his chest and lap at his blood like a cat would cream. I feel the calmest I ever have in my life. I could spend an eternity here. In front of him.

For the first time, perhaps ever, I feel in control.

CHAPTER 15

LOVELY

'What is it you want, Fury?' Charon asks me for perhaps the millionth time.

How his toes don't cramp after all this time, I know not. From where I'm lying on the table, staring at the intricate woodgrain of the beams of the vaulted ceiling, I can't bring myself to care. Nor do I care for the city that is being decimated, according to Leander. Kane sometimes sits on the other side of the door, giving updates on the wraiths. He reports out of boredom, he assures us, though part of me suspects he relishes the gossip. He informs us that Leander is beyond dramatic, and while the Underworld *is* being trashed, the wraiths are not so organised as to launch an attack on the river, nor would they be inclined to do so.

Me, meanwhile—I'm fat on Charon. On his delectable blood. On his company.

'I only want you,' I tell him in response for the millionth time before catching myself. 'In chains.'

The minute movement of his shoulders exerts only the slightest strain on his restraints, the bone chains groaning with friction. 'You have me. Is my submission not sufficient?'

'Consider it payback.'

'Then your vow against vengeance is to the wraiths' detriment alone?'

I raise my eyebrows, not answering but turning to face him. His features are schooled into calm. He must be sick of my questions. About what he is, where he came from, his mission, my mission—none of this he will answer, only saying my help is crucial to appease the wraiths. He tells me this often. His plan is that with the help of Hero and Leander, brokering the negotiations between Fury and wraith might still be possible and perhaps come to less bloody forms of revenge.

His plan is half-baked at best. As if the wraiths would accept anything less than brutal retribution. There's always the same obstacle too. Without my submission, my instincts may take over and cause more damage than needed. Though Charon does little to demand the failsafe of my submission or even put much effort into his assertion that his plan is a good one. Rather, he's content in his chains. It niggles at me.

Despite having lived an eternity, no one's put him in chains before. Though it's all a farce, as he could shake them off like daisy chains if he wanted. He's changed tactics, since I'm not going to submit by force. He just needs to wait me out. There's no other way.

I chew my lip. This is how it goes inside my brain, round and round in circles.

He watches me. Amused.

It drives me crazy.

Though Charon maintains that it's the Fury bond fuelling my desire to be near him, it might give him pause if he suspected how truly under my skin he is. Even this close to him, he consumes my every thought. And the sight of him standing in chains—well, *that* image makes my toes curl into the sandy surface of the room. A wave of goose bumps passes over my arms.

Charon tilts his head. 'Are you cold?'

I shake my head and peer out the window that covers an entire end of the house. The river drifts past peaceful and serene, while the world around it is anything but. I should be pondering how to help the plight of the wraiths rather than how Charon looked when I sliced his shirt off. It must be the bond, I tell myself. I love Tino. My friend of forever, who would protect me from all the bad things that have ever happened to me. It's all I've ever wanted. To be safe. Yet here I am with another man—if Charon can be defined as a man. I'm not certain what he is, but I'm sure he must have the parts....

There goes my mind again. I should be figuring out how to help Charon and the wraiths. Perhaps once that is done, I can even figure out how to control my Fury abilities and return to the living world. Not remain here, holding the ruler of the Underworld captive and wondering what form his naked body takes.

Letting out a huff, I get to my feet. This is all Charon's fault for not crossing any sort of line in our relationship and easing a single iota of tension between us. For never putting his hands on me for a thousand years. I hate him for it. I'm wretched with the knowledge.

The ice dagger remains clutched in my palm. I swing it furiously while I pace. Charon remains in his usual stance, hands wrapped around the chains, stretched upwards enough that his toes are revealed beneath the shadows that cloak him like a garment, his antler crown stored on the table on which he healed me. Although he presents as human—*ish*—every now and then, a flicker of the glow of the souls from the river casts light across his features, and a faint buzz of his skeleton beneath his olive skin flitters in, then out, as if he's unsubstantial in some way.

'Why are you angry? Your face is all scrunched up,' he remarks, corner of his lips twitching.

I stop pacing and stare at him. Not answering, I move closer, bringing the knife to his throat, though he doesn't flinch. Reaching my other hand out, I trail my fingers over the black silklike shirt he's wearing, though I can't tell if it's fabric or shadow. When my caress grazes his abdomen, his body jerks as if to escape me, his lips parting, and I drop my hand.

'Am I so terrible?' I ask.

The unnatural blue eyes he fixes on me are so intent, I have to break their hold before he admits that, yes, I'm awful.

Concentrating instead on my fingers as they thread through the whispering shadows along his chest, I muse, 'I was trying to figure out what this material is. Or whether it even is material or shadow. Without the cloak, you have fewer shadows, though they never entirely leave you, do they?' I steel myself to bring my gaze to meet his once more. 'Is that you, Charon? Are you made of shadow? Would you slip through my fingers if I held on to you too tight?'

He takes a visible swallow, and for some reason, the sight of it turns my insides molten. I've never been filled with so much longing in a single moment that it's agony in my chest coupled with a devastating sorrow because this is a line he will never cross. My submission would make me his, but he'll never be mine.

My eyes fall to his lips, my chest against his. He's so close, though he doesn't move. Frozen. His analgesic scent swarms my senses. I'm not brave enough to close the distance. I'm certain that even if he allows me to steal one kiss, the grim truth remains that he'll never allow himself to be mine. Unwanted hands on my body are a familiar intrusion to me. I would not wish it on anyone in return. I drop my gaze before stepping away from him.

The bone chains grind together under the burden of his weight. I pretend that he's fighting the urge to break free and put his hands on me. I so wish to pretend with him. Play make-believe that what I feel for him is more than a bond, that he desires me in return. My unbeating heart threatens to shatter. Tears rise and collect in the corners of my eyes. Strange that the ability to cry has returned to me. And now I'm weeping over a love I never lost because it was never mine in the first place.

Smoothing my hand along the black silk wrapped around my middle, I attempt to pull myself together. The Ferryman will not witness me cry—not over him. Not ever.

I take a shuddering breath that fills my lungs like rapid gunfire. It's been too long since one of us has uttered a word. Sooner or later, I'm going to have to release him and devise a real plan. But my brain refuses to work. Since the moment I stepped foot in the City of the Dead as a damned Fury, the dreaded bond hasn't allowed me a moment's peace.

It takes several gulps to bury the emotion until I can no longer taste its bitterness. When I have the courage to lift my chin, it's to find Charon slouched in his chains, totally relaxed, eyes travelling the length of my body. He really shouldn't look at me that way.

He clears his throat. 'I suppose I should finally

address the elephant in the room and ask what on earth you're wearing.'

I follow suit and glance down at the bloodstained neon tie-dyed leggings. I appreciate his attempt to lighten the mood, so I give him a twirl. 'Why? Don't you like them?'

He cocks his head as if considering. 'I prefer you in black.'

Of course he does.

'Spin again,' he commands.

I pause. Then I do as he requests.

As I spin, the water around me shifts, glimmering as if wrapping me in a cocoon, urging me to dance. I continue to twirl as bubbles pop in my ears at the movement. Perhaps in this one simple act of submission, I am now his. Though after a moment of whirling, I easily come to a halt. When I do, my body is transformed. No longer in my leggings, I'm now draped in black silk and shadow, but not like the toga the guardians once wrapped around me. This garment has a full, lavish skirt hanging in folds from my waist, thin straps with a low back to allow for my wings, and a plunging neckline.

I clasp my fingers to my mouth, this time spinning slowly to admire it myself. It might just be the most beautiful thing I've ever worn. The harsh red of the scars adorning my arms is a bleak contrast to its splendour.

'You didn't give me sleeves,' I say quietly, now tracing their rough texture.

'Why would I do that?'

'Because this dress is fit for a princess, and I don't live up to the title. My scars—they're proof of my greatest weakness.'

'On the contrary. They're a reminder that you're stronger than all you've endured.'

The dress is suddenly too tight. How does he expect me not to long for him when he says things like that?

He must sense my hesitation, because he continues, 'Of course, it is in my ability to make you a dress with sleeves.'

'No,' I say quickly. 'I like how you made me sound. Like I'm strong.'

The water around us stills. There I go, letting my emotions rise to the surface, allowing the moment to get away from me.

In an attempt to lighten it once more, I gather the hem of the dress and swish it around, dipping into a half curtsy. 'Does it come in any different colours?'

He smirks. 'Spin for me, Fury.'

I do as I'm told and spin again. The water shifts and glistens around me almost like glitter settling onto my skin. When I stop, my dress has transformed to that of pure spun gold. It illuminates the dull grey of the Underworld.

'You should see yourself,' Charon says.

Then a full-length mirror shimmers into existence by the window of souls. The reflection staring back at me takes my breath away. I could be a character out of mythology. The gold, liquid as if water itself, ripples across my skin, the flame of my hair flickering and crackling, the scars on my arms making me appear even more fearsome. I'm beautiful and terrible all at the same time.

'You look like a warrior,' Charon whispers.

I do. Too bad I don't feel like one. But I don't want to trivialise his efforts. I turn slightly, stretching out my wings. 'Or an angel of death,' I muse.

Charon chuckles.

I turn fully and arch an eyebrow, settling my hand on my hip. 'Shall I twirl once more? Is that part of the spell?'

'And if I told you I just enjoy watching you move?'

'Oh.' My stomach dips. 'Well, in that case.'

I spin for him again, allowing him to transform the fabric with no more than the water around me and the magic of his being—the same magic that's woven into me, flowing through my veins too. I stumble to a stop, and the dress is now pure white with no straps at all, the neckline a soft heart shape tight around my bust. The skirt flows out from my waist, its bottom nothing but the fluffiest, softest feathers that feel like wisps of cloud between my fingers. They hold their shape despite the water surrounding us.

'*Now* you're an angel.'

I grin at him, swishing the feathers. 'Who knew you're a seamstress.'

'I'm many things.' His sharp-toothed smile is sardonic. 'As are you.'

I gulp, then startle when a knock thuds on the door. I spin so abruptly, a few feathers shake loose and scatter over the silt floor, their whiteness in stark contrast to its blackness.

'Master,' Hero's musical voice sings, full of caution.

'I told you, we're not to be disturbed,' Charon growls.

'Master, the wraith Kane sends word from the city. The wraiths are on their way.'

'Guard the river,' he commands.

'Master, they're not coming for the river.'

'Then what are you—'

'Charon.' They barely ever use his name. 'They're coming here. They're planning an attack on your home. They are coming for the Fury.'

Charon's eyes flick to mine, then to the door. 'Guard the river, Hero. Tell Leander the same.'

'But the wards will not hold out against them all. You should meet them, *talk* to them. Calm them before they destroy your home.'

'Guard the river, Hero. I won't say it again.'

I've stopped breathing, but there's no further argument from Hero. They must have left to carry out Charon's orders and relocated to the river.

Charon's mask of perfect relaxation remains fixed in place. He flexes his palms, eyes on me. 'What now?'

What now indeed.

I should free him. He's barely my prisoner anyway.

'The wraiths are on their way' is apparently the only pointless observation I have to offer.

'So it would seem.' His tone is casual. Too casual.

I should release him.

'You're not worried?' I ask instead.

He shrugs, earning another complaint from the bone chains. The creak of his captivity is almost a drug. I shudder, an acidic taste rising on my tongue, something close to possession. 'Remain in your chains, Ferryman. You are mine, remember.'

And then I turn my back on him, snatch my knife, and stand sentinel over the river. I roll the dagger in my palm. If the wraiths are coming, I will be ready for them.

I shudder as the white feather dress melts away, transforming into a raiment. A dress of the finest spun gold once more, marking me as a warrior.

CHAPTER 16

LOVELY

Charon stays quiet as I keep my eyes on the river, though his breath is cold on my neck from all the way across the room, sending goose bumps over my body so vigorous, it leaves me trembling. Or perhaps my shaking is due to the dread that the wraiths are on their way. And I have no idea how to fight them. I've taken to my usual vigil of the waters in the distance, a habit of a thousand years. Now I drop my stare to my dagger composed of ice and carved like a flame from where I've moved to sit.

Charon is many things. I am too. Lovely and Fury.

I close my eyes, squeezing them tight while trying to figure out how I can be both. Which choices are my own. The wraiths don't trust him anymore. I should be the one to bargain with them.

A deep rumble breaks the silence of Charon's home, powerful enough to shake the walls, though they remain intact. For now. Must be the wards Hero mentioned being pummelled. The stench of mutiny is hard upon the air.

'It won't hold them forever,' Charon says into the silence.

I grind my teeth. Though I don't answer, I spin on my ass, facing the door instead of the river, my fist clenched so hard around the hilt of the knife that it creaks under the duress.

Another shake of the ground—the deep rumble of Titans clashing. A vague memory from my Fury sisters flits across my brain; an incarnation of me has been present at a gruesome battle before. The clanging of metal and crunching of bone is familiar to my ears. But their Fury rage doesn't surface now—it's not natural to fight the wraiths. That fact does not fill me with confidence.

'Fury,' Charon snaps when I don't acknowledge him. 'I should meet with them.'

My jaw is so tense, my teeth groan. The clink of the bone chains distracts my attention from the fracas headed our way and my own indecision on how to face them.

'I could break out of these at any point.'

'That's the test,' I snarl at him. 'Stay where you are.'

Charon's eyes burn into me as if he would set me aflame if I wasn't already.

The silt around the room quakes in shimmery

judders. My focus trained on the door, I rise to my feet and plant them into what I hope is some kind of fighting stance. This is ridiculous. I have no idea why I'm commanding Charon to remain chained or why he's bothering to listen to me. But every one of my previous decisions keeps me rooted in place. That I ran away. Leander's confession that The Ferryman needed me. His own command that I fix his world. I have to do something. I have to try.

The door shudders on its hinges. The wards have been breached. My breaths come rapid fire. I should try to run, but I'm frozen in place. All I ever seem to do is run. Run from fights, run from myself. The liquid gold of my dress morphs in slow, languorous drips, moulding around my limbs, gold armour shielding me, even wrapping around my scars.

'Not funny,' I mutter.

'You'll need its protection more than any dress if you plan on facing the wraiths without my assistance,' Charon returns without irony, his eyes now fixed on the rattling door as it finally gives way.

I attempt to give a nod as I clutch my ice dagger tightly. There will be no running. I will bargain, or I will fight.

The wood shatters, though the gap isn't big enough for the monstrous creatures to fit through. A giant tarantula leg whips wildly through the gap, trying to find purchase. It had to be the fucking spider.

The wall quivers as Dorian, the wraith tarantula,

retreats for a moment of reprieve that's followed by a boom. The mammoth-sized elephant knocks a gaping hole through the wall, and the spider scrambles through, the tiger flanking him.

Dorian pauses to gape at Charon in chains for a mere moment before he huffs, ignoring The Ferryman being held prisoner.

The elephant rears as if to charge while the other two wraiths clear a path. My breath is stolen. There's no way I'm winning against an elephant. Plus, with Dorian and the tiger flanking the only exit, I have no possible means of escape.

The tiger snarls, snapping its monstrous jaws. The elephant is about to charge when a new thundering hit rumbles the floor of the Underworld—great paws running at speed. Kane pelts full force into the side of the elephant, sending the silt and shadows into a frenzy. With a howl, he snaps his jaws around the wraith's neck, rending rotting flesh from rotting bone.

'Traitor!' the tiger roars before pelting in my direction.

Two giant paws strike my shoulders, but thankfully the armour does its job, and its claws only sink into the metal and flatten me to the window. Remembering the knife in my palm, I slash at its face. It releases me with a yowl so terrible, it jitters my bones. It slinks away, observing me afresh, the gold of the armour glinting in its dead eyes, and then begins to circle. I match its pace, holding my dagger, which is now dripping black sludge, defensively in front of me.

'I'm not your enemy,' I say, attempting to reason with it. 'Let's talk. You will not take your vengeance from me by force.'

It snarls, not bothering to even converse with me. Dorian joins the circling motion, pincers dripping foul-smelling shadow, the stench that of a ripe corpse. It lunges. I slash. Both of us miss our mark.

'We will test your theory.' Dorian's voice is a creaking, agony-filled thing. 'You are ours. The others will be through the barrier soon. There is nothing more in your Ferryman's power to protect you.'

A howl from Kane, and when I glance to find him, he's being propelled into a nearby building in a bone-crunching toss. The mammoth-sized elephant eases into Charon's home, tumbling more bricks out of place.

The tiger slashes at my ankle, but its claws slide off the protective gold of the armour. I spring away from it, slash at it once, then again at Dorian.

'I will not serve you,' I grit out through clenched teeth.

'You are Fury. You will do as bidden. If The Ferryman is too weak to do his duty, he is of no use to us.'

This time when Dorian dives, my slash finds its mark, slicing right through one of his pincers. His rage is pure noise, his yell combined with the rumble of eight feet hitting the ground in quick succession.

'Fury,' Charon yells.

'Don't' is all I say without giving a single thought to why.

The next moment, both Dorian and the tiger are charging, no longer concerned about the cuts I'm landing. Shadow and sludge fall from my blade to the floor as they loom over me.

The tiger finds its mark first, jaws clamping over my wrist, crushing the armour around my skin. The flash of pain is white hot, forcing me to my knees and to drop my knife. My scream is so vicious, its timbre is a stranger to me. Yet when Dorian's broken pincers break through the armour and sink into my shoulder, somewhere, far off, I know I scream again.

With everything I have, I fight against the pain Dorian is inflicting. He's an old wraith; his murder happened during a war still entrenched in memories of the living. A soldier sliding in slick mud. Piles of bodies. Campmates of living skeletons. The children walking through the prison, peering at him through barbed wire fences.

'Stop!' I shriek, trying to pull away from him. Megaera's memory burns on the backs of my eyelids, whispering to me the melody of generational curses. Songs of damage to be lamented in lifetimes of suffering. 'No! Charon, help me!' I cry, relenting.

The pressure on my right arm is released, and I

peek an eye open in time to witness the tiger being thrown across the room and out of the hole in the wall. Charon isn't wearing his cloak or crown, but his entire being is swallowed in shadow as he turns to the wraith.

Dorian releases his vice-like grip on my shoulder, then turns on Charon as if to trample him. Charon catches his legs and throws him to the window, which cracks while the remaining walls shudder.

'You come into my house!' he roars as the spider comes for him again, only for Charon to lock his palms around Dorian's legs once more.

Dorian flails, attempting to throw The Ferryman off. They tussle, Dorian uselessly trying to pull his limbs from Charon's grip, as if The Ferryman's touch is causing him agony. *He's trying to escape.* Charon's hands remain locked in place, pulling his limbs further apart.

Clenching my palm over my bleeding shoulder, I force myself to stand. This all feels wrong. Blood pounds in my ears. I careen against the cracked window.

With the sickening tearing of limbs comes a human-sounding scream. From Dorian. Charon has torn one of his legs off, though not the same one that Kane once did to attempt my freedom. When Charon tosses it aside, it disintegrates as it flies through the air. Dorian wails, thrashes, pleads, but Charon isn't done. Leg by leg, he rips Dorian apart until only his body remains. The Ferryman takes a pincer in each hand, then tears his body in two. The wraith known as Dorian fades away into nothing.

The silence of the Underworld is a wounded creature in itself. Awful. Heavy. The tiger and the elephant slink away. Cautious. Each careful step in retreat measured until they're absorbed into the dim gloom of the Underworld.

Charon remains rooted to the spot, though he's turned from me, so I mark only the quick rise and fall of his shoulders. The shadows covering his olive skin fade to their normal quicksilver writhing. I'm still too terrified to move a muscle. I can't comprehend what just happened here.

When he turns, he's masked whatever emotion he was battling with a simmering calm. He stalks over to me, his eyes roaming my body, then lingering on my shoulder. 'You're hurt.'

His hands are on me, his elegant fingers examining the fine planes of gilt armour, the shuddering cold of his skin permeating the metal. My breathing falters as he searches every inch for a chink. Our chests rise and fall in quick tandem as panic holds him in its clutches.

'Charon.'

He glances around for the blade and finds it close by, thick with wraith blood. He wipes it on his leg. 'Here.' He motions for me to take it.

I don't. 'Charon.'

'You're hurt. You need to heal.' He slices across his

wrist, bringing his blood to the surface in perfect black beads.

I take his wrist and run my thumb across the wound, smearing the blood. 'Charon. I'm not in danger.'

His frantic eyes find mine, and the cool shock of them feels like being hit with bolts of lightning, the ferocity flashing within them frightening. He takes a step closer to me, a huge sigh leaving him. He moves forwards, forcing me backwards until my wings find a shaky wall. His right hand snakes into my hair before cupping the nape of my neck, his grasp keeping me in place as he brings his forehead to mine and closes his eyes, letting out an unsteady exhale. That wonderous saline taste frosts my bottom lip, and I'm forced to lick it.

I sink into him, allowing my hands to smooth up his chest until I'm cradling his face in my palms. 'What happened here?' I whisper. 'Did you force Dorian's soul to go on?'

'No.' His voice is rough, on the cusp of cracking as his grip tightens. 'I tore it entirely. There is no *on*. Not for Dorian.'

CHAPTER 17

LOVELY

Charon's breaths continue as jittering inhales followed by exhales of physical agony. He's uncloaked, no crown, exposed, his icy forehead pressed to mine. With his eyes squeezed shut, he's the most human I've ever seen him, the most unguarded. For lifetimes, I've dreamed of being in his arms, and now that I'm here, I might just shatter into a thousand pieces. That heady scent of his is dulling my senses and wrapping me around him. His pain interweaves with my own. When his lips part, the noise that leaves them is pure anguish. He tries to pull away, but I hold him fast, powerless to release him in this moment.

'I cannot' is all he manages to say.

'You can,' I soothe. 'Talk to me, Charon. Tell me what happened.'

He shakes his head, bringing up his long fingers to massage his eyes.

'Please,' I whisper. And then again and again until the word is a litany of begging, my palms still on his cheeks, his chest pressed against mine.

'I cannot.' This time he manages to extricate himself from my grasp, leaving me standing there.

Without him close, I'm more aware of the ache of the wound in my shoulder, the blood dripping down my arm and off my elbow in a steady trickle. In another extremely human gesture, he drags his hand down his face with his back to me.

I take a tentative step towards him. 'You tore Dorian's soul? Unmade him? For me?'

Clearly it's the wrong thing to say. Charon turns, unbound wrath burning in his expression. 'You left!' he bites out. 'You were gone from this place—not for a lifetime, or a thousand years, but tens of thousands. I have lived without you. Abandoned.'

Chilled by his anger, I stop my advance.

But he closes the distance, gesturing between us. 'Us? This thing you desire of me—it will never be. Yes, yes, Fury, we spent a lifetime together, ten lifetimes in the ten human minutes before your friends tore you from my world. Time which passed as, what? Weeks in the living world upon your return to life?' He cocks his head. 'You didn't even consider it, did you? The expanse of time that passed here. Do you really think the city I built with my own hands crumbled in mere weeks?' Desperation seeps into his voice. 'I have spent eons dwelling in my mistakes, witnessing my home fall. And for what? Scraps of communication from you in which you denied me. Deigned to talk to me only to ask how you may separate yourself from this place. Spoke to me when you were in the arms of another.'

I choke on my reply, the words stuck in my throat, burning. In the wake of Dorian's execution, Charon's mask of calm has slipped and revealed the depths of my betrayal to him along with it.

'I.... What you're assuming... it never happened. We kissed, but I was never truly with him. Not since you. I broke it off.'

Charon laughs, though there's nothing funny about it, running his fingers through the black shadows of his hair. 'Yes, quite. I'm all too aware you felt you couldn't do the deed with your Fury bond in place. Don't worry yourself—I'm not the voyeur you believe me to be. You forget, I've had Furies bound to me before. I was not interested in their exploits either.'

Despite already knowing that, his words still wound me.

'That wasn't what I meant, Charon. It wasn't about the bond. I realise that now,' I protest, though my words are weak with the quavering of unshed tears, recognising the truth of them. I've been fooling myself that how I feel is due to a bond or a case of Stockholm syndrome. 'It was about you.'

'It matters not.' He stalks to the broken table and

reclaims his discarded cloak, throwing it over his shoulders in a whirl and concealing his face within the depths of his hood. 'The mistake was mine. Not yours. It seems my time spent in the company of human spirits has schooled me in the ways of loneliness.' He snatches the antler crown and settles it on his head. 'I am no human spirit. I forgot my role, and my city paid dearly for the error. I'm still failing. Because of you.'

There's no warmth in the sentiment. No confession of tenderness. Only ice.

'You're right... I never should have left.'

He steps closer, the antler crown casting shadows against the flame of my hair. 'I committed the greatest crime against my duty as Ferryman. I unmade a soul. For you. What are you going to do about it?'

I bite my lip. The bond between us vibrates, hot and demanding my submission. Charon and Tino may both be far from my reach now, my chance of love and safety long gone, but foolishness has always been my path, one only I may set right.

Swallowing, I square my shoulders. 'Regret is not something I feel for failing to submit to you. I will not willingly be your servant. I refuse to mean only that to you.'

'Fury—' he growls.

I hold my palm aloft, halting his words, amazed it doesn't shake. 'Let me finish. I also understand what you're unable to give me. While I will not be a tool of death, I will fix the problem I've created. If there's another way to appease the wraiths, I will find it.'

Before I crumple into a heap, I stalk around him towards the gaping hole in the wall.

'It's not safe for you in the city,' he warns.

'After what you did, no wraith will dream of touching me,' I respond coolly.

As I leave, I hear him utter, 'For now.'

My legs are trembling so hard that even standing, let alone walking, is a challenge as I exit the house. Kane is nursing his wounds, licking a behemoth front paw, though he rises to his feet with ease as I approach.

'That was… intense.' He chuckles.

'You were listening?'

'Only to the good bits.'

I sigh. 'Walk with me to the river?'

He inclines his head, remaining at a steady pace by my side.

'It would appear that our Ferryman is quite at your mercy.'

'He despises me,' I correct.

'And no less at your mercy.' He chuckles again.

'Did you see what he did to Dorian?'

The matted, rotten fur along Kane's huge spine shudders. 'It was a perversion of nature. The wraiths have slunk to their holes to lick their wounds for now. But the actions of their protector and champion both speak a thousand words, and their anger will return tenfold. Not for you alone, but for your Ferryman also.'

I take a hard swallow. 'It won't come to that. He'll simply unmake them.'

Kane snarls, blackened teeth gleaming in the gloom. 'It's a line he will not cross again. The Ferryman is the Shepherd of Souls, not the Destroyer of them.' He tuts. 'A Fury refusing to kill. The Ferryman doing the executing. This world is coming undone. There will be only chaos.'

I'd rather not dwell on what that chaos will mean. For me. For Charon. My body is weak from the wound in my shoulder, and I wish to speak with the guardians. As we near the river, their luminescence casts sheens of pinks and blues against the hue of the souls they keep sentry over.

The guardians are huddled close, their whispers almost a melody carrying across the waters. My chest aches over how good it is to be in their company again —then a wash of shame showers me for how I've been depriving them of Charon for days. It's partly because of his absence that the wraiths planned an attack on his home.

When they notice me standing next to Kane, their skin glitters, a constellation of twinkling stars, as they both glide over.

'Sweet Lovely.' Hero wraps a tentacle around my arm to better examine my wound. 'You're hurt.'

I'm still wrapped in sheet gold that hugs my body

like a second skin except where Dorian bit my shoulder, the metal there peeling away to reveal gore. Where the tiger crushed the material to my forearm, the gilt material crinkles like tinfoil, bruising my wrist.

'Not badly, thanks to Charon.'

Hero blinks at me. I presume they want to ask me what happened, but for whatever reason, they don't, which only fuels the flames of my guilt.

I slide my palm over Hero's limb. 'Hero, I'm sorry.'

They merely guide me closer to the river. I wince at the movement, craning my head to observe the two large holes in my shoulder, blood still oozing. 'Why won't it stop bleeding?'

'From a wraith, I take it?' Leander asks.

I grunt in response.

'They're toxic to Furies. To all, in fact. Lucky for you, there's a cure.'

Leander leaves us, and Hero helps me into a seated position on the bank. Kane curls around my back so I have something to lean on when my head becomes light. I drape my wings over him, and after a moment of observing the passing souls, my eyes become heavy.

'And The Ferryman?' Hero asks lightly.

'His home is destroyed,' I tell them, my eyes never leaving the river. 'As is Dorian.'

Hero sinks a little lower until they've settled into the silt beside me. 'This is grave indeed,' they state.

Kane snorts in agreement. I dry swallow.

'How does The Ferryman fare?'

I recline into Kane, not minding the rotting smell permeating him. There's almost something comforting to him that is so totally different from Charon and keeps me in my body rather than takes me out of it.

'He's furious. At me,' I finally reply as Leander approaches. I shuffle a little closer to Hero. 'Please, will you tell Leander? The words are too painful to repeat.'

Hero blooms cerulean. At the river's edge, Leander dips a small kylix before bringing it to me and pressing its rounded handles into my palms.

'Drink,' Leander urges. 'Much like with your wounds before, the river will heal you.'

Another stab of guilt spears me over how the guardians aren't aware of what I've been taking from The Ferryman for purely selfish reasons of obtaining an illusion of power, nor do they quite know how complicated our relationship is. How he'd clung to me in the moments after he'd destroyed Dorian. I drink the rancid river water without complaint. Its effects are immediate, my shoulder itching with healing.

'Did The Ferryman have to heal many Furies this way?' I venture, then take another sip, retching at the putrid taste.

'While the Furies were not generally attacked by the wraiths, as The Ferryman mostly protected them through the bargains, accidents did happen.' Leander muses on the river for a moment. 'You forget, Hero and I haven't been here for all time. After we came, it became our role to tend the Furies if they were injured. They mostly roamed the city when they were in residence. Their time spent with The Ferryman was sparing and mainly only to broker bargains and report on their missions.'

'We should go to him,' Hero says to Leander.

I push the kylix into the silt so as not to spill any while breaking into my old habit of counting souls, catching glimmers of the lives they lived. Full, rich, filled with love. I try to pull at the memories of the Furies, attempting to recall occasions when they were healed by Charon himself rather than the river water. Diving into their deepest memories, I try to stay away from the most intimate, though they surface regardless. Long fingers against Alecto's inner thigh, sharp teeth biting into Tisiphone's lip…. I shudder, then lock them away, wishing I'd never looked.

'I'll watch over her,' Kane tells them, his voice a deep rumble against my back.

'Why are you being so nice to me?' I ask through a yawn as the guardians drift away.

'I have to admit, I feel somewhat responsible for you.'

The idea of a shadow wolf turning protector makes me smile, distracting me from the heat in my centre the Furies' memories brought. I curl so my face rests on Kane's belly, the rhythmic rocking of the boats lulling me, and I fall into a dreamless sleep.

RUNNING MY FINGERS THROUGH PRICKLES OF GRASS, MY FACE buried in the stuff, it smells of deep earth. Across my cheek, soft suckers gently *pop, pop, pop*, reminding me of falling rain. It had rained the day I buried my father.

My eyes snap awake, and I sit bolt upright, my gaze snagging on the shared glance thrown between Hero and Leander.

'Were you... sleeping?' Hero asks.

I arch my spine, nodding as I wobble to my feet.

'How has slumber found you here?'

But I don't have the answer to their question. Instead, I motion to the reem of black fabric in Leander's tentacles. 'What's that?'

Leander runs a limb over my exposed shoulder. 'We thought you might wish to change.'

'Good idea.' I glide my fingers over the smooth gold. While it makes my body look awesome, Midas touched, it only serves as a reminder of all I'm not. I'm no warrior.

Hero moves to my rear, tentacles sliding over my shoulders and around my ribcage. The material is so snug on me, I stifle a laugh, wiggling at their probing caresses. After a moment, Hero drops their tentacles.

'Sorry, Hero. It tickles.' I turn slightly to face them. 'What's wrong?'

'Erm, the armour is unremovable.'

I frown.

'There's no edge to clasp onto. You will have to speak with The Ferryman.'

My eyes bulge. 'He'd rather claw his own skin off than be in my presence right now,' I squeak. Hero and Leander's shifty behaviour only confirms the sentiment. 'Perhaps I'll remain in the armour for the time being.'

Leander agrees and drops the fabric to the ground, then drifts away after retrieving my discarded kylix.

Finally, I turn my back on the river and force myself to gaze upon the destroyed city. Not many buildings are left standing, most reduced to piles of rubble. Only a wall of shabby houses remains, shielding the river from the destruction.

'Tell me, Hero, why don't they come for the river?'

'They're not monsters,' Kane answers before Hero has the chance, brushing against me as he eases from his sitting position. 'They're souls in pain. They harbour no ill will for the spirits passing on. Their deaths were so brutal, the sole memory they each dwell on.'

I push my fingers into Kane's fur, and he gasps at the contact, though it's not a flinching inhale. Rather, it's a sigh of relief.

Closing my eyes, I feel it as his pain rises to the surface. The awful clinical room, cold green eyes, the slice of a knife. 'You're still in pain.'

He turns his huge wolf head, bringing his hollow

eyes to mine. 'It will be my constant companion. You're the reason it no longer consumes me.'

I bite my lip. 'I'm sorry I can't help them. Is that weird, given they would tear me apart?'

'It's in the nature of Furies to want to help them,' Hero chimes softly.

But my focus remains on Kane. Strange, how I've come to care for this rotting creature in such a short time since my return. I'm bonded to him. Not with the same intensity I am to Charon, but it's there all the same.

I extend my other arm so both palms are sunk deep into his fur and bury my face in his chest. His rot fills my nostrils as his pain rises to the surface once more. I have no fear of Kane, so I allow his agony to seep into me, only wincing slightly when the slices slash at my knees and I hear the grind of the bone saw. I take it all in so that for a moment, Kane is free of his memory.

The wolf's breath shudders. He butts his head against mine, and we stand forehead to forehead as I exhale his pain. When I draw my embrace away from his body, the anguish underneath his surface simmers a little less intensely.

'You do me a great service,' he rumbles. Quiet. Reverent. He drops to his haunches, lowering himself into a bow. 'I am your servant, Fury.'

I stroke his moth-eaten ear. 'My friend, you do not bow to me.'

As he pushes up to his full height, I stroke his face, surprised by my own words. By how the golden bond that lives in my chest flares with light, filling me with satisfaction. And I want to bottle this moment with him.

Cerise shimmering catches my eye. Leander has returned. Hero is frozen in their observations of my interaction with Kane.

'Am I interrupting something?' Leander asks.

Kane comes to a sit, head balanced on my shoulder, and it gives me strength.

'I have a plan,' I tell them.

CHAPTER 18

TINO

The dark of the unbroken morning swallows Lee whole. I'm left panting on the soggy shore, desolate. I should have read the signs. She was too calm. I wanted so much to believe, to write it off as relief that it was finally over, that moving forwards was possible. We would find a way to sever her connection to Death, to cure her of her affliction, even.

I fall onto the wet sand, struggling to suppress the sob that's threatening to break free. After everything, I've lost her.

In an attempt to ground myself, I pull out my phone, relying on the fact that I won't cry if I'm talking to someone.

Lisette answers. 'Tino.'

'She's gone,' I croak. 'I've lost her.'

'What do you mean?'

'I knew she wouldn't be able to live with it. With killing someone. She's gone back to Death.'

'Tino....'

'She'd rather be a prisoner for the rest of her life.'

'Tino!' Lisette snaps me out of my despair with her urgency. 'We don't have much time. Those sources I told Lee about before, the unfriendly ones? Well, I received a call from them only moments ago. Listen to me very carefully.'

I pull myself together, and as I listen to the words that rattle out of her mouth at breakneck speed, I check my watch. Only half a minute since Lee dove into the claiming sea.

CHAPTER 19

LOVELY

Hero and Leander's words of warning ringing in my ears, I clutch onto Kane's matted fur as he pelts through the wrecked streets of the Underworld, as we concluded it was better that I ride on Kane for swiftness as well as safety. In my golden armour, seated on a giant shadow wolf, I almost suit the part of a warrior. I will certainly need the nerve of one if I'm to pull this off.

Kane slows as we near the wreck of Charon's home. He's done nothing to fix it except fashion himself a chair from which he stares out towards the river. The front wall and door lie in rubble, the huge hole still blown through it. I eye the shaky-looking supporting wall to my right.

I slide off Kane, then grasp his muzzle in my hands. 'You know what to do,' I whisper. 'I imagine it'll be obvious where to find me.'

He dips his head and runs towards the centre of the city, howling as he goes, his cries drawing Charon's attention.

When I enter his home, Charon stands to observe me, his blue eyes glowing in the depths of his hood.

I swallow as I move towards him with what I'm hoping are steady steps.

'We have a problem,' I say, glad my voice carries confidence.

'Oh?'

I stretch my arms wide. 'The armour. I can't remove it.'

As he closes the distance in two strides, I hate the need that swells inside me, how I can't help but inhale his deep opium scent and wish to drown in it. But now is not the time. I have to shut the want out. To find my own strength and hide no more.

'Don't you think it better to keep it on?' As he says that, he slides his hand over my shoulder, knitting the material until there's not a scratch on it.

I tilt my head to better consider him. 'It's beautiful. But not convenient for what I have planned.'

'And what do you have planned?'

'I'm to meet with the wraiths. Kane is to arrange it.'

Something dangerous flickers in his eyes. 'I will come with you.'

'No. You can't,' I argue, ignoring how his palm

squeezes the place on my shoulder where it still rests. 'Right now, they're scared of you. Fear and mistrust will not be conducive to negotiations.'

'The wraiths cannot be bargained with unless you plan on more death in your beloved living world.'

'We'll see.' His immediate argument dies on his lips as I interrupt. 'Kane will be there to protect me.'

'You trust the wolf?'

'I do.'

For a second, a lifetime, an eternity, Charon and I hold each other's gazes. His shadows—in control or out of it, I'm not sure which—slither around the gold armour, hugging the contours of my body. Darkness pitted against flame, a battle of night and dawn. Am I just as much a drug to him as he is to me? Something to desire and keep at a distance both. Does it pain him to hold me as much as it does me to be held?

'Your plan,' he inquires finally. 'What's your leverage?'

'That,' I reply, chewing my lip, 'is something I can't tell you. For now. Let's hope this works.'

'I don't like this,' he murmurs. 'This is my city.'

'You asked me to fix it. I believe this will. But you must stay out of it.'

He mulls it over, reading the unspoken words between us. 'What is it you need of me?'

'First, I need you to remove the armour.' I'm glad my voice doesn't betray the blood rushing in my ears as I speak, the hungry growl in my belly. I manage to keep my tone all business. 'Do you need me to twirl?'

Silence echoes between us once more as Charon considers me. 'What did you have in mind?' His voice is steeped in such shadow, my mind reels at all the possibilities before catching his meaning.

'Something loose, arms bare... and red.' This time I can't help the faint quiver in my voice.

'Hm.' He steps closer again. 'Turn around.'

That golden bond in my chest pulls taut as I follow his order, keeping my eyes on the shadow we cast as he steps between my wings to come so close, the tips of his antlers loom over my head. The flame of my hair sparks and smoulders, the tang of smoke lingering around us. His breath is glittering frost on the back of my neck. I close my eyes, forcing my body not to shake. I have a plan to execute, and it needs my attention, but he is so very distracting.

I jump when his fingers slide down my arms, the gold of the armour melting away and revealing my bare skin. 'Am I the flame to your ice?' I murmur.

He doesn't answer, only makes a soft growl in my ear, causing goose bumps on the exposed skin of my neck.

For a moment, I worry he'll leave me completely bare, but as I survey my body, the sheen of silken fabric becomes a waterfall of crimson wrapping my limbs, held in place by straps so fine, they almost cut, a neckline so plunging, it almost grazes my navel and splits each side of the skirt, leaving my legs on view.

I am truly a sacrifice to the wraiths.

'You're walking into the lion's den, Fury,' he warns, voice low. 'What will you cost me this time?'

'Much, I imagine.' I half laugh, feeling a little light-headed.

His palms land on my arms, and he spins me to face him. 'Now, what was the second?'

'What?'

'You said the first thing you needed was to be stripped of your armour.'

I take a moment to consider how true the statement is.

'Now, what is the second thing you require of me?'

'Oh, that.' I step out of his grasp, collecting my scattered thoughts. 'I need you to build me a room. Large enough to house a wraith comfortably.'

'A room.'

'A building, I guess.' I wish he was uncloaked so I might read his expression. 'One with a front door big enough for a wraith to enter and a smaller door for me at the rear. It doesn't need to be grand. It should be nothing more than a single room.'

Of all things, Charon laughs, making me wish even more that he was free of his hood. Though it's not a laugh of mirth but one dripping with mockery.

I put my hands on my hips and tap my foot. 'You're making fun of me.'

He stops laughing and gives me a taunting bow. 'On the contrary, I live to serve.'

He's being facetious, but I don't pay it any mind right now. 'And the building?'

He shakes his head a little, faint reverberations of a skull flickering within his hood. He gestures towards the blown-off end of his house, and I walk through it to follow him into the city.

We walk a long way, past destruction and debris, the water around us glittering with the dust of broken homes. After a while, we come to a place where the river is obscured from view. It is a dull and monochrome spot. My crackling hair creates shadow monsters of the piles of rock.

My nerves must be getting to me more than I'd hoped, as I startle when I turn to him and find his scrutiny hard on me.

'Is there a problem with the location?' he asks.

I shake my head, though in truth, I'm a tad nervous at being so far from the river. He turns in a circle, assessing the space around him, flinging stray rocks as if they're nothing even though they're the size of cars.

He sighs. 'The wraiths will more than likely destroy it as soon as it's built.'

I remain silent. That might be true.

'And time is of the essence? You need this built now? In one go?'

I meet his stare. 'Do you have something better to do?'

His gaze lingers, then trails my neckline achingly slowly, igniting my blood. Charon huffs a dry chuckle and paces some more before he raises both palms towards a pile of rubble. The ground shifts, and silt stirs while rubble shakes, seeming to fold in on itself until it resembles something made of bricks. The new brickwork reconfigures like in a game of *Tetris* until they slot in perfect conjunction with the colossal grind of stone against stone, and a wall stands some twenty feet high.

I pace forwards and place my palm on it. Solid. Part of me was expecting to swipe my fingers through the mirage. Charon is already working on a corresponding wall double the length of this one. I wander to the middle with a view of touching the other wall, but he's already storming to the halfway point. As he meets me, he raises his arms to the sides, invoking walls that rise from the silt, matching the narrow wall's height and then some. I peer at the lofty ceiling in awe as a great pitched roof lays itself in tiles of black slate, wooden beams sliding across the vaulted ceiling to support the structure.

It's hard not to be impressed, and a laugh escapes my lips. When I straighten my neck to speak, he's already moved away from me. He built the walls around us, and we're now standing in a sealed box. My stomach dips at being trapped with him. My hair is the only source of light in the dark. As he reaches the end of the room, he places his palms on the wall, and his shadow grows until his antlers graze the ceiling. As he descends to the floor once more, he arcs his arms, and in their wake, two huge wooden doors appear, fixed with great iron bolts.

My feet move of their own volition, and I press my palm to the rough texture of the timber. 'It's amazing,' I whisper. It's real wood, not a dream of it. 'You've never been to the Earth's surface?'

'No.' Charon strokes his hand against the grain of the other door before rubbing his fingers together.

'I've been wondering, how do you know what buildings of the living world should look like? The wooden doors. The vaulted ceiling. Every building here in the city.'

'Hm' is the only noise he makes for a while as he takes a step away and appraises his work. 'I've watched the river for many years. Beheld many memories. They are my inspiration.'

I'm floored by this revelation. How much Charon is inspired by the human world. That he would care so much to make things that are familiar so they might find comfort in the City of the Dead. In all our years spent side by side, I never asked.

As if sensing a question coming that he doesn't want to answer, Charon continues, 'It's rather a crude building. But the wraiths will have noticed its construction. They'll be on their way.' He walks away, pausing near the middle, perhaps noting now that he's turned away from me that I'm its only source of light. 'I take it you find it suitable.'

I lock my fingers together in front of me. 'It's perfect.'

'Perhaps, if you're successful in whatever endeavour you have planned, I might make some improvements.' The faintest flicker of hope sparkles in his eyes.

This must be something he enjoys doing, it dawns on me with a jolt. My mind can't help but drift to the memory of the pearl that he created when I requested the bath, as well as Hero and Leander's disapproval when they told me it was of his crafting. Charon had imagined it would be something I might enjoy, so he fashioned it for me. When he observes a soul, he sees what might make them happy. Even me.

'I would like that,' I say through the lump in my throat.

He lingers. 'You're sure I can't stay?'

'I'm sure,' I force myself to say.

He turns and stalks to the rear of the hall, and as he nears the furthest corner, a small door appears. He walks through it without a backwards glance.

I take a fortifying breath and push aside my worries about why he's even listening to me, though he must truly be at the last straw with the wraiths. I consider his earlier words. For me, only weeks have passed, but he has endured lifetimes of unrest. This has to work. I *must* make this work.

I make my way to the large wooden doors of the entrance, rest my open palms on both, then take a step in retreat. I lower myself to the ground and wait for Kane.

CHAPTER 20

LOVELY

At the dull *thud* on the wooden door, I scramble to my feet and ease it open. Kane looks as though he's gone a few rounds with a tank. A gash on his brow drips sludge into his eye, making me want to heave. Pressing down my nausea, I push the door further open to let him in, but he remains panting where he is.

'Jesus. What happened to you? They didn't believe it?'

'Many didn't.'

My heart sinks.

'But Maya agreed to come as an envoy.'

'Maya?' Hope seeps into me at the name.

'The tiger.'

Shit. Maya is the sole other wraith who bore witness to Dorian being destroyed by Charon. If there's anyone who wishes a little vengeance on me, it's her. 'Why Maya?' I whisper.

Kane raises a wolfy shoulder. 'The others are aware of what happened, so they are fearful it's a trap and that The Ferryman lies in wait. Maya is angry enough to chance it.'

There's too much to unpack for me to properly consider everything he's told me before Kane is speaking again. 'Will you receive her?'

'Yes.' Taking two steps, I open the other of the double doors, allowing them both entrance.

Kane nods. 'I'll remain close.'

He pads off a little way to collect her. He's worse for wear, with shadow still oozing out of a slash in his belly. I wouldn't fancy his chances against the tiger right now.

With both doors wide open, the full gloom of the Underworld cascades in. Kane omitted that while Maya is the only one who'll speak with me one-on-one, more wraiths have gathered. The mammoth of an elephant, a caribou, an eagle, as well as wraiths I've never seen before, like a buffalo, a scorpion, and perhaps the most terrifying of them all, what appears to be a massive wasp. When forming my plan, I hadn't given much thought to all the different forms they might possess.

I drag my gaze to the giant tiger stalking up the three steps of the building, her orange coat wilted to more of a dusty silver beneath the grime.

Kane slinks in behind me as I retreat, allowing the tiger into the hall. He gives a warning growl, which Maya returns. The cries of the wraiths sound like nails on a chalkboard.

I hold my palms aloft, showing I'm free of weapons this time. 'Maya, I'm so grateful you have come.'

She snarls again. I turn a circle around her with Kane behind me while she follows suit in a predatory stance, not willing to let me out of her sight. Full circle completed, I close the doors, depriving the wraiths of their show and locking myself in with a snarling wraith of a tiger.

She halts her prowl, glancing around the room, which is pitch-black save the flame of my hair.

'The Ferryman is not here.' She almost sounds surprised, though not as surprised as I am to find that her voice, though cracked, has a West Indian lilt.

'Just me and you,' I reassure her.

'And your pet dog.'

Kane offers a growl for the comment.

'I need *some* protection,' I point out. 'I'm taking a big risk here.'

She snarls.

'But no more souls will suffer because of me.'

'What happened to Dorian was an abomination!' she cries with a hiss.

'Let me rephrase: No soul, living or dead, will suffer again because of me.' She begins stalking me again, and my breathing picks up speed—I'm sure she'll pounce any minute. 'Maya, please listen to me. I will not be a harbinger of death. If you tear me apart, so be it, but I will not accept your mission of vengeance.'

She hisses again, clearly weighing her options. 'Your lapdog told us you plan to ease our suffering. How will you do that without avenging our deaths?'

The words are dry on my tongue. She might laugh in my face, or worse, eat me anyway. Charon will be so annoyed. I lick my parched lips and stop our dance. 'By offering myself to you.'

She stops her prowl once again.

I fight the tremble in my bones. Remind myself this plan is my own. 'It might not be as sweet as vengeance, not at first, but I'll ease your pain. It will be slow, but I will endure it. For each of you.'

Maya is stunned.

'It's true,' Kane growls. 'She will take it into herself. Try—you have nothing to lose.'

'Speak plainly, Fury. Did you not execute your dog's murderer?'

'I did. That horror is something I refuse to endure again. And despite the bloodshed, Kane is still in pain. Though no longer ravaged by it, he suffers enough that I may still offer him relief. It will take longer with you, but I promise I will continue until you find a semblance of peace.'

Maya sits, tilting her head. 'You have no idea what you promise. This will not be gentle.'

A wave of relief fills my chest. She's listening. I can do this. 'Do you know much about Dorian's death? His human death?'

Kane stills behind me. This is not something I shared with him, nor Hero and Leander, when I discussed my plan.

'Wraiths do not talk of such things.'

'It was awful. Obviously. Many died, as he did, in one of the worst atrocities witnessed by mankind. He festered in that for more than eighty years. His killers are long dead.' I bring my palm to my chest. 'The people I would have killed in his name—they would have been innocent.'

'So. Was. He,' Maya hisses.

'Then Dorian is no different from his killer. None of you are. It goes on, and it never ends. I will not be party to a legacy of death.'

'So, you offer yourself in their stead?'

'I do.'

Maya gently rises, takes a tentative step towards me and then another. I command myself to remain still until the rot of her breath is on my face, and then I motion behind me. 'Back, Kane.'

The wolf slinks off, nestling into a corner, though he remains alert on his feet. Ready to intervene.

'I-I'll take as much as possible for me to bear,' I say, quiet and afraid.

Slowly, I raise my palms, fingers splayed, before sinking them into Maya's fur. She snarls at the contact. So much pain. A cry wrenches from my throat as her agony rises. The flashes come fast—the moonlit beach, alcohol sour on their lips.

Tears escape. 'It's okay,' I urge, as for Maya, having my hands on her skin does not truly ease her suffering. The wraiths demand blood.

With a roar, Maya bares her teeth and sinks her jaw into my shoulder. My own screams shatter the air, my knees instantly buckling. Though I'm no longer in the sanctuary of the hall of the Underworld. I'm on a beach, kissed by moonlight. That's what I focus on—the moonlight. Not the unwanted weight on top of me. I let the terror fill me. My assailants are many. I stare at the moon—so pretty. I try to count the stars. I inhale it all in for Maya. Swallow it. Every punch after they were done with her, every kick to our abdomen, our face. Until I feel my lip pop and my mouth fills with blood and I'm choking on it. My back is raw from friction burns as I'm dragged into the sea. Only, this time there's a certain comfort in being drowned. The water flooding my lungs is a familiar sensation. At least the ordeal is over now.

'Enough,' I cry, pulling my grip from her chest, tearing the skin where her teeth are lodged in my body. Her jaw pops, and I'm free. I fall to the ground with a thump.

Kane instantly bounds forwards to stand over my body while I clutch my mauled shoulder.

Maya retreats a few paces, my blood dripping from her fangs, shaking her head as if casting off a dream… or a nightmare. Her pants are fewer as she eyes me cowering beneath Kane.

'I will tell the others of what you offered me here today.' Her eyes are wide with shock. 'We will talk again.'

With that, she prowls to the doors and knocks them open with her head before disappearing down the steps.

Light-headed, I press my forehead to the cool silt floor. It worked. I can't believe it worked. I could do it; I found the strength to endure her pain. My eyes become heavy, and I'm aware the ground around me is covered with blood.

Kane pushes his head under my unmarked arm. 'Let's get you to the river, Fury.'

The arm attached to the shoulder Maya mauled is completely useless. My fingers refuse to twitch. So, with my one good arm, I have to yank myself onto Kane and hold on for dear life. As he nudges his way out of the hall, the wraiths have thankfully dispersed. Kane sets off at a careful trot.

'Do you know your way to the river?' I ask.

'Of course. It calls to me.'

'It does?'

'Fear not, Fury. I will not answer.'

'One day, you might.'

'One day, I might.'

I let my eyes fall closed, soothed by the rhythmic rocking of our journey until the gentle tones of the guardians gliding on still waters beckons us.

'Oh dear.' Hero.

Despite my doziness, I smile.

'She's quite delirious,' Leander chimes as they wrap their limbs around me and ease me to the river's edge.

'Rude.' I smirk, incapable of opening my eyes while my head flops about listlessly.

My fluffy existence is ruined when foul river water is tipped into my mouth.

'Drink,' Hero and Leander both encourage.

I do, gulping disgustingly large amounts of the stuff, my fingers tingling as sensation returns.

Finally, I peel my eyes open to find Kane standing above me, Hero and Leander floating nearby. I laugh, pushing the empty kylix to the floor. 'It worked. It really worked.'

'The wraiths have not yet agreed,' Kane reminds me, party pooper that he is.

'They will.' I rise to my feet. 'I'm certain of it.'

'You will endure *that* for an eternity?' Kane demands.

'Wraith!' Leander chastises.

'A thousand times over.' I beam, nonplussed. 'This is how I save the city.'

'Is The Ferryman such a poor master?'

I frown at the wolf. 'This has nothing to do with him and everything to do with not wanting blood on my hands.'

Kane huffs but makes no further comment.

I refuse to take this as anything other than a win. Even the tiny strap of my dress has survived the mauling, though my neck and arm are caked with blood—as is my dress, though luckily, the stains match the colour. How does one wash in a world of water? Grasping the edge of my dress, I use the fine material to scrub my arm, delighted when the blood comes away.

'Ha!' I laugh, making quick work of the rest of the blood.

Hero and Leander exchange a glance. 'Are you quite well, Lovely?' Leander queries.

I take their tentacles in my grasp. 'I'm happy.'

Their bioluminescence flares in a shower of shooting stars.

'You're happy?' Hero smooths a limb over my cheek.

'So happy, Hero. *Sacrifice* is something I'm made for.'

Leander joins their partner, running limbs over my hair and skin. In praise. Adoration. Admiration. The sensation fills me.

'I'll rest now to be ready for when they come again.'

Turning to Kane, I now mount him with ease.

Hero splutters, 'W-will you not report to The Ferryman?'

I shake my head. 'Not yet. It's too soon. Will you keep my secret for now? I don't want to put you two in an awkward position.'

Hero hesitates.

Leander does not. 'It's one we'll keep for as long as we're able.'

I beam at them and urge Kane forwards. He travels in the direction of the hall without prompting, already in tune with my wishes.

After a little while, passing the giant rubble piles, broken trees, the remnants of streetlamps, the world that once was, a thought passes my mind. 'There's a wasp amongst them.'

'Mmm. A new addition, if I'm correct. Cristobal.'

'Cristobal,' I repeat. What a lovely name. What pain must he have endured for his spirit to claim the form of a wasp? 'I will receive Cristobal next.'

Kane's footfalls falter. 'Why the wasp?'

'He's the one I fear the most. I need to assure myself what I'm capable of.'

Kane dips his head with a grunt, arriving at the hall once more. We walk in side by side in silence. Kane does a lap of the hall, disappearing into the darkest corners. I watch his circuit of the parameter until he stills near the top of the hall.

'Do wraiths find any sort of rest?' I ask him.

'In a sense.'

When I embrace his jowls and smoosh my face against his, he sighs. 'Rest, then,' I tell him.

He turns in circles a few times before settling, and once he's curled up like a true domesticated hound, I move around and position myself by his belly, his gentle breaths soothing me. Bringing my head to his shoulder, I draw my eyes closed and sleep.

CHAPTER 21

LOVELY

Cristobal's screams are a thousand church bells decimating my ears. Or they could be my own. Pure white floods my vision. Blistering agony. A giant stinger rips the flesh of my thigh from hip to knee. *This* scream is definitely mine. Opening my eyes, I'm pinned to the ceiling of my sanctuary by the wasp, not lost in the nightmare of Cristobal's memory. Kane circles, snarling, below where I'm pinned, his blackened teeth catching the glints of my sparking hair. The acrid taste of gunpowder on the back of my tongue fades with Cristobal's brutal memory.

'Enough!' I scream.

Cristobal withdraws, his stinger tearing muscle as it's yanked from my leg, and I plummet through the water, landing on Kane with a crunch of wing. I scream some more as my wolf yelps, desperately trying to keep my leg attached. Cristobal hovers nervously, not saying a word. My vision is already covered in black spots.

'Kane. The river,' I rasp, my words pale ghosts in my throat.

'Do you need me to carry her?' Cristobal's voice is a low hum.

But Kane is already moving, not caring how I'm holding on so tight, his fur is loosening from his flesh.

'I'm... not... going... to... make....'

Kane lets out an awful howl as sorrowful as a dirge as my fingers begin to lose their hold. I slip, falling off Kane's hindquarters into the many limbs of the guardians.

'Hold on, Lovely,' they croon.

As I'm placed on the silt, my leg, which feels like it's alight, hits the ground with a thud. I cry out, the effort of my shriek too much. All that's left is whimpers bubbling from my lips in an unrestrained stream.

The relief of the river water is soon brought to my lips, and I drink until every drop is gone.

'More,' I demand. I drink a whole second cup before my leg has stitched itself together.

Kane paces, the agitation rolling off him in waves. The guardians soothe my aching limb, their tentacles helping the healing effects of the river by easing the knots in the newly grown flesh. They can't contain their worry either. Their bioluminescence pulses in a steady strum as if warning away a predator.

I dry my mouth on the back of my hand. 'It'll get better. This first wave was always going to be the worst, when the pain is freshest.'

'You haven't even scratched the surface. The true number of wraiths who reside in the Underworld is a mystery.'

'I have nothing but time,' I remind him.

'It will break your spirit,' Kane snarls.

I'm surprised how much the notion of my broken spirit bothers him. 'Do you think so little of me? I'm strong enough. For this, I'm strong enough.'

A low growl rumbles in his throat.

'Please, Kane. I'm only tired now. I need to rest. We'll hit a rhythm, I promise. Right now, I need to prove myself to them.'

I stand, whole again. A small rest is all I need. I mount Kane once more, and we return to the sanctuary, leaving the laments of the guardians behind us. Kane watches me with woe-filled eyes before curling into a crescent moon, allowing me to collapse into his side, my face buried in rotting fur, my wings draped over his spine, giving him a chimera-like aura.

Kane's transformation lingers in my mind for a beat before all thoughts fade into nothingness.

I PACE THE HALL OF WHAT I'VE COME TO CHRISTEN 'THE sanctuary.' My haven in the City of the Dead. Kane's head nudges open the door. I stop my pacing and eye the wolf.

He slides in through the gap. 'It's Jamal.'

I nod. The caribou. The child. If anyone's pain deserves easing, it's his, though the memories of our last encounter plummet through me. The memory of seeing my intestines outside my body leaves me with a nauseous taste in my mouth, my saliva suddenly thick.

Kane now nudges both doors open, allowing Jamal entrance to the hall where I've bled over and over again. The silt must be rich with the stuff by now. I'm surprised poppies haven't sprung up and turned my sanctuary into the monument of a battlefield.

Jamal's nerves are apparent in each slow, tentative step. He stalks forwards on trembling legs, his eyes averted. His nervousness makes my task easier.

Emboldened, I step towards him. 'Don't be afraid,' I reassure him, running my fingers over his snout. Memories rise quickly to the surface. I make my voice soft. 'I know how to help. This is a part of me I'm willing to give,' I say through the tears already collecting in my eyes as his memories course through me.

With a shuddering exhale, he spears me with his antlers, their sharp ends slicing through my soft belly. I keep my focus on Jamal, keen to ease the poor boy's suffering. I let his death consume me until I'm totally out of my body and living his final horrific moments. In the process, my fingers clamp onto his face, and I learn a glimmer, not only about his life before but also about his wraith form. Jamal had been so small in life, unable to protect himself, that in his wraith form, he became large. A caribou.

More memories flit through my brain, deeper than his death. It was December when Jamal died, and images of a Christmas picture book in his tiny hands flicker like overexposed film spinning free of its spool —something too insubstantial to grasp onto.

'Fury,' Kane growls. 'Enough.'

I peek my sleepy eyes open to find I'm slumped over Jamal's sloping forehead, his antlers so deep into my body, they protrude out of my back, their shadows casting finger demons on the walls of the hall. My arms hold on as tight as my strength will allow.

'No.' I tighten my grasp. 'Let's keep going.'

I push my face into Jamal's shorthaired hide, my tears mixing with his fur in a mangle of rot and damp hair. His body shudders beneath mine, his memory slipping beyond my grip when Kane lunges, snapping at Jamal and causing him to jerk away. The wet slurp of his antlers slices through my insides as if they're butter as I'm dropped to the floor.

'No!' I cry again. holding my palm towards Jamal, trying and failing to clutch onto him, wanting to take every ounce of pain he suffered and make it vanish entirely.

Kane stands protectively over me while Jamal staggers a pace in retreat, shaking his head. Pieces of rot and decay fling from his antlers, splatting against the wall of the sanctuary as his skin shudders. My mouth drops open, and Kane's breath hitches.

A layer of rot slides from Jamal's haunches, leaving something of a normal-looking caribou, tanned skin peeking through the sludge of shadow.

'What the...?' Kane whispers.

My head spins. The glistening pool of crimson I'm lying in spreads further and further across the floor, creating a lake from the depths of a nightmare. 'Kane,' I slur.

Breaking free of his wonder, he turns and shuffles me onto his back, my stomach tented over the ridge of his spine so that my feet are visible from under his belly. The rough drag of his matted fur against my wounds returns me to my body in a startling cry. Then Kane is out the door and bounding to the river, alerting the guardians with his customary yowl.

The glow of the journeying souls comes into view, and Kane skids to a halt so suddenly, I slide off him and land in a heap. A whimper escapes my parched lips, my eyes rolling in their sockets, needing the relief of Hero and Leander's soothing caresses. I reach a weak arm in the direction of the river.

'What is this?'

The dark voice rattles my bones, and through my blurred vision, The Ferryman is the Grim Reaper standing on the banks of the Styx. Hero and Leander linger nervously behind him. Charon kneels at my side, his cool hand on the nape of my neck, elevating my head as his eyes zero in on the wounds in my chest and stomach. My spirit is almost certainly leaving my body.

He turns to Hero and Leander, his tone blade sharp. 'What has been happening here?'

'She has been healing the wraiths,' Leander ventures, their voice meek. 'It seems to be effective.'

Charon's eyes flash on me, his free hand cupping my cheek.

'You're missing your scythe,' I murmur, delirious.

He scoops me in his arms. The sudden woosh makes my head spin, and I clutch onto his cloak.

'Master,' Hero calls, 'we need to heal her.'

But Charon doesn't answer, doesn't spare his guardians a glance. His eyes are fixed on me and filled with withering rage. I'm too weak to argue. My own slow blinks could be taking seconds or hours; the time spent in his arms moving away from the glow of the river is a mystery to me. As we cross the threshold of his home, I barely have the fortitude to observe if it's been repaired. My only care when he's placed me on a hard table, my mind drifting, is foolishly wishing to be in his arms again. That wish will only hurt us both. I'll never truly have him, and he will never believe I would willingly choose him.

What strange thoughts to dwell on when you're bleeding out on a table.

When his blurred form clouds my vision again,

he's uncrowned and uncloaked. My sanguine smile is laced through my words when I say, 'There you are.'

'Drink, Fury,' he commands softly.

I do. It's not river water.

BURYING MY FACE DEEP INTO SILK, IT FAINTLY SMELLS OF opium and is as soft as goose down. I peek my eyes open to be met with a view of the river, golden orbs bobbing along its gentle current, Leander gliding gracefully above it. On one side, my arm is resting under the pillow beneath my head. I'm in bed. The fact has me bolting up, trying to make sense of what befell me. My tattered red dress has been replaced with a loose black shift, a deep-cut V in the back to accommo-date my wings.

Swinging around, I see that Charon is seated at the end of the bed, facing me, his shoulders leant against the high footboard. Uncloaked, one bare foot tucked under himself, the other rooted on the ground as if ready to sprint from me at any moment. His brow is furrowed, making him appear less fearsome and more... adorable.

'You were sleeping,' he says, and I'm not sure if it's a question or a statement.

'That's not supposed to happen, is it?'

He shrugs. 'No one knew what a Fury free of the

yolk of servitude would be capable of. It appears you're bending the Underworld to your will.'

'You don't sound worried.'

'It's low on my list of concerns.'

'Oh.'

The conversation stalls, and I examine him for any trace of what he's really feeling. Turns out, his human face is as hard to read as his hooded one. It flickers gently, and for some wild reason, the reminder that he is not wholly human does something to my insides I don't care to examine right now.

He lets out a sigh and sets his sights on the river. 'I should be furious with you right now. Why was I not part of your plan? Why did you go to Hero and Leander instead of me?'

The question throws me entirely off balance. 'They said their role was to heal the Furies. I assumed....' I trail off because he does look furious, though I'm not sure if it's with me or because my reasoning makes sense, and he isn't sure why he's angry about it. Not wanting to provoke him, I change tack. 'It's working. The wraiths are calming. Rebuild this city, Charon.'

'You will spend eternities at their mercy, swallowing their pain.'

'Better than a legacy of bloodshed.' Bracing myself, I take his hand.

He lets me, threading his fingers through mine. I allow the thrum of the bond to pass through me, another pain to absorb, something else I must steel myself against if I'm to be successful. 'This is what I was made for. Allow me this. The living world does not need to be fed their pain. Let me swallow it.'

His eyebrows knit so tight, they forge deep lines in his brow, but eventually he nods.

I breathe a sigh of relief.

'But you will no longer be tended by Hero and Leander. You will come to me.'

I swallow hard. 'Why?'

He breaks his reverie with the river and turns his intention on me, universes alive in his stare. He turns my hand in his own, his icy fingers tracing the lines etched in my palm. That warm trickle of longing coats my limbs.

'So that I may be of some use in your schemes,' he finally replies. 'Please, Fury, allow me this.'

Because he said please, I nod. He makes a small noise of agreement in the back of his throat, drops my hand, and walks away.

Now that he isn't consuming every bit of my attention, his restored home is revealed to me. The bed isn't like the one he crafted for me before. This one, situated near the window, is simple and much more befitting his home. His chair sits a little way off from its end. The single purpose of the large table in the middle of the room has clearly been to provide a space where he can heal me.

Charon gestures to the door. 'You've forged quite

the guard dog. Kane has kept sentry for the duration of your slumber.'

I grin at that. 'For the sole purpose of eavesdropping, I assume.' I make towards the door.

'Where are you going?'

I fumble, believing his previous gesture was my dismissal. 'I should get back to the sanctuary.'

Charon's eyebrows lift, the corner of his mouth turning up. 'The sanctuary?'

'It's what I've taken to calling the building.'

'Hmm.' His eyes drift away from me and to the bed he obviously made for me.

My cheeks become hot. 'Well, I better go,' I mutter and leave before I say or do something stupid.

True to his word, Kane is waiting outside. He rises to his feet as I exit, then waits.

I clear my throat. 'Following my meetings with the wraiths going forwards, I'm to be brought to The Ferryman and not the river,' I say with as much dignity as I can muster.

Kane's smirk is evident in every inch of his being.

'Shut up,' I snap, moving to his side to mount him, and we return to the sanctuary.

CHAPTER 22

LOVELY

I pound the floors of the sanctuary, counting the distance in steps from door to rear exit—106. Nerves jitter my bones, though it's not from the next wraith who is set to stalk through my doors but rather from how I'm to be brought before The Ferryman after. I silently curse myself for agreeing. I'll no doubt be in a vulnerable state and likely do something stupid to expose myself.

Kane escorts in the eagle. As soon as he's told me his name, it flies from my brain in the same instant. My head isn't in the game. I need to focus.

The eagle chatters, expressing gratitude. I smile. Or did I? I can't think. Hating how distracted I am by the anticipation of being healed by Charon, I throw myself into the task at hand and lose myself in the eagle's awful death. Though his beak struggles to make proper purchase on my neck; it happens in a series of brisk snaps. I flit in and out of his psyche in a jarring agony. For the first time, I push the wraith away, grappling with his grimy oil-slick feathers as he tries again to take hold. Through the fog and violence, I'm vaguely worried he might cleave my neck clean in two.

Kane, sensing this, joins the fray until we're a blur of sludgy feathers, teeth, and blood. Kane nips my ankle in his haste, and I slip, bringing my face directly into the path of the eagle's beak, and with a horrifying pop, he plucks my eye from its socket.

I stagger out of range, clutching my eye, blood running down my face and into my mouth.

'Fuck. Oh, fuck,' I cry.

'Fury, my apologies.' The wraith's voice is gravel steeped in panic.

Kane snaps at him to retreat.

'Kane. Don't.' I beat my alarm into submission, suppressing revulsion that my eyeball is now cupped in my palm, sinew slipping between my fingers. 'No apologies needed. An accident.' I choke down the need to heave. With my free hand, I fumble my way to Kane and pull myself onto his back.

He leaves the eagle with a snarl before sprinting the journey to Charon's home. I have half a mind to tell him to make for the river instead, as for some reason, this injury feels like one I'd rather Charon not witness—though I fail to voice it. All too soon, I'm sliding from my seat on Kane and standing at The Ferryman's door.

A grotesque urge to laugh rises in my throat at how ridiculous I am with one fist raised, knocking on an ancient entity's door with my eyeball clutched in the other, but it seems this is where my life has taken me.

When Charon opens the door, he's uncloaked. His eyes widen. Clearly he wasn't expecting me to be standing on my own. He probably also wasn't expecting me to be without an eye. He takes my free hand and leads me inside.

Though I'm light-headed, it's not the gravest injury I've sustained. I walk to the table and pop myself atop it, my legs swinging, as if being without an eye is the most normal thing in the world.

'There's nothing sexy about being Fury,' I joke.

Charon looks murderous. With gentle fingers he attempts to move the hand cupping my eye.

'I wouldn't do that,' I warn him. 'My eye is completely free of its socket.'

'Fuck me.' His fingers are cool on the side of my face.

I giggle. 'Did you just swear?'

Though he doesn't answer, merely tilts my face this way and then that, some of the rage melts out of him. Releasing me, he drags a dagger towards him. I'm unsure if it's the same ice dagger with the flame-carved hilt I abandoned after the attack or if he's pulled it into existence from thin air.

Bewitched, I stare as he slices at his wrist and offers me the pearls of his precious blood. Careful to keep one hand to my eye, I take his wrist with my other hand and drink, lowering my good eye so I don't have to watch him watch me.

The purity of his blood is bliss, its ice spreading through my bones, my cells singing with so much life, I might burst. Every inch of my body is aware of him, struggling to be close to him, as desperate as roots straining their fingers to find water. His shadows wind deeper from my wrist to my elbow, as treacherous as poison ivy. I drink deep.

With every passing moment, my eye eases into its rightful home in its socket until I'm blinking rapidly, eyes downcast as my vision returns. Without his cloak, Charon's bare feet are exposed. I stop drinking and slowly drop my hand from my face, the golden thread that binds us going crazy in my chest.

Charon examines my fixed eye. The whispers of his touch are enough to send my insides molten. *It's just the bond. It's just the bond. It's just the bond,* I repeat over and over in my mind. Though I'm healed, I'm more light-headed than ever as he takes a piece of cloth and begins to wipe the blood from my face.

'You don't have to....'

He tilts his head. 'You want me to stop?'

Yes. No. I don't know. I take the cloth from his fingers, trying not to grimace. 'A mirror would be good.'

He steps away, and with a wave of his hand, a full-length mirror appears on the wall. I keep my eyes on his perfectly sculpted shoulders as he moves away to observe the light of the river. Looking into the mirror, I'm thankful to find that my eye appears much the way it was. Luckily the bloodstains are lost on the black shift dress I'm still wearing. I wipe the blood from my cheek before moving on to my arm and hand until I'm free of the sticky stuff.

'What will you rebuild first?' I ask, needing to fill the silence.

'Perhaps the cathedral. It's home to a thin spot. The spirits deeply enjoyed it there.' His voice is quiet and contemplative.

'I thought they'd all moved on. That the wraiths alone remained.'

'While many moved on, I suspect some still hide within the city limits. Though I know not where.'

I turn to observe him. 'How was it for you? Having to move them on?'

He doesn't answer.

The bed still lies near the window, though I know he doesn't sleep. Why keep it? My heart flutters in the desperate hope that I might be the reason it remains. That the memory of me in it is a call to him too.

I'm filled with the urge to fidget. I motion towards the door. 'I should go, then.'

He remains silent, so I leave, dragging my feet only the slightest amount.

Kane rises to attention as I blow out a breath, closing the door behind me. The wolf scans my face, a sigh leaving his chest when he registers my restored eye. I'm grateful he doesn't ask about Charon or note how my blood is on fire, my skin vibrating.

'To the sanctuary?'

'No. Let's take a walk.'

SHARP TEETH EMBED INTO THE FLESH OF MY SHOULDER, images swarming hot and sticky against the back of my eyelids. Yet my thoughts are unable to stay rooted in the scene.

The Ferryman is a problem.

Three times now, I've visited Charon. Each time is the same. I drink from his wrist, we have minimal conversation followed by his quiet dismissal, my blood on fire every time I leave him. Then Kane and I stalk the ruined streets of the Underworld to burn off some of my energy. Sometimes we pass a wraith who eyes us with silent caution. On our last stroll, we came across a large area cleared of rubble. It must be where the cathedral is planned, though the foundations have not yet been laid. Charon's rebuild of the city is stop-start. His hesitation caused a new kind of anger to settle into me. Charon is waiting for my plan to blow up in my face.

The worst of it is how my simmering annoyance

takes my head out of the game with the wraiths. I should be focused on the jaguar in front of me, not the chilly healing session that will follow.

Something's wrong.

I snap my eyes open, crying out and pushing the wraith from me. They stumble away. My fingers fly to my neck and find a huge chunk of it missing, the blood spurting out violently like a Halloween prop. The pressure reminds me of a child sucking a drink through a straw, and the revolting noise is all I can focus on as the wraith scrambles to apologise.

Kane pushes the jaguar out of the way, then nudges me onto his back before I collapse. I stretch out to rest between the blades of his shoulders, my feet dangling on either side of him. My blood sinks fast into his fur. The Underworld is spinning, a grim carousel, so I shut my eyes.

'Are you trying to get yourself killed? Is your aim to provoke him?' Kane growls.

My brain is candy floss, inconsistent and intangible. 'Take me to the river,' I mumble, my tongue feeling too big for my mouth.

Kane slams into The Ferryman's door. I collide with it, smashing my wrist, and shoot eye daggers at the wolf. When Charon throws open the door, I fall in through the opening and slump at his feet. Charon follows suit by casting a disapproving glance at Kane. When he pulls me by my wrists, my head flops to the floor before he manages to haul me to my feet.

'Get off me.' I try to yank out of his grasp, my head lolling everywhere. I feel stupid and next to passing out, though I don't miss his exasperated glance at Kane. 'Take me to the river. I want Hero and Leander.' I crumple into a heap, finally freeing myself.

Charon crouches in front of me. Maybe it's my blurred vision, but something akin to sympathy blooms in his eyes as he takes my head in his palms. 'There's no time.'

He pulls me into his arms, shutting Kane out with a slam of his door. Charon perches me on the edge of the table where I usually sit, but my useless head won't stop flopping forwards. He growls as my head wobbles, and my cheek presses against the cool skin of his chest.

Charon doesn't have a shirt on. My taffy brain doesn't quite compute the information.

He fists a bunch of my flaming hair at the nape of my neck, keeping my head in place. I stare at him while his concentration is on the knife in his hand as he slides it across the skin a centimetre below his collarbone, leaving a trickle of black blood in its wake.

His gaze finds mine, and then he steps closer, pushing between my legs. My body goes into revolt as he brings my lips to his skin. It's a stupid idea to keep my eyes on his as I drink from him. Nor is it a good decision for him to whisper, 'Good girl.'

His voice is smoke, and my toes curl, wrapping themselves around his calves. As my wound heals, my hands snake to his hips and around his back, wishing to discover the cool of his skin. The flesh of my neck is stitched together, but I drink still, not wanting this moment to be over, his blood warm and metallic on my tongue. I want to keep feeling how his breaths are shallow against my belly, how my hips are stretched wide for him. I exert pressure through my fingertips, urging him closer to me. He yields, fingers sliding further over my face and into my hair. The heady earthy scent wraps around us, richer than ever before, decadent vanilla and mouth-watering almond making our embrace even more dreamy. An illusion. The world, my injuries—they fall away, everything reduced to the point where my lips meet his skin.

In a fluid motion, he pulls away, dipping his arms low around my waist and hoisting me free of my seat. My legs instinctively wrap around his hips, and my arms wind around his neck. I'd been so ravenous, I'm sure my lips are bloody. As he spins me away from the table, the treacherous bond prays he's taking us to the bed.

But he stills, his luminous eyes on my mouth still moist with his blood. 'Why did you ask for the guardians?'

I smooth my fingers over the cliffs of his cheekbones. 'Because your indifference towards me is too much to bear.'

'Do I seem indifferent, Fury?' His words are so soft, they hurt. His gaze remains caught on my mouth.

'Not now.' I graze my nose along his, stealing his oxygen. Or whatever it is that sustains him in this watery place. 'Must I be almost beheaded to get your attention?'

Charon laughs, his whole face alive with it, though my disappointment lingers when he drops me to my feet. He peers at me, his height hooding his eyes. 'I shall do better to not be indifferent.'

My stomach sinks a little. I take a step away. 'A little conversation will do.'

He nods. His bare chest is impossible not to stare at, all hard angles sharing the same flicker of blueish-silver skeletal shadow when the light catches him just right. He clears his throat, and he's once more clothed in his uniform of black.

'Are your clothes made of shadow alone?'

'Yes.' He cocks an eyebrow. 'You're surprised?'

Yes. He never fails to surprise me. I clear my throat, sure I'm staring. 'I should….' I motion towards the door, 'Kane was quite annoyed by my carelessness.'

'One moment.' His gaze travels the length of my body, leaving a replica of the red dress in its wake. He turns to the river. 'Until next time.'

My gown ripples in the water, its silky material batting against the spindly legs of the wolf at my side.

'Kane,' I start.

'Yes, Fury.'

'I want to meet with the wraiths, but not in the sanctuary, and to talk, not to heal them. I want to get to know them.'

Kane huffs a laugh. 'There isn't much to get to know.'

'I could have said the same about you.' I give him a self-satisfied grin. 'At first.'

'Okay. I'll round up some wraiths once I've escorted you home to the sanctuary.' He practically cocks an eyebrow at me. 'It's not as if they hold parliament or anything.'

I let out a laugh because, actually, I *did* believe they have some kind of organisation. 'Perhaps they should.'

'Fury, there's no organising pain. Let them be.'

I stare at him, guilt throbbing at me, suddenly worried I'm doing a bad job.

'I will do as you ask regardless,' he relents.

When we arrive at my hallowed hall, Kane tells me to stay put until he returns, and I slip inside alone. I chew my nail in the dark, wondering how true it might be. That all wraiths will forever be consumed by their pain. Yet Kane appears to have found some purpose by my side. I would even go so far as to call him a gossip.

When Kane pounds on the door, inviting me outside, I find he has amassed a party of five wraiths, Maya amongst them, who congregate at the foot of the small stairs leading to the hall.

'Thank you for meeting me.'

The water is thick with anticipation. Maya snarls some.

With a fortifying exhale, I confess, 'I was hoping we might spend some time together. Forge a kind of friendship?'

The wraiths exchange perplexed glances. 'We assumed this was in relation to Tessa,' Maya growls.

Tessa, the jaguar. She's not joined the rest of them for our convocation.

'What would this have to do with her?'

'She's worried she hurt you,' Cristobal answers.

'Nothing I can't handle.' I give what I hope is a reassuring smile.

Kane huffs.

'The river heals me,' I say in response to their confused stares. 'Please don't worry yourselves about me. I called you here to talk about how you're doing. Are you pleased with my work? Will you accept me?'

Maya is practically agog. Cristobal's wings flap, lifting him from the floor where he rests.

'You serve us well,' Maya assures me after a while. 'While it's not vengeance, our spirits are soothed somewhat.' She spares a passing glance at each of the others. 'We will accept you.'

They all buzz or bow or stomp in agreement. Warmth blooms in my chest.

'Happy to hear that,' I tell them as Maya settles into a seated position. 'I was thinking you should visit me again soon. For another session. And Cristobal too.'

Maya cocks her head.

'Your pain is never fully healed,' I explain. 'I wish to keep on top of it. If we do it this way, I believe that in time, the process will be less traumatic—for all of us.'

Shock tremors across the party, and their hollow, beady eyes turn on one another. Cristobal buzzes in approval. A nearby bull stomps.

Maya speaks again. 'And those you've not yet received?'

'I will continue to do so. I have no plans to stop.'

The bull acquiesces with a bow of his head. Strange to be seated here in the finest dress I've ever laid my eyes on, surrounded by violent spirits. I have never felt quite so at ease. I feel no hesitation with them, no ulterior motive.

Kane stands protectively by my side, black eyes like shiny buttons. With him positioned as my protector, the meaning of purpose floats in my mind. How important it is to the soul to have one. Even in death, are the wraiths still chasing theirs?

'You speak well, Maya. Perhaps you might help me?'

She tilts her head.

'The wraiths need a leader, someone who might speak on their behalf, raise their grievances. You've come forwards twice now when someone needed to step up. Maybe you should be that figure?'

'I do not speak for the desires of all here.'

'Of course. Your job would be to learn. To speak with the wraiths. Consider it. Discuss it with the others.'

She nods, and a quiet comfort settles over me. They stay and talk for a while about my plans. About The Ferryman's part in them. I ask them to cease their campaign of destruction so that he might rebuild and the lost spirits may make their homes here once more. They agree.

Something I've never felt before washes through me as I survey the group around me. Pride. Hope, maybe? I did this. Something good. Not through force but in a way only I know how.

A small smile ghosts my lips. The Ferryman was wrong. I don't need to fight—I can heal instead.

CHAPTER 23

LOVELY

The gash in my leg winds from the top of my inner thigh down to my knee. A result of my second meeting with Cristobal. Thankfully, with this subsequent session, the wound is less vicious, though it smarts all the same.

I limp to the table, then ease myself into a sitting position. I hitch my knee up to examine the wound through the slit of my dress, wincing as I push at its edges. It's angry, with gooey sludge coalescing along the perimeter of the gouge. Cristobal's pain was lessened but still there. Where it will forever linger. While my Fury sisters all granted vengeance, they never removed the pain, not fully.

The notion whirs in my head as I mutter, 'Shame that the wraith wounds are toxic. This one might have healed by itself otherwise.'

When I glance up, Charon is staring at the cut. I

feel oddly on display with one knee drawn to my chin while the other dangles over the table's edge. I want to chastise him for not talking when he promised he'd try, but the water around us becomes charged with something dangerous I have no name for.

This wound isn't urgent. I'm in no danger of perishing from it. He nears me, taking the knife from thin air. Sparks flare in the neon of his eyes, a silent challenge. A new game. He holds it out for me to take, but I shake my head. The corner of his delicious mouth twitches. He rests the blade against his wrist before looking to me for confirmation. I shake my head again. He brings it to his chest. I nod, and he takes a laboured inhale.

The shadows fall away, revealing his chest. He pierces his skin, leaving a trail of blood before stepping forwards. He nudges my knees apart with his legs, and I gasp. He drops the knife, threading his fingers into the flames of my hair to observe me as I use him to heal myself.

The water around us takes on a languid quality, thick and dreamlike. I take a slow blink as he moves back, catching my lip with his thumb to reveal some of his blood. Which, in turn, he brings to his own mouth. The sight makes me shudder.

Although I asked for his conversation, I don't have a damn thing to say. My body is a tightly wound dynamo in danger of cracking.

His shadows magically appear, covering him

though they taper off at his elbows, which is strangely the sexiest thing I've ever seen. He lowers himself into his chair with a casual grace. 'So, you're making progress with the wraiths?'

'Yes,' I croak, throat dry. 'Maybe it's time to rebuild that cathedral you've been procrastinating on.'

'Clever,' he chuckles, averting his eyes to the river.

Realising that I'm still sitting indecently on the table, I pull myself together and hop off to make a sharp exit, needing to be far from here and the pull of our bond.

***

I MEET TESSA, THE JAGUAR, AGAIN. THIS TIME I SPEAK WITH her before I dive into her death. We map out some better expectations. Then, like the sacrificial lamb, I lie down, shifting my dress to offer her the tender side of my belly just below my ribs where she's to sink her fangs. I welcome her into my arms as if she's a child, my fingers sliding into her matted fur. I soak in her pain, used to the blows of death. Something different and distant tinkles in my veins through her nightmare, a promise wrapped in dreadful expectation.

When she finishes, she rears up, a little dazed. I share her sluggishness, a dream difficult to shake. When I examine the wound, I find four perfect puncture marks. Barely any mauling, as if she'd been perfectly still. When she shakes her fur, some of the rot drips to the floor in stagnant pools that melt like butter into the silt of the Underworld. What is absorbing all this decay doing to the city? My hall has taken on a coppery musk from the blood spilt. She doesn't say anything as she slinks out of the sanctuary.

Kane's silence is a loaded beast of its own as I mount him. We make our way to The Ferryman without haste, his paws landing dully in the silt. I chance a peek at Kane as I approach the door, and his head cocks. If a wolf made of shadow, putrid flesh, and bone could raise a judgemental eyebrow, he would be doing so in this instant. When I knock on the door, then enter, Charon is already without a shirt. My neck flushes at all the implications of a wraith seeing him this way—their master, changed as he is.

The door closes behind us. Charon marks my hand clutched to my side, and he tugs at the side of my dress to inspect the damage, how urgent my injury is. I'm panting, anticipation rolling over me. I tell myself I must have punctured a lung. That it's not the way Charon is descending on me that steals my ability to control my thrumming chest. His home in pitch dark-ness, Charon drives me into retreat until my ass hits the table, and I slide my palms up his bare chest. His fingers smooth along the backs of my legs, lifting me to sit, and I lock my fingers around his neck. No words are spoken between us, only the crackling of fire permeating the heavy silence.

He brings the knife of ice and flame to his collarbone, his sharp features thrown into stark relief from the sole source of sparking light. I shake my head. His eyes widen. The shadows wrap even tighter around me. He moves the blade to the base of his neck, and I nod. As soon as the cut is made, the knife clatters to the table, and my mouth is on him.

His hands drop to my knees to trail up the lengths of my thighs, leaving a wake of chilled fire on my nerve endings before he digs his thumbs into the dips where my hips meet my groin. I jolt, lost, a burning flame. I bite into his skin as if I've turned wraith. He clasps my lower back, claiming me, sliding my body closer until I'm flush against him. Charon is a starved man forbidden from eating at a banquet, and I'm the ripe fruit almost rotting just beyond his grasp. A peach he refuses to devour.

Fully healed, I reluctantly pull away. Our gazes clash, the rise and fall of our chests ragged against each other. His luminous eyes never leave mine. Lost in the moment, wrapped in abandon, I jerk forwards to claim his mouth. He retreats. I have no time for mortification as he grasps my neck in his huge palm and smiles, sharp teeth and all. He holds me there, my swallow a dry thing against his grip. I'm barely able to breathe. To think.

As my mind catches up, my nerves settle. This is still a game of submission. One I'll never win. I wrap my fingers around his hand that still holds my throat, realising this is all I'm ever going to get. I prise his fingers away inch by painful inch, the spark of challenge fading from his visage. Without saying another word, I leave his home.

———

It appears I have hit my stride with the wraiths. We're working out how we fit. They understand where to bite, where to strike, and for how long. I rarely must call enough. Their pain is my pain. My flesh is their flesh.

Now when Kane and I walk the streets of the City of the Dead, sometimes they murmur, 'Sweet girl. She tastes so sweet,' in hushed reverent tones.

As well as the improvements to the sanctuary, progress is slowly being made to the cathedral. The wraiths have done nothing to sabotage the construction. Three walls now stand. One wall, huge and arched, contains an exquisite stained-glass window in the centre. A woman with a flame of red hair is depicted with a gigantic wolf by her side. It makes my knees weak every time I see it.

And then there's Charon. Whatever it is I'm doing with him, this battle of wills is getting a little out of control. I'm not quite sure why either of us is entertaining our arrangement. It's more excruciating than any wraith bite.

My meet with Maya has gone well, though her bite has gone so deep that the tips of my fingers are losing sensation, but she's not what consumes my thoughts as Kane and I ride out. Once we arrive at The Ferryman's abode, I slide from my seat upon my wolf. In the two steps to his door, it opens before I have chance to knock, revealing Charon bare from the waist up. I'm in his arms before the door slams behind us, my good arm clasped around his neck, his hands hooking under my thighs, wrapping me around him before stalking to place me on the table where he heals me. Touches me. Drives me to the brink of insanity.

He slashes his throat, and in a heartbeat, the knife clatters to the table. His icy fingers dance along my legs, urgent and grasping under my knees, pulling me to him. I bring my lips to his neck, drinking deep, sucking at his skin. I use my good hand to clamp him to me, my nails driving into the flesh of his shoulder blade.

The pressure of his grip on my upper thighs is driving me wild. I lock my knees around his waist. Sensation fizzes into my affected hand once more as I lift it, yanking him to me, and bite down hard on his neck. At the forcefulness of my action, his palms slap the table behind me so that he doesn't topple onto me, as ravenous as I am. But it's the moan leaving his throat, light and barely there, that is thoroughly the last straw.

I release him, shocking him with the recoil, to push his shoulders back, then use my knees as leverage so our positions are reversed. Now he's perched on the table while I straddle his lap. For a second, my stomach dips with the certainty that he'll push me away, but then his hands slide around my waist, dragging me to him, his shadows winding relentless, freezing phantoms around my limbs.

This time when I bring my lips to his neck and bite, it's not for the purpose of drawing blood but because I want to, because I enjoy the rise and fall of his chest against mine and the golden thrum of our bond shimmering within me, winding so impossibly tight, I might explode. My bites turn to kisses as shallow gasps leave his throat, and I trail them along his jaw. That saline taste of my death is on his skin as I savour him.

His fingers dig into the skin of my back, bringing my own blood to the surface at the same time that I bite his lip. I cannot breathe. I swallow that fear and kiss him on the mouth. He's all ice and sharp teeth. He is Death. The end. Oblivion. And oh, how I lose myself in its sweetness. Opium fills my nostrils, becomes my oxygen. If only for a moment of weakness, he's mine. I will claim him with all the hunger of a person starved.

He groans again, his mouth leaving mine. This time it's *his* teeth, *his* kiss at *my* neck. I shift my body closer, sinking further into his lap. I *feel* him.

Then Charon snaps and shoves me off him.

CHAPTER 24

LOVELY

From my place on the floor, I stare at him, panting, not sure if I'm mortified or furious. Charon's chest heaves as he runs his fingers through his black hair. His whole entity is flickering, that faint skeletal shadow coming through in bright shades of silver and blue as if my effect on him is so awful, he might just unmake himself in the process.

'Forgive me.' He closes his eyes. 'I let things go too far.'

He offers me a hand. I knock it out of my way, preferring to scramble to my feet without his aid. 'I can't keep doing this, Charon. This, whatever's going on here. You want me. You don't want me.'

'It's not about you.'

'Of course it's about me! I know who you were and what you did to the other Furies. I have their bloody memories. What's wrong with me?'

Charon's eyes widen. 'It's different. This is differ-ent.' He motions between us with a furious hand.

'What, all because I'm not your servant? Because you don't have control over me?'

'Of course that's the reason!' he bellows, the walls of his home shaking. 'You are the fucking undoing of me!'

Charon drags his palm down his face, turning his back on me. I snap my mouth shut.

His pacing lasts a moment before he rounds on me, pointing an audacious finger in my direction. 'There were rules—rules we always followed. The Furies before, they knew their role, and I knew mine.' His tone is brusque while vexation ravages his features.

I scoff. 'Yet part of your role was to satisfy them? Then perform your role, Ferryman, because I am not satisfied.'

He pummels his eye sockets with the heels of his palms. 'Don't you take enough?'

My jaw drops. The anger seeps out of me filled with a coldness to rival his touch. I swallow hard. 'This is the last time. You were the one who wanted this. The water of the river is just as capable of healing me. Hero and Leander tended the Furies before. Clearly it was the better arrangement.'

'Fury,' he protests, attempting to catch my arm, but I'm out of here.

I storm out and into the city, Kane at my heels.

Charon doesn't follow. I stomp away with little worry of being at risk from wraith attacks. The wraiths listen to what *I* say now.

'Not a single word from you,' I snarl at the wolf.

For a while, he lets me stew in my ruminations. Who needs The Ferryman anyway? I broker my own deals with the wraiths. Healing myself on the banks of the river will be no chore. Let him watch over the souls and build his silly little buildings.

'His blood makes you stronger,' Kane interjects. Apparently, I'd been muttering aloud. 'The river is diluted.'

'It will do,' I snap. 'The wraiths' anger is much more manageable now.'

Kane is eyeing me, however.

'What?' I demand.

He huffs. 'Obviously this was going to blow up.'

'Stop it.'

'Was he good at least? Tell me it was worth it.'

'Kane!' I chide, though his audacity forces a smile. 'We never.... That's actually the problem.' I sigh.

'Disappointing.'

'Exactly.'

I weave my fingers into Kane's fur as he brushes against me. His rot stench is no longer so jarring on me; must be a result of sleeping with my face buried in his coat. I slow my pace and drop my head to lean against his body, taking comfort in his proximity.

THE RIVER WATER SPLUTTERS OUT OF MY MOUTH AS I attempt to force it down my throat. It's god-awful stuff. It's drinking vinegar after sipping fine wine. I choke, coughing and spilling the vital liquid, my face aching from the frown. But I need it to heal the claw marks running in jagged canyons along my thigh.

I push the kylix into the silt and recline on the riverbank to let the full healing effects take hold. One benefit of not speaking to The Ferryman is that I enjoy the company of Hero and Leander much more often, their presence infinitely less confusing than his.

Hero massages my newly healed leg. 'Remarkable. You are truly remarkable, sweet girl.'

'Thank you, Hero.' I beam, allowing them to work out the kinks in my fresh muscle.

Leander adjusts my head as they settle their limbs over my shoulders, easing some of the tension there, suckers clicking in slow circles against my skin. I let my eyes drift closed at the sweet attention.

'Who would have thought it,' Leander chuckles, 'when you were a scared little thing in your cell. Look at you now. You are a lioness.'

I laugh. 'Do not do me a disservice, Leander. I am the lamb.'

The guardians join me in my tittering. Their laughs are melodious, the passing boats shining a little brighter for their mirth. I stretch out my limbs, and Leander strokes the flame of my hair while Hero moves to massage my feet. Honestly, moments such as these make it easy to understand why the Furies before preferred the guardians' company to The Ferryman's.

'Lovely.' Leander motions to the row of freshly built buildings lining the river.

I'm unable to recall what shape they took before they were destroyed, but now they're a row of perfect chocolate box cottages complete with paned windows and thatched roofs. 'This is because of all you've achieved.'

'Hmm,' I muse. 'When did Charon learn how to thatch?'

The guardians' tinkling laugh makes me grin again. I've never seen them like this before, like all is right with their world. I don't want to dampen their spirits by pointing out that though their master has mostly rebuilt the city by the river, the cathedral sits unfinished. Part of him must still be waiting for me to fail.

I sigh. I'll have to talk to him soon. The wraiths have requested residences, though they're falling short of specifics. My gaze snags on Kane, who is as good as dozing a little way along the river.

Hero stops their massaging, allowing me to sit up as they hover closer. 'The wraith rests,' they whisper.

'Fitfully,' I confess, glancing at my wolf friend. 'Though he's never truly asleep, I sometimes have his nightmares. Always the same room, the same green eyes. Is there nothing more to do for him?'

'Kane is more than given the royal treatment, sweet girl. His vengeance done. His pain soothed. He has even earned a place at your side.'

Hero's words placate me. But there's something else. The beauty of being parted from Charon, from him not consuming my every thought, is that it's given me a little perspective. Kane's residual pain bothers me; his vengeance is done, yet the memory of the cold, evil eyes of his killer still lurks beneath his skin. The rest of the wraiths are calming, but still, I feel like there's something a little out of my grasp. Something I'm missing.

Annoyingly, Kane was right. While the river water heals me, it's not as potent to aid me in absorbing the nightmares of the wraiths. It's manageable but tiring. I'm healing a little slower. After Charon's sessions, my body sings with life, leaving Kane and me to stalk the Underworld together. These days I must lie for long stretches on the bank of the river to recover. Of course, the guardians fussing over me also causes me to linger. I'm ashamed to admit that there's something regal about being so taken care of. Should I be comforted by the notion that a little of my old self remains? And that if I'm being truly honest, I still wish it was Charon's hands doing the looking after.

THE MAMMOTH-SIZED ELEPHANT'S NAME IS MAMET, AND she's one of the oldest wraiths I've encountered. Her memories are little more than fire. A screaming, spitting wall of flame and rage. But this is the third time she has graced my hall. At first her thirst for vengeance was so old, so dormant during her tenure in the City of the Dead, that she was robbed of language.

As I face her now, shadow dripping from her tusks and a rotting garland haloing her enormous head, I wish I was fortified a little with The Ferryman's blood. The only way to connect fully with her is to be impaled. It's not pleasant.

'Mamet,' I greet her, beaming. I open my arms wide and welcome her once more into my arena.

'Fury.' She tilts her head. Under the smoke and gristle, her voice has a gentle French accent.

I run my fingers over the soft space of flesh centimetres above my navel. 'Here, Mamet, if you will.'

She ambles forwards, and with each heavy footstep, the silt makes a cloud around her until she reaches me. I smooth my palms along her forehead and let out a giant breath as if I'm about to have a needle at the doctor's. That's what I tell my brain. *Just a scratch. Just a scratch.*

The contact of her skin makes cloying heat rise in my bones. Flames fan my face. The scent of burning flesh scorches my nostrils. When her tusk slices through me, I cry out. Or I believe I do, plunged as I am deep into Mamet's memories—so deep in her fiery death, I have no sense of self. Her screams are my screams. Her confusion-laced terror is hot and terrible on my tongue. A wall of heat so encompassing, the roughness of wood splintering against my back, my shoulders arched so far, unnaturally stretched, and an ache in my core I cannot place.

Through the flames come flickers of faces, angry with dirty smudges on their cheeks and babes at their hips, a yowling mob baying for blood. I blink through the smoke, trying to make sense of it. There's something they're shouting. I disconnect from the clawing smoke choking me, the fire melting the flesh of my face. There's a word they're shouting. I don't recognise it, spit out in another language. Yet something innate reveals its meaning to me: *witch.*

A scream strangles in my throat as my palms are cut against the rough rope binding my hands—or is that the tough skin of the wraith? I'm moving. Have my bindings come loose? The vision is becoming unstable. My eyes drift over the crowd, their faces a blur as I seek out one in particular.

Growling—the flames are growling. But I hold fast to the binding. There's someone I'm searching for. I long to gaze upon her one last time. There—I spot her. She's not shouting. Instead, she's crying, silently, privately.

'Vivienne.'

The tearing of flesh jolts me into the reality of the sanctuary. Mamet is thrashing around the room, and Kane's mouth is clamped onto my ankle. I'm being tossed through the air like a rag doll and caught in a tug of war between creatures. When I glance down at my chest, Mamet's tusk, originally impaled at my navel, is now sitting under my sternum.

A quiet 'Oh' leaves my lips.

Mamet throws her head forwards, and I land with a splat on the ground.

She continues to thrash about the room, shaking the walls as she hits them. Kane is standing sentry over my body, biting and rearing when she's close to trampling me. The scene unravels before me, though I make little sense of it. My hands are slick, covered with blood, its coppery flavour flooding my mouth. When I grasp my stomach, it's to find a gaping hole through the centre of my body. I need to attract Kane's attention, but the black spots are coming in fast. When I open my mouth to speak, nothing but a splutter of blood comes forth, soaking the floor.

There's a splintering of wood. Mamet must have broken free of the doors.

'I can't move you,' Kane is saying distantly.

I'm so tired.

'Hang in there, Fury. I'm going to get help.'

How long Kane's been gone becomes an intangible

thing. How long have I lain dying? The wraith wounds are toxic. Will my soul simply drift to the river? Or will my injury unmake me entirely?

When I'm scooped up, floating through the air, I assume the former.

CHAPTER 25

LOVELY

For someone who's dying, I'm remarkably comfortable. Maybe that's how effortless it is to pass on. To slide from one life to the next, like floating on a bed of satin. My brain is cotton wool, my hand heavy and lazy as I drag it along my chest, finding that the angry edges of the wound remain. When I frown, the motion aches. Surely I'm dead. I would have hoped that being dead meant not walking around with a hole through my middle.

But I'm already dead, resident of the Underworld.

Forcing my eyes to open, I'm met with a neon blue stare. Now I'm even more certain I'm dead, because Charon doesn't appear furious. Instead, his eyes are soft. Unable to lift my head, heavy as it is, I swivel my eyes in their sockets, soon discovering why I'm so comfy. I'm lying on the bed, not the table, my wings folded beneath me.

Charon is stretched out beside me. 'We thought we lost you for a minute. It's been difficult to encourage you to drink.'

I part my lips to speak, but my mind is fuzzy. Whatever I was going to say perishes on my tongue. Charon shifts above me, moving his body to form a cage over mine as if to protect me from further attack. His eyes trail the length of my chest, assessing the injuries that are reluctant to heal.

His gaze is on the hole in my chest when he speaks again. 'After eons alone, I never knew true loneliness until you.' The words are soft and adoring, and in the haze of my injury, they take on a dreamlike quality.

My lips stretch into a lazy smile. 'That is an awful compliment.' I'm surprised to find my own voice is light and filled with mirth. Though I'm healing slowly, I am healing. He must have fed me his blood. 'Why don't you tell me how you really feel?'

Charon runs a sharp nail from my jaw to my chin, tilting it so his gaze is inescapable. 'I'm beginning to believe there is strength in gentleness.'

My breath catches. His gaze lowers, his fingers following, trailing a line that's alive and freezing under his caress from my jaw, between my breasts, and all the way to my navel, pushing the tattered fabric of my dress aside to better examine the gashes in my skin. I don't shrink in shame. It's natural to be exposed to him. Right.

'Look at you,' he murmurs.

'At your mercy,' I say, even more weightless now. 'Just like you always wanted.'

He shifts so he's lying next to me again. In a slow blink, he's cut his wrist and is offering it to me. I shake my head.

'This will heal you faster. No more river water. I was foolish,' he says.

I let the words hang there for a moment. 'What will it cost you?'

He tilts his head, his other hand cupping my face, his thumb ghosting my cheek. 'Nothing I'm not willing to be parted with.'

'Like your dignity?' I joke.

He smiles, a glorious, sharp thing. How am I to deny him anything when he smiles at me like that?

He raises his wrist again, and this time I take from him what I need.

When I wake, Charon is still lying next to me, though all the intimacy has vanished. He's careful to not touch me, not even bearing to spare me a glance. Instead, his eyes are fixed on the ceiling.

'I've been foolish.'

'You might have mentioned that.' I smirk, turning fully onto my side to gaze at him.

'No more river water,' he tells me, at last turning

his attention on me. 'I will be there, and I will heal you.'

'They're not aware it's you who heals me. What we do, how we are with each other.'

He stares at me a beat. 'This city is mine. Loath as I am to admit it, I've been neglecting my ward and everyone who resides within it. I care not if they discover it's I who heals you. As for appearances, I'll be cloaked.'

Although it makes total sense, disappointment blooms in my stomach. I need his blood, but the intimacy is killing us. My body is fully healed now, though I'm sore as hell. My crimson dress has been restored while I slept. Rising to sit, I'm making to move when his hand shoots out and clasps around my wrist.

'Stay,' he says. 'Stay with me. Don't return to the sanctuary.'

Our gazes clash. His expression seems almost fearful I might say yes. With his high cheekbones and sharp teeth flickering in and out of existence, how might I rest easy next to him with what my body demands of him? What my heart demands of him. It may no longer beat. But I'm a fool to downplay this as my bond. We're not meant for each other. I can't keep putting myself through this with him, hoping for scraps of affection. Though it pains me to recognise it, Charon is right. Our lines are all blurred. Even if he were to cross his line and get physical with me, it wouldn't be enough. He's done the right thing by removing that act of intimacy between us. Why replace it with another?

Slowly, I shake my head, saying, 'That won't do, now will it?' and he releases his grasp.

'I hate watching you leave.'

The rawness in his words almost shatters my already shaky resolve.

I force myself to my feet. To put the distance between myself and the being I so desperately long to be close to.

As I reach the door, I cast my gaze over my shoulder to meet him where he's still reclined on the bed.

'I need you, you know,' I tell him, my own honesty making my voice shake. 'For what comes next. I can't do it without you by my side.'

Charon's gaze turns hot, his crystalline eyes churning. I worry he might demand I reveal my schemes, my intentions, or deny me the aid I need when I already take so much from him. Dragging my eyes away from him almost hurts, but I do, setting my focus on the glowing river.

'Then by your side I will be.'

The thread between us shimmers. I take a deep breath and leave.

Kane stands upon my exit, and I deflate in front of him.

'Do you mind?' I gesture to his back.

'Not at all.'

Grateful, I climb onto my seat a little below his shoulder blades and wrap my arms around his neck. Alive but exhausted. 'Will you take me to the river?'

He plods forwards, understanding that I need quiet right now. My eyes slip closed. I drift in and out of consciousness at his gentle pace, not paying much mind to a waft of a crisp scent under the grime of Kane's coat, one that makes me think of chilly winter mornings. My mind must be getting lost in a dream.

When we arrive at the river, Hero and Leander crowd around me, snatching me from my reverie, searching for my wound as I slide from Kane.

I wrap my arms around their bodies. 'It was a bad one, my friends, but I'm already healed.'

They sink a little closer, waiting for me to explain.

'I came here to talk. The Ferryman will be tending my healing again, and as much as I hate to say it, I fear he's right to take it back over. However, his manners are extremely lacking, and my muscles are sore.' I grin at them hopefully.

Hero blooms at the compliment. 'Please rest, Lovely.'

Without a moment's hesitation, I lie on the bank and close my eyes, then peek them open again to address Kane. 'Please find Mamet to check if she's okay.'

Kane bites down on whatever objection he had on his tongue, but he makes me aware of the displeasure my concern causes him by skulking off at a snail's pace. It doesn't bother me, however. I allow the guardians to smooth their limbs down my legs, up my arms, working out every kink and bringing me to the brink of sleep.

'What happened to make The Ferryman intervene?' Hero asks from their place at my feet.

With a sigh, I tell them, 'Kane had to bring him to my rescue, in a sense. Something went wrong, and I was hurt badly. Almost as badly as the first time Kane dragged me here.'

I turn the event over in my head. What had gone so wrong? In my own mind, I was getting into a good rhythm with the wraiths, especially after multiple sessions. Their deaths don't weigh quite so heavy over them now. It takes seconds of me rubbing my forehead before Leander shifts and takes over massaging my temples, the tips of their limbs releasing the pressure there.

Vivienne. The name pops into my brain before falling away again like sand through my fingertips.

'Mamet was distressed,' I confess. 'My injury was a bad one. Tell me, if Charon had not come to me when Kane called, what would have happened? Would I have simply drifted on?'

Hero and Leander exchange a glance.

'It doesn't work that way here,' Leander says.

There's a fragile caution in their manner, a sense of words being carefully selected.

'What would happen? I'd just lie there until I'm healed?'

Silence.

'Please tell me. Explain to me what I'm risking.'

'Your soul could become so tattered, so torn, that The Ferryman has no choice but to put you in a boat and send you on,' Hero confesses before coming to an abrupt halt.

'And?' I urge.

'He would not wish us to scare you. You've been doing so well, Lovely. Your plan is a good one. The Ferryman has been busy lately. He's built more. The wraiths haven't destroyed anything in a long time.'

'I appreciate that your instinct is to protect me, Hero, but I would rather have all the facts. My methods are... unorthodox, I'm aware.'

'Exactly,' Hero chimes. 'No one may predict the future. These are unprecedented times. It's only what he suspects.'

I sit up, agitation rolling off me.

'There's a chance you'll turn wraith yourself,' Leander interjects before I demand the truth once more. 'If you are ripped apart in agony, not healed fast enough, you'd be consumed by your own death.'

The air leaves my lungs. I stare at Leander. Through them. So many things slide into place. The Ferryman's need to check my wounds, the urgency, why he would share his blood with me when he is so set against being near me. The stained-glass window of the cathedral. It's not a sign of devotion. It's my tombstone.

I sink my head into my hands. How have I been so blind?

'Leander, you say too much.' Hero sinks a tentacle over my shoulder.

'No, it's better I know,' I tell them. Although my head is spinning to such an extent, I'm not sure I believe my own words.

I'd never given much consideration to any lingering effects to myself I might be causing, only that I needed to help. It was my sole course of action not involving bloodshed. Charon was so desperate, he went along with it. Now he believes he has no choice but to be my personal blood bank. He *doesn't* have a choice, because what option do I have other than to continue?

'What a mess,' I say into my palms.

'You are doing a good job, Fury,' Hero soothes, smoothing a limb over my hair and tilting my chin to them. 'You are strong. You are fire. You can do this.'

I nod, hoping the sense of strength I'd carved for myself would soon return. 'Please don't tell him what I've learnt. I need some time to process it myself.'

They hesitate but agree.

WHAT WILL NOT WAIT, HOWEVER, ARE THE WRAITHS. THEIR need is constant. Kane warned me once how this endeavour will break my spirit, but little did he suspect at the time how close to the mark he was. For the first time, I'm worried. So much so, it's difficult to conceal as I fiddle with my fingers while Charon lingers in the corner of the hall, fully cloaked and crowned. I hope he simply believes me to be nervous because he's observing.

Maya prowls into the hall.

I swallow my fear and walk halfway to meet her. 'Maya, I brought you here because I wanted to explain a change to the arrangement.'

She eyes Charon, suspicion infusing her gaze.

'Pretend he's not here,' I say with a smile.

Her eyes snap to me, and I might as well plough on.

'I told you I'm healed by the river. Well, it's sometimes quite an arduous process. So, The Ferryman will be here to tend my injuries, but not to interfere in any way. You have my word.'

She snarls as my next words tumble out of my mouth. 'And because of that, you will be permitted to stay, too, oversee each transaction, as is anyone else you deem worthy.'

Charon's head whips my direction. I try to keep my focus on Maya and not his eyes boring holes into the back of my head. I need to fix this somehow, to free him of this corner he's been caged in.

Maya drops into a bow. 'I do not like it, but I will accept it. I will communicate it to the wraiths.' She pauses. 'It's natural you have your reservations after Mamet.'

I wring my hands in front of me. 'Is she okay?'

'She will not speak of what happened. Shame is her company right now.'

Not wanting to push, I offer the barest nod. I only want to speak to her to ask who Vivienne is. Instead, I force myself to focus on what I'm dreading. 'Perhaps, to settle everyone's nerves, let's resume with someone I'm quite comfortable with. Cristobal, perhaps?' Who would have believed the easiest wraith to appease is the wasp?

Maya bows and leaves to update the wraiths about the change. I shake out my hands and am heading to the rear of the room when Charon comes towards me.

'I know,' I tell him, trying to wave him off, 'but you said you didn't care about them witnessing you healing me, and we're all a bit on edge right now.'

'That's not what I was going to say.'

'Oh.' I stare into the depths of his hood, half wanting to shrink away from him, aware of what he suspects will happen to me. How he believes this peace to be temporary. 'What, then?'

He glances at Kane, who sits in the other corner. 'Is the wolf necessary now that I'm here?'

Despite myself, I smile. 'Yes. Kane is absolutely necessary to me.'

Kane chuckles, and I delight a small bit at the annoyance in Charon's eyes.

Charon lowers his voice, his eyes snagging on my lips. 'You seem nervous.'

'Yes, well,' I attempt nonchalance. 'Anyone would be with you breathing down their neck.'

He takes a step closer. 'Do you need to prepare?'

He holds out an open hand, and I'm suddenly too hot. 'That usually comes after,' I tell his palm.

'Fury, you were severely injured. Perhaps it would be best to fortify yourself somewhat?'

'Yes. I suppose you're right,' I agree, knowing that the fragile peace of the Underworld rests on a knife edge.

I work to disentangle my desire from the weird knowledge I have about why he's doing this. I step into his orbit. Shadows wrap seductively around my body. Determined to not lose myself, I set my jaw, promising myself not to stare at him.

He brings the knife to his wrist. It's like crystal glinting off the black pearls of blood contrasting the olive of his skin. I wrap my fingers around his arm and bring it to my lips. Instantly my worries are satiated, and every fibre of my being is focused on him, in tune with him. My tongue pushes against his skin, drawing more blood. Charon's free hand wraps around the nape of my neck. I make the mistake of opening my eyes to find Kane staring.

I pull away, stumbling a few paces in retreat. I

brush my lips with the back of my hand as Charon surveys me with keen eyes, giving nothing away. His blood gives me clarity, steels my resolve, and everything at stake settles on my shoulders, not with pressure but with determination.

Nothing has changed, Lovely. I need him; he needs me. Business.

I turn away and stalk to the double doors, then throw them wide. Maya prowls forwards, circling around me, eyes fixed on The Ferryman. Cristobal buzzes in, his giant moth-eaten wings flapping against the wall so quickly, they're blurred in the gloom, and I'm forced to retreat several paces to accommodate him.

'Cristobal, my friend.' I don't hesitate to put him at ease, coaxing my hand along his side.

The first ripples of anguish rise to the surface, then crash and recede at my edges. Cristobal buzzes in excitement. Keeping my focus on him, I offer him a nod to proceed, not sparing a glance at Charon, whose stare is burning into me.

My warning words to Kane had been to remain vigilant. He might have to moderate the wraiths and The Ferryman both when I'm deep in Cristobal's psyche.

'Let's begin,' I say to Cristobal, surprisingly confident. With him, I'm on solid ground.

I place my hands on the bulk of his body, soaking in the immediate hit of that night I have travelled to often and fall into that moment. The air there is balmy, alive with cicada song, the gunmetal instantly cold on the side of my head. With the rush of fear, my other body is distantly taking a stinger to the thigh. I cry out, crushing the tips of my fingers into Cristobal's abdomen.

The faint whiff of burning stings in my nostrils. The agony of those final moments floods through me. I know my farm is on fire. The cartel wants it, but I need to be strong. After all, I have a family to feed. The pain hits as sharp and deadly as a spear to the heart. The anguish. The certainty that they are all dead. No one escapes, and it's all my fault.

I groan, soaking it in, letting it become part of me. My family has perished, and it's my fault. I should have agreed. Better they be homeless than dead. Through the grief, the devastation, the crushing weight of guilt, I catch a glimmer, a tinkle of laughter —a girl in a waterfall. Her laugh. Her beaming expression.

Cristobal's body shudders. I scream, the stinger tearing through flesh.

'Enough,' I whimper, pulling myself free of the memory.

My psyche tumbles into the room, and I find I'm lanced to the wall. Cristobal is eager to pull away, letting me slide into a heap. Kane leaps in front of me, but there's no need, as Cristobal retreats, Maya with him. The Ferryman slams the double doors behind them.

My panting breath echoes in the stillness of the hall. It went well. Charon didn't unmake anyone. Closing my eyes, I let my head fall back against the brick, relief pulsing through me. Icy fingers grip my leg as Charon turns it this way, then that, examining the wraith's mark. The wound is angry, but it hasn't gone the whole way through.

Charon, hooded and crowned as he is, almost takes my eye out with a sharp spear of his crown, ill practiced at healing me this way 'This is what you've been doing all this time,' he mutters.

Kane prowls behind us, observing.

'This was nothing.' I half laugh, wincing. 'A success.' My head is spinning, though, trying to pick apart Cristobal's fading memory. There was something else. Flashes of a waterfall. Images I'm certain are not connected to his death.

Charon shifts and hits me in the face with an antler.

'Do you mind?' I grab it, shoving him away from me.

Kane turns stock still as Charon falls on his ass.

'Why are you being so precious?' I bite out. 'You've seen me injured a million times. You're the one who's going to take my eye out with that thing.' I gesture to his crown.

The Ferryman stares at me while Kane gapes in

shock. Charon rips the crown from his head, tossing it aside, and then lowers his hood. 'It's one thing to observe your injuries, and quite another to witness you receiving them.' He speaks fast, low, and with a deadly lilt. 'He almost removed your leg.'

'Don't be so dramatic.' I lean forwards, getting in his face. 'There isn't even an exit wound.'

'This—' He waves a hand at the empty hall. '—is courting madness.'

Balling my hands into fists, I shout, 'What else do you want me to do, Ferryman? I'm bleeding over here!' I've never yelled at anyone the way I do at Charon, instead always twisted myself, made myself small and apologised for existing.

He drags a hand over his face, skull shadow flickering wildly, and lets out a noise of pure frustration. He reaches into his cloak and slits his wrist with the dagger before shoving his arm in my face. I grab his wrist and yank it to my mouth. I drink while we both stare daggers at each other, my chest rising and falling rapid fire, his face twisted into a sneer.

Why I'm so angry becomes lost in my swirling mind, though I bite down hard and hope it hurts. As I do, I pull him forwards with such a jerk that his hand lands heavy on the brick beside my head. The slap reverberates in my ears. My mouth fills with his delicious blood. His expression changes, shifts from something furious to one no less hot and demanding—until the tension in his shoulders melts, and he's dangerously close.

He blinks and leans back on his heels, glancing at the ceiling for a moment. Through the haze of our argument, my leg is healed. I drop his wrist so suddenly, it lands on my freshly healed thigh.

It stays there for a beat. Relaxes. His palm smooths over the sensitive virgin skin. Shuddering, I drop my gaze to where his hand rests.

'You're so soft,' he whispers. Then he's on his feet, collects the discarded crown, and is out of the sanctuary.

I slide my legs in front of me and rest my forehead on my knees. Why is this so hard?

A dull thud tells me Kane has planted himself in front of me, and he has something to say.

'You two need to pull yourselves together,' he says, tone mocking. 'You're both lucky the wraiths weren't witness to any of that.'

'Because he's undermining me? Or the other way round?'

'Both,' he huffs. 'Fury, you just put the ruler of the Underworld on his ass.'

I chuckle. 'I caught him off guard. The wraiths have attacked him before.'

'You're referring to the wraith he *unmade*?'

I recall the fight through the hazy filter of a memory long passed. At the time, it appeared as if

Dorian was trying to escape him rather than battle him.

I blow out a breath. I might as well tell Kane. He's my friend, after all. 'He believes I'm going to fail, Kane. He's keeping me glued together until the day comes.'

Kane cocks his head, and tears gather in the corner of my eyes.

He nudges my foot with his nose. A small gesture of comfort. 'From the outside, I'd venture to say he'd do anything possible to keep that from happening.'

I sniff, half smiling at my wolf. When did he become so thoughtful?

CHAPTER 26

LOVELY

When *did* Kane become so thoughtful? The notion plagues me as I amble alongside him through the city. We're going to meet with Maya. I study him. I've spent so much time with him, I hadn't noticed. His eyes, which were once flat, hollow things, now have a black sheen not present before. Shadow no longer drips incessantly from his sharp fangs. Even his fur isn't as matted.

We sit in a newly constructed square with Maya. Charon has also built a water fountain in the centre. It's a testament to the wraiths. There is a congregation of animals at its centre, a tiger, an elephant, and a boar holding a decanter with water flowing from it. I ponder how he's made a waterlike substance in a liquid world.

Dipping the tip of my finger into it, I bring it to my

lips. Not river water. It doesn't taste of anything. Only the gentle splashing of the droplets in the pool tinkles around us. Maya is staring. I snap my attention back to the business at hand, but her words are difficult to absorb.

She's explaining that the wraiths are satisfied with how the meet with Cristobal went. She mutters something about them still being somewhat nervous, how she will remain present for now. Her appearance is all I'm able to focus on. Does her fur shine a little brighter? More orange than filth? Are her ears a little less moth-eaten?

'Something the matter, Fury?' she asks.

I've been frowning. 'No, nothing wrong. In fact, I must ask The Ferryman something. Right away, actually. I'm sorry, Maya. I'll send for you again soon.'

She eyes me but nods.

I walk away, picking at the edges of my nails, pushing hard into their beds, but they do not break.

Kane trots at my heels. 'What troubles you?' His breath is hot on my shoulder, and it doesn't stink.

'We need to return to the sanctuary.' I quicken my pace, breaking into a run.

'I hate to say this, but you're alarming me.' But I don't respond, not daring to give voice to my plot just yet.

When I fling the doors of the sanctuary open, Charon is standing in the middle of the hall, shadow sleeves pushed up to his elbows, of all things.

My heart sinks at the sight of him. 'What are you doing here?'

I've come to such a sudden halt that Kane crashes into the back of me and sends me careening into the hall and onto my knees in the silt.

Charon arches an eyebrow. I scramble to my feet and throw a glare Kane's way. He has the good sense to look guilty.

'Improvements.' Charon raises his arms towards the side of the building.

I walk a little further in to view the three large arched windows in the wall. They're fancy, the kind I'd expect Juliet to call Romeo from.

'It was so gloomy in here,' he explains.

'Practical, though,' I say, wishing to defend this little place of my own.

'Still.' He flashes me a sharp smile. Which automatically means he'll get his own way.

I bite my lip. This must be a peace offering for insinuating I'm out of my mind. Perhaps his being here isn't the worst thing after all.

Business partners, Lovely. We're both in the business of maintaining the Underworld.

'They're beautiful,' I tell him. Coming to his side, I place my hands on my hips and school my features into a natural expression. 'Your timing is perfect, actually.'

His head snaps my direction. 'So soon.'

Not wanting to lie outright, I make no protest as

the shadows melt to cover the length of his arms once more and he retrieves his cloak and crown, disappearing beneath his hood.

Kane's jaw swings open, but I spear him with a glare, silently saying, *'Make a sound, and I'll personally unmake you.'*

Charon's eyes flick to the double doors before returning to mine. A thrill dances over my body as he cuts the skin of his wrist before giving it to me again. My hands shake. *All* of me trembles. I remind myself that he already hates me, already believes I'll fail—he's waiting for it, actually. A shudder climbs my limbs at how angry he'll be. At me. At Kane. Possibly so furious, he'll erase a soul from existence.

Releasing his wrist, I step away. Meet his eyes and, with a swallow, reveal, 'You probably shouldn't be here when I do this.'

'Do what?' The shadows drown out the light his windows have created.

'What needs to be done for this to truly be over.'

He closes the distance I put between us. 'No. Whatever you're plotting, my answer is no.'

'I *know*, Charon,' I say softly. 'What I'm doing can't last forever. It's only a matter of time before my spirit breaks entirely or I become a wraith myself.'

Kane scrambles to his feet, but I motion for him to remain where he is, and he slowly lowers into a tense sit.

'You won't,' Charon argues, the faintest tips of his

fingers catching my hips. 'I won't allow it. I am the master of all, and I will not allow you to break.'

'But you're not the master of me,' I remind him, biting my lip. 'Will you really spend eternities watching me being pulled apart? You couldn't even endure it once. What about the next time something goes wrong? When I slip up, or a wraith makes a mistake with me? What will you do then?'

His silence tells me everything.

Dropping my gaze, I speak to his clenched fists. 'You have to let me try.'

'Tell me first, Fury, and I might leave. You used me, so speak.'

I chew my lip and turn to the wraith wolf lingering in the corner. 'I'm going to cure Kane.'

The oxygen leaves the room. Kane is ready to riot, springing to his feet, clearly intending to pounce.

Charon extends a hand to keep the wolf at bay. 'You will attempt no such thing,' he warns.

'I've been seeing flickers in the other wraiths too. Memories beyond their deaths—they're under there. If I cure them, they won't need to come to me to ease their pain. They'll finally move past their violent ends. Kane may be calm, but his hurt still lives under his skin. Let me turn their fury into something *good*.'

'Mamet,' Kane growls.

I nod.

'What about Mamet?' Charon asks, still not

allowing Kane close. 'The wraith who almost split you in half?'

'It was the first time I've ever gleaned something more. A powerful memory. A name.'

'She almost killed you for it,' Charon says, but his resolve is already fissuring before my eyes.

'I trust Kane. With my life. More than anyone. If the cure doesn't work for him, whose pain I'm most familiar with, then I'll concede that the experiment is a failure. But if you stay, you might intervene too soon, or distract me, and this is going to be painful. For Kane as well as me.'

Charon finally lowers his arm. 'I will stay. This is my city. I may not be master of you, but I am master of the wolf, Master of Boats, and the master of my blood. You stole from me, Fury. Successful or not, you'll require my assistance in the aftermath, and Kane might be in no state to send for aid. So, I will stay.'

Grinding my teeth, I dip my head. I want to argue, but he's right. I turn from him to Kane, who is cast in a sorrowful repose as I approach him. 'I'm sorry, my friend. I leapt into this plan without talking to you first.'

'Nothing you ask of me would I ever deny you, Fury.' He pushes his head to mine. 'He may be my master, but you are who I follow. Anywhere,' he whispers.

Tears gather in the corners of my eyes. I squeeze

him to me. 'I trust you with my body more than anyone. That's why this will work.'

His skin shudders, and when I thread my fingers into his fur, his pain doesn't sing like that of the other wraiths, but it's there, simmering beneath the surface.

'I have no desire to hurt you.'

'Be that as it may—' Gritting my teeth, I smile. '—you know what must be done. My shoulder would be best.'

When I press a kiss to his forehead, the golden shimmer of our bond ignites. One I believed was reserved for Charon alone, yet Kane is caught firm within its embrace. Closing my eyes, I let my fingers sink through his fur to his skin. The pain rises as a wave, then crests and falls into my body until the sanctuary fades away and I'm surrounded by plastic-wrapped walls, my skin prickling with the chill of a surgical table.

A distant cry echoes, and my shoulder crunches as though bitten by a giant beast, though my arm is not yet a limb removed in this room I've been trapped in countless times before. This is the memory where I live. Only green eyes, the stark antiseptic sting of the room, and the cold slice of the blade. Terror fills me. He's coming for more. My only wish now, in my final moments, is for him not to eat in front of me. But he does.

Me observing my own flesh being consumed is part of the ritual.

I search for scraps of myself so I may examine Kane's memories and not become lost in his demise. Kane's death was one of the slowest. Devoid of anything other than terror—no shame, no regret, just sheer terror. Despite the knife, the strangest sensation of being crushed fills my chest. I push deeper into Kane as if plundering his memory of those final days, hunting for a remnant. Anything else.

Kane fights the intrusion with every cell of his tortured soul until my head cracks against stone, and I blink, black spots in my vision. I'm in the safety of my sanctuary.

'It's okay, Kane.' Tears slide down my face.

His growls are so violent, they shake the foundations of my hall.

My arm hangs listlessly on one side, but I cling fast to him with the other. 'Let me in, my friend. Don't be afraid.'

The hall shimmers out of view once more, my world mixing with Kane's—the revolting whir of the bone saw, the sickening crunch of a femur. I have the vague awareness of being flung like a rag doll. A fleeting expectation that I'll sail against the opposite wall and likely out of Charon's lovely window flits across my mind. When solid arms slide against my waist, I sink to the cool metal of the surgical table. Then through it.

Less myself now, more wolf, I'm prowling. Snow is thick under my boots, the crunch of fresh snow crisp, though I'm shifting now, onto my stomach. The air tastes so clean, it's enough to get you high. For a moment the frost in my beard is reflected in the lens, and I grin to myself, disbelieving the sight before me. A huge white wolf is staring right down the barrel of my lens. The most majestic creature I have ever beheld. It throws its head back and howls.

Awe ripples through me, rushing so fast, I might pass out.

The world turns dark, and I fall through the tundra of Ellesmere Island.

***

If I were the speck that birthed the beginning of the known universe, I would be a bright, fidgeting fleck in the blue of Charon's eye.

Rushing into my body, I'm keenly aware of three things. My teeth are clamped on skin, there's blood in my mouth, and I'm in someone's arms. Slowing the rate of my drinking is near impossible, for I am starved. I squint just enough to glean that I'm on the floor of the sanctuary with Charon's knees around me. My wings fall limp on either side of us as he holds me to his chest. A very cold chest. Without releasing his arm that I'm practically mauling, I relax further against his body.

His lips ghost along my neck, stopping at my ear. 'Open your eyes, Fury.'

With a final lick of his arm, which causes Charon to tighten his free hand's grip on my stomach, I open my eyes and peek at Kane.

Kane is standing. Barely. His long legs tremble as he rises to his feet as if he's a baby deer. He shakes his body, rot and sludge and shadow dripping from him and splattering the walls around him, the stench giving way to a pine scent, until nothing is left except pure white. His eyes shine amber. He is a beacon in the grayscale of the Underworld, alive and radiating with brilliance.

My jaw drops. 'The wolf from my dream,' I whisper, wanting to fall to my knees before him because, surely, he is a wonderful dream in this decaying place.

'The wolf of Kane's memory, I imagine.' Charon's words frost my neck. 'You did it. You found a moment outside his death, then dragged it kicking and screaming out of him. You transformed Kane from terror to awe.'

I spin, meeting his neon eyes to make sure I'm hearing him correctly. He must have cast off his crown and hood when he came to steady me. He's not exactly smiling—it's something both more and less than that when he says, 'Congratulations. You've cured your first wraith.'

CHAPTER 27

LOVELY

About three seconds is all it takes for me to have my arms around Kane's neck. Not a trace of rot on him, he now smells like the promise of winter, snow, and crisp air. His new scent sinks into my lungs, and he rests his head on my shoulder, letting me stay there until I'm ready to release him.

Laughter bubbles out of my throat. 'We have so much to do.' My head ping-pongs between the two of them. 'We need to meet with Maya. We should start with Mamet... and Cristobal. I already have a flavour of the memories I should search for with those two. Then it's a case of discovering with the others.'

'Slow down, Fury.' Charon holds a shadow-ridden palm aloft. 'You need to rest.'

'How is rest possible?' I laugh, unable to mask my glee. 'There's so much to discuss.' My mind spins, my thoughts coming rapid fire. 'Obviously, as soon as they set their eyes on Kane, they'll be convinced. Just look at you.'

Kane puffs his chest out. 'I'm something to behold, am I not?'

'Wonderous.' I beam. 'But—' I turn on Charon. 'You're a problem.'

At his affronted expression, Kane laughs. No longer a bristling sound, it's a full roar. The joy of it makes me giggle too. Kane is pure awe. So much so, I have to clutch my stomach to keep myself from keeling over.

'Are you two quite done?'

In fact, I only stop when Kane ceases laughing himself to talk to Charon. 'Ferryman, few have seen you as I have. Witnessed you care for the Fury. Most behold you bathed in shadow, raising buildings, fashioning a world around you, tending the souls of the river. You are the Shepherd of Souls, but you are a cold master.'

I glance from Kane to Charon, preparing to launch myself in front of my friend, for Charon is coiled and ready to strike.

After a beat, he eases onto his back foot, giving a nonchalant shrug. 'Then I will not be draped in shadow. I will be as I am now.'

Kane arches a perfect wolf eyebrow, surveying The Ferryman without his crown and cloak, black garments clinging to his form, his olive skin smooth and perfect.

'Charon, I understand what you did. You anchored me. I admit I'd have failed if you didn't, but I'm sure Kane will now serve as my anchor. You need not expose yourself in such a way.'

Charon's bare feet drag in the silt as he comes towards me, arms open, shadows dropping away from his forearms. 'Did I miss something? Does the wolf's blood hold the power to heal? Are my arms so terrible to rest in? Am I so offensive to you now?'

My mouth drops open to argue that he's more than aware what our issues are. How it's our proximity that's the problem. But Kane's biting chuckle cuts me off.

'Oh, this is about to get interesting.' The wolf smirks.

THE WALK THROUGH THE UNDERWORLD IS QUITE DIFFERENT with Kane by my side in his new form. Actually, he doesn't quite walk by my side. The tip of his nose rests at my shoulder. He is a bright, shining diamond, fur glistening and catching the glints of my flame. We are twin stars, and I've never felt more powerful than with the white wolf of the City of the Dead flanking me.

The wraiths' curiosity wins out, and many lurk from the shadows of the city as we approach the square where we meet with Maya, whispers filling the waters.

Maya is already waiting as we enter the square. She's pacing. Agitated that I haven't called, I imagine. Her jaw swings low as her eyes land on Kane, a small crowd gathered around her, though none of them dare come near either of us.

'Apologies for my delay, Maya.' I gesture to my wolf. 'As you see, my latest endeavour proved fruitful. It's a gift, one I plan to share with you all.' Taking my time to meet each of their eyes, I make my way around the gathered circle, giving them my gaze in turn. 'There will be no more suffering, my friends.'

Murmurs erupt from the crowd. Maya's attention is fixed on Kane. I might as well finish what I came here to say. I suppose that's the problem with being awestruck—it has the tendency to steal your words.

'Hopefully it will take no more than two sessions to cure your suffering. As you know, The Ferryman is now present at the sessions. For the cure to work, he must anchor me. Please do not be afraid. There's nothing to fear from him. In fact, he'll be revealed to you as never before. Uncrowned and uncloaked.' My declaration earns another murmur from them. 'He, like I, serve you, my friends. We will make this city a home fit for all.'

No shouts of joy or elation sing out. Instead, tremors of shock ripple through the Underworld. As I turn to leave, I say, 'I request an audience with Mamet.'

Leaving them to gossip amongst themselves, I

whisper to Kane at my shoulder. 'You're useful for holding a crowd's attention, I'll give you that,' I tell him.

'I believe you're quite capable of doing that yourself.'

'What's it like for you? Do you feel as wonderful as you look?'

He chuckles. 'It's strange. I'm certain my death was a terrible one, but I cannot recall it. Now the soft bites of snowflakes caress my cheek, I hear the crunch of snow beneath my boots, taste an air so clean, I'm high on the stuff, the sense of amber eyes of the wolf that day peering at me from amidst the white.' He bows his head. 'It was the best day of my life.'

'That's quite a day to live in.'

'Indeed.'

As we round on the sanctuary, the changes to my home stop me dead in my tracks. It's been raised, five more steps now needed to reach its doors. I turn to Kane. The wolf shakes his head, mischief in his eyes. He settles himself neatly at the bottom stair.

'I'll sit this one out,' he tells me, leaving me to ascend by myself, nudge the doors open, and slide inside.

Charon is still here, shadows dripping from his elbows. The hall is now flooded with gloomy light, as the windows he'd installed in one wall now have their mirror image on the opposite wall. The man himself is at the rear of the building, erecting what appears to be some kind of extension. There's something about the way his knee pops, his toes digging into the silt as he raises his arms to slot bricks into place that has my stomach dipping and warming.

'Why the sudden interest?'

He turns and stalks towards me, light in his eyes. 'Well, it dawned on me how this is a single room. Where are you sleeping, on the floor?'

'Kane makes for quite a comfy pillow.'

Charon shakes his head. 'You and that wolf.'

'Yes, yes.' I tap my foot. 'I would marry him if I could.'

He shoots me a glare.

'It was a joke.' I throw my hands up and stalk towards the new door, curious about his endeavours. The extension is a small room with a bed, not as elaborate as the first bed he made for me but less basic than the one he threw together in his home. This one is designed for the comfort of my sleep, not mocking, not an emergency, but useful and beautiful all the same.

In the corner is a highbacked chair deep enough to accommodate my wings, and there is a woollen rug next to it large enough for a giant wolf to slumber on. My first instinct is to gush over him making me pretty things. But I stop myself and recognise this for the win it is. Charon may not have been convinced that my healing the wraiths was a long-term solution. The miracle of Kane transformed, however, has given The Ferryman pause that I might be able to pull something of this magnitude off. I step over the threshold to peer around.

Charon lingers in the hall. 'I promised I'd improve the building.'

'Thank you,' I say. When he doesn't make any move to leave or say anything else, I assume he must want an update on my meet with Maya. 'I've asked Mamet to come.'

He leans a shoulder against the frame of the door. 'And?'

'I've warned the wraiths of your changed presence.'

'Oh.'

He's quite the conversationalist today. Our gazes heat, though I might be imagining the smirk on his lips. The shadows slink around his being in a lazy kind of way. Does every creature in the Underworld find him quite so annoying?

'Does it bother you to expose yourself to them? After being The Ferryman for eons, are you ready to be Charon?'

'I suppose we'll find out.'

'You don't seem worried.' I grip the soft mattress where I've taken a seat.

'Do I ever?'

No, I guess he doesn't. Only once have I seen him wear his worry. When he'd torn Dorian's soul to shreds. His biggest mistake. I remember how he'd searched my body for injuries with panicked hands afterwards until I'd stilled them.

Casting the recollection off, I march away from the bed into the main hall to wait for Mamet. I sit in the centre while Charon fidgets about the room, creating flame-housed sconces between the windows and a little platform at the front of the hall with two stone steps, as if I'm to give sermons.

'Please desist in the improvements. What's the platform for?'

He shrugs, settling on the step. 'It suits the space.'

A knock pounds at the door, and Kane peeks his head round. 'Mamet is here.'

Thank God!

I throw the double doors wide, a beatific grin on my face, the hem of my elaborate red dress swirling around my calves as I make way for the mammoth-sized elephant. Maya prowls in her wake.

'I assume the offer stands?' she growls. 'My presence is accept—' She breaks off.

Tension blooms in the air. Charon is off the step and by my side. The wraiths appear thunderstruck. I chance a glance at him to ensure he's not doing anything awful or scowling as he so often is when I'm around. But if anything, he's at total ease to be so revealed. His shadow self is restrained at a minimum, and he's clothed in black silk, which serves as a brilliant contrast to his olive skin, his forearms still exposed. His mouth holds a secret of a smile, the cliffs of his cheeks dangerous. The wraiths would only recognise him by the luminosity of his eyes. Between the sudden transformation of Kane and Charon, I sympathise with the wraiths' shock.

'The Ferryman looks different, and I understand this will take some getting used to, but I promise you, he's a crucial part of the process.'

'You flatter me, Fury,' he drawls, making my neck flush.

The wraiths, unknowing what to do, offer him a sort of bow.

He waves them off. 'Let us begin.'

As I beckon Mamet forwards, she dips her head to me. 'I must admit, Fury, I'm nervous. Our last meeting left me unsettled.'

'I apologise for your uneasiness. Trust me, the power to do this is mine.'

With Kane a beautiful shining beacon of hope, giving off as much light as the flame of my hair, it's hard for her not to be convinced.

I point to the soft spot above my belly button. 'Same place,' I tell her.

Nerves dance along my skin, the rush of sensation that comes with possibility. I feel a confidence in myself with Mamet. With her, it's not *what* I'm searching for but *who*.

Charon takes his place behind me, nestling in the gap between my wings. His cool hands slide over my shoulders, thumbs hard against the nape of my neck. I smooth my palms along Mamet's wrinkled forehead, the familiar ache appearing with the first whiffs of smoke.

'Now, Mamet,' I whisper, and as her tusk plunges through my belly, I fall from the sanctuary straight to a burning stake in my French village. Angry faces hurl abuse through the licking flames, the heat so unbearable that even the capacity to scream is stolen from me, and my teeth crack in my jaw. The tugging sensation at my core is something new. A grunt in my ear sends goose bumps cascading along my left arm, and for a moment, I flicker between a fiery death and the French countryside.

My eyes roll back into my head at the vision. I'm sinking, grasping through leathery skin. The urgency of clasping onto one vital memory pounds between my eyes, hot and sharp. Tiny elephant details of the tapestry in the mansion, the finest thing I've ever laid eyes on. Until her. The daughter of the marquis has a heart-shaped face, doe eyes, and the most exquisite dimples. Her skin is softest at the sweet spot of her inner thigh, and when I place my lips there, she giggles so uncontrollably, my heart swells with love. She is divinity itself. When she grasps each cheek, she pulls me to her and kisses me on the mouth. I melt into her, losing myself. It might be the happiest day of my life. When her fingers slide between my legs, I moan her name.

'Vivienne.'

Charon's breath is ragged in my ear, his blood cool and metallic on my lips. Awake again, I tilt my head to sink it onto his shoulder, taking a moment's reprieve. Mamet's memory pools in my stomach. My own chest rises and falls to match The Ferryman's. Hell, if any of the other wraiths' memories are so intense, I'll turn feral.

It doesn't help that Charon's hand is heavy on my chest. It travels achingly slow to my navel, the tips of his fingers denting my fresh flesh, checking that the hole in my stomach is healed, but my mind is lost in Mamet's final moments revelling in her lover's touch. Before I tell my brain to do differently, my palm is on top of Charon's, pushing it lower. His inhale hitches on my neck, a sort of groan in his throat. I have to bite on my bottom lip not to make a returning moan when his fingers find the same soft skin of inner thigh Mamet was so fond of.

'Fury,' Kane whispers.

My eyes snap open to the three wraiths before me. *Holy shit!* I attempt to scramble to my feet, but Charon clamps his hands on my stomach and drops his forehead to my shoulder. Is he dying of embarrassment?

'Heavens above,' Maya marvels, but she's not shocked by my inappropriate display with The Ferryman. Mamet isn't merely casting off her shadows. She's shrinking, no longer mammoth sized with strings of rot hanging as awful bunting from her tusks. It slides away with sickening slaps that reverberate around my sanctuary, leaving leathery grey skin and shining black eyes in its wake.

'Vivi...,' she intones, her legs trembling, before she tumbles to the floor. Although whole, cured, she's a shaking mess.

None of us are sure what to do about the elephant who is now stumbling around the hall, falling, then rising, only to fall again, tusks carving away brick-work. All eyes are glued on Mamet, except for Charon, who's apparently hiding behind me. The rise and fall of his chest is so rapid, I worry he was also plunged into Mamet's psyche and is as flushed as I am at her memory.

Kane sidles next to me. 'What's wrong with her?'

At this point, I'm being quite rude laid out on the floor, unmoving between Charon's legs. When I try to free myself of him again, he holds me fast.

'Erm, her best memory is quite an intense one. It's happy, that's for sure,' I reply from within Charon's grip, which is still a vice locking me in place. 'But it'll take some adjusting for her to live within it.'

The penny drops for the wolf, and his expression turns almost comical.

'Get the door for her, please! She should probably lie down in a dark room for a while,' I call out. We all should.

Kane springs into action. He gives Maya some

direction about how Mamet needs some time to acclimatise. They both act as walls for Mamet to ping-pong between as they leave the sanctuary.

As soon as the doors close, Charon releases me from his grasp, and I swivel on my knees to face him, noticing my back is sticky.

He leans back onto his elbows, letting out a groan. 'I need to get to the river.' His voice is as rough as gravel.

'What's happened to you?' As I lay my hands on him, the shadows fall away, revealing a hole in the centre of Charon's chest, black blood oozing from him. The tusk must have gone straight through me and into him.

All colour seeps from my cheeks. 'Charon! Are you going to die?'

'You can't kill what was never alive.' He chuckles, then winces. He holds out a palm. 'A little assistance.'

I heave him to his feet, taking some of his weight. The silvery blue of his skeleton flickers faintly, a constant buzz under his skin. His eyes find mine, and something sparks, then lingers between us. Mamet's ghost caresses my lurid desires. His gaze shifts to his hand planted on my shoulder, the faint outline of his bones on constant display. He sets his jaw, and we make towards the rear door.

Although I'm sure he could manage on his own, he lets me walk him to the river. Thankfully, the wraiths have dispersed from the sanctuary steps, so our path is an unimpeded one. His soft gasps demand my full attention, my mind blank of all useful conversation. Only the slight shame that he is injured while I can think of but one thing: Mamet's memory and how best I can place Charon in it. I'm starting to understand why the other Furies took human lovers. His distance is truly maddening.

'Ferryman?' Leander's musical tones snap me out of my ridiculous reverie.

When the guardians approach, he accepts their help, and I keep pace beside them. As they wrap their limbs around him, the shadows fall away from his chest, revealing the extent of his injury. The edges of the wound have turned a garish purple colour.

'Master, what happened to you?' Hero cries.

Charon doesn't slow his purposeful gait towards the river. Hero smooths a tentacle over his bare arm as if admiring the luminous skeletal frame beneath his skin.

'All will be well,' he tells them, though he winces with every step.

At the river's edge, he raises his right hand, bringing all the boats to a tinkling halt. He eases himself onto the bank, and the guardians let him go, lingering a little way, tentacles twitching as if concerned for the progress of the boats. Without a backwards glance, Charon lowers himself into the water and disappears into the river.

'Never seen that before,' Hero and Leander chime in unison, dumbstruck.

The boats continue their journey. I stare at the vacant spot where he sat only a moment before. A wave of panic rushes through me. He didn't even say anything—no instruction on where I'm to find him or what to tell the wraiths.

'Did I just kill the ruler of the Underworld?' I inquire, though Hero and Leander have relaxed their limbs, unfazed now the boats are moving again.

'I'm sure a wraith dealt the blow and not you,' Leander offers, which is completely unhelpful.

I sink to the ground, a plume of silt shifting into the water around me.

'He's not dead.' Hero wraps a limb around me. 'I'm sure we'd all be unmade if he were to perish.'

They drift away as if that was a comforting statement.

Slowly, I cross my legs into a comfier position and wait for him to return.

CHAPTER 28

LOVELY

After sitting and waiting for so long, when I finally stand again, an impression of my ass remains in the silt. I drag my feet the whole way to the sanctuary, not bothering to give a farewell to the guardians. We're not unmade, so I guess Charon will return when he's ready. What do I tell Kane? Or the wraiths? Yes, the cure works, but we might kill The Ferryman, unmaking the whole Underworld in the process. Happy days.

Slipping through the front doors of my hall, I'm met with the sight of Charon in the middle of the hall, fashioning some sort of monstrous iron chandelier. My jaw drops. *The fucking audacity of the creature.*

'Where is Kane?' I demand.

Charon gestures towards the extension, though his focus remains on the task at hand. 'He rests. I made him aware you were with the guardians so he didn't worry about your whereabouts.'

Worry about my whereabouts? 'And what of you?' I gesture to his being, his skin no longer revealing the electric current of his skeleton. 'Did the river just birth you again or something?'

'Something like that.' Charon flashes me a rare full smile. Those teeth.

Heat liquefies in my belly. 'You know, you're stunning when you smile' spills from my lips. God, what's wrong with me? Bloody Mamet and her stupid happy thought.

Please, please, please let him brush it off, I think as I attempt to escape to the extension and cringe myself into oblivion.

'Oh?' He intercepts me as I try to walk past, abandoning his ridiculous chandelier. 'I should smile more? Any more suggestions for improvement to my being?'

I want to die.

A business arrangement, Lovely. That's what we have. I square my shoulders. 'We should discuss the predicament we're in. No cure, and I might turn wraith after such constant exposure to their toxicity. Cure, and you may be so injured, the whole Underworld will be unmade.'

Now I kind of want to smack his smile from his face as it curls further on his lips. 'Makes the notion of forever more exciting, does it not?'

'You're not taking me seriously.'

'On the contrary, your concern for me is adorable.'

'Ferryman.'

'Fury.'

'It's not concern for you,' I protest. 'If the Underworld is unmade, I will be unmade, and Kane will be unmade…. You know how fond I am of the wolf.'

'Ah, yes. The wolf, of course. Well, let me assure you, for the sake of Kane. I cannot and will not die. The cure is a good plan. No need for discussion.'

His eyes dance across my face, a sharp tooth digging into his bottom lip. The liquid sensation in my core intensifies before trickling south, his nearness bringing the faintest whiff of opium. Calm settles into me. 'Good. I'll leave you to… whatever that's supposed to be.'

I inch around him, trying to figure out the question plainly written on his face in the knit of his brows.

At the last moment, he asks, 'What was Mamet's memory?'

This time, it's me who smiles. 'That is between me and Mamet… and Vivienne.'

It gives me too much satisfaction to slam the door behind me, though not before ordering Kane from the room where I sleep where he had been peacefully resting, telling him that The Ferryman is in need of company. I, however, am not.

THE CHANDELIER TURNS OUT TO BE EXQUISITE. CHARON crafts little wraith forms into its edge. Eternal candles sit within the centre, so when he raises it to the hall's vaulted ceiling, it casts the shadows of animals onto the tops of the walls.

I've taken to leaving the doors of the sanctuary open when I'm here, welcoming any wraith to approach. Charon has raised the building even more, so now there are ten steps to my doorway, though he won't tell me the meaning behind it.

It would be impractical to add seating given the nature of the healing ceremony, so instead I lie on my back, wings outstretched, Kane at my side, the shadow animals dancing along the ceiling. A distant memory stirs, one of my dad and a night-light that had a similar effect. The safety only my dad brought me when I was young, on nights I had nightmares. How he'd sneak me a hot chocolate to calm me, its warm taste the flavour of comfort. I feel that now. Safe.

Charon's head blocks my view. 'You're crying.'

'These are happy tears.'

He frowns.

'Let's call Cristobal to us. They're too nervous to approach on their own.' I run my fingers through Kane's fur. 'Perhaps you should speak with Maya. Reassure her that any wraith may request an audience and that we will listen to all.'

'Of course.' Kane rises and trots down the steps.

Charon takes his place at my side, observing the show of shadows for a moment until I'm forced to break the silence.

'Did you talk with Maya about their request?'

'I did. Residences that resemble homes with beds. Simple enough. I've already begun. Though they have little in the way of pleasure at the moment, I believe that will change as more wraiths accept the cure.'

Something in the way he says it makes me lose interest in the shadow show. 'You spoke with Mamet?'

'I did.'

Urgh, I could ring his neck.

'Care to elaborate?'

'Her request was very specific.' The corner of his lips twists the tiniest amount, as if he is attempting, and failing, to conceal his amusement. It sends the golden cord in my chest shimmering like harp strings.

'Tell me.'

'Perhaps it's between me and Mamet.'

'Charon.'

'Fury,' he mimics, though the way his eyes sparkle reveals he's delighted and will tell me anyway. I merely need to wait him out. 'She asked me for a four-poster bed, dark mahogany, with a canopy of black velvet.'

'Aha!' I clamp my hand over my mouth to keep the laugh from tumbling out of me, heat ravaging my cheeks. 'She's an elephant wraith—the bed….'

'Massive,' he finishes for me, chuckling himself. 'Quite something to behold, believe me.'

Our laughter is impossible to contain as we descend into fits of giggles, and I'm crying real tears again.

Slowly but surely, the wraiths approach the steps of the sanctuary of their own free will. It's hard for them not to be captivated by the bright yellow body of Cristobal when he flies so often above the city's rooftops. Charon and I run a smooth operation. We're over ten wraiths down, and there's yet to be one I've not been able to cure. Only three wraiths have required two sessions for me to root out the source of a good memory. Only once has Charon had to disappear into the river, when Maya, in the throes of transformation, clasped onto him, dislodging a rotten claw deep into his thigh.

What shocks me is how five of the wraiths we've cured were ones I'd never met before, giving credence to Charon's belief that many spirits are hiding in the inner workings of the city. As he rebuilds from the wasteland it had become, I understand a little more how the city works and is seemingly infinite, though when I fly high, the outer border where the river lies and the guardians remain is in plain view. He builds endlessly inwards, the city folding in on itself in a mass of endless passageways, like brain neurons, defying real comprehension. Limitless housing for the dead who wander.

Cure them we must, one by one. They stalk and prowl and skuttle into the sanctuary, stares fixed on The Ferryman now exposed to them, the luminous silvery blue flickers of bone beneath skin on display. Then I take them into my arms, using my body to free them of their pain, Charon's palms cold on my shoulders or my waist, depending on where the wraith must bite or claw or impale. Kane and Maya stand guard, their keen eyes on us. Kane tells me the wraiths gossip about the sight of The Ferryman's death-dealing palms against my bare skin, and I eye him, suspecting he does little to quash the swirling rumours.

The cathedral is raised at last, though it holds little resemblance to what it was before, and no lost spirits frequent it yet. Charon insists on carving the pews by hand after imagining the wood into existence. I run my fingers over the splintered edge of his work-in-progress, pushing my thumb along the rounded edge of the bench. The huge stained-glass panel at the end of the nave of a Fury with a giant shadow wolf no longer seems quite so mocking.

'Will you change it?' I gesture to the glass with a chisel he's left lying around that I'm excavating silt from beneath my nails with.

He stops sanding and gives the glass his attention. 'I suppose I should.'

In the blink of an eye, the shadow wolf is brilliant white.

I gasp. 'Why bother with all the tools if it's so easy?'

'Where's the fun in that?' He smirks, resuming his sanding.

Forever is a long time. I guess he must occupy himself somehow.

'I was thinking about Kane,' I confess, changing the subject. He's off with Maya somewhere, probably spreading more rumours.

'Of course you were.'

'I'm hoping to do something nice for him. As you've done for Mamet and some of the others.'

'What would he like?'

'He hasn't said, and he'd never ask. But I want to surprise him.'

The steady grind of his sanding comes to a slow halt. I'm sitting on the ground a little way away from where he works, so his expression is hidden from me. I only imagine the pained pinch of his eyebrows. Even the notion of it forces me to bite my lip.

'What did you have in mind?'

'A mountain,' I say to his back. 'With snow on it. Kane loves snow.'

'You want a mountain.' He turns so fast, I startle as he snatches the chisel I'm playing with out of my hand, pointing it at me before turning it to his own chest. 'You believe I can just *build* a mountain for your favourite wraith.'

Blinking twice, I feign innocence with a coy tilt of my head. 'Something beyond your imagining, Ferryman?'

He scoffs, dropping his tools, and stalks away. 'She wants a mountain. Not a hill or a plateau. A mountain. I'll show her a mountain.'

Leaning off the edge of the pew, I fix my eyes on him as he mutters to himself, expecting him to stop, but no, he snatches his crown from a nearby pew, cloaks himself, and is out of the cathedral. Baffled, I run after him. Surely he's not going to do it now.

He doesn't venture far. Is he going to plonk a mountain down in the middle of the city?

With his palms raised in front of him, shadows rippling across his skin, he shifts the silt, the ground thundering, the buildings tumbling away to make way for a rocky peak that appears in the shuddering surface and rises, the colossal creak of the ground transforming beneath us until we're both staggering in retreat to make way for its gargantuan size.

Wraiths gather behind us, watching the summit disappear amongst swirling clouds as its monstrous body grows. Snow cascades down the mountainside, thick and pure white, tapering off onto the silty ground where we're all standing. Kane comes to my side, jaws agape, Maya at his rear. The Underworld is silent, that hushed sort of nothingness only possible with the gentle falling of snow.

Charon drops his hands, oblivious to the gathered crowd, his focus on me alone. 'Behold, a mountain.'

No one quite knows what to do about his display of power. The nonchalance of it. So, I choose to ignore it and The Ferryman with it. Instead, I push my fingers into Kane's fur and beam at him. 'A gift, my friend— for you.'

His amber eyes reflect the brilliance of the snow. The silence that hangs around us all is broken when Kane throws his head back and howls. He pelts into the fresh snow, sending plumes of the stuff everywhere. Most of the wraiths who are gathered are uncured and therefore unable to share Kane's delight, but Maya joins in with the revelry. The vivid orange and black of her fur against white sends the Underworld into violent technicolour.

'Will you not join them?' Charon asks from my side as we watch the wraiths' paws sink deep into the snow as they bound about.

Mulling it over a moment, I tell him, 'No. It's not meant for me.'

'Fury. It is all for you.'

My head snaps his direction, only to find he's already walking away through the crowd of wraiths, who give him a wide berth. My brain refuses to wrangle those words into comprehension right now, so I take them at their most literal and step onto the freezing snow. The sensation bites into my toes, the frost creeping into my veins, as Maya and Kane continue to frolic. Kane is more like a giant puppy than wraith of the Underworld.

My heart, or what's left of it, swells. Gathering the hem of my dress in my fist, I leave the cool of the mountain and run through the city streets to the sanctuary. Or maybe I should go to his home? Yes, he would head there and not to the sanctuary. Silly of me.

Slowing, I'm about to change course when a shadowy figure lingering at the foot of the base of the sanctuary catches my attention. Those bloody steps Charon insists on adding to now stand at fifteen.

I abandon the idea of finding Charon and cautiously approach. The caribou's muscles are taut and ready to flee.

'Jamal?'

His hooves clatter on the lower step he was lingering on. 'I was hoping to find you.' His voice is low.

'Of course.' Keeping my own voice gentle, I ask, 'To talk, or do you want to come inside?'

'I... I'm fearful of it. Many of the wraiths are. I was torn apart once.'

My heart breaks a little for him. Jamal is a spirit who does not visit me. Not since that fateful encounter. 'There's nothing to fear, I promise. A little discomfort is all, but you've seen Kane, right? And Maya?'

The caribou nods.

I swallow. Jamal was only a child when he died. The only child wraith I've come across. His death is seared onto the backs of my eyelids. 'You don't have to do anything you're not ready for, Jamal.'

He scuffs his hoof on the bottom step.

'Perhaps you would like to come inside? Then decide how you want to proceed.'

As we ascend the stairs side by side, a creeping panic settles over me. I'm missing both a Ferryman and a wraith. And while Kane's protection is now more of a token in the rituals, I can't do this without Charon. Though I don't hold out much hope he's in the sanctuary, I might as well double-check first. At least that way, I have Jamal in the building.

Despite telling myself this, I'm disappointed to find the hall empty. I usher Jamal further in. 'Please make yourself comfortable. I need a few moments to prepare.' I point at the giant chandelier, aiming to distract him from his nerves. 'Isn't my chandelier marvellous?' I ask, leaving Jamal staring at the ceiling as I slip into my room with a view of escaping through the side door.

To my total surprise, Charon is lying on my bed, one arm slung over his face, crown and cloak on the floor. Despite the intrusion, I'm relieved I don't have to skulk around the Underworld to find him. Though I'm not about to show him that.

Popping my hip, I tell him, 'Quite the display you put on out there.'

He waves an elegant hand. 'A trifle.'

'Yeah, well, I have a customer,' I say for want of a better word, 'so speak now if you're not up for this.'

He finally drops his arm and sits. 'Where is the wolf?'

'Still frolicking on the mountainside. Let's do this without him. But....' My words falter. God, I've gotten so good at this. Why am I nervous? 'It's Jamal. It's not going to be an easy one.'

'Fury.' Charon takes my face in his palms. 'I've witnessed you succeed on dozens of occasions. This is no different.'

'Charon, he's just a child.' A tear spills from my eye and runs along Charon's hand.

He brushes my cheek with his thumb. 'Allow me to speak with him. He wouldn't force you to unwillingly swallow that horror.'

'No. I have to help him.'

'Then I'll be right behind you.'

'Okay. Good.' I steel myself. 'We've got this. Business as usual. Please wait here for one minute before you come in. He's a little skittish.'

Jamal is pacing the hall when I enter. 'Jamal, are you ready?' The incline of his head is so slight, I would have missed it if I'd blinked. 'The Ferryman will join us now. He'll be here to help me. He's not going to touch you.'

Jamal's nerves permeate the room like a fog. It's hard not to be swallowed by them. As Fury, I've bent my calling to my will, transformed it from something fuelled by anger to one of kindness. But Jamal's fate is ash on my tongue. Loathing swells in my chest on behalf of a boy robbed of his life.

As Charon takes his place behind me, I fix my attention on Jamal, 'Just hold on, okay? Whatever happens, don't let go.'

'I won't let go.' Jamal's voice shakes.

Jamal lowers his head and spears me, popping through my skin and organs with such force that behind me, Charon's feet stumble until his back collides with the wall, though I don't stop falling until I land with a clatter under the kitchen table. Quick to pick myself apart and not wanting to linger in Jamal's agony, I search for the key, remembering the book— the memory I'm sifting through his brain to find. I tell myself to ignore the ringing in my ears that doesn't belong. The hand clasped tight and bruising around my ankle. The stale scent of alcohol on angry lips.

Focus on Jamal. The book. What was the book? *'Twas the Night Before Christmas*. My brain reels because I'm not there under that table anymore—I'm dancing through the pages of a book. I'm flying.

Now, Dasher! Now, Dancer! Now, Prancer and Vixen. On... On... Comet....

'Drink for me, Fury.'

My throat is parched. I drag my tongue against Charon's skin before biting down and letting my mouth fill with the relief of his blood. His chest rises against my back, solid and real. My eyelids are so heavy, they've possibly transformed to lead. I lean my head against his shoulder so I don't have to go to the effort of holding it aloft, those torn parts of myself knitting together in fresh flesh. I drink, anchoring myself in him until his breath is cold on my ear.

'Open your eyes and behold what you've done.'

Panicking, I snap my eyes open. Nothing in this world or the next prepares me for the boy, his small arms wrapped around my waist. My chest rises and falls, a misshapen rhythm of a failing heartbeat. I smooth my palm over his rough hair. 'Jamal.'

'I won't let go.' He utters it over and over, trembling in my arms where the three of us are lying in a heap on the floor.

'You didn't, Jamal. You didn't. Look.'

He peeks his eyes open, taking in the miracle that he no longer holds his wraith form. Blinking me in as if it's the first time he's laid eyes on me.

Charon shifts behind me, and I rise, helping Jamal to his feet.

He wraps his arms around me again, his head resting on my stomach within our embrace. I hold him as tight as my arms will allow, my chest still an unsteady shudder of restrained tears. When he's ready to let go, I release him. He has the biggest brown eyes, or perhaps I'm out of habit of being around humans, but he's so innocent. Though now, Jamal only has eyes for Charon.

'I'm ready,' he says simply.

When Charon is cloaked again, Jamal slips his hand into mine as we approach the stairs of the sanctuary.

'Fury,' Kane calls, taking the steps three at a time, 'I heard your scream....'

Though I have no recollection of screaming, he, Maya, and a few other wraiths have come running. Their silence now is a wholly different beast to their awe at the snow. Jamal shrinks at my side. Charon leads us on to the river. A procession of wraiths follows.

As we approach the banks, the crowd attracts the guardians, though they instinctively observe the reverent hush. Their gaze settles more on me than on the wraith child. From the depths of the river, Charon summons a small shining boat and offers Jamal his hand.

'You're doing the right thing,' he tells the boy. 'You will live again, Jamal. This life will be a better one.'

Encouraged, Jamal releases my fingers. For the first time since Dorian, Charon puts his hand on a wraith and helps Jamal into his boat.

We all stand on the banks of the river in a stillness

so complete and witness Jamal journey on into the next life.

Hero and Leander drift close, their tentacles ghosting my arms.

'Sweet girl,' they whisper in unison, 'how did you do that?'

CHAPTER 29

LOVELY

Having performed two incredible acts of power in such a short amount of time, and Kane being an awful gossip, I shouldn't be surprised at what I find. I'd retreated to the sanctuary for a nap after promising the guardians I'd return to give them a blow by blow, as they were also puzzled about the appearance of the snowcapped mountain. But when I opened my doors to visit them, I immediately snapped it shut again.

Now I pound the floor of the sanctuary in a perfect rectangle, sending tiny plumes of silt into the water while muttering, 'Where is he?' every five paces.

Eventually, the creak of the door to my private rooms signals the return of Kane, and seconds later he enters the main hall, Charon at his heel.

'Finally.' I grab the crown off his head, throw it to

the floor, and shove his hood away, revealing his classic pinched expression.

'What the...?'

'We have a serious situation on our hands, and given that this is as much your fault as it is mine, you need to be here to deal with it.'

He smooths his palms down my arms, chilling my agitated skin. 'I saw. Not afraid of being torn in two, but you're too timid to face a crowd?'

'Hundreds are out there,' I hiss.

He arches a brow. 'I don't expect they'll all bite at once.'

'You're not helping!' Bordering on shrill, I stamp my foot.

'Well, let's not keep them waiting.'

He shoves me out the double doors by my shoulders until I'm stood face to face with hundreds of wraiths—rhino and giraffe and gaur and a hundred other species, many of whom have crawled out of the gaps of the city to gawp at me. At us. They stare at Charon uncloaked too. His bare feet, his almost human body. The gentle occasional flicker of his skeleton beneath. They crowd the steps of the sanctuary, shoulder to shoulder, still and silent.

Unsure what to do, I take half a step forwards, and as I do, the crowd ripples into a slight part, the stench of their rot riding the wave of their movement, though their hope cuts through the foulness, leaving its fresh taste on my tongue. A shifting tide.

Faltering, I reach behind me to clasp Charon's hand, lacing his long fingers between my own. 'Don't you dare leave me,' I whisper.

The next steps I take, he takes with me, the crowd parting wider, following us, their eyes shifting to our joined palms. Whispers echo through the water.

'Sweet girl.'

'We heard she tastes so sweet.'

Beside me, Charon clenches his jaw.

'You can't touch them, can you?' I mutter at a volume for him alone.

He dips his head to my ear. 'I can, but the reputation of the Master of Boats is an old one.'

The crowd stretches on. And on.

***

From my place on the roof of the sanctuary, knees held against my chest, wings relaxed and draped on either side of the pitch, the sprawling City of the Dead is a sight to behold. The sanctuary now twenty-five steps above the ground, the view it allows me is one I do not regret. The river stretches around the borders of the city a little way to my right, and to my left, the mountain casts a shadow of a criss-cross onto the roofs below. Charon's most recent addition has been Victorian-style streetlamps, flames and all, dotting glistening globes throughout the expanse of grey. Every now and then, the orange flash of tiger hide slinks around a corner. Or the white flickering orb of a lost soul dances along a street.

The spirits have begun to come out of hiding, escaping their boats more frequently, choosing to linger in the afterlife rather than journey on with the decline in wraiths. Following Jamal's passing, an exodus of wraiths followed suit. Mamet, Cristobal, and dozens more, free of the horror of their deaths, all decided to discover what awaits them in their next life.

Charon stands on the bank of the river, one shadowed hand halting the flow of souls while the other raises a boat from the depths of the bloodied waters. The wraiths peer on with reverence and a smattering of fear, the silence palpable through the city as a wraith passes on, hopefully to a good life followed by a better end. The possibility of happiness tinkles on the waters.

While there's an unfathomable horde of wraiths hidden in the limitless bounds of the Underworld, the numbers of the uncured dwindle. Maya and many others remain to bask in the new life breathed into the City of the Dead.

It's been hard work, and Charon has been lost to the river over a dozen more times. Though I've never been able to heal another wraith to human form, I've cured so many, I've lost count. These days the cases are so few, it's pretty much limited to the new wraiths who climb from their boats and seek me out immediately, demanding their vengeance. The work they entail is mostly swift, their anger not festering bile but a quickly snuffed flame, their human memories all too easy to pull to the surface.

'You finally tire of the wolf.' Charon takes careful steps towards me across the pitch of the roof, toes clinging as if he might suffer harm should he fall.

'Never.' I rest my chin on my knees. 'It's just so peaceful from up here.'

He remains standing, which signals he's here to talk, his preoccupation with the mountain indicating that what he has to say isn't good. 'I've spoken with Kane, and Maya.... The guardians also.'

Apprehension prickles along my spine.

'It's time we plan for your departure from the city.'

'What?'

'Your first trip to the waking world. We're all in agreement. For the first time in a long time, the city is at peace.'

Blood rushes in my ears, his declarations defying belief. I barely have the words. They're *all* in agreement. They've been plotting behind my back.

I'm going to murder the wolf.

'Exactly,' I manage as soon as I've gathered myself. 'A peace of my making. I will not abandon them.'

'No Fury was ever bound to the Underworld alone.' He sighs. 'True, there being only one of you complicates matters somewhat. Logistics must be considered, of course. Time being one of them. It passes quicker here. But I'm used to managing wraiths, and most of your quarry are new. There will be a small backlog when you return, nothing unmanageable for your skill. We're sure that after you return from your first sojourn, things will settle much faster in subsequent trips, reassured you will come... home.'

My mouth must be hanging open or something else ridiculous, because rather than coming to his senses, Charon plunges on with his spiel.

'My only request of you, Fury, is you limit your sojourns to the waking world to days at a time. Perhaps five at a maximum. It may be a little jarring for you to adapt to at first, but your predecessors did in time. The good news is, your absence on the surface will hardly be noticed. The sting of your departure will be keener here.'

The shock will not shake itself free. 'But my Fury powers—they're unchecked. Who knows what damage I'll do.'

Charon finally brings himself to gaze at me, his brow pinched in pain. Or am I just the eternal fool? 'You've bent those rules truly out of shape. There will be no danger, I'm sure.'

'Why are you saying this? Have I not proved myself as Fury?' Regaining something of my self-possession, I heave myself to face him, hot and tearful. 'This is my home, Ferryman. I assert my right to belong here!' I shout, stamping my foot and dislodging some of the slate roof tiles.

'Are you not pleased? Despite your lengthy tenure

with the wraiths, in the living world, mere minutes have passed.' His voice drops a note. 'Your human will be waiting for you.'

My whole world tumbles in front of me. Tino. It's been so long since I reflected on my past life. And now Charon is offering me what I once begged him for—one lifetime to be spent with him. My plan has finally come full circle. I may be both—Fury and Lovely. Living one lifetime with the people I left behind.

The noise that leaves me is so raw, I buckle, clutching my chest.

Charon almost takes a step towards me before thinking better of it. 'Fury, what more do you want?'

Choking down the scream I want to release, I attempt to pull the broken pieces of myself together. I want to yell at him, at myself. At the mention of Tino's name, the strong version of myself falls apart. I'm not the saviour of the wraiths. I am poor Lee.

Pulling on every bit of dignity I have, I force myself to full height as I tell him, 'I will not abandon my city. This is *my* city,' I grind out through clenched teeth.

Flying off the roof and towards the river, I allow my own pain to rise, crash against the surface, and swallow me, leaving the beads of my tears in my wake. When I land unsteadily on the banks of the river, Hero and Leander rush to meet me, my sobs echoing around us as I collapse into their limbs.

'Why?' I cry, dignity be damned. 'Why doesn't he want me?'

They shush and calm, smoothing their limbs over my skin and hair, wiping the tears from my eyes. They talk and talk in musical tones that slide through me as I gaze at the river until they've almost convinced me that a break from this place is what I need.

When I trudge to the sanctuary, utterly spent, I lie on my bed, staring at the ceiling with Kane snoring in the corner. It seems I've brought sleep as well as peace to the Underworld. The guardians' advice echoes over and over in my head. A Fury is a creature of two worlds. I have proved myself. They're certain I'll return. Even The Ferryman is convinced of it. So why am I not comforted? Don't I deserve love? Doesn't Tino deserve an explanation? What about Marie?

Old thoughts and feelings rise and fester.

Sleep will not find me.

AFTER MY FIGHT WITH CHARON, I'M HIDING. OBSERVING shadow creatures who dance along the ceiling. At the slow whine of the sanctuary door, I arch my back from where I'm lying to discover who's creeping in. It's the last person I want to see. Charon mostly passes through the city in full regalia still, though he discards it as soon as he's safe within the confines of the sanctuary.

'The wolf?' His voice is so quiet, I might have missed it if I weren't so annoyingly attuned to him.

'Told me I was a bore, so I suspect he's off on your damned mountain with the tiger.'

'Right.'

I press my fingers to my eyelids. If he's come here to impose a trademark one-sided conversation comprised of his one-word answers, I'm going to lose my mind.

'Long have I dwelled on what you said,' he continues.

How insightful. My lingering hurt and anger at him lurks underneath my skin, ready to bite.

'The wonders never cease.' With a view to escape, I rise and dust myself off.

'You do belong here. This place is your home. Of course it is.'

'You just want to be rid of me.'

'That is not what I wish.'

'You told me to leave.'

'As is your right!'

'Fine. I'll leave. Happy?'

'I don't understand,' he grinds out, massaging his eyes while I pace in front of him, needing to release my pent-up emotions.

'You didn't even ask me, *Ferryman*, what I wanted. If I wanted to go back, if I was ready to leave, to return to the arms of my human lover who I abandoned! You colluded with Kane—and *Maya*, of all creatures—to set me free into the human world as if you're in control of my actions. Like I am your prisoner again.'

Charon's head remains clutched in his hands. '*Fuck.*'

I stop my march, pausing to discern him, as if by staring enough, I'll unlock the secrets of such a cold master. He's so angry, his edges shake, and though he's not wearing his cloak, shadows wrap around his arms and drift away again, plunging the room in and out of darkness.

'Why are you here?' I demand. 'Can't we ignore each other like civilised beings?'

'The guardians,' he says into his palms.

'What about them?'

'They are unhappy with me.'

I let out a sardonic laugh. 'They sent you? Go fuck yourself, Charon. I'm leaving.' If I don't escape now, I'll say something I'll regret. Though when I turn to leave, his palm lands on my arm. When I attempt to shrug out of it, he tightens his grip. 'What do *you* want?'

'I should not be a creature with wants.'

'No? What about what you *don't* want?' I'm so furious, I have no idea what's flying out of my mouth. 'You don't care about *him* anymore? How he might have his hands on what's yours? You're indifferent, right? The Furies had human lovers, didn't they? Doesn't matter how many I take as long as they're not you, correct? Because when you don't have the control, you're not interested.'

'Watch your tone, Fury.'

'Or what, *Ferryman*? You'll put me in chains? You

no longer want me on my knees? No longer wish me to serve you? Has that imagination of yours finally faltered?'

His hand on my throat is so sudden, it takes a moment to register that my feet are sliding into the vast space of the sanctuary. His eyes glowing with rampant fury, he snuffs out every candle of the chandelier. My stomach dips at the display of power, fearful for a moment that he'll unmake my being from existence just as easily.

While I worry over my death, his mouth locks onto mine. Powerful. Hungry. Claiming. His long fingers bruise my face as he devours my lips. His low groan undoes me—the sound of a man tasting the fruit he's long denied himself, all his ice dousing me. His heady drugging smell wraps itself around me, no longer a scent alone but a taste, saline and as addictive as any narcotic. My fingers claim any skin they find, but he circles my wrists in the vice of his grip, yanking them low around my back.

His kisses slow. When he pulls away, his eyes are hooded, as frosted as a cold night. 'On your knees,' he commands.

And like a good little Fury, I obey.

He sways, then paces away, backing up until his shoulders hit the wall. The tiny dimple one of his fangs dents into his lower lip is enough to make me wild. With a tiny motion of his head, he beckons me. I sink to all fours and crawl to him. If a look were to unmake me, it would be his right now. As I close the distance, the heavy weight of iron manacles around my wrists slows my progress while my breathing quickens with anticipation.

'Beg,' he whispers, his voice smoke.

Liquid heat in my stomach melts lower, my nails clawing against cold silt. 'Please, Ferryman. Let me serve you. Please you. Just tell me how I might.'

His head tilts, eyes closing in ecstasy and agony, chest heaving. With a soft clink of metal, the length of chains pulls taut, leaving me a few agonising inches from him.

A sly smile crosses my face. 'Charon,' I purr, enjoying this new game.

When he drags his fingers across his face, revealing his anguished expression, my stomach sinks.

'I cannot,' he mumbles.

With a click of his fingers, the chains are gone— and so is he.

CHAPTER 30

LOVELY

'What do you think I should do?' I ask the wolf beside me as we promenade along one of my favourite cobbled streets, with its twinkling streetlamps and many bay windowfronts, the occasional spirit bobbing along. Sometimes a technicolour wraith passes me with an incline of the head.

Kane measures his words with care. 'I believe a return to your old world would be good for you. I'd miss you, of course,' he's quick to add.

I haven't seen Charon since he fled from me, and while the memory stings, it isn't the reason I'm seriously considering returning to the living world. A light has been switched on in my brain. The image of Tino abandoned on the beach will not leave my mind. While my argument with Charon was over how I wouldn't abandon the city and the wraiths who live in it who depend on me, the flaw in my argument is hard to deny. Tino was the most important person in the world to me—still is—yet I abandoned him.

That morning on the beach feels like a million lifetimes ago. I have shed my skin many times since, died a thousand deaths. Built my armour and become the person I always longed to be. No longer poor victim Lee, desperate for someone to hide behind. I walk in a city of my building that without me would not be standing. I fixed the Underworld, cured the wraiths of their agony—surely there's some good to be done in the waking world too. How have only moments passed there when so much has changed here? Is Tino still staring at the same breaking dawn? Does Marie still lie on her hospital bed?

A glint of silver lettering catches my eye, and I dart across the street to press my nose to the glass of what has the appearance of a sweetshop.

'When did he do this?' I say out loud, though to no one in particular.

As I push the door open, a bell tinkles overhead. My eyes devour the gilded counter, the lemon-candy-cane-stripe décor, rows of jars lining the walls. It's beautiful but empty. There are no sweets or candy floss, nor ice cream in the case.

'It appears your Ferryman has been watching the river some.'

'He's as much yours as he is mine,' I sigh, adding weights to the Victorian-style scales. Without any sweets to balance, it rocks to and fro with a violent clunk.

'Ah yes, despite my close quarters, he must have addressed me all of three times.'

I scowl at Kane. 'Besides, he's hiding from me. I should get this journey over with, I suppose.' I move the weights to their original place by the side of the scales. 'I so miss eating. When I escaped before, everything I ate, I threw it all back up. Why is that?'

'Your Fury ancestors were before my time. Perhaps because you had not accepted your calling, you were something halfway. Without an anchor, human food is intolerable to you.'

'And now? I still haven't accepted the calling in the traditional way, and The Ferryman has no hold over me. So, what is my anchor?'

Sensing my sadness, Kane pushes his head to my shoulder, his fur, once coarse, now feather soft, the scent of freshest winter lingering on him. 'Allow me to be your anchor. It would be my honour.'

'I'll miss you, too, my friend.'

***

THERE'S NOTHING LEFT TO DO BUT PREPARE TO LEAVE.

I let Kane take his walk up the mountain with Maya, as she's much more in the mood for frivolity. I head to the sanctuary before seeking out the guardians to find out how I leave and wish them goodbye for now. I'll return soon. I stare around my simple room, at the bed, the chair, the wool rug where Kane sleeps, not sure why I came here. It's not as if I have anything to pack.

The frame of my door creaks behind me. Charon. Shoulder leaning against the wood, arms folded across his body with his ridiculous forearms on show. Kane's right—I should go to the surface and let off some steam. Not with Tino—that would be unfair—but someone. Anyone at this point.

Charon clears his throat. I fight my blush because I'm only staring at *forearms*. Hardly a crime.

'I realise what a fool I've been,' he says, clear as always, when he's foolish in so many ways. 'Your submission is the last thing I desire. You spoke of wants, and that is something I have not wanted in a long time. Having you in chains before me only served to remind me of that fact. No matter how tempting you looked in them.'

Oh. Well, that's good to know, I suppose. Though understanding the reason behind the rejection doesn't remove the sting of it. There's nothing more to say on this. Hopefully when I return, things will be a little easier between us. The tension eased. My own foolish tears rise, hot and stinging, to the corners of my eyes. This must have happened to every Fury before me—him remaining beyond their grasp. Now I, like them, am seeking solace in the human world. When I return, my desire won't be so excruciating.

Eventually it will wither, and he'll be happy with me at arm's length.

'As Ferryman, I should not be a creature who wants. My role is to serve the city,' he says in response to my silence. 'But I do want you, Lovely. I want you by my side, I want your time, I want your smile, I want your conversation. Most of all, more than anything, I want your heart. Though I have no right to desire it so.'

I've lost the ability to breathe.

Freeing himself of the doorway, Charon continues, 'Often, I think of that time when I first kissed you after I healed you. When I told you it was different with you. You believed I only desired you compliant, and I didn't correct you. It was then I knew, and at every moment since, that I am totally, *wretchedly* in love with you. You changed the shape of this world with your gentleness, and like this world, I fell to my knees before you.'

My lips part as he hooks a slender finger under my chin. 'You have earned your place here ten times over. A thousand times over. You deserve to return to the man you love. Yet each moment you stay here in the city we built together gives me hope that what compels you to stay isn't the result of a bond you never wanted, nor is it the urge for me to satisfy a need out of duty.' His free fingers find mine, and he slides my palm to his chest, where every quick breath he takes vibrates beneath my hand, his words tumbling through me. 'I do not want to satisfy a need. I must be *the* need. Lovely, I *want* to be all you ever need.'

How strange that words may kill and fix in the same instant, those last few frayed edges of myself soothed and brushed away. Making me so whole I might burst. 'You called me by my name.'

'You have never been my Fury. You are a creature of your own creating. Though I am wholly yours.'

After such a speech, how do I find the words to tell him I've loved him so long, I have no idea where to start? How do I say I have died inside him a thousand times and been reborn a stronger version of myself? That I am strong not because he stands in front of me, but because he stands beside me? I find no pretty way to say any of those things, so I kiss him.

This is not the furious kiss of before or a moment of weakness. Charon kisses me deliberately, unguarded. His hands sink to my waist to pull me to his chest. It is the cold kiss of death—ice and abandon and addiction lie within him. Everything the wraiths of the Underworld fear about him, I long to fill myself with—from the shadows that envelop me until my world is pitch-black to the low rumbling growl building in his chest.

He's hard edges and sharp teeth, and when my tongue is nicked, the taste of blood in my mouth, he pulls away, an apology on his lips.

'No,' I tell him. 'You don't have to be gentle with me. Gentleness is mine, and I do not wish it in return.'

When he kisses me again, the force of our collision sends me backwards. My stomach dips at the realisation he's taking us to the bed. As we move, he's not removing my dress but rather *unmaking* it until I'm bare before him. His mouth never leaving mine, I might pass out with the need for air, not helped by the savage groans clawing their way from my throat.

When my calves hit my bedframe, I fall onto it, breathless, and he takes a moment to admire me from where he stands.

'Charon.' I smirk. 'The shadows.' It's wholly unfair to be naked when he is not.

He drops to one knee and then the other, hooking his fingers behind my knees and pulling me to the edge of the bed. *Holy. Fuck.* If I don't come apart the second he touches me, I'll be surprised.

His hands linger on my knees, holding them apart and just *looking* at me.

I'm a mess.

So, when he takes an ankle, drawing it to his shoulder level, and places a freezing kiss there, I let out a gasp so loud, I'm sure the Underworld will have heard me. He works up my leg agonisingly slowly—kisses and licks and *bites*. His sharp teeth on my tender skin is a song through my body, the sweetest melody. Observing him on his knees is a power bordering on dangerous. By the time he's reached my inner thigh, my chest is heaving with such laboured breaths that when he finally gives in and gives me the release I need, I unravel all too quickly.

———

'CHARON?'

'Yes, Fury.'

I push myself onto my elbow, barely believing where I am. The Ferryman without crown, cloak, or shadow, here in my bed, elegant fingers tracing over my shoulder to where skin meets wing, my leg pulled over his waist. The faint flickers of his ribcage are blueish and silver beneath me, the knowledge now mine that his eyes glow extra bright right before he comes undone.

'Are you a god?'

He laughs, and it fills me with such joy, I'm almost sorry the sound is so hard won. 'No. Though I have met one before. He changed much. He was born with an unusual ability, one in a million, and that's a high number, for the birth of gods is not common. He had the ability to walk both worlds.'

'Hades.'

He nods. 'I'm no god, Fury. I have always simply *been*. As long as there have been humans, there has been me. I am a constant, an element, an idea.'

'An element,' I murmur, kissing his neck. 'I like that. You know, in the living world, Charon is grotesque.'

'How nice of Hades to paint me so. Gods are vain creatures.'

He grabs my knee, pulling me astride him, before rising to meet my lips.

There's so much more I want to ask him. 'Who gave you your crown?'

'I cannot remember.' I gasp when he bites my breast. 'The first humans were a very long time ago.'

When he kisses me again, all questions slide right out of my head. 'Stay with me, Charon,' I say between kisses. 'Make the sanctuary our home and never leave my side.'

He kisses me deeper, his cool fingers sliding into the flames of my hair, holding me so close that I can be in no doubt that he feels the same way. Not only that he wants me forever by his side, but that I am his home in return.

CHAPTER 31

LOVELY

When Charon and I finally emerge, I'm half expecting a parade. Much to my disappointment, it's only Kane who mentions anything.

'You two were enough to cause an avalanche,' he says.

I gawp at him, heat colouring my cheeks. 'Where have you been?' I deflect.

'On the streets,' he laments, his tone pious, though when I level him with a glare, he becomes cagey.

'You stayed with Maya, didn't you?' I grin.

'Her company is not a bore like many of the others. Mind out of the gutter, Fury. We're not all as feral as your Ferryman.'

For once I don't argue with Kane about Charon being mine. Or being feral. Pricks of happiness only that he is both of those things. Kane stalks off with a dramatic roll of his eyes. Probably to find Maya.

When I return to the sanctuary, Charon is outside, and the building has been raised a few steps. I give an eye roll of my own. 'What is it with you and these steps?'

'You never ask me for anything.'

'So, you give me steps?'

He shrugs, dusting non-existent sweat from his brow. 'You enjoy the view from the roof. More steps improve your view.'

Warmth pools in my chest. 'Charon.' I lay my hand on his arm. 'I think I have enough steps.'

'What else do you want?'

You. Only you, you silly element. But I suppose he's all too aware of that now, and he won't take it as his answer. I glance at the sanctuary raised above the city as if it's some grand building. 'Kane should have his own room.'

He sighs. 'Hardly a gift.'

Right. 'I want a home. Not somewhere for me to cure the wraiths alone. The hall will be necessary still, but a bedroom with a bed large enough for us to lose days in, with a bathroom and a bath with a view of the river. A room with a big fireplace where we'll sit and be... and a room for Kane.'

He grins. 'Your wish is my command.'

CHARON DOESN'T BUILD ME A HOME. HE BUILDS ME A palace. A sprawling maze of rooms, a ballroom with a crystal chandelier boasting over twenty thousand crystals that shimmer in the light of my hair, a bathroom with a giant clawfoot bath big enough for two nestled on a balcony with a view of the river. Kane doesn't just have his own room—he has his own wing.

The main hall still serves as a receiving room for new wraiths. I'm glad that without me mentioning a word, Charon doesn't alter this place, an unspoken language passing between us. It's a point of origin, the moment it all began to change.

The ruler of the Underworld now walks by my side uncloaked and uncrowned through the thriving streets of the city. The only time he wears full Ferryman regalia is when he's urging a wraith or soul on down to the river. He is very much now Charon to the residents. Recently, he's been experimenting with flowers. The city streets are lined with bluebells and lily of the valley.

I drop to my knees, and he lingers at my shoulder as I tinkle the delicate white flowers on their stem with the tips of my fingers before bringing it to my nose, though they have no fragrance.

'Though I observed a spirit's memories, smell is something beyond imitation. Smell and taste are outside my grasp.'

When I glance at him, he's frowning. We've

paused outside the sweetshop. At first glance, the gilded lettering above the door is in swirling cursive but a series of patterns and not actually the name of a shop.

'I observed it once, in the memory of a passing soul.' He gestures to the building. 'It seemed an interesting memory. The soul was young, I believe, though the human spirit is inclined towards nostalgia, so I might be mistaken. I'd hoped the souls who linger here might enjoy its presence.'

A lump wedges in my throat at the lengths he'll go to ensure the afterlife is a pleasant one, but whoever charged him with this role has put him forever at a disadvantage. He's never been human; his perspective is limited.

As I enter the olde-style shop, with its pastel pinstripe walls and empty jars, Charon remains close behind me. 'That's why there's no food in the Underworld, isn't it? Because you can't imagine taste.'

Charon's eyes linger on me for a while, as if he's considering a hard-to-wrangle thought that is also difficult to suppress. Instead, he says, 'There's no need for food here. Hunger doesn't visit my realm.'

I smother a grin. 'My dear, food is so much more than hunger. It's not about satisfying a basic need to survive. There's joy in eating.' I spin on the spot, hands splayed at the empty shelves. 'A sweetshop isn't about surviving. It's about pleasure.'

He advances, arching a perfect eyebrow and

running his long fingers along the side of my face. 'My dear?'

'Would you prefer Ferryman?' I smile, biting my lip.

'No. I like "my dear" fine.'

When he beams at me in return, it's impossible not to kiss him. To fill myself with his oblivion until the scales tip and I lose myself into nothingness, an asteroid falling through space. He rarely touches me in full view, but he allows himself a moment of indulgence before he draws away.

Grabbing one of the jars in both hands, I turn to him. 'We should fill this place up.'

'As I said, I have no context for food.'

'That's where I come in.' I grin, wolfish. 'I'll describe them to you, and you fill the jar.'

A faint veil of amusement passes over his face. 'All right. You describe them to me, and I will create sweets for you.'

A laugh escapes my lips. The prospect is a little ludicrous. Make sweets for who? Wraiths? I imagine Kane crunching sherbet lemons in his massive jaws and release another giggle.

First, I describe the physical appearance of sherbet lemons. That's the easy part. Now for the taste.

'They taste... fruity.'

Charon cocks his head. 'Fruity? If that's the best you've got, this is a doomed experiment.'

How do I describe a taste to someone who has never eaten anything?

'You really have zero point of reference? You have no sense of taste at all?'

'I do have the sense of taste. I've simply never eaten food.'

'Well, what have you tasted?'

He shoots me a pointed glance. *Oh, right.* The colour creeps into my cheeks. 'What did I taste like?'

'Sweet as they say,' he murmurs.

That's not distracting at all. I stare at the jar, my stomach doing somersaults, and I must resist the urge not to push him against the counter and have my way with him. But in some strange way, it helps.

'Sherbet lemons taste sharp but refreshing.' I massage my jaw. 'More sour than sweet. The tang gets you just here. But it's an enjoyable sharpness, the kind that makes your mouth water.'

Charon places his hands on the jar, and it fills with little lemon-shaped sweets. I take off the glass lid and fish one out.

'Moment of truth,' he says as I eat the treat.

An explosion of flavour fills my mouth, and while it isn't exactly as a real sherbet lemon would taste, it comes pretty close. Sweet and tart at the same time, wholly delicious. I jump on the spot, elated, my wings taking out some of the jars in my excitement in a clattering crash. Charon only tuts and returns them to their original state.

'They're amazing!' I fish another from the jar. 'You should taste this.'

I hold it out to Charon between my pinched fingers, and he pops it into his mouth. As soon as the sweet hits his tongue, his eyes widen, and the silvery blue flickers of his skeleton under his skin go crazy. For a moment it takes me aback, but then his lips are on mine, the sherbet lemon he was eating in my mouth. And I sink into him. The taste of his oblivion is a little less, with the sticky sweetness, and I remain in the moment with him, appreciate his hands on me without my stomach dipping as if falling off a cliff. The candied scent of lemon mingles with his drugging essence.

He pulls away, crunching what's left of the sweet between his sharp teeth. 'What's next?' He grins.

I'm elated that his smile is a little easier to win these days.

We continue to work through the varieties, me describing sweets and Charon filling their jars before I sample them. Some are total misses but taste so good, I don't tell him he's wrong. Fizzy cola bottles are hilarious to describe and even more so to sample, as Charon is intent on sharing every creation in the manner he did the sherbet lemon. Some he takes several attempts at. When I tell him chocolate tastes as good as sex feels, he gets it right first try.

Unsurprisingly after this, we become far too distracted to continue creating sweets.

THE SWEETSHOP HAS BECOME ONE OF MY FAVOURITE PLACES in the city in which to idle. Charon has created little rose-flavoured bonbons in the shape of actual roses that are quite literally to die for. Now the glass jars are filled with a cacophony of brightly coloured treats. Quite without shame, I help myself to bonbon after bonbon. Sometimes it's hard for me to reconcile The Ferryman who is now my partner with The Ferryman who once took me prisoner, though I suppose he was there all along, in the sculpting of the bath, in the unending chalk. I refused to acknowledge it at the time, unready to accept him.

Outside, a wayward spirit bobs past, bright and shining. On their way to the cathedral, I imagine, attracted to the thin point in the veil. This spirit halts and bobs in retreat, dancing in front of the window. Spikes of golden hue flare, threatening to become limbs.

Sensing their excitement, I come out from behind the counter and open the door so they may enter the shop, observing them with curiosity. The brass bell Charon installed over the door—though as far as I know, no one else aside from myself, Kane, and Charon has ever stepped foot inside—chimes a welcome. A wayward spirit rarely interacts with anything other than the spots in the city where the points between the living and dead worlds are at their weakest. Their mission is their unfinished business and passing messages to the other side. The wraiths were consumed by vengeance, the wayward souls with their lost voice.

Charon loves crafting things from the memories he observes in the boats, things to make the souls feel at home, but none have taken notice of his efforts before this moment. The spirit becomes a little frenzied in front of the jars, worrying they might knock them off the shelves I put myself between the spirit and the sweets, careful my wings don't interfere.

'Here, let me,' I say.

The spirit settles a little, and I run my fingers across the smooth jars, lingering a moment on each. When I reach the sherbet lemons, the spirit bobs about like an excited kid. Maybe they are. I unscrew the top of the jar, take out a sticky lemon treat, and hold it in my palm. The spirit bobs about, a spike stretching like a solar flare, and something akin to a mouth appears. I pop the treat into its mouth, only pausing for a moment to ponder how odd this is.

The spirit stretches like taffy being pulled, more limbs appearing, until it's a glowing orb with arms and legs. I take a step away from the bizarro creature until a head and body appear, becoming the form of a woman in her early twenties with mousy brown hair in a short bob framing angular features, her skin glowing the slightest amount.

'Sherbet lemons remind me of my grandpa,' she

says after a while, her eyes full of loving reminiscence, her voice distorted as if trapped underwater. My mouth must be hanging wide because the spirit chuckles, then frowns. 'It was so urgent I talk to him. I was his only family left. What will he do without me?' Her eyes glisten.

When I lay my hand over hers, it's surprisingly solid. 'I'm sorry for your loss.'

She nods.

'Do you want to tell me about him?'

'He loved sherbet lemons.' She giggles. 'One of my favourite memories is of being a little girl, when my mom was still alive. He would always sneak me a sherbet lemon. It became a symbol of him. On the day of her funeral, I was so sad that she was gone. But when my grandpa gave me a sherbet lemon, I knew that despite it all, I was going to be okay because I was going to live with him. Is that bad? That I was relieved at my mother's funeral?'

'Not at all,' I assure her.

She grins, shaking her head and perusing the array of treats. 'May I have another?'

'Sure.'

This time when I unscrew the lid, she takes one herself and pops it into her mouth, closing her eyes and savouring the memory of her grandpa.

Excitement bubbles inside me. 'Do you want to stay here a while?'

She happily agrees, and I leave her the open jar

of sweets and set off to find Charon. I go on foot at first, but I'm quickly frustrated by my own slowness and take flight. Surveying the city from a height, I keep my eye out for the long shadow that only he casts.

I find him by the river, monitoring the steady procession of souls. I'm a little breathless, and as I pretty much crash-land into his arms, he must steady me by my elbows.

'There's a way to help the wayward souls,' I manage to wheeze out between pants.

His brow furrows.

Unable to rescramble the words coherently, I take him by the hand and lead him to the sweetshop. His jaw drops at the sight of the human-looking soul sitting within the walls, demolishing the sherbet lemons, then snaps it shut again so loud, his teeth crack.

'H-how?' He stumbles on the word.

'It's the power of the sense of taste—I'm sure of it. It distracted her from her unfinished business. Charon, taste, smell, the things beyond your imagining— they're some of the most powerful human triggers. Together, we might help the wayward souls too. I imagine more souls will move on.'

'We already have record numbers of wraiths moving on, even more souls being recycled.'

I take a moment to mull on this. 'You once told me that the growing population meant that magic was stretched more thinly. What would it mean to have even more souls recycled?'

Charon shrugs. 'More magic, I guess.'

'What would that mean for the living world?'

'Not sure.' His eyes meet mine, mischief and mirth alive in them. 'But that doesn't mean you should stop.'

CHAPTER 32

LOVELY

The bathtub is a cast-iron monstrosity so big it can fit my wingspan as well as the over-seven-foot ruler of the Underworld, and it has the most magnificent view of the City of the Dead from the floor-to-ceiling window it faces. Charon has given me an upgrade. This tub has a winding arch of a tap from which oil-like water flows, so now I can actually take baths and not just mime taking one.

A fresh pearl sits in a divot in the side of the tub. If I run it across my skin, a lather of iridescent bubbles will trail across my naked flesh. But what I love the most is dragging it across Charon's body and watching how the flicker of his essence responds to the sensation, as if it's his very pulse. His life is not measured in heartbeats but in the moments when I'm touching him.

Due to the size of my wings, he lies between my

legs with his back to my chest, also watching the bright hustle of the city below us. No longer shades of grey, the city is a sprawling multicolour painting of memories, glowing orbs of souls mixed with the vibrant splashes of the wraiths, orange and stark white, feather and fur. Every now and then, there is a human-looking spirit walking alongside them. Their gentle hum reaches us even up here, as if the city is bustling with life.

The city that I built. Not with my bare hands, but with my very soul by giving it everything I have, and it flourished, nourished by my own blood. Not just a sanctuary for lost souls, but a place for them to find true peace. While many choose to move on, many find reason to linger. Not out of vengeance or loss or frustration, but because they are finding happiness in the afterlife.

Charon takes the hand I'd been trailing over his chest and brings it to his lips, reverent, placing a soft kiss on the tips of my fingers. In this moment, and the many we have shared like it, I'm so happy, I could cry. In the land of the living, my friends joked that I was obsessed with The End, but my end was only the beginning.

'Can I ask you a question?' I say, breaking the easy silence between us.

'I don't know, can you?'

But I don't match his playful tone. An old thought

has been weighing heavy in my mind, and I need answers.

When I don't respond, choosing to worry my bottom lip instead, Charon continues. 'You may ask me anything, Fury. You know that.'

'It's about my dad.' He sucks in a breath. 'You met him, right? Before he passed on. Did you know he came to me once? To warn me about you.'

'I did,' he confesses in a low voice. As he tilts his head, I notice his eyes are closed, my fingers still steepled at his lips as if he's in prayer. 'I was there the moment your father's spirit climbed from its boat. I saw his final memories, the bliss he chose to live in. They were all of you.'

'Really?' I whisper against his neck.

'I'd met you before, of course. When you were a shivering drowned thing. Terrified. Like you all were for those three minutes when you thrashed in my river to heed the call of becoming a Fury.'

'I have no memory of that,' I tell him.

'I know. It is the way of things. Or *was* the way of things. But that day when his spirit was passing, I observed the best moments of you through his eyes. The sound of your laugh, him reading you a bedtime story and the joy of watching your eyelids grow heavy. The night light in your bedroom that brought you so much wonder.'

My throat is thick. 'The chandelier? With the wraith animals?'

He nods. 'I thought it might remind you of him, of happy times. His soul must have recognised that there was a time when his best memories were not so filled with joy. It's why his soul escaped its boat to talk to you one last time.'

A tear escapes, rolling down my cheek and onto Charon's shoulder. 'I wish I'd gotten the chance to speak to him a final time. To tell him that I loved him too.' I hesitate, looking into his eyes. 'He's moved on to his next life... do you know who?'

'No. And he wouldn't know you even if I did.'

I nod, dropping my head to his shoulder, letting my sadness wash through me. Acknowledging it as the love that it is.

'Fury, I should be apologising to you.'

'Why?'

'Because I'm the reason he sent that message. He climbed out of his boat because of his disjointed memories, but he warned you of me because I pursued him.'

'You chased him?'

'Not as such. You were only a child in his memories, but you were so vibrant. This big smile as you laughed with such abandon, all that wild hair flying around you. You looked like a flame in the dark, and I wanted to know you. My first Fury in so long. My petrified heart longed to know more about the woman who would be gracing my shores once more. I might have mentioned before that souls with unfinished business tend to avoid me. I am The End. I'm afraid I quite alarmed him.'

A small sigh escapes me. So typical of The Ferryman to expose my raw parts and heal at the same time. Pulling myself flush against Charon's back, squeezing him with my knees, I place a kiss on his neck before nipping him and then kissing him some more, tasting the addictive saltiness of his skin. He drops his head back onto my shoulder, his deep exhale of contentment reverberating through my ribcage.

'After all this time,' I say to him between kisses, 'how can I still be falling more in love with you with every moment that passes?'

'Does it have anything to do with the extra rooms I keep building you?' I slap his shoulder, relieved to be back in a light mood with him, and he chuckles. 'No? Must be the dresses.' And because he's laughing and I love that, I wipe my tears and slap him again. 'Not sure where this violent side of you has come from,' he teases, escaping my grasp and turning to face me. As he does, a small table with a bowl of fruit appears to the side of the tub.

The strawberries Charon creates are gargantuan. I never bothered correcting him that he was way off with the sizing. There's something luxurious about eating strawberries the size of my hand while in the tub.

He observes me for a while, a slight puckering between his eyebrows.

Oh no, the strawberries are a bribe.

'Uh-oh.' I put my strawberry down, 'What did Kane do now?' Kane has become the prankster of the Underworld.

'The wraith has done nothing, just his usual antics,' he assures me with a chuckle. 'Fury… Lovely. It is time for you to return to the land of the living.'

My mouth drops open.

He doesn't wait for me to respond, instead cupping my face with his hand. 'You have no need to earn your place here. I'm not sending you away.'

'T-this is my home.' I stutter, not knowing what to think. How to feel.

He nods. 'It is, and it will wait for you. As will I.'

I thread my fingers through his. 'Why do you want me to leave?'

The corner of his mouth quirks. 'Trust me, I don't. But people are waiting for you. Time may pass slowly there, but it passes all the same. There will be a day when the people you left behind will be gone, and your chance will be lost for all time. I would not see that happen to you.'

For all the certainty I feel in my city, returning to my old life fills me with a weird kind of fear. 'Charon, I wasn't a good person in life. I made some awful decisions.'

'Lucky for you, you have an immortal life to fix that.'

Charon takes a huge strawberry and starts eating,

fangs in soft flesh, letting the juices fall into the oily water with tinkling drips. His eyes glow especially blue when he eats. I'm not quite sure what it does to him to experience a sensation he wasn't built for. I lean forwards and kiss him before he takes another bite.

His intoxicating opium scent mixes with the sweetness of the strawberry, and his sharp teeth against my tongue threaten to send me rabid. But his words are consuming. A seed that was planted long ago takes root.

I pull back. 'How long has passed?'

'About seven minutes.'

Which is about seven hundred years in the Under-world. Less time than I spent as a prisoner. Yet so much more has changed.

'Why does it feel like I've been here so much longer this time?'

'Well, your body is here, too, not just your soul.' Charon shrugs like it should be obvious. 'You're more grounded here now. Plus....' He pauses. 'Things are different. The fabric of the Underworld has changed, and you've been the one to change it.'

Who would have thought in their wildest dreams that I'd have the capacity to change a whole world? Little Lee who was scared of fights and dabbled in drugs.

I need to address the giant elephant in the room.

'I won't be returning to him, you know. But I do

owe Tino an explanation. A better explanation anyway.'

'I know that,' he says, a slight smile on his lips. 'I doubt he'll make you scream the way I can.'

Colour rises in my cheeks. I clear my throat. I know it was meant to be a joke, but it lands heavy on my chest. 'You don't have to do that, you know. He and I were a mistake. I loved him, always, as a friend. I thought he was what I wanted because I was always so scared, I wanted to hide in him. It's not like that with you.'

'Oh? And what is it like with me?'

I stare into his neon gaze, his face serious now, betraying nothing, his arms wrapped around the curve of the bath.

I don't smile, matching his visage. 'It's like you stripped everything away. I was bare, and you forced me to look at myself, to see what I was capable of. You never underestimated me. You never worried I might destroy myself. Even when you thought I could turn wraith, you gave me room to walk my own path.'

Something sparks in those cool eyes. 'You're wrong.' He edges closer. 'I was terrified. I still am every time I hold you in my arms when you take a wraith's awful death and replace it with something good. *You* terrify me, Fury.'

Then he kisses me, and nothing else matters. He pulls me onto his lap and breathes me in like I'm air, and in that moment, I'm not sure he'll be capable of letting me go. He kisses me like he'll never see me again.

'It's not enough,' I moan into his mouth, stopping kissing him and smoothing back the tendrils of black shadow that make up his hair. 'I can't leave you. I would love to see my friends again, but it's not enough.'

He leans his head back against the rim of the tub. 'We could.... No, stupid idea.'

'What is it?'

He frowns. 'A human memory I've seen many times before.' He squeezes his hand into a fist in front of me. My eyes land on it, and we both watch as his fingers curl away one by one. 'Be my wife.' In his palm, there is a perfect circle of black onyx.

For the second time, I'm lost for words.

He must think me aghast, as his next words betray a hint of panic. 'It would not be an act of submission, but an act of commitment on both sides. That you would return. That you'd never have to explain your-self to me. No matter the construct of time, we will always return to each other.'

He holds up the shiny ring, and I take it carefully in my fingers, afraid it might shatter.

Charon continues, 'Even if you chose to move on to your next life one day, this vow would hold. There will never be another for me. You are the last Fury I will ever create.'

My breath catches. While I can't imagine ever not

wanting to be with Charon, even I can't deny I cannot truly grasp what forever feels like. 'You don't have to make that vow.'

He hooks his finger under my chin, catching my gaze. 'You don't need to marry me for me to know there will never be another. There was the ocean of eternity, and then there was you.'

'Yes,' I cry as my eyes prick with tears. 'I will marry you.'

He kisses me again. This time he doesn't stop.

***

I MARRY CHARON ON THE BANKS OF THE RIVER, IN THE dappled glow of souls passing from one life to the next, knowing with absolute certainty that I am in the exact place I was always meant to be: not at the feet of The Ferryman, but by his side. His equal.

Despite their uneasiness at being by the riverside, the banks are thick with a procession of wraiths and human spirits alike. They gather side by side to witness something never seen before in the infinity of the afterlife.

Charon, while crowned, is sans cloak, out in the open, allowing all to see the crinkles in the corners of his eyes when he looks at me walking towards him, Kane at my side. The whole of the Underworld is free to see the points of his fanged teeth as he openly smiles with joy at the occasion.

A weird buzz of energy surrounds the water around him, a being of The End now with a dual purpose: that of Ferryman and that of husband. The bond that binds us has long felt blurred out of all recognition. I can only call it love. The heat that blooms across my skin, the smile that I cannot help but wear, is pure, the truest love I have ever felt. For I don't want anything from this creature in front of me —not protection, not safety, not retreat, only to be by his side and face what comes next together.

His cold fingers lace through my warm ones, pulling me closer, as if I'm the air he breathes. The guardians flank him on either side. On instinct, his shadows wrap themselves around my wrists, writhing along my forearms to my elbows while the flames of my hair wrap around the bones of his crown. My pure white gown contrasts his shadows to perfection in a style I've come to adopt in my kingdom. The straps are fine and sharp, creating dents in the flesh of my shoulders, the neckline drawing low into a deep V-neck that exposes my navel, my scars proudly on display. The train stretches on behind me for a mile. The dress of pure red that signifies my service to the wraiths replaced today with a blinding brilliance that is a symbol that I am totally his.

His hands remain cool in mine, and I feel the wraiths' attention trained on our connection, perhaps wondering how I can bear his touch. When he brings my fingers to his lips, kissing them with such soft reverence that he closes his eyes for a moment, their shock is a light gasp playing on the water, and even I am amazed by his open display of affection.

He straightens, bringing his eyes to mine, and speaks softly. 'Fury. *Lovely.*'

I beam even brighter at the sound of my true name on his lips.

'Though I am not an expert in the ways of marriage, I believe that there is an exchange of vows. And I wish to make my vow to you first.'

My breath catches at this, how he's willing to prove, even after all this time, that to see me submit to him is the last thing he desires and that he would bind himself to me first. He surrenders himself.

'I vow this to you, Fury, Lovely, my love, that I am yours from this day until the end of my days. I've been blessed with many names—The Ferryman, Shepherd of Souls, Master of Boats. Ruler of the Underworld. It is my greatest honour to call myself your husband.'

The universe that lives in his eyes makes them flare the way they do when he tastes something particularly delicious or when he reaches the peak of his pleasure, and the sight sends goose bumps cascading down my bare arms. Around us, the bioluminescence of the guardians swirls like nebulas in a night sky, and the hushed murmurs of spirits float on the river, gently rocking the boats.

Clearing my throat, I return a vow, following his

lead. 'I vow this to you, The Ferryman, Charon. The love of all my lives. That I am yours from this day until the end of my days. Sometimes it feels like I died a thousand deaths to reach you, but know this: I would gladly die a thousand more if it meant I could call myself your wife.'

Charon's chest rises, and he releases one of my hands to slide his around the nape of my neck, pulling me into a kiss. Shock reverberates through not only my body but in a wave through the crowd that surrounds us, though it quickly melts into my core, and I hook my free arm around his neck and draw him closer to me. Kane woops and sparks a trail of similar calls from the wraiths in attendance, the stomp of their feet sending a shudder through the very earth we stand on. And Charon kisses me some more, sending my head spinning, making it feel like my soul may well loosen from my body.

A small noise behind us brings Charon back into himself as Hero remarks, 'Master, the rings?'

'Ah, yes.' From a closed palm, he reveals the simple band of pure onyx and slips it onto my ring finger, pausing as it settles into place. 'Would you prefer a diamond?'

'No. This is perfect.' I move to kiss him again, but Leander makes a disapproving tut, and Charon places a band of pure pearl in my palm. Pushing the ring into its place on his finger, I notice that while his skin is swathed in ever-rippling shadow, they avoid the brilliance of the ring. It shines like a glint of sunshine on the darkness of his being.

'They are joined!' the guardians announce in unison behind us.

The wraiths and spirits cheer, and the ground tremors beneath us once more, the City of the Dead alive with celebration.

Charon turns to his subjects. 'Now there will be a period of revelry which will last for a hundred years in honour of a unified Underworld.' His voice carries, smooth and powerful, and a silence of anticipation ripples through the creatures of darkness.

When Charon snaps his fingers, music cascades through the empty streets of the city, something from a bygone era, haunting and beautiful. It sings to the spirits, and one by one, they bound into the city, tumbling with elation at the promise of a new age as they go.

The guardians drift away, Kane having disappeared with the revellers.

Charon holds out a hand. 'I would like to dance with my wife.'

His words send a thrill through me. Wife. I'm a wife. I place my hand in his, and he sweeps me into a waltz along the banks of the river.

'I never knew you could dance,' I say.

His lips twist into the hint of a smile. 'There is not much I can't imagine.'

'Indeed.' I grin, and I kiss him then without restraint.

When he pulls back, his face is a tapestry of emotions, a sad glint in his eyes. As I turn to observe the revelry taking over the city, it dawns on me what he's done.

'Clever,' I breathe, half about to protest, not fully wanting this moment. Not now.

He catches my chin and brings me round to look at him. 'You will be back before they realise.' It's a lie, and we both know it. His worry puckers lines at the edges of his eyes.

Flapping my wings, I rise up to rest my forehead against his, plunging my hands into the depths of his shadow and holding him to me. 'It'll hurt me to be apart from you.'

'And I from you.'

I kiss him, tender and hesitant. 'How do I go back?'

He gives a sad half smile. 'Easy. You go up.'

CHAPTER 33

TINO

As I slide my phone into my pocket, the sun succumbs to the new dawn and crests over the horizon. I contemplate what to do next, gingerly rising to my feet when a shimmer on the surface of nearing water catches my attention. It starts to bubble as if that patch of the sea is reaching the boiling point. My heart thunders as the sea hisses in protest. I almost don't want to dare give thought to those hopes.

My trainers become soaked in the surf. The water parts, and Lee's red hair flicks across the rising sun as she bursts out of the sea, taking a huge inhale as if starved of oxygen. She flounders a little, orientating herself, water spluttering from her lips, then swims to shore. As soon as her eyes meet mine, her lips split, and she's beaming at me.

I pelt into the freezing waters. The shock of the

cold steals my breath away, but I don't care. The water drenches my jeans, making them heavy, slowing my progress to her, but I can't help but smile despite the resistance. All I care about is having her back.

She finds her footing as she reaches me, then throws her arms wide and wraps them around my neck while I pull her tight to my body. I almost can't believe she's in my arms. There's no killing this girl. She's laughing, her stomach rocking against mine, although I'm crying tears of joy. I close my eyes and drink in the moment. savouring how sturdy she feels, how real. Like home.

'I can't believe you escaped,' I whisper into her soaking hair.

She pulls away, now taking my hands in hers, and although she's smiling, there's a sadness in the glaze of her eyes. 'I have much to tell you,' she says simply as we walk towards my car.

Now that she's fully out of the water, I notice what she's wearing: a white dress, elegant, with thin straps and a plunging V-neck, seemingly already dry and hugging close to her figure. The sight of her looking at home in such finery makes me take a hard swallow.

'I didn't escape,' she reveals, catching me staring as we walk along the beach, sand clinging to her bare feet. 'And I'm not staying, Tee.' She turns to fully face me, her expression beaming and at odds with her words. 'I almost don't know where to start.'

'What happened down there, Lee? What did he do to you? What's with the dress?'

She bites her lip but doesn't answer my question. 'Have you heard from Marie? How does she fare?'

My brows knit at the unusual choice of words. 'No change. Still in a coma, I'm afraid. The theory that she'd be cured as soon as you executed that... wraith, was it?'

She confirms it with a tilt of the head, though her eyes remain on the horizon.

'The wraith's murderer was untrue,' I finish.

She rubs her head as if she'd forgotten what she'd hypothesised only days ago. Then I recall how much more time has passed for her in the hands of the beast who caged her. Who, if she's to be believed, has now released her. A thousand thoughts cross my mind as I struggle to keep Lisette's rushed words at the forefront.

'How long were you gone?' I ask, breaking her from her reverie.

'A long time,' she muses, the corner of her mouth lifting a little. Her cryptic answers are beginning to grate. 'We should go and tend to Marie straight away. No time should be lost. I'll explain more on the way.'

At least convincing her to go to New Orleans won't be a problem. 'Sure.' I lead the way off the beach. 'I'll drive. We'll go grab our passports, get you a change of clothes, and hit the road.'

For the first time, she glances at her body and

smooths her hands along her dress, a mild surprise coating her face as if she's only just remembered she's wearing it.

'What?' I prompt. 'Is that official Fury garb?'

'Something like that.' She smiles again without offering further explanation.

We walk the remaining short distance to the car in silence. As soon as the doors are closed, I turn on the heater full blast to fight against the chill in the air and my bones.

I may not know how much time has passed, but one thing is for sure—I'm not a fan of the changes in her. I worry how much Death has sunk his fangs into her.

THE DRIVE IS PAINFULLY AWKWARD. LEE GAZES OUT THE window as if she's never seen dry land before. She's bone dry, while I'm sodden still, and she will not stop twining her fingers into her curls.

'Are you hungry? Shall I stop somewhere and grab some food?'

'No, thank you.'

I chance a glance at her sitting like royalty in my car, her skin a creamy white, her eyes bright and alert as if soaking in each thing we pass like they're rare delights.

'Are you really Lee?' I whisper, almost hoping that

this is the only plausible explanation to the difference in how she holds herself.

When she turns to me, her expression is soft. 'Of course it's me. Why would you say such a thing?' Her voice is strained as if she were attempting to tame a wild beast.

'Talk to me, Lee. A few hours ago, I found you drenched in blood, muttering to yourself outside a flaming prison. Time passes differently there, I realise, but you have to talk to me.'

'Sorry.' She shakes her head a little. 'It's so disorientating. The time slip. It's so much more substantial this time.'

She does appear a bit dazed, so I go with some simple questions rather than the big open-ended stuff. 'You said you didn't escape. Which means he set you free?'

'In a manner of speaking.' She tilts her head, and I try not to scream as she organises her thoughts. 'He didn't set me free because I wasn't a prisoner. He urged me to return.'

Something acidic rises in my stomach. That means nothing good. 'Why would Death want you to return?'

'He's not Death.'

'The Ferryman, whatever. Do you have another mission?'

'No mission. Only to help Marie, and....'

'And?' I urge, trying to ease my foot off the accelerator. Her calm manner is driving me crazy. Lee was always guarded, hard to read, but there was always a sort of frenzy about her. Nothing like this.

'To see you, of course.'

I scoff. 'You expect me to believe Death sent you to see me.'

'He's not Death,' she repeats gently.

'Lee!' I slam my hand on the steering wheel. Guilt over the outburst pounds through my veins the next instant, though she doesn't flinch.

There are no cracks in the facade, only a quiet chuckle creeping past her lips. 'Yes. I suppose now I'm here, I'm a little concerned you won't believe me.'

'Try,' I plead.

And so she does. She explains how the Underworld was in ruins when she returned, the wraiths were rioting, demanding vengeance, and The Ferryman was furious at her. That she refused to be an instrument of death, how she found another way.

I listen, trying not to cringe when she tells me she realised she could ease their pain by allowing them to feast on her, how she takes their agony into her being. I ignore the heat in my own veins when she tells me how the blood of The Ferryman healed her. That her way worked, but it was flawed, and she was in danger of becoming wraith herself.

She explains her relationship with Kane, the wraith who first charged her to pursue his murderer, how he had become her greatest friend and protector in the Underworld. How with him and The Ferryman beside her, they forged a new path. She discovered a cure for the wraiths.

I try to ignore the expression of pure joy on her face when she tells me the City of the Dead is alive and thriving because of her, and the sick dread in my stomach because she doesn't recognise what is so crystal clear to me. That even in death she's managed to surround herself with beings who would only use her.

When I glance across at her in the passenger seat, I'm distracted by her slender fingers fiddling with a band around her finger. Must be some kind of tether to the other side.

'And what of Dea.... Where's The Ferryman in all of this?'

'He's not my jailer, Tee. He's my husband.'

The words are a brick wall slamming into my chest. My hands lose their grip on the steering wheel while Lee loses control of her perfect composure and lets out a shriek. The car beside me swerves into a luckily empty outside lane, horn blaring as I regain enough self-possession to pull over onto the hard shoulder, killing the engine and clutching the car keys in my shaking palm.

I sit there, my heaving chest torn between the terror of almost hitting another car and horror at what she's confessed.

After a pause, she speaks again. 'I'm sorry to drop it on you like that. But things are so much different now. I love him. I really love him. You always said you wanted me to let something good happen to me, and I finally have.'

I stare at her earnest expression, eyes wide and hopeful in anticipation of the response she's expecting.

'You're happy? Being there in the Underworld? With him?'

'I am.' She nods.

I think I manage to give one in return and turn the key in the ignition. The car roars to life. I need to get her to Lisette as quickly as possible.

CHAPTER 34

TINO

A little over twenty-four hours later, I'm standing in an airport, waiting to fly to New Orleans. I'm caught between horror, resolve, and flickerings of uncertainty.

Now wearing jeans and a T-shirt, Lee resembles something close to normal, though her hair hangs in wild tresses, and she stands there unbothered by the fact that the multitude of scars dancing over her forearms is attracting the stares of those in close proximity.

Oblivious, she gabs away at me as if she hasn't a care in the world. About how she's staying for three days, that, as it's the first time she's left the wraiths, she's nervous they'll miss her. Apparently, she left them during some sort of revel. She chatters on about the changes she's made, how there's food and flowers with scents for the first time ever. How she imagines herself as the link between humanity and the eternal.

She talks of white wolves and snowcapped mountains and strawberries the size of her fist, but she never talks of him. Her exuberance is almost enough to make me falter. It's probably the happiest I've ever seen her, the most comfortable in her own skin. Then I notice her staring off into space, a banal sanguine smile on her face. She must be talking to him in her mind. My skin crawls at the depths of the hold he now has on her, and I steel my resolve.

***

THIRTY-SIX HOURS SINCE LEE WAS REVIVED FROM THE depths of the sea, and she hasn't eaten a morsel nor drunk a drop of water by the time we've touched down in New Orleans. Her plain refusal to eat has helped me shake the lingering doubts in my mind. Lee loves eating.

Lisette is waiting for us in arrivals. Lee breaks into a jog to greet her and throws her arms around the shorter woman, clutching her tight.

'It's so good to see you.' The warmth in her words is genuine, though Lisette's eyes remain firm on mine, and my heart hammers in my chest as I give her the barest of nods.

'And you.' Lisette holds Lee by her elbows and

takes a deeper drink of her altered appearance. 'You look incredible. I love your hair wild this way.'

Lee beams.

'Do you mind if we head straight to the hospital?' Lisette asks.

'Not at all.' Lee gestures for Lisette to lead us. As we walk to the car, she continues, 'I leave again in a day.' Her eyes catch mine. 'I'm sorry it's not more time for now. But I'll return in a day or two, so long as all goes well, if you don't mind waiting in New Orleans for a few days?'

My mouth drops open. 'So soon?'

She shakes her head. 'I keep forgetting. Acclimatising to the time change will take getting used to. But yes, I hope to be back much more often... if you'll have me.'

'You know I will, Lee.' The words come out tight, but if she marks my tension, she gives nothing away.

'Where's Lorna?' she asks Lisette as we make our way to the car.

Lisette doesn't miss a beat. 'She's tending Marie's shop in her absence. Tell me more about your latest trip to the other side.'

So, Lee does. Her happy, carefree chatter fills the car as we drive away from Louis Armstrong Airport. Lisette is more responsive than I had been during my silent listening and is happy to question Lee more on The Ferryman's role. We learn how he can be hurt by the wraiths, that he's consumed by the river. How he creates all in the Underworld, and the limitations that restrained him until Lee.

My palms sweat, and I wipe them against my jeans as, all too soon, the hospital comes into view.

The busy halls of the hospital take on a dreamlike quality with Lee gliding between me and Lisette and staring at each person we pass as if they're a wonder of the universe. It strikes me how strange she must view the waking world after being surrounded by the dead so long.

As we enter Marie's room, Lisette asks for the information we've both been waiting for Lee to divulge.

'Did The Ferryman give you the cure for Marie?'

As Lee steps around Marie in the bed, she spares Lisette a glance, something mischievous dancing in the glint of her eyes. 'No. In the end, he didn't need to. I now understand far more about the wraiths, about Kane in particular.'

She gently lowers herself to sit by Marie, smoothing delicate fingers across the now full grey of her braids, our friend having aged overnight by the soul sickness.

'What will you do?' I ask.

Lee keeps her attention fixed on the woman in the bed. 'What I always do. I'll remove the pain.' She leans forwards and presses her lips to Marie's.

We wait a beat and then two. My body sags, shoulders hunching. When Lisette gasps beside me, I see what she sees. The grey is whirling within Marie's hair, swirling like smoke and receding until there's nothing left but the black of her natural colour.

Righting herself, Lee sighs, her breath rattling, and like a candle in the wind, something inside her sparks and flickers. She clutches her chest.

I put a gentle hand on Lee's shoulder. 'Are you okay?'

'Fine. I'm used to worse.'

But her hand remains over her heart.

'Why hasn't she woken?' Lisette asks from the other side of Marie's bed.

'She needs a little time is all,' Lee replies, eyes soft with an empathy I've never witnessed in her before. 'She will be well, Lisette. I promise.'

Lisette gives a sniff and bows her head, accepting Lee's arm around her shoulders when she moves to comfort her. 'Thank you,' Lisette murmurs.

Lee rests her cheek on top of Lisette's curls.

My phone buzzes, lit green with a text from Lorna. One simple word that makes my stomach dive. *Here.* Lisette must feel the simultaneous vibration, though she doesn't need to check the text—she knows what's coming.

'Let's head to the shop.' She links her arm around Lee's waist and leads her to the door.

In this moment, I'm not at all who I think I am. I'm paralysed. Thrown back in time to a moment when my friend was dying in my arms, leaving me powerless and trembling once more. Their footfalls move in slow motion across my vision. One, two, three steps towards the door, and then it opens. A hooded figure revealed lying in wait, a stretch of golden cord shimmering in his hands. Lee takes an instinctive step in retreat from the threat, but Lisette is quick as lightning, taking the hand that rests on Lee's waist and shoving it violently between Lee's shoulder blades. She catches her other wrist, and the figure darts around Lee, then jerks and binds her hands together without mercy. Lee cries out against the strain.

'Will it hold?' Lisette lingers at the figure's side, brows knit, while I attempt to unwind myself from this immovable knot I'm in.

'This was designed to restrained gods. It will hold your Fury.' His voice is broad with an Irish accent.

'What's happening? What's happening?' Lee chants in quick succession, struggling against her bonds.

Finally, I'm shocked into myself in a whoosh, and I step forwards. I clasp her cheeks in my hands, her skin scorching beneath mine. 'Lee, we're going to help you. I won't let you be claimed by Death again.'

Her eyes widen in panic. 'No,' she whispers before turning frantic. 'Tee, no—let me go. I don't want this. I *want* to go home.' She struggles mightily, flexing her arms. The binding cords fizz in the air around her.

'You don't know what you're saying,' I tell her, trying to soothe her writhing. 'When we've broken your connection, you'll understand it was all an illusion.'

'No!' She fights against us with shoulders and knees, knocking Lisette over, and Lorna comes into the room from where she's been standing guard in the hallway to help us restrain her.

The Irish witch, for I'm now sure that's what he is, jostles me out of the way and comes to stand in front of Lee. His fingers hard and bruising on her cheeks, he brings her face around to meet his.

His expression is furious, but upon connecting with him, Lee stills in her effort to escape, as if magic understands magic. We all quieten, waiting for lightning to strike.

He slowly tilts his gaze to find mine. 'I find no traces of compulsion on her.' His words are soft, as if he's delivering a terminal diagnosis.

Lee deflates as she speaks to him. 'I'm no prisoner of the Underworld, witch. I love him. The Ferryman is my husband.'

The witch observes her where he holds her between his palms, as if she's a precious jewel to be treasured or studied. My stomach lurches as a possessive expression flashes across his face.

'This wasn't the plan, Gareth,' Lorna barks. 'Let's get her out of here before a nurse comes in.'

In a fluid motion, the witch, Gareth, heaves Lee over his shoulder in a fireman's lift and stalks out of the room. The rest of us scramble after him.

CHAPTER 35

LOVELY

Bound by my hands and feet, I sit perched on the foot of the bed I once called mine in Lisette and Lorna's apartment, struggling to control my breathing. *This is all a terrible misunderstanding.* If the raised voices in the next room are any indication, the witch is the only one who seems to be arguing my corner.

'I told you, there are no traces of compulsion on her,' he insists in his stern Irish accent.

'You'd know all about compulsion, wouldn't you, Gareth?' Lorna bites.

Pause. 'Do you have something to say to me, Lorna? After I came to your assistance, knowing it's what *he'd* want.'

'Does *he* even know you're here? That I called?' Lorna's words are venom. I've never heard her sound so angry. Gareth's silence is all the answer she needs.

'That's what I thought. You can't be so arrogant as to think you know everything about all that is magic in this world.'

'I know a shitload more than you do, little girl. I've lived your lifetime three times over. And if you're going to do this ritual on a being who's not willing, prepare to pay the consequences.'

'Is that a threat?'

Gareth's ferocity matches Lorna's, and from the anger rife in his voice, I can almost feel the point of his finger jabbing into my chest through the wall. 'That is a creature with the might of the Underworld behind her. You want that on your heads? Then you're bigger idiots than I believed you to be.'

Silence. Although I never would have thought it of her, I half expect to hear Lorna start throwing punches, or at least some furniture.

At last, Tino's voice, calm and collected, eases through the tension. 'We appreciate your concern, Gareth. But I know Lee. She would never have given in to this. Perhaps it's not compulsion but good old-fashioned brainwashing, or addiction, or a token. She's wearing a black ring. Wouldn't let me remove it.'

His words break my heart. That is how he sees me, how he's always truly seen me—as someone who's fragile, easily led, in need of protection. And in my past life, I did nothing to discourage it.

Gareth's words are softer now. 'She wears a ring because she said she's married.'

'That's what she believes,' Tino counters.

For the first time, tears pool in my eyes.

Gareth's sigh is so huge, I hear it through the wall. 'As far as I know—and that knowledge is limited, given Furies should be extinct—they walk the line between both worlds, tied to the Underworld through the Styx and our world through our food.'

'Lee hasn't eaten or drunk anything since she came back. Before she left, she just threw it all back up.'

'I suggest you encourage her to eat or drink something from this world—something natural, no junk food—before you attempt the ritual. The more time she spends here, the more grounded to this reality she'll be.'

Lisette chimes in, 'But she said she ate in the Underworld too. It wasn't the Styx.'

'Pomegranates?' Gareth asks, sounding a little alarmed.

'No, anything. Strawberries, chocolate, all sorts,' Tino tells him.

'Really?' The surprise in Gareth's voice is evident. 'Then my information truly is outdated. Be careful.'

Gareth's footsteps move away, and my heart sinks that my only seeming ally is leaving. Lorna's hushed voice sounds, but I can't hear what she's saying to him. The door cracks open, and Tino comes in.

'Tee, please, let me go. Whatever you have planned, I don't want it. I choose Charon.'

He crouches in front of me. 'Lee, you can't see it

right now, but once we've cured you, you'll see that you were being controlled.'

'Cure me?' I splutter.

Tino smiles. 'Yes. You'll be human again, and we'll be together. You won't need to be scared anymore. I'll look after you.'

The water in my eyes breaks, and the first tear trickles over my cheek. 'You have this all wrong. My place is in the Underworld. I'm so sorry I hurt you, Tee. I'm so sorry I did that. I can be both, though. We can still be friends. I'll visit all the time. But the Underworld is my home now. You need to let me go.'

He smooths the tear away from my cheek. 'Time. That's all you need.'

I shudder at the reversal in my fortunes, how lifetimes ago, it was Charon who spoke those words to me. How in one sense, Tino is right. My whole life, I had people deciding my fate, and it took my second death for me to carve my own place in these worlds. I almost can't blame him for not believing me even though I want to be furious. Tino is clinging to a version of me that still existed a matter of weeks ago for him, before I ever went to the Underworld.

Lorna comes in holding a glass of water. Her face is almost sympathetic at the sight of me bound. 'Please drink.' She holds the glass to my lips, and I edge my face away from the liquid.

I'm not averse to the food and drink of this world —I just haven't craved it since being back. But now that I know it'll help anchor me here, I do not want to partake. I need to stave off their plans for as long as possible to convince them that I'm in my right mind.

'Don't make this any harder than it needs to be, Lee,' Tino urges, but I refuse the liquid again.

Lisette, who'd been hovering in the doorway, comes to my side and grasps the side of my face, nodding to Tee. 'Come help me, Tino.'

'No, no!' I shake my head, ridding myself of her hands.

'Is that really necessary?' Lorna asks.

'Let's get this over with as quickly as possible.' Lisette's words are fast and sharp. 'Do you think I like seeing her like this? It's horrible. This isn't who I am— keeping someone hostage. Either we choose to believe her and let her go, or we put her out of her misery and get this done. Which is it?'

Tino nods, resolute.

My stomach sinks. 'Tino, please, you're my best friend. Please don't do this to me. The Underworld is the one place I've been happy. This is what I'm supposed to do. Please don't take this away from me.'

But he grips my jaw, holding my head up, and though I struggle against them, they hold me fast.

'I love you, Lee.' Tino's voice wavers. 'This is because I love you.'

'No!' The water is cold and fresh on my tongue, somehow totally different from anything else in the Underworld, no matter how I'd describe it. The tears slide down my face as I'm forced to drink, catching breaths as the glass empties. 'Stop. Charon. Help. Me,' I manage to get out between glugs, feeling as pathetic and as much the victim as I ever was in the living world. I'd resisted calling on him for so long, powerless as he is in the land of the living, believing too much in my own new ability to negotiate.

His voice immediately sounds in my head. *'What's happening, Fury?'*

But I can't even think a response. All I can do is cry until I become limp in their grasp.

Lorna takes a step away, the water finished. 'Jesus,' she mutters when they release me. 'Tino, are you sure about this?'

I crumple into a ball and weep, betrayed. When I peek my eyes open, the three of them look aghast at the sight of me, feet bound and hands tied behind my back as I tremble on the bed.

'I'm sure,' he says, eyes turning hard. 'As soon as it's done, things will go back to normal. She'll go back to normal.'

He can't know what he's saying. Does he not believe what I've become for the Underworld? That I have the ability to cure, to create—that I take so much joy in the world I fashioned myself? Does he not remember who I am in this world? Someone broken and haunted.

'Maybe we should give her a few moments,' Lorna suggests.

Tee nods. 'Okay. But Lisette is right. The sooner we get this done, the better.'

They leave me shivering, curled up on the bed, closing my eyes against such a betrayal, while at the same time not being able to blame them. How could they believe anything different? Every one of the poor choices I made when I was alive has led me to this point. Running, always running from my calling. Too afraid to confront the dead until Charon held the light in my eyes and forced me to acknowledge all that I'm capable of.

Goose bumps cascade over my body, the water bringing life into my veins.

'*Fury?*' Charon's deep voice sounds in my head again. '*Lovely. What's happening?*'

My teeth chatter as I begin to explain what's happened. How as soon as I released Marie from her bargain with Kane, curing her the way I do the wraiths, sucking that misery from her lifeforce, I was captured.

'*You are Fury, break free of your bonds.*'

'*It's not that simple,*' I tell him, struggling like a trapped animal, the rough crochet blanket chafing my skin. '*The ropes are bound in some sort of magic. A witch was helping them. He said the ropes are enough to bind gods.*'

Charon's rumbling growl fills my chest.

'*Charon, they plan to cure me. To sever my link to the Underworld.*'

'That is not possible.'

I squeeze my eyes shut, and a lone tear escapes, rolling over my cheek and soaking into the bed. *'They seem pretty confident. I'm scared. I want to come home, Charon.'*

'Break free, Fury.'

'I want you to know that I will find a way back to you.'

'Fury!' Charon's voice comes hot and urgent through our connection. *'You are no ordinary Fury who can be bound and held like a common god. You remade the Underworld as you saw fit. You fractured your very soul to save this place. Rise, creature of the City of the Dead, right hand of Death. I may be the Shepherd of Souls, the Master of Boats. But you, my love, you are the Master of Wraiths, and their strength is yours. Your connection to me will not be broken.'*

In the way only Charon can evoke, his words are a balm and a quickening all at the same time. They caress and bruise, satiating me and yet filling me with the desire to acknowledge that I am powerful, and I will not sacrifice my home so easily. I strain against the golden bonds. They flicker and flare as I pull at them with all my strength, the skin of my shoulder blades tearing.

I release a scream as the wings hidden within my human form break free. The bonds crackle as if splintering, and my wrists feel the slightest of spaces open between them.

The effort makes me call out in a battle cry. The

echo of my Fury sisters joins the fray, outraged at my shackles.

Tino flings the door open, jaw dropping at the sight of my wings stretched out behind me, my top in tatters.

The bonds snap back into place, leaving me panting and no less a prisoner.

CHAPTER 36

LOVELY

Tino helps position me on the end of the bed so that I'm sitting once more. My brain wages war with itself over whether to threaten him or appeal to his reason. Which one will work in this moment? For I know he won't leave me alone again after witnessing my bonds almost snap.

'We need to speed up the plans, Lisette,' he calls out, his amber eyes widening. 'Bring more water.'

'Tee…,' I start. Reason it must be, as I can't find it in myself to be mad at him. My purpose is to heal, not to cause harm.

He grasps my face gently, his fingers sliding into my hair, and I gasp at the hurt in his expression. How much it hurts me in turn to see him this way.

'I never get to save you,' he says. 'Please, just let me save you.'

'Tino, I don't need saving. I never did. This is where I'm supposed to be.'

'You cannot mean that. To be so surrounded by death.'

'You told me once that I can't always surround myself with the dead and the dying, but Tino, what if that's what I'm supposed to be doing? That is my calling. I wanted to know my role, and I found it. But I can be both. I'm made for this world too. I just want my friend back.'

For a moment, a flicker of hope flares in my chest that he's going to waver, but then Lorna walks into the room with a glass of water, and that moment passes like sand through my fingers.

'Hold her,' he instructs, and Lorna helps him to clamp my head back.

I set my lips in a grim line, unwilling to budge.

'Please, Lee,' Lorna begs, tears spilling over her cheeks as they struggle with me.

My heart lurches. But I know the second I open my mouth to plead with them, they'll force fresh water down my throat.

Eventually Lorna calls out to Lisette, who prises her fingers between my clamped lips and forces an opening for Lorna to begin pouring the water through. I splutter, choking, doing anything but swallow, but in the end, I can't help it when the cool liquid slides down my throat.

I sink my eyes closed and do something I have not

done in many lifetimes. I retreat into myself and detach from the reality of what's being done to my body against my will. The Master of Wraiths does not feel like a fitting title, as never once did I shy away from their pain, never did I try to detach myself when I was living every ounce of their agony. I welcomed it, made it part of myself. No, master is not fitting. I am the Mother of Wraiths, for I love them as if they were my children.

I reach out to every wraith I've cured who remains in the watery depths of the Underworld and feel them through the golden thread of my bond, a tiny piece of myself that I have given each of them woven like a finely spun spider's web. I feel them all now.

On the backs of my eyelids, I can see Kane on the top of his snowcapped mountain, thrashing against the stormy summit as if trying to break free of the Underworld to save me. His gleaming teeth snap through the water, leaving trails of vibrating bubbles. Maya at the edge of the river, prowling, searching for an opening, as if a boat will suddenly ferry her back to the waking world and not on to her next life.

And Charon.... I cannot bear to pull on that thread. Tears pool in the corners of my eyes, and I weep for the world I am willingly bound to, the world I gave my heart and soul to, the world that is powerless to help me in the land of the living.

Easing my eyes open once more, I slacken my hold on those golden cords and relinquish my cries to my children, to the being I love. I will not be the cause for their further suffering. If I can do nothing else, I can protect them. I shut it down and face the people in the room, a sense of calm coming over me as Lorna moves the glass from my lips. I fall back to the bed, neither panting nor pleading. I curl into a ball and stare at the wall.

They, on the other hand, are breathless from the struggle, all eyes hot on me. Lorna is silently crying.

Lisette's voice is hoarse when she says, 'I'll get the chalk.' She stalks out of the room.

THE ROOM IS SWELTERING HOT.

The bed has been overturned and leant against the wall to make way for the chalk circle I've been placed in. Not just any circle—a huge ouroboros. The sweat glistens on Lisette's forehead at the effort of her penmanship. She's not a natural artist, but the giant snake devouring its own tail is clear.

The pure beeswax candles at each of the four corners of the room flame unnaturally high, creating a heat which has the three of them dripping sweat. I feel the flames as Mamet once did, licking viciously at my skin. I must be seeing things in my delirium, because I could have sworn the chalk snake just winked at me.

'*Fury.*' Charon's voice is tinged with alarm. '*What's happening in your world?*'

The edges of the snake glimmer in the candlelight. *'They're doing some sort of ritual. I'm sat in the belly of a serpent,'* I say in my mind, my thoughts like sticky tar. I have no idea why I chose those words. I have no idea why I didn't just say ouroboros. In fact, I have no idea how I even know that word. It's been such a long time since I examined the memories of Furies past, so detached am I from them now, but a haze of shuddering images flickers through my mind. Not just one but thousands of images of the great snake devouring itself, its scales a shimmering electric blue. The colour of Charon's eyes. The colour of exploding stars. Death and creation made the same.

Panic floods my veins, acidic tasting on my tongue.

'What does it mean, Charon?'

'It's my symbol.' For the first time, there's a fear in his voice. Somehow, he doesn't need to tell me anything else.

'It's the door to the journey on, isn't it?' The flashes of a thousand memories told me as much. This is the last things the Furies ever saw before their souls were recycled. Passed on, dormant through the generations, waiting to be reactivated.

'The cycle of life moves only one way. Forwards. The eternal cycle of destruction and rebirth. Nothing truly dies.'

I shudder as Lisette steps into the circle.

'Are they going to kill me?'

'They're going to push you back into the cycle. Or at

least they're going to try. Force your immortal heart to the fragility of life once more.'

Lisette starts chanting, and the flames of the candles shoot into the air, instantly blackening the ceiling. I can't understand the words coming from her mouth, but the chalk snake shimmers and begins to slither around us in a continuous circle. The widening of Lisette's eyes tells me she didn't expect that to happen. She anoints my head with water, and I scream at the agony of its touch burning like a brand.

Lisette takes a step back, almost toppling over the churning ouroboros, then quickly rights herself when Lorna comes to steady her shoulders, not missing a beat with her chanting. Lorna looks a little green. Tino stands terrified by the door, attempting to shield himself from the extended flame. I realise they are all little children who have no idea of the forces they're messing with.

Lisette places her hand on my chest, and I scream again. Her palm feels like it passes right through my being, phantom fingers rooting around in the cavity of my chest. Her unwelcome digits tapping into my soul, my essence, feel as painful as any cut, more agonising than any violation I've experienced.

'Stop!' I scream.

The agony catches, and my hair sparks, the full flames of my Fury form trying to protect me from the horror of my soul being grasped and wavering inside my body, the perversion of it. My wings beat against the borders of the chalk snake. Though fear trickles into Lisette's eyes, she does not stop.

The golden thread that binds me, not just to Charon but to every creature in the Underworld, rises to the surface of my skin. Gathered under the pressure of Lisette's fingertips, it looks like veins shining neon blue, an estuary of my soul. My psychic connection to every being I've healed.

'Charon!' I scream out loud, but he doesn't answer.

Lisette's phantom fingers fill that cavity in my chest, threading those golden cords into her greedy grasp. They wail against her intrusion like tortured spirits flying through my very body, resisting being pulled from their host. It burns like the pits of hell, and I should catch fire from it. Lisette twists her fingers against my skin the tiniest fraction, and all that golden light inside me cracks.

The bond I shared with Charon, his hold on me as Fury, sputters and dies.

The bonds of the wraiths howl, and the noise leaves my mouth as if I'm channelling the dead. A final lamentation of the Underworld.

The sound is so haunting, Tino and Lorna clap their hands over their ears. The door to the bedroom door flings open with a thunderous crack, throwing Tino out of its path, and reveals Marie, feet planted, eyes wide, gun drawn and trained wholly on Lisette.

'Get your hands off her,' she all but shrieks. 'Now!' she yells, cocking the gun.

Lisette releases her grip. I crumple to the floor, panting, hurting. The spirits of the wraiths howling inside me settle and content themselves to licking their wounds.

Marie's hand trembles as she flits the gun from Lisette's direction to Tino, Lorna, and then back to Lisette. 'What the *fuck* is going on?' she grits out between her teeth.

Lisette's hands are raised in surrender. 'Marie, lower the gun,' she says gently, voice wobbling. 'I'm your friend.'

Marie's eyes dart around the room. 'I woke up in the hospital.' With her free hand, she rubs her chest. 'I was called here. The hurt was incredible, like my soul being torn in two.'

She is wraith touched. That realisation slams into me with the force of a brick wall. When I'd been calling out for the help of the Underworld, while Kane thrashed against the storm of the mountain peak, while Maya considered plunging into the river to save me, Marie heard my call.

'Thank you,' I whisper, the relief so intense that I practically deflate, nose touching the wooden floorboards.

'Break the circle,' Marie demands.

'Marie—' Tino starts.

She interrupts, so furious her voice shakes. 'You fools! You incredible fools. You have brought Death to my doorstep.' Her eyes level on mine, serious, flat, fearful. I've read her all wrong. Marie is not furious—she is terrified. 'He waits for you. On the shore.'

Without hesitation, Lisette breaks the line of the chalk snake with a scuff of her boot, and I scramble to my feet. Forcing my wings and hair into submission, I fall into step with Marie, who feels it necessary to keep me under armed guard, frantically rotating her gun. The trio follow at a distance, crestfallen.

As we descend the stairs of Lisette and Lorna's apartment, my brain tries to make sense of who is waiting for me on the shore. It cannot be Charon. It just can't be him. His place is in the Underworld. He's not made for the living world. How would he even get out?

My whirring thoughts are stilled, however, the moment I step foot out into the street. It's filled with people, an eerie quiet settled over them, no one talking, everyone staring up at an inky, starless sky.

'What's happening?' I whisper to Marie, who's walking sidestep, swinging her gun-toting hands back and forth so she can maintain protection of me while keeping a mistrustful eye on those behind us.

'It's one in the afternoon, Lovely.'

I gasp, staring at the shadow draped over the sun. A darkness has come to New Orleans. Its residents stand frozen. As we weave in and out between them, I examine their upturned faces, their open mouths and wide eyes. With growing horror, I realise they're not rendered immovable by the shock of day turning to night—they are human statues. Time has ground to a snail's pace.

A fizzing sensation travels over every inch of my skin. Charon *must* be here. The Ferryman, an idea, an element, a creature as old as humanity itself, has stepped foot in the world of the living for the first time. And the land revolts at his intrusion.

The stagnant taste of death rides the still air, cloying and mixed with a scent all too consuming for me as we near the banks of the Mississippi. Opium, rich and heady, and I breathe it in like oxygen.

The stench of decay becomes so rich, Tino, Lisette, and Lorna hang further back, unable to move closer. Only Marie and I progress. The sound of one of the girls retching behind me trails in the distance. It's probably Lisette, as I know Lorna has the stomach for death. I've seen it in her memories.

There, on the riverside, a hooded figure waits. A black abyss frays its edges, the water bubbling as if boiling behind him. The grass around him has blackened to a char, the infection spreading out to withering trees like a plague crawling over the bark, lampposts bending as if overcome by heat and hanging like drooping flowers.

I don't think. I run. Run straight into his arms.

As I do, my human form burns away. I am wings and flame as I fall into him.

'I thought I lost you,' his shadow-drenched voice says into my ear.

'Never.' I clutch onto him, abandon, oblivion, home. 'You'll never lose me. But how? How are you here?'

He pulls back, tracing the edge of my face with the tips of charred fingers. 'You've broken every rule of my world. It was time I broke a few of this world's.'

I lean into his touch; Charon retains no human form here. In fact, he's terrifying, a seven-foot mass of shadow and bone, the skull and skeleton flickering of home no longer a bluish silver hue. Here, blackened bones are on display, shadows writhing over their surface like mercury. Across his eyes sits a tattered bandage as if protecting him from the blinding brilliance of the living world.

'You came to rescue me?'

He chuckles. 'Turns out it was a wholly unnecessary endeavour.' He threads his arms around my waist to keep me close. 'You had it under control.'

'Apparently, my collusion with Kane did some good after all. Marie is wraith touched; I called out to her.'

'Incredible,' he muses, adoring.

I let myself rest against him, my head on his chest, his arms around me. What a pair we are, flame and shadow mingling in the space around us. Wing and bone. Creatures of the dead. My home, my meaning, my calling—I embrace it all.

After a while of holding me, he takes a step back. 'I must not linger in this place.' He motions to the decaying world around him. 'While I'm creation in the Underworld, here I'm destruction alone. Some rules even I cannot bend.'

I peer up at him, into those eerie bandaged eyes. But I don't recoil, do not want to. If this was his form always, I would love him all the same. 'Will there be consequences for you following me here?'

'Undoubtedly.' He grasps my face. 'You are a cost that was too much to pay.'

I beam, though my expression soon drops, seriousness settling over me. 'The bond between us is broken. My tie to you as Fury.'

'And yet here you are, in my arms.'

I nod, still clutched in his grasp.

'That is all that matters.'

'Time to go home.' I thread my fingers into his.

Charon gives a nod to the group behind me. 'I have a strong suspicion they would listen to you this time.'

I glance back at my friends. Marie has thankfully stowed her gun and is standing the closest, although she has slunk back towards the others to give me and Charon some privacy. Lisette stands with Lorna's arms wrapped around her. Tino sits on the dying grass. They're all waiting intently, like they've been watching as I rested in Death's arms. That's all Charon will ever be to them, as he once was to the wraiths. Death. The End. When to me he is simply everything. They look part devastated, part contrite.

'It might be good for my reputation if they didn't see me drag you back to hell.'

At that, I bark out a laugh, then nod.

'Come home to me, Fury.' He rests his forehead against mine.

Then he's moving backwards into the water, and for the first time, I notice the dead fish floating in the river. I wonder how his appearance will be explained in the rational world. If they will even recall it. Then Charon is gone, and the shadow eases from the sun as if melting away, and slowly the people statues of Woldenberg Park thaw and begin carrying on with their normal lives, only noticing with confusion the dead grass, the limp lampposts, and decayed trees.

Having forced my wings and hair back into myself when the world woke up, I take a fortifying breath and turn back to my friends. Marie places a hand on my shoulder as I pass, while Lisette averts her eyes.

I plonk myself next to Tino, who is staring at the charred grass. 'I'm sorry, Tee.'

He snorts, and though he sounds derisive when he talks, he can't keep his voice from shaking. 'I'm the one who should be apologising to you.'

'True,' I muse, ever so slightly bumping my shoulder against his. 'For this. But it's me who's sorry for everything that came before. I've always loved you... as a friend. And I am so sorry for using you, for everything I put you through. If you'll let me, I want to try and make it up to you.'

He takes a deep breath. 'He's not even a man. Not really. He's a thing.'

I try not to let his spite bristle me. 'I know,' I say, and he brings his honey-coloured eyes to mine. 'Surprising as this may be, this isn't about him. It's about me. Where I fit. What I want to do with my life.'

'You'd rather live with the dead than with me.'

'Haven't you been listening? I *want* to be both. I'm needed in the Underworld. I love it there. I love that creature you just saw and every other creature in the City of the Dead. With all my heart, my whole soul.' I tentatively place my fingers on his arm. 'But I also love you. You're not just my friend, you're family. Is there any way we can get back to that place?'

His exhale is shaky, jittery, but he takes my hand and holds it. 'I don't know. Maybe.' He leans his shoulder more into mine. 'I would like that. Perhaps in time, we can.'

Slowly, ever so slowly, he eases his arm around my shoulders, and I allow myself to lean on him. We have a lot of healing to do, a lot of work for him not to see me as defined by my former human self.

Luckily, I have nothing but time.

CHAPTER 37

LOVELY

I didn't stick around for too much longer after that. It was an awkward goodbye with Lorna and Lisette, followed by a bone-crunching hug from Marie, who now looks fully restored—not a trace of grey hair in sight.

The aurora borealis of the descent into the Underworld whooshes past me. Our bond is broken, so I can no longer hear Charon in my thoughts, can no longer reach out to him through the ether, but that only makes my longing to be in his arms even sharper, the need for him even keener.

With this descent, I'm not heading for beyond the borders of the city. My aim is true. I'm guiding myself straight towards that open square right in front of the sanctuary. One thing I can't control is the speed of my descent. I'm still falling like a shooting star, the water streaming around me pelting faster as that instinctive feeling I'm about to hit the bottom fills me.

As I crash-land, silt blooms around me like a cloud of smoke, but the impact doesn't hurt. I could be falling into bed, it's so soft. For the first time in my life, landing somewhere doesn't fill me with dread. I stay lying in the silt, wishing to weep. I'm home. Home that isn't a person I'm trying to cling to, hide behind, lose myself in—but a home where I belong.

As the silt clears, eyes are on me, my loyal wraiths who crashed against the borders between the living and the dead when I was in danger, and in the middle of them all, those neon blue eyes.

Charon.

Standing, I throw my arms around his neck, and he holds me close. Without cloak or crown as he so often is now, he's out in the open, looking wholly human except for his size and that flickering of bone beneath his skin's surface, draped in shadow that tapers off at his elbows, revealing his ridiculous forearms that somehow do things to my stomach I have no words for. I've changed him as much as he has changed me. Now we are precisely what each other needs.

'Sweet girl.' The words come in whispers and chants through the crowd of wraiths, expressing their elation at having me back.

I do a quick scan of the city; it seems intact, which means Charon was able to avoid any riots in my absence.

Unable to restrain myself to do what's proper, I kiss my husband. Ripples of shock pass through the wraiths, and there is a small shuffle of retreat away from me. But I don't care. I can't wait, and he doesn't make any move to stop me.

Instead, he deepens our kiss. His sharp teeth catch on the edge of my tongue, and I drink in all his death. Feel wild as his hands grasp me, sliding around my ribcage to converge at that point where my skin meets wing. In this moment, I want only him, need him close. The shirt of my Earthly clothes was ripped when my wings tore through in the descent, my hair catching flame.

'Take me to bed,' I murmur through our kisses when I have the opportunity to do so.

His returning growl makes my core heat even further. 'While I would love nothing more, there is some business to be done. Hence, the crowd.'

Breaking away from him, I pull back to survey the wraiths, feeling a little guilty to find Kane was near Charon's side. I reach out and smooth down the brilliant white fur on the side of his face, and he offers me a sort of bow. Wow. He must be really pleased to see me to not be offering any words of reproach for ignoring him, no matter how joking they may be.

Charon holds out a hand. 'Wife.'

'Husband.' I take his palm in mine, and he leads me up the *many* stone steps of the sanctuary. The wraiths follow at an easy distance, crowding the steps of our home.

'What's going on?' I whisper.

The corner of Charon's mouth curls into a half smile. 'You'll see.'

As we walk, my mortal clothes melt away to a gown of spun gold that looks like liquid rippling around the curves of my body. It's my usual style, with tiny straps and plunging neckline. The red I normally wear has become a symbol of my service to the wraiths; I've not worn gold since Charon armoured me.

When we reach the top of the steps, he turns me out to face the crowd and releases me to the quiet expectant hush of the wraiths. Does he expect me to make a speech? A debrief from the surface? I suppose it was a bit of a disaster. They were clawing at the fringes of this world, trying to get me back. Hell, the ruler of the Underworld left for the first time ever. I do owe them an explanation.

I only wish he had warned me a little that I was to give an address. But when I cock my head to find him, he's taking his antler crown off a nearby plinth. He holds it in his hands, between our bodies. *He* actually looks a little sheepish.

'I should have done this long ago,' he says.

Though I don't have a heartbeat, something lurches in my chest. It might be sickness, because then he raises the crown above my head and nestles it into the fire of my hair. The flames crackle around the antlers as it settles into place, and the chill of a rushing power flows through me so strong, I have to close my eyes for a moment. That same immortal image of the ouroboros settles onto the backs of my eyelids. It's like seeing for the first time. I see *everything*. I see that moment between death and life. I see it all. And it is so beautiful, it chokes me, my chest heaving as its weight sinks into me.

When I open my eyes to meet his, the neon stare of galaxies, and he grins that rare sharp smile, I know in the depths of my soul that I'm transformed again, that the possibility of creation lies within me too. I became an idea, an element, when I accepted the crown of the Underworld.

Around us, the wraiths stoop into low bows, their foreheads touching the silt. Slowly, Charon drops to his knee in front of me. Words flee my brain. I'm trapped in this moment—no, not trapped. I wish to live in it. He takes my hand and brings my fingers to his lips, an act of submission that fires every single goose bump on my body.

When his eyes meet mine, his lips part. 'My queen.'

The breath I've been holding judders out of me, and he must know I'm about to fall apart, because he doesn't release my hand, only rises to stand by my side and lifts our joined hands.

'The Queen of the Underworld. No longer is this the City of the Dead. It is the City of Light.'

The wraiths roar, stomping their feet, dislodging the silt. The ground trembles underneath us.

Charon's voice drops so that only I can hear. 'Long may she reign.'

Frenzied, the wraiths bound back into the depths of our city. My city.

Finally alone with him, I turn to Charon, shaking my head slightly. He's taken leave of his senses.

'What does this mean?' I gesture to the crown.

He wraps his arms around my waist, clearly relishing me being back in a dress, and kisses my neck. Which is so distracting, but I need answers before I melt into a puddle.

'Charon,' I probe.

'I am still the Master of Boats,' he says between kisses, letting out a groan as I thread my fingers into his shadowy hair.

'But I'm now Ferryman?' I ask, my brain getting foggy.

'We are both Shepherd of Souls.'

My eyes widen, and I force myself from his arms. 'You mean I get to see the source?'

'Yes.' He grins again. 'I will take you to the source.'

'How? How is this possible? The rules....'

'It is my gift to give.' He cups my cheek. 'With the might of the Underworld at your call, your Fury ability to walk both worlds, you will never be captive again.'

I take a swallow at the power he's given me and wonder what sacrifice he's made to make it so. 'What about the new wraiths? Are there many to cure? I should go to them.'

'There are some. And they are safe. Maya and Kane have been working out a system. Kane will tell you all. You have time.' He sighs. 'Now, can we please stop talking?' His thumb snags on my lower lip.

Before I have the chance to answer, he kisses me, lifting me from the floor, and I wrap my legs around him as he carries me indoors.

Once we're inside the darkened hall of the sanctuary, his urgent kisses turn even more rabid. Strong fingers push into the tender flesh of my thighs until I'm gasping into his mouth, our breaths coming in synchronised shallow pants. I'm an immortal creature, a Shepherd of Souls, but that doesn't stop me from pushing against him, my need so deep, I lock my feet around his back and kiss him so hard that I feel the edges of my being fizzing.

He carries me backwards until my back hits the wall, my wings spreading wide, the whoosh of my breath leaving me shaking the foundations. My exquisite gold dress melts into nothing as Charon's mouth becomes fast and furious until he bites down on my nipple, and I cry out.

Yanking his face to mine, I continue to kiss him. I want to tell him that I need him, that I can't wait, but I don't want to come up for air. I just want to sink into him, to lose myself in that opium scent. But he reads my mind, my words of instruction unneeded as his shadows drop away and he pushes inside me.

That feeling is so good, it should unmake worlds. That moment when we break apart to witness how it feels for the other. That slow easing of bodies coming together. I lower myself onto him, wanting to soak up every moment of him, to memorise the feeling of him deep in my body. But as I bite my lip, the pace gathering, I know it's impossible to hold on to. That sensation has a duality. I want it to last, but at the same time, I want it to continue into that wonderful quickening I feel in every cell. I long for that loss of control. To see that sparking moment when I know, with absolute certainty, that he is about to come. That his unnatural blue eyes will fire like the furnaces that power the universe when he does, that the power to bring him to his knees is one only I possess. That I hold him in my palm, and he holds me in his. In that moment, we are both at our most vulnerable, and he is totally, unbearably mine.

As I come, I bite down on his bottom lip, and his moan is so low, so intimate that it's better than any roar. I pepper his neck with kisses, though it's too much effort to prise myself off him, and Charon must detangle us. I feel like a rag doll in his arms. So much has happened.

He smooths his hands along my cheeks. 'You should rest.'

I have nothing left in me but a nod.

He scoops me up like a princess, and my wings trail behind us as he walks up the stairs through our home. He's unmade my dress, but he takes care to ensure his shadows are draped around me, though there is no spirit wandering these halls who would observe me.

In our bedroom, he lowers me into bed, and I can already feel consciousness slipping from me now that I'm home.

I reach out a floppy hand, twining my fingers with his. 'Stay,' I command, though it's soft and slurred.

Unable to lie behind me on account of my wings, he paces around the bed and gets in front of me. I wrap my arms around his torso, his shoulder my pillow, and hook my leg over his hip. I sleep like the dead.

***

I FINALLY LET CHARON LEAVE OUR BED, DESPITE THE FACT that he's dropped my Fury moniker and is constantly referring to me as *my queen*: 'Your kingdom awaits, my queen.' 'We should perhaps move from this bed at some point, my queen.' 'Do you like that, my queen?'

Lord, those words in his mouth—they just do something to me that is beyond unjust. Like his surrender has only deepened my own. That last question had practically been growled between my legs. 'Yes, I do like that. Don't stop, my king,' I'd replied. Apparently, those words do something to him too.

But being Queen of the Underworld is a calling I couldn't have avoided, not that I wanted to—I only needed to satisfy my hunger for him first. After, he shows me what he's created at Kane and Maya's request, their system for the new wraiths in my absence. It takes my breath away, and that twinkle in his eye at my pleasure in what he's built only steals it once more.

The building can only be compared to the Colosseum in Rome, a huge circular structure buried in the depths of the city so very far from the river. Kane and Maya bound down the corridors, excited at what they're part of. A duty and purpose they carved for themselves. I feel like a gladiator preparing for battle as they lead me to the arena.

Some human spirits sit in the stands in small groups, watching the chaos below. For it is chaos, shadowy rot-filled wraiths crashing about the arena, toppling stone walls with mighty bodies or shredding sail-like ribbons dangling from poles at intervals around the edges. Even some cured wraiths, recognisable by their bright shocks of colour, tumble around the arena with the shadow beasts.

'Are they fighting?' I gasp.

'They're playing,' Kane answers. 'Those wraiths are all rage, no brains. They're no match for us.' He and Maya join the fray, whooping as they go.

Their entrance into the carnage signals mine and Charon's presence to the brawling wraiths. Delighted by our audience, they lead the uncured wraiths on a merry dance around the arena. Even Charon seems amused, though his smiles are for me alone.

The city had been long in my absence, and though Kane and Maya are doing a fine job of keeping the wraiths occupied, with Charon intermittently rebuilding the Colosseum they destroy, I wish to return to my duties as soon as possible.

As Charon had expected, when I turned my hand to curing the handful of new wraiths who had built up while I'd been gone, their rage and vengeance were so close to their surface that it had been all too easy for me to dive into their psyche and find a moment of happiness to bring them into.

Though that didn't stop him from demanding that I rest once my task was complete. I'd promised I would, but instead I find myself drifting towards the river in search of the guardians. It's been too long since I've seen them, and my question has been burning in my mind since I saw death incarnate standing on the banks of the Mississippi.

The golden, soul-filled hue of the river is no longer the only light illuminating the gloom of the city that is now alive with colour and eternal flames, but the sight of it is no less awe-inspiring. That gentle passage of magic from one life to the next—on it goes. Charon and I oversee that onward tide of life.

'Lovely,' the guardians chime together, and I run into their many arms.

'Or is it Your Majesty?'

'Or our queen?' they ask alternately, mirth in their voices.

'Heavens, no,' I laugh. 'You are the only two beings in this entire world who call me by my human name, and I would like to keep it that way.'

'Your wish is our command.' They give mocking bows.

I wave them off, then join them on their route along the river. They drift over its surface, gently rocking the boats, on the lookout for wraiths or wayward spirits seeking to escape the journey on by demanding sanctuary in the city.

'We're sorry we were not at your coronation,' Hero says after a while of comfortable silence. 'Your sanctuary is too far from the river for us to stray.'

'The Ferryman did discuss having the ceremony here, but the river tends to make the wraiths uncomfortable. He'd blessed us with the wedding. We urged him to use the sanctuary,' Leander continues.

'Charon talked to you about that?' I ask.

The guardians' laughter tinkles through the water like music. 'In your absence, our counsel is the only one he can seek,' Hero reminds me.

'Who else would he talk to? The wolf?' Leander chuckles like that notion is ridiculous. 'It was like old times.'

'Sorry I returned,' I tease them.

'Hush now,' Leander titters.

'Speaking of Charon.' I stop walking and express my concerns to the guardians. 'He left the Underworld for the first time ever?'

The guardians pause, hesitating. 'Yes,' they say in unison.

'How did he do it?'

Hero speaks, though it is with tentative words. 'He raised a boat, a huge black monstrosity with a rotting paddle. Halted the progression of souls and forced his way up the river.'

I stand with my mouth open, dread pooling in my stomach. I have to give voice to my fears. 'Hero, did he make me queen as an insurance policy? In case some-thing happens to him for what he did?'

'Sweet girl.' Hero cups my face with a suckered limb, and I lean into the comfort of my friend. 'He was already planning to make it so. Everything changes, even him. He was merely ensuring the future of his world.'

I want to tell them I couldn't do this without him, but the words feel like a lie on my tongue, so I don't say them. Instead, I take a second to marvel in the truth that, if I needed to, I could. Despite how much I want him to be by my side always.

'Do you think it will happen?' I ask them instead. 'Will I need to rule alone one day?'

But they don't answer. Hero drifts off to return to the gentle sway of the waters, and Leander tells me, 'Lovely, the eternities are long. You have no comprehension of it yet, but you will.'

The eternities are long. So, he and I will be too.

EPILOGUE

LOVELY

The ends of my waist-length curls tickle my skin. Despite this being my fourth visit (or third successful one, following my disastrous first journey), my hair returning to wild tendrils snaking around my shoulders is something I've yet to get used to.

Tino pulls his car up to a stop outside my mother's house, and I release a huge breath as I eye the front door. I can face down the most terrifying wraiths—mammoths, lions, great hawks—unfazed, but the sight of my mother's chipped white front door is enough to terrify me.

'Thanks again for picking me up. And the clothes.' I gesture to the pale jeans and black T-shirt I'm wearing. 'I don't think my mom would have appreciated me wearing a crimson silk dress for the first time she's seen me in months.'

We've been able to work out a system where I tap out a message to Marie at the thin point of the veil in the cathedral, which is then drawn to her through the wraith's touch, and she, in turn, lets Tino know I'm on my way. It's always that beach in Wales, and he comes equipped with a change of clothes for me.

'I would have paid money to see her expression,' he chortles. 'To be fair, the last time she saw you, bat wings were protruding from your back, so she might not have been too shocked.'

I really laugh at that. Somehow, I've managed to have everything I wanted, and Tino has let me back into his life to prove myself as his friend. True, some-times his gaze lingers on me a little too long, and the want in his eyes makes my chest twinge with guilt. Other times, it's more a look of wonder at how changed I am, no longer closed off and trying to make myself small. I tell him how I feel and smile all the time.

The living world is just so... bright. When I'm back, I soak up Tino's idle, normal gossip, wanting to hear about every minute that's passed even though I've been seeing him on a monthly basis, and he tells me that his life isn't all that eventful. I smell the spring flowers and try to memorise every scent, and Tino and I can lose hours discussing how we would describe them best, though he finds it superbly weird. As a result, the Underworld is in bloom, not just a sanctuary for souls but a haven, a place filled with peace, not suffering.

We FaceTime Marie and Lorna, and they fill me in on their much more interesting lives. Marie is looking for a new spirit guide, and back home, I found a cured wraith who is up to the challenge, a beautiful Ridgway's hawk who now mostly spends their time perched on the roof of the cathedral. Lisette still can't face me, though I have faith that one day, at the encouragement of her girlfriend, she will. Though I'll never find an Earthly way of repaying what I did in the prison, the lives of the guards I took, I believe that every wraith's vengeance I heal goes some small part towards the debt of life I incurred. I can only hope that in their next lives, the guards lived long and happy. That I'll never know is a regret I must always carry.

Over our lifetimes together, Charon has changed his opinion about the chains, even if it's just for play. I finger the tender skin around my wrist, but it's best not think about *that* parting gift while sitting here with my friend; I can already feel the blush flaring up my neck.

When I told Tino I wanted to reconcile with my mom, pride filled his expression. He made a call. And here I am.

'Wish me luck.' I beam, reaching for the handle.

'I'll be here in case you need a quick getaway.'

I laugh and roll my eyes, getting out of his car. My running days are behind me.

Before I even reach the front door, my mom is on the doorstep and throwing her arms around me. Her chest wobbles against mine with barely restrained sobs.

'It's really you,' she cries.

I hug her back. 'It's really me.'

She puts me at arm's length, then cups my cheeks. 'You look incredible. Are you well?'

'Better than I've ever been.' I place my fingers over hers, and fresh tears spring into her eyes.

She ushers me into the house, offering me tea and biscuits, looking scandalised when I refuse.

'The last time I saw you,' she starts, sitting to face me on the sofa, 'you grew wings.'

I nod.

'Tell me everything.'

So, I do.

ACKNOWLEDGMENTS

Thank you, the reader, for coming on this journey with me. In many ways, *Daughter of the Drowned* was a hard book to write. Lovely was such a flawed, broken character. She was a character of my heart, and my rebellion about all the so-called strong FMCs I was reading in fantasy.

Don't get me wrong, these characters can be beautifully written—we need those stabby, snarky women represented in this world. But I was starting to feel like these characters were implying that strength could only be found at the sharp end of a blade, or that you needed hope and grit from page one. I felt it important that Lovely be none of those things, that her inner strength be hard-fought and that violence never be in her nature.

What I never expected was readers approaching me on social media after *Daughter of the Drowned* released, telling me how much Lovely's character resonated with them, how her struggles helped them feel seen and understood. So, my first and overwhelming thanks go to those readers, for letting me know how important it was to tell this story and that there are so many different types of strength in this world. As I was writing *She of the Shadows*, it became obvious that there was only one way I could end Lovely's tale after everything she'd been through—brilliantly happy. To all my flawed, dark readers who identify with Lovely, I hope I've done her justice, and that her happy ending shows you how deserving you are of your own.

To my wonderful content editor, McKinley—how will I ever write another book without hoping that you'll be there to edit it? Your commentary will never fail to make me laugh and smile, and also wonder at how a soul can be so like my own. You are brilliant and make my work stronger, and I'm so thankful for every edit.

Thanks so much to everyone at Hot Tree Publishing for their belief and hard work in making this dark duology a success. Kristin, you are consistently amazing and have the patience of a saint. You must have had your head in your hands at points while editing book two—I promise I looked for repetition! Alas, nothing gets past your expert eye, for which I'm eternally grateful.

A massive shoutout to my beta readers, Jessica, T.H., and Andrea. Your comments gave me so much joy. And to my final eyes, Kim, thank you for your wonderful comments… and sorry about the nightmares!

To my wonderful 'author friend' Maria Dean, may

we always be by each other's sides in this crazy journey. Also, to those wonderful women of TikTok and Instagram who've worked so hard to champion me and my work—Laura, Kimberley, Becci, Ash, Kirstin, Katie, Carina, Sophie and Stacey to name a few. You girls are pure gold. I'm so grateful for every share, every tag, every mention.

Finally, my incredible thanks to my family. To my little girl, Ivy, who is such a shining light in even the darkest of times. To my partner, Ben, whose own strength has wowed everyone in recent times—including me. Your ability to get things done is astounding. Your loyalty blows me away. May we always laugh in the face of adversity together. And thank you for building my website *exactly* how I wanted it—I love it so much. To my mom and sister for being my unfailing champions and following me to book fairs.

This book, as well as my recent reality, has really caused me to reflect on strength and resilience, and my final word is to my wonderful parents, who are an unshakable foundation in my life. I truly don't know what I would do without you both. I love you.

About the Author

Kerry Williams is a UK author based in the heart of England and writer of romantic fantasy novels.

Copywriter by day, she gets lost in a world of magic at night, either in her writing or in what she reads. Her creative roots were cultivated by the writing of the unforgettable Anne Rice, and she also adores the work of Erin Morgenstern, Holly Black, and J. K. Rowling. These days you will often find her with her nose buried in a romantic fantasy book.

She graduated from Brunel University with a 2:1(hons) in Creative Writing. She is an avid cat lady, die-hard tea drinker, and eternal stargazer. Always known to her family as a daydreamer, she and her young daughter, Ivy, can often be found looking at the moon.

Join Kerry's newsletter: https://bit.ly/ KerryWMailList

Visit Kerry's website for her current booklist: https://kerrywilliamsauthor.co.uk/

instagram.com/kerrywilliamsauthor

tiktok.com/@kerrywilliamsauthor

goodreads.com/kerrywilliamswrites

About the Publisher

Hot Tree Publishing loves love. Publishing adult romantic fiction, HTPubs are all about diverse reads featuring heroes and heroines to swoon over. Since opening in 2015, HTPubs have published more than 300 titles across the wide and diverse range of romantic genres. If you're chasing a happily ever after in your favourite subgenre, HTPubs have you covered.

Interested in discovering more amazing reads brought to you by Hot Tree Publishing? Head over to the website for information:

WWW.HOTTREEPUBLISHING.COM

facebook.com/hottreepublishing

instagram.com/hottreepublishing

tiktok.com/@hottreepublishing